Wicked Little Witch

J.S. Rodriguez

Literal Publications

Contents

Content Warning

Some contents within this book may be triggering or disturbing to some readers. This book is intended for mature audiences only. Reader discretion is advised.

This book contains themes and descriptions of loss/death of family, scenes of trauma, anxiety, PTSD, mentions of domestic violence, sexual assault, murder, torture, graphic gore, kidnapping, captivity, forced proximity, and descriptions of death that may be distressing to some readers. Please prioritize your mental well-being and do not read if you are sensitive to these topics.

Epigraph

The universe decided to grant me a mate, something a monster like me doesn't deserve. I didn't give a shit if I deserved it or not, I'm taking her and making her mine. Then the universe decided to play a twisted game with me and made her the very thing I despise the most in this world, a filthy little witch and the daughter of my enemy. The perfect way to make a man like me pay for his sins.

I don't know whether to kill the wicked little witch or bend her over and fuck her before tossing her aside.

One thing I am certain of is that I refuse to mate her.

Prologue

"Mom?" I scream, running down the stairs. Please be okay. I finally hit the last step, calling out again as I slow down, gripping the banister. "Mom?"

I pause at the eerie silence; with shaky legs, I step down into the entryway. I flinch when the floorboards creak under my foot, squeezing my eyes shut, and my body tenses before looking back up the stairs. I want nothing more than to run back up and hide with my younger sister.

Keep going, Mom needs you.

Paralyzed with fear, I break into cold sweats, I let out a slow, shaky breath. Tiptoeing, I step into the dining room; it's empty. In here, everything seems untouched.

I slowly crept past the table, heading into the kitchen, where the scene changes drastically, making my blood run cold. It's as if someone was throwing things around; plates and vases are shattered all over the kitchen floor.

"Mom?" I call out as I stand in the middle of the shattered glass. Looking towards the hall that led to the living room, the last place that she could possibly be. I'm shaking violently as I inch forward. I wrap my arms around my midsection seeking some type of comfort.

"Don't be a baby. Mom needs help." I whisper to myself, watching my feet as I avoid the broken glass. I finally reach the opening to the living room and pause, trying to listen for any movement. My heartbeat pounding loudly in my ears makes it difficult. It's too dark to see anything.

"Mom?" When there's no response, my fingers that are trembling uncontrollably slowly reach for the light switch, tears running down my face, my breathing fast and rigid.

I take a deep breath and let it out slowly as my fingers pause on the light switch. I'm too scared to flip it on, but I know I have to. Did the big, scary man from upstairs hurt her?

I flip on the switch at last.

My eyes quickly take in the scene before me. The recliner lay sideways on the floor along with the bookcase, our books scattered everywhere. I slowly step around the couch, and my heart skips a beat when I see her, face down between the couch and the coffee table.

No, no, no.

No.

Why?

"Mom?" I cry out, tears blurring my vision.

"No, Momma, please." I fall to my knees, and I start crawling towards her. I grab her shoulders, shaking her slightly.

"Please wake up." I'm about to turn her around to see her face.

"Isabella?" A little voice stops me.

I stand to see Luna staring at me from the hallway.

Chapter 1

Present day

I gasp as I sit up, clenching my chest tightly as I frantically look around, wiping the beads of sweat off my forehead with the back of my hand. I realize I'm in bed, so I take a deep, calm breath. My alarm starts blaring loudly, with unsteady fingers, I reach over to push the button turning it off. I rub my face hard, trying to wake myself up.

"Just a dream," I mumble to myself. "It was just a dream." My fingers begin to massage my temples, trying to ease the throbbing pain.

If I hadn't run and hid like a coward, I could have saved her. I could have killed him before he murdered her.

I am the one to blame for her death.

"Hey sis." I look up to see my sister leaning against the door frame leading to my room, brows furrowed together, and the corner of her lips curled downward in a deep frown. "Is everything okay? Looks like you saw a ghost."

"Yeah, I'm fine. Just a nightmare, no biggie." I shrug my shoulders, looking away from her. I didn't want to tell her the nightmares are coming back; no need to cause concern for something so small.

"You wanna talk about it?" She pushes off the doorframe and sits on my bed, grabbing my hand.

"Nope." I squeeze her hand before letting go as I sit up, leaning my back against the headboard, closing my eyes. "But what's up?"

"My friends are going to the movies, and they asked me if I can go with them. It starts around seven tonight."

"Sure, why not? I'll be working anyway." I turn to face her. "You look pretty." I smile as I look at her outfit. She's wearing a pretty baby blue sweater and black jeans. She looks a lot like Mom, unlike me, she has long, brown chestnut hair. We share the same small button nose and pouty lips, but she has a round face with hazel eyes, she's slender with soft curves, my body is curvier than hers, and her brown skin is a shade darker than mine.

I work out a lot, though, to make sure I can take care of us, a big part of me enjoys it. Luna is the complete opposite and despises the idea of working out, the thought of being sweaty is gross, her words, not mine, but she has always been more girly than I ever was. She's popular at school, always happy and cheery, a real people person. I, on the other hand, am quiet, never had many friends.

"Well, there's a boy that's going too, and I really like him," she says, pulling me from my distracted thoughts.

"Oh, yeah?" My smile widens. "Is he cute?" I lean forward, playfully shoving her shoulder with my hand.

"My gosh, yes! *And* he's a football player!" She squeals loudly, fanning herself, making me laugh.

"Ohhh! Is that why you've been going to all of those football games lately?" I wiggle my eyebrows at her, teasing her.

"Duh!" She throws her hands up as if it were obvious. "Have you seen how good they look in a football uniform? They're so yummy, it should be illegal."

"Uh yeah! I was once in high school, too, you know, and I do agree with you. They do look good." I kick the blanket off me to sit next to her. "But be careful. I don't want to see you get hurt."

"I know, I know. I will be. He keeps asking me out, but I keep saying no." She pouts a little and looks away from me.

"Why?" I arch my brows.

"Cause," she says, voice full of frustration. "He's a player. He probably slept with all of my friends already, and I don't want to be just another girl."

"Remember, players have feelings, too. They'll change for the right girl." I grab her hand, threading my fingers through hers. "I understand that it's a scary thought, the idea of being hurt. But honestly, you should always go after what you want. Never be worried about what-ifs. Yes, you might get hurt, but you never know. It could be worth it."

"You really believe that?" She looks back at me, eyes wide with hope.

"Yes. Plus, if he hurts you, I'll kick his ass." I wink at her.

"Bella!" she groans. I always tell her that if anyone messes with her, I'll kick some ass, and I mean it.

"No, but seriously, if he does hurt you, he's not the one for you, and he doesn't deserve you."

"You are the freaking best!" She gets up, starts jumping happily, and grabs her phone from the back pocket of her jeans and calls her friend.

"Emily, guess what! I'm going to say yes to Caleb and go on my first date!" She squeals loudly, making me cringe and leaves the room.

I shake my head and get up to get dressed for the day, changing into a pair of my overly worn joggers, a T-shirt, and running shoes that are barely hanging on, but it seems like every time I saved enough money to buy new ones, Luna needed something else for school.

I step outside and look around the neighborhood. We live in a line of townhomes, and the opposite side of the street is wooden.

It's such a beautiful fall day out, the windy air has a bit of chill to it. I close my eyes, taking a peaceful moment of silence, reopening my eyes, I take in the autumn landscape bursting with vibrant orange leaves, I inhale deeply, enjoying the crispy scents in the morning air. It's my favorite time of year. So, instead of running on my treadmill, I decide to enjoy the outdoors today.

I start stretching my legs, warming up first, and then start a slow-paced jog, going towards the woods. I watch as the leaves slowly dance their way down to the ground and listen to the crunch of leaves as my feet pounded against the earth.

I smile, enjoying the beautiful colors and the melody of the birds singing in the trees all around me, and the way the sunshine's through the canopy of trees is so magical and ethereal.

I slow my jog into a walk as I enter my favorite place to be, a large open space in the woods with a large tree in the center of it. I lay down at the base of the tree and start laughing as I gather the leaves off the ground, throwing them in the air, and watch them sway their way back down, landing on top of me.

After a few minutes of tranquility, I jump up and start running again, even though all I want is to stay here and shut everything out, at least for a little while, but that isn't possible.

We settled here after moving around so much because it's surrounded by young demons. It's what Luna needs, friends who could teach her what she needs to know, since I could never do it.

My magic is full witch, and even my witch magic is different. I'm just a freak. Plain and simple. I'll never fit in. The fact that I didn't need spells unnerved them. They always said something felt wrong about me. I'm completely fine with it now; I learned to live with myself being different.

When I make it home I take my frustrations out on the poor punching bag.

After an hour of boxing, I strip out of my sweaty clothes, and turned on the hot shower. I groan as soon as my sore muscles feel the hot water.

I start mopping the floors and shaking my ass to the rap music blaring on the speakers. Jen and I are closing the bar tonight, so we thought we'd leave the music on and have some fun while we cleaned up. I've been working here for about six months, and I have a love-hate relationship with it.

The best part, witches and demons stay away from here. It's the human side of town, and that is exactly why I chose to work here. Thankfully, they think humans are beneath us, which I never understood. I like them, and they don't judge me for being different.

The bar I work at is small but cute, it has a dance floor, pool tables, and of course, a large bar. We mostly get locals, but once in a blue moon, there's someone driving by taking the backway instead of the freeway.

I head to the bathroom and wrinkle my nose, nearly gagging. Eww, it stinks in here; I cover my mouth and nose with my hand, wishing I didn't have to clean it, but its my turn tonight.

I go to the mirror first and stare at my reflection. I look so freaking exhausted, that's for sure. I have my work uniform on: a black miniskirt and a white tank top. I hate it, but my creepy boss loves it. I have long dark hair, with forest green eyes that stand out on my brown skin, high cheekbones, full pouty lips, and freckles that scattered around my small nose and under my eyes.

I grab the elastic from my wrist and put my hair in a high ponytail. I go to the first stall after putting on gloves and grabbing the cleaning supplies. Alright, time to clean up. Cleaning bathrooms in a bar is the worst, especially in the men's. It's almost like they don't know how to aim while drunk. Pee is scattered all over the walls and floor. I scrunch my nose as I start to clean the toilet.

Jeez, did they even aim at the toilet?

When I'm finished, I go to the dance floor and close my eyes, my arms waving in the air, and I dance to a couple of songs, waiting for Jen to get done, enjoying myself.

"Shake that ass!" Jen shouts at me as she cleans the bar top.

"Dammit, baby, you didn't tell me you could move like that; you're like our very own Shakira." Damon comes up behind me and grabs ahold of my hips. He works as the bartender, while Jen and I are waitresses. I allow him to dance with me for a couple of minutes before pushing him away, laughing.

"Well ladies, I have myself a hot date tomorrow, so I'd better get going and get some beauty sleep." He walks away from me; I hear a bit of disappointment in his voice, and his shoulders are slightly hunched. I watch him until he opens the door, I couldn't bring myself to feel bad, I never showed him I wanted anything past being co-workers. He wants more, but I refuse to give him what he wants.

"Damn Bella, you missed out on that fine piece of ass," Jen says as soon as the door shuts behind him.

"He's just not my type." I shrug.

"Girl! That man is everyone's type." She sighs. "Well, unless you swing the other way, which no judgment here if so."

"Nope. I am one hundred percent straight." I laugh, shaking my head. I don't see why he isn't interested in her. She's pretty with short blond hair, blue eyes, and a killer jawline. Heck, she belongs in a magazine or on a runway.

"Any plans for tonight?" She finishes and throws the cloth in the sink, washing it before hanging it up to dry.

"Plans?" I snort. "Funny, I never have plans other than work." I walk over to the radio and turn it off, and walk toward the break room. It's small and dark. It's more like a closet, no windows, a tiny table pushed in a corner with two chairs, and lockers where we keep our stuff during our shifts, which don't actually lock.

"You should come out with us tonight!" She follows, and I turn away from her, grabbing my things.

"I'm way too exhausted for that." It's true, but that isn't the actual reason. I don't want to get too attached to anyone. There's no point and it's dangerous, especially with a human.

"You say that every time I ask you to hang." I turn around to face her, my lips pursed. She folds her arms over her chest, and her eyes narrow as she stares at me. She gets angrier each time she asks me to hang out.

"I know, but I'm not that kind of person, at least not at this moment in my life." I shake my head, I feel bad, but we could never be friends. No matter how much I want it. It's not good for someone like me to have any type of relationship. My father's goons are always looking for me, and if they ever found out I grew close to someone, they would use them to get to me. I can't allow them to think I care for Jen; she couldn't defend herself, nor can I risk her knowing I'm not human.

"You are twenty-one! It's the perfect moment in life! I never see you go out. All you do is come to work and go straight home."

"I wish it were, but that's not the case for me. I can't let my little sister be alone all night. I have a sister to take care of, Jen. You know that." I throw on my jacket and grab my purse, swinging it over my shoulder.

"She's seventeen. I'm sure she'll be fine alone for a couple more hours so you can go out and have some fun with friends."

"Jen, thank you, but honestly, I'm way too tired after a ten-plus hour shift to do anything like that." I rub my forehead with my fingers to soothe my headache. I lean my shoulder on the brick wall, looking at her, letting her see my exhaustion.

"Why do you need to work so many hours?" She swings her keys around her index finger.

"Bills, Jen, bills, that's the only way I can pay them." I take a deep breath. She will never understand, I don't even know why I'm explaining myself. She only works to keep herself busy because her family is rich, or at least well off. She likes to show off just a little, not that she's trying too, but she gets excited about the gifts she receives for simply passing a test.

"I hope Luna knows how lucky she is to have a sister like you."

"Me too." I smile. "Alright, you ready to head out? I have a warm bed calling out my name, with promises of a good night's rest." I push off the wall.

She laughs and nods. "Yeah, let's get out of here."

She skips to the exit, and I follow her. I hate that I'm envious of her life. "God, Jen, you have way too much energy."

"I'm just excited! We got some really great tips tonight." She grins over her shoulder at me before opening the door for us. We step outside, and I lock the door.

"Heck yeah, we did! It was a good night for tips." I look around feeling off, I'm not really sure why. We're alone out here. I clear my throat, looking back at her, feeling completely anxious, I shift leg to leg. I have a feeling that I need to get home as soon as possible. "Well, have a great night."

"You too! Are you sure you don't want a ride home?" She wiggles her car keys in between us.

"No, but thanks." I give her a tight smile as I start walking away backwards.

"Alrighty. Nighty night." She waves at me before turning around and walking toward the parking lot that's completely empty, except for her ridiculously expensive car.

I shiver at the cold breeze. Shit, I quickly zip up my jacket and begin walking. I blow out a breath and stop. I spin around to call out to Jen, changing my mind about that ride, but when I look, she's already driving away. I groan loudly.

Just my luck.

I start walking, wrapping my arms tightly around myself, trying to get warm. I wonder what my life would be like if I were ever free from my father. Will we ever not be in hiding? Scared? Running? I used to dream about finding my mate, knowing he'd protect me. But finding a mate is pretty rare. I stopped dreaming long ago; it's useless.

It's *stupid.*

I can't just sit around and wait for a knight in shining armor to save me. It's never going to happen. It's not like I'll find him here out of all places, I don't even know how to find him. I wasn't old enough for my mom to teach me something like that.

Heck, I never even had the chance to date. I mean, when I was sixteen, there was a cute boy, and he asked me on a date after he kissed me.

I shake my head at that memory. It was a horrible and slobbery kiss, but I never made it on that date.

All I want now is to make sure Luna is happy and safe. The dreams that I had for myself vanished when my mom died.

I'm about halfway home when the hairs on the back of my neck stand up, and an unpleasant shiver shoots down my spine. I get that feeling every time someone is watching me. I look over my shoulder, but the dark alleyway is empty.

But I know better. Only because you don't see anyone, doesn't mean no one is there; it just means they are hiding in the shadows, watching and waiting for the opportunity to strike. I swallow nervously, but I keep my facial expression natural.

I need to get home. I have a protection barrier around the house that keeps anyone with evil intentions out. I turn the corner and head down the main street. I have nowhere to hide, all the stores are closed this time of night.

That's when I see them up ahead, blocking my way. There's six of them standing shoulder to shoulder watching me, shit. I turn around, but stop when I see another group blocking the other side of the street. I'm trapped; there is nowhere for me to go. I have to fight; it's my only way out. I eye them; they're covered head to toe in black. I can't see their faces due to the black masks. As I call to my magic, I feel the heat of it rushing through my body, heating my veins. I lowly groan at the feeling, I rotate my head side to side, cracking my neck. I look up at the group and smile. They begin running at me at full speed.

Once they are close enough, I lift my right hand, palm facing out as I unleash my flames in their direction. The flames enter whatever opening they find through their bodies, usually the nose and mouth. I tilt my head to the side as I watch in fascination as they scream in agony. Their skin slowly turns black as my flames burn them from the inside out.

I turn to the side and hold out my left hand, my palm facing the other group, my flames shot out, repeating the action. I can easily kill a dozen or so at once within minutes. I usually don't use my flames, but every time I do, it feels amazing.

"Fuck me," I whisper once I hear someone mumbling a spell coming from somewhere behind me. I look over my shoulder, and see a tall wizard. I can't make out any details since he's wearing a black cloak. He's walking towards me, and I can feel his gaze on me. I can sense his magic, it's strong.

He'd be able to block my flames. We can go head-to-head, but I don't have time for that. I need to get to Luna, and we need to get the hell out of here. My father found me. I'm surprised he sent this warlock. Why didn't he come himself?

I know if I make it home, he can easily break down my protection barrier, and they will find Luna. I can't let that happen. No one knows about her, and I prefer to keep it that way. I knew this day would happen. My mom prepared me for this moment before she died, but training is nothing compared to this. My body is completely froze with fear. If he gets hold of me... No, don't think about that.

What do I do?

Run.

I swallow the lump of fear that's slowly forming inside my throat, and I spin around to run in the opposite direction; I have to lead them away from Luna. I know they will catch me in no time, so I reach into my jacket pocket to grab my cell phone and dial Luna's number.

"What's up? Are you on the way home?" Her voice is low and scratchy, like I woke her up. I blink the tears away, it isn't the time to cry. Everything will be okay, just don't panic.

Be strong. The last thing you want to do when you're being attacked is panic. I can hear my mom's voice inside my head.

"Bella?"

She sounds more alert now.

"Luna, there's no time to explain, but they found us." I can hear the pounding of footsteps getting nearer behind me. I don't even have to turn around and look to know they're catching up to me. "Shit, they are catching up fast."

"Wait, what? Who? Are you okay?" I hear a loud grunt. "*Fuck,* sorry, I smacked my toe."

I shake my head, she is too clumsy for her own good.

"I'm being chased. Luna, listen, do you remember where I put the address? The one we would need in case of an emergency?" I already memorized the address, but I know she didn't. She has never taken it seriously.

"Yes, I'll grab it now."

I can hear the sound of papers shuffling around. It's buried underneath a stack of important paperwork in a small lock box. There's also cash in there for emergencies like this.

"Okay, good. Get the cash too." I try to keep my voice calm as my vision starts to blur from the tears in my eyes. Please be okay.

I taught her enough, didn't I?

Oh God, I should have been harder on her.

"Got it! I'll meet you at our spot." She sounds completely out of breath, just from moving around my room.

"Luna, there is no time. You have to go straight to the address. Use the cash and take a bus."

"We'll meet at the bus station, right?" I hear the slight panic in her voice.

How do I tell her I'm not meeting her?

How do I tell her that I can't outrun the large group?

"Bella!" she snaps.

"No Luna, there's too many. I can't outrun them, and I can't lead them to you."

"No!" she cries out. "That's impossible. You're the strongest witch I know! Mama used to say that all the time."

"Calm down, Luna. Freaking out won't help us. There are too many, I'll drain my magic if I take them all. You can do this; we have practiced for a reason. We both knew this day would come. We cannot let my dad know about you."

"I can help you!"

I almost laugh; I would have if we weren't in a dangerous situation. She isn't that powerful, we're complete opposites. She doesn't have any special abilities, thank fuck. Hell, she couldn't even fight, as clumsy as she is. She isn't made for this.

"No, you can't. Just go to that address, that's Momma's old friend, Trisha. She will help you. I will come and find you as soon as I can."

"But what if they hurt you, Bella?" she whimpers softly.

"They won't. My father needs me, but I also know they'll hurt you without a doubt in my mind. I will come find you, Luna, I promise."

"Bella, someone's here," she whispers.

My mind swirls with panic, and my feet stop moving.

No, no, please no. She can't fight anyone off. I feel the anger running through my veins, removing all panic. I slowly turn around and see the group of six stopping ten feet away. They look at each other and then back at me.

"Run Luna. RUN, NOW!"

"I'm scared," she cries out, pissing me off even more.

I shake my head, calming myself down. This isn't the time to cry like a baby, but it isn't the time to yell at her either.

"I'm coming, okay? I'm coming! Just have to deal with one small problem," I hiss out as I eye each of the men before smiling sweetly at them. I shove my phone into my bra as I slowly walk toward them.

I inhale deeply, feeling my nostrils flare as I crack my neck, baring my teeth at them. My fingers light up with flames, and they all turn around to run. But I'm faster. The flames rush out of my fingertips, wrapping around each man, quickly entering their bodies. I watch as their flesh slowly turns dark before they fall limp to the ground. They didn't even have time to scream.

My head tilts to the side to look at the warlock who is slowly walking toward me with his hands out in front of him, palms facing me. His eyes narrow at me, mouth moving quickly from the spell he's casting. I growl with anger when my flames slowly wrap around an invisible shield that he must've casted around himself.

My brows furrowed in confusion as he begins to back away instead of fighting. I smile, realizing he can only cast one spell at a time. He can't keep his shield up and hurt me at the same time, and his backup is gone.

I lift my other hand and at full force, I blast the flames at him. They wrap around the shield, swirling around it at high speeds to the point that I can hardly see the warlock. It looks beautiful but deadly. My hands and fingers are round as if holding a ball, and I tighten my fingers together; the flames mimic my hands and tighten against his shield. I can see his arms trembling and his body slowly falling to the ground as his shield grows smaller under the pressure. He isn't strong enough to hold his shield.

His frightened eyes look back at me as his arms fall limp to his sides, and he drops to his knees. I watch as my flames surround him. His body starts convulsing at the force of it. There's so much entering him at a quick and deadly speed that his body explodes.

I gasp as a few pieces of the melted flesh smack against me.

I never knew that could happen.

I push down the regret; they attacked me, so I shouldn't feel bad. I start running as fast as my legs can go. I don't let go of my power; the magic is still rushing through my veins, ready for me to use it again, even though I shouldn't. I've used so much that my body starts to feel overloaded.

God, please be okay!

"Bella!" I hear Luna scream.

I blink, remembering I put my phone on speaker. Reaching in my bra, I take the phone out.

"What is it? What's wrong?" I shout, angry at myself. *Why the hell didn't I just go straight home? I should've known if they are watching me, they know where I live. I could be there protecting her.* "Luna? Luna!" I hear movements, and then a loud groan. "I'm almost there!"

"Awww, how freaking cute," a deep male voice I don't recognize says into the phone, making me flinch.

They have her...

"Who the hell are you?" I almost cry out in joy when I see my house up ahead. "If you hurt her, I'll kill you!"

"Such a violent little thing you are, but it's a little too late. You should have taught her how to use her powers; it could have helped her. She probably would have gotten away! She's not nearly as strong as you, but if she knew what she was doing, she would have put up a better fight." He laughs wickedly.

"What did you do? What do you want?" My blood runs cold, and I grab hold of my throat as it tightens.

"Oh, don't worry, she's not dead."

I let out a breath.

"Yet." Then, the line goes dead.

I run up the porch steps and push the door open.

"Luna!" I shout as soon as I open the door.

"We have you now." A voice sings behind me, and I feel myself tense as his warm breath tickles the back of my neck. "I must say, I'm surprised you made it this far. You're a sexy little thing." He grabs my jaw tightly, tilting my head back.

My hand grips his wrist, burning it. He hisses, losing his grip. I quickly spin around, putting distance between us. I look around the room, but there are no signs of Luna. Looking back at him, my upper lip curls into a snarl.

Short black hair, dark brown eyes, his nose is a little large, and his lips are on the smaller side. A large scar starts underneath his left ear and down across his throat. Someone tried cutting his head off his shoulders, which, at the moment, I wish they had succeeded.

"Fuck you." I spit in his face. I pick up my knee and knee him right in his dick. His eyes widen as he drops, groaning. No matter how powerful a man is, that always seems to work.

I feel a small pinch on the right side of my neck; my hand reaches up to find a syringe in it. I close my eyes, feeling lightheaded. I take a few deep breaths to control the dizziness. The medicine or whatever they are using burns quickly due to my flames still swirling inside me and making it less effective.

"Why the fuck isn't the shot working?" He groans on his knees, holding his junk. "It should've knocked her ass out cold, dude."

"You can't take us all down. That should make you too weak to use your powers on all of us." A tall woman says, walking into my line of sight. She's wearing all black leather and has short purple pixie hair. If she weren't actively trying to hurt me, I'd say she looks pretty badass.

"No, maybe not. But regardless, I'm not going down without a fight."

She runs toward me with her fist in the air. I jump in the air and my foot slams into the side of her face, her body twists to the side at the force of my kick, and she lands face-first on the hardwood floor. Before she can recover, I jump onto her back, wrapping my hands on either side of her head, and twist hard. I shiver when I hear the loud crack. I let her go, making her head hit the floor with a loud bang.

The man wraps his arms around my waist, and he picks me up, throwing my body hard against the wall, causing me to cry out in pain. I'm pretty sure the hard impact dislocated my shoulder. My knees buckle, and my ass hits the ground.

"You fucking bitch, you killed her," he growls. His voice is deep and animalistic. *I bet he's a shifter.* He grabs me by my hair, pulling me up until I'm on my knees, making me flinch at the sting. My hands are around his wrist, but he ignores the burn. He backhands me hard, making my ears ring, and I can taste metallic. I moan, closing my eyes, seeing stars floating around my vision. I swallow the blood, fighting off the pain, blinking a few times. I look up at him with a smile.

His eyes widen in shock. *Yeah, I'm a crazy bitch.*

"Where is she?" I jump up, my right hand reaches out, wrapping around his throat, and my flames shoot out, melting the skin. He hisses in pain and throws himself backward landing flat on his back, but he's too late; the damage is already done. I release a small flame and it's going to be an excruciating death unless I call it back.

"What did you do?" He rushes out, voice full of panic. I'm sure he's already feeling the pain.

I stand slowly, stepping closer to him. I place my foot on his throat, pushing down with enough force to choke him.

I release some pressure. "I won't ask again. I can stop the pain," I hiss, knowing my flame is causing him a shit ton of pain as his entire body is twitching, and tears are running down his face.

After a few minutes, I call to my flame, and I know when it burns out by the smoke coming out of his mouth and the way he begins to cough.

"He took her." He chokes out.

"Who is he? Is it my father?" I crouched down, looking into his dark eyes. Hmm, maybe not a shifter as he would have shifted by now.

"Yes. He knew you were too powerful to catch, so he took your friend, knowing you'll go after her." I straighten stepping away from him. Of course he did. He's been watching me, but at least he thinks she's just a friend.

"Where did he take her?" I move towards him again. I place my foot against the side of his face, pushing his head into the hardwood floor. Too bad I'm not wearing heels, that'd be so much fun.

Chapter 2

AZRAEL

I stare at a dark-haired beauty walking by, before looking back down at the cute redhead sucking my cock. I close my eyes, trying to come. She's been at it for a while now, and I'm growing bored. I'm not sure how her mouth is still working.

The waitress comes over and sits down beside me on the red velvet sofa, offering her wrist for me to drink from, which I gladly do. The humans who work here either hope they'll one day be turned into one of us or are addicted to our bites. It can be addicting; it's like a drug to humans.

"Doll face, sit on my lap," I say to the redhead. I only ever call them nicknames since I can never remember their names as there's never any need to. I look over to where my cousin Darren is, but he is long gone. I roll my eyes. I shouldn't be surprised, bastard ditched me.

"Yes, my prince. Whatever you want." She moans as she crawls onto my lap, straddling me. She reaches between us, guides my cock to her entrance, slowly sinks down on it, and starts moving her hips, and riding my cock. "You like that?" She groans breathlessly.

"Shut the fuck up," I growl in annoyance. Her voice annoys the crap out of me, and I was close to coming before she opened her mouth. She narrows her eyes at me before extending her fangs and biting into the waitress's wrist.

I grab her by the hips and fuck her hard. I feel her pulsating around me. I groan at the sensation and pull out, my fingers wrapping around my cock. I pump twice before coming all over her lower abdomen and bare breast. She starts groaning in annoyance since she didn't get off; I shrug my shoulders and push her off as I stand, throwing cash on the table.

"Thanks, doll face." I wink at her before teleporting home. I remove my clothes and hop into the hot shower to wash her scent off me. Once I no longer smell her, I turn off the shower just when my phone begins to ring.

"What, Stella?" I begin drying myself with my towel.

"Always so cranky, jeez! Have you heard from Darren?"

"Nope." I grab a pair of sweats and put them on, running my fingers through my wet hair.

"Neither have I. I think something is wrong," she rushes out.

"He can take care of himself." I hang up as I sit on my leather chair, and rest my ankle onto the opposite knee, leaning back. I grab a cigar off the side table, cut the tip off, and light it.

I watch it warm up before taking a long puff as I stare out the window in my room, looking into the dark night. It's a full moon tonight. A witch's favorite night, and when they are the most powerful due to the moon's energy or some shit.

Tonight is the anniversary of my mother's death. She died because of a witch. I fucking despise witches. They can all fucking burn for all I care.

"Azrael! Don't you ever hang up on me again!" I roll my eyes as I hear Stella's high-pitched voice yelling right before she kicks my bedroom door open.

"Oh yes. Do come in, my dear sister!" I puff my cigar before blowing out the smoke.

"How can you be so childish!"

"What do you want? I am not in the mood for you." I turn my head to look at her.

"Do you not know what day it is?" She huffs and then pouts like a child, and I'm the childish one... right.

"Of course, I fucking do! What the Hell do you want?" I snap.

"Did you call Father? I did, but he didn't answer." She throws herself onto my bed.

"Yes, I spoke to him earlier and he's busy." He always makes today the busiest day of the year since Mother passed away, and I know it is to keep his thoughts busy.

"Well, I am worried about Darren. He never stays at a girl's house." She rolls to her side and looks at me.

"That is true, but he can handle himself, sis; he'll be fine."

"No, I don't have a good feeling, and I won't leave till you get up and help me find him."

"Fine!" I growl through clenched teeth.

Chapter 3

BELLA

I left the man unconscious on my living room floor. I decided not to kill him, which might bite me in the ass later, but whatever. Before I knocked him out, he told me where to go.

I jump onto my motorcycle, turning it on, and smiling as it roars to life, vibrating underneath me. I just got it about a week ago, and I haven't had much time to use it.

He took her to an abandoned building about twenty minutes from here.

I don't know what is going to happen when I get there, but I'm not scared. As long as my sister is safe, then that's all that matters.

The roads are pretty much empty. I drive as fast as I can, my skirt flying up from the wind, showing my underwear, but I don't give a shit. The magic running through my veins keeps me warm from the cool air.

I pull up to the building and park the motorcycle, hopping off as I look around. I'm in the middle of nowhere. It's a large two-story brick building with a few broken windows. It looks old and abandoned. The grass and weeds are overgrown.

I walk through the overgrown grass that leads me to the large double doors. Not caring about being loud, I lift my left leg and kick down the metal doors, breaking them off the hinges with the help of my magic. No point in hiding, they know I'm coming.

I stand right outside the building, looking inside. I freeze, and all the air disappears from my lungs. I try to keep my face void of any emotions. There, right in the center of the room is Luna, tied up on a metal chair. The only light in the entire room is pointed right at her, and the rest of the room is pitch black. I roll my eyes. *Seriously*?

I start walking to her. Yes, the awareness is obvious to me that this is what they want, and it's a trap, but I couldn't care less about any of it. I just need to be close to her.

"No, Isabella! It's a trap, run," Luna cries out, her eyes puffy and red from all the crying. She starts struggling against the ropes.

"I know it is, Luna. But I'm not leaving you here alone." I smile at her, trying to be reassuring.

When I get close to her, all the lights flick on, and my father walks behind Luna, grabbing her left shoulder.

"Hello, daughter of mine." He grins. "You grew into such a beautiful young lady. I don't know what is so special about her, but I'm glad you are here."

Seriously, he doesn't know she's my sister. She looks so much like mom. I was so sure once he saw her, he'd know.

"She's a close friend of mine. Please, let her go. She has nothing to do with this." I put my hands on my hips, lifting my chin. "You finally got me right where you want me."

"Well, I guess I don't need her anymore now that you are here. But only if you stay."

I already know he isn't just going to let us both leave.

"I'll stay. I won't fight. Just let her go." I nod, looking him in the eye.

"No, Bella! We can fight them all and leave." She starts thrusting around. I can sense that she's trying to use her magic, making me frown.

"Shut up!" My father grabs hold of her throat, choking her slowly, making her go red in the face.

I snarl and rush toward him.

My hand hits the center of his chest over Luna's head, using the force of my magic to throw him, and his back slams against the wall. I tilt my head to the side as I look at him. I slowly look around, and I see at least a hundred or so men and women; they look like soldiers. He must think highly of me, gathering so many to fight me if needed.

I know I can't fight them without risking Luna's life. I won't lie, I am thinking about trying to take them all on. The dark side of me thinks it'd be fun. I take a deep, calming breath, and glance down at Luna. She's hunched over trying to catch her breath. Kneeling down in front of her, I start untying the ropes that are tightly wrapped around her ankles.

Luna hisses in pain, and I see her skin is raw due to her struggling against the rope.

"Luna, listen to me; you need to run. You have that note still with you?" She nods; her large eyes are filled with tears. I look at the red handprint around her throat that my father gave her and instantly feel sick to my stomach. "Good, now go. My bike is out front, so go straight there, okay? Do not stop for anything. If a cop tries to pull you over, use your magic to control him."

"But you said…"

"I know what I said," I snap, and pinch the bridge of my nose. "Just listen. Right now, ignore all the rules, okay? Do anything you need to do to get there." I untie her wrists, and she is finally free.

"Please don't make me go." She shakes her head, her lower lip trembling. "We can both make it out if we fight." Luna lets out a loud sob that echoes around the large room. I stand up and pull her up with me. She throws her arms around me.

"Not without risking your life, and that is not something I'm willing to do." Out of the corner of my eyes, I see my father moving as a man tries helping him up. "I love you. Please listen to me. It's not the time to argue. I'll find you again, I promise." I whisper lowly in her ear.

"Okay." She nods. "I love you, too."

"Now go." I push her toward the door. She takes a step, but my father's voice stops her from going further.

"Not without this," my father says as he digs into his front pocket and pulls out something long and shiny as he walks toward us. Once he stops in front of me, I can make out two silver chains of some sort.

"What are they for?" I narrow my eyes on the chains, an uncertainty feeling unfurls in my chest.

"It stops you from using your magic. Let's call it insurance." The thought of being chained up like some kind of monster sickens me. I push it aside; for Luna, I don't have another choice.

"None of you will follow her. Got it?" I try to sound strong, but it comes out low and weak, like my voice is breaking.

"Deal." He nods and steps in front of me. "Hold out both hands."

I gulp, but I do as he demands. I watch as he clasps each chain against my wrists; they look like bracelets. I pinch my lips together. I just gave up my powers. I'm trapped in his claws.

I turn to face Luna as my chest tightens. I push her out the door and mouth, *go.*

I watch as she slowly backs away, and I follow. Someone steps in front of me, and I laugh. "Fuck off, I'm not leaving, but I will watch her drive off."

"Let her be." My father nods and the man backs off but stays close.

I snort. "As if you could stop me anyway."

I pause beside the broken doors, and watch her as she climbs onto my motorcycle. It roars to life. My mom taught me how to drive one, and I taught Luna a year ago.

She turns to look at me with a sad expression.

I love you, I mouth. I smile at her, trying to comfort her, trying to look strong. In reality, I feel like I'm breaking.

She smiles back as she wipes the tears off her face, and she turns the bike around and then speeds off. My heart tightens as she disappears from sight. I bite my lower lip to keep it from trembling.

I tense when I feel hands gripping my shoulders, almost like a gentle caress.

"Don't touch me," I push my father's hands off, turning to face him.

"Don't be like that, sweet daughter of mine, it's nothing personal." he smirks. Before I can say anything, his fist comes flying and connects to the side of my face, hard. With my ears ringing and stars dancing in my vision, I fall hitting the ground with a thump, and I don't even bother fighting off the darkness.

This time, I let it consume me.

I groan as I roll to lie on my back. I look around, but it's completely dark. I can only see outlines thanks to the candles glowing. I'm like ninety-nine percent sure, they threw me into a damn cell, due to the chilly air and the lumpy mattress. I rub my hands together, trying to warm my cold fingers. They're so freaking cold that I lose all feeling. I sit up, and when I do, a sharp pain stabs the side of my head. Fuck that hurts like hell! I scrunch my nose. It smells like something, or someone, died in here, and their flesh is rotting.

Okay, don't panic...

I need to find a way to escape.

My dear father could have at least put me in an actual room, Jesus. I don't remember much about him except that he was a complete asshole to my mom and that he wasn't bad with me. My mom knew what he had planned for me was pure evil, and after she found out she was pregnant with Luna, she packed our things. We left, and we have been on the run since then. I was around four, so it's all I have ever known.

Mom truly loved my dad, but he grew evil after his sister was murdered; ever since, he'd been crazy with the need for revenge. I was only a year old when his sister died, and he wanted to use my powers to get revenge when I got old enough. But my mom didn't agree. She tried to change his mind, but he wouldn't listen; he knew how powerful I would be. How did he know? I have no damn idea.

My mom told me that no matter how strong I become, I would never defeat the man who murdered his sister because he's the Vampire Prince. She told me how strong he is, and the only reason his sister was murdered was because she was caught stealing.

My mom told me he forgave her the first time she stole, but when she tried stealing again, he killed her on the spot. I truly believe it was justified because he did give her a second chance.

How the *fuck* does my father think he can defeat the actual Vampire Prince? I don't know, but he is delusional, fucked in the fucking head. I have heard how sinister, ruthless, and powerful the prince is. Women also talk about how handsome he is, eye roll. I have never seen him before, so I wouldn't know.

All I know is I will never help my father. Not only because it's a suicide mission, but I wouldn't kill someone who didn't deserve it.

I hated my father with all my heart; I'll never forgive him. He's the one who sent that man to murder my mom.

When I was younger, a stupid, naïve little girl, I used to dream that he would forget about his hatred and revenge so we could be a family again.

I get up and start looking around, wondering if there's any way out. I see a few windows, but they're useless since they aren't in my cell.

"Hello?" I call out. *A girl has to eat, damn.* I spin around after hearing a low groan.

I'm not alone.

Maybe they can tell me where we are. "Hey, do you know where we are?" I ask whoever is in the other cell. I hear a grunt, but there's no reply. "Asshole," I mumble. I inch closer to the wall and slam the back of my head against it, *what the fuck am I going to do?*

A low chuckle cuts the silence, making me grin like an idiot.

"I don't know what you did to land in this hellhole, but me? Nothing!" I throw my hands in the air. "Heck, I wouldn't even have gotten caught, but I had to protect my sister. You see, my father wants to use me as revenge for his sister, and I refuse to help. Now here I am locked up because I don't want to be a part of his stupid revenge. How is that fair?"

"Shut up!" the man interrupts me, in a low growl.

"So, you do talk? You know, it's rude to interrupt someone talking."

"I don't care, little girl."

"Little girl? Who the fuck do you think you're talking to?" I snap, placing a hand on my hip, and narrowing my eyes into slits.

"You have a filthy mouth, little girl. "

"You're an asshole." I stomp toward his cell and grab hold of the bars with both hands.

"Yes, I am, but at least I'm not a whiny little girl."

"I am not whiny."

"You actually are. All you've been doing is complaining."

"Ha, so you were listening."

"Not like I had a fucking choice." He growls and out of nowhere, I see a pair of bright green eyes, almost as if they're glowing.

I gasp and step back, but fingers wrap around my wrist over the cuffs, and he yanks me forward until my body slams against the bars.

"Let me go!" I growl, baring my teeth. I yank on my wrist, and he lets me go making me fall onto my ass. I hiss at the sharp pain slithering up my spine. "You asshole!"

"I only did what you asked." He chuckles. I stand, backing away from him.

I plop down on the dirty little mattress and start thinking about Luna. *Did she go to the address like I told her to? Is she okay?* I wish there was a way to know, but until I get out of here, I won't.

I wish I were stricter with her like my mom was with me, but I wanted her to have the freedom I had always craved.

She's seventeen, four years younger than me. She's definitely a wild child. I was forced to grow up since my mom died when I was sixteen, and I had to provide for us at a young age.

I started telling her why we were on the run when she turned fourteen, but she never took it seriously. She always said if my dad were looking for us, he would have found us already. But I knew he was looking for me and that he would find me eventually.

I did teach her how to run, though, so she should be on the way to my mom's best friend's house. Trisha should be able to teach her how to use her demon powers and give her a safe place to stay. Mom wanted me to go there if anything happened to her, but I didn't listen, thinking I could do it alone. But if I had listened, we wouldn't be in this situation. Maybe I should have gone there after my mom passed, and Luna would be safe.

I lay my back onto the dirty mattress, thinking of my mom. I remember one day, about a week after we ran from my father, we found a small apartment, and the first night we were there, we built a little fort where we slept. There, in that fort, she braided my hair and told me magical stories.

She always told me not to be ashamed of who I was. That I was unique and special, so I needed to be proud of being different.

I'm the only halfling that was mixed with both witch and demon. I tried to keep us around demons for Luna's sake so she could learn more about her kind, but they hated me and refused to help me.

I'm hated for what I am, and I try to be okay with it. But deep down, I'm lonely and hurt.

God, I miss you, Mom. I close my eyes and doze off.

"Izzy! Run now!" My mom screams from the kitchen. I run, but not away from her, I run towards her.

I stop dead in my tracks when I find her fighting with a large man. His back is towards me, but instead of helping her, I turn and run scared. I have to hide with Luna. My vision starts blurring from the tears. Fear runs through my veins, turning my blood cold, making my body tremble, and my heart pound like a drum in my chest.

"Luna," I whisper to my sister when I finally make it to her room, I grab her small shoulders and begin to shake her; she groans lowly, brows furrowing. "Get up, we have to hide."

"But Bella, why?" my sister whines. Rolling over, she starts rubbing her eyes. I hate that she's so whiny; Mom spoils her too much.

"Luna, it's not the time. Let's go. Now." She grumbles but finally gets up, and we both rush to her closet. There's a hidden door in the back of it that my mom had made for us. She gets down on her knees, but before she goes in, she turns to look at me with tears in her eyes.

"What's happening?" she says, her lower lip trembling.

"Nothing, Luna. Go, now." I motion my hands towards the small door. She nods and crawls inside. I start crawling in, but a loud, high-pitched scream stops me. I swallow the lump of fear in my throat and close my eyes. I should be helping her instead of hiding. "Close the door and do not open it, no matter what, unless it's Mom or me."

"But you need to come in too," she cries out.

"Stop being such a crybaby and shut the door!"

"But..."

"Stop!" I shout, grabbing my hair, pulling at it, and squeezing my eyes shut, taking a few deep breaths. When I hear the door shut, I turn and leave.

I shut the bedroom door and slowly tiptoe down the hall. I can hear things being thrown around, one moment, but another moment later, there's nothing but silence. I pause, praying to hear something, anything.

I'm paralyzed with terror when I hear footsteps thumping up the stairs. I need to hide, but my limbs refuse to listen to my commands, and that's when I see him, a large man. Large doesn't even begin to describe him... he's a freaking giant. He looks extremely scary; he tilts his head to the side as his gaze slowly sweeps over me. I whimper and step back, his lips slowly curl into an evil grin, like he's enjoying my fear.

His eyes are completely black, no white in them at all. He has a large scar running from his left eye down to his upper lip.

"Look what we have here, Daddy's little princess. You know he's been looking everywhere for you. I don't think he cares if I have a little taste of you first." He licks his lips with a long, pointed tongue.

"Get away from me," I say as I start backing away, holding my hands up in front of me. My arms are shivering violently. I bite my lower lip hard to keep myself from crying.

"Oh, come on, sweetheart, I'll make you feel really good." He starts to freaking laugh, like a maniac. Like I'm not trembling in fear. He reaches me in two long strides and grabs hold of my upper arm tightly.

I know I should use my magic, but my head is hazy from the fear. I can't even think straight.

"Damn, you look like a fucking angel, my sweet." His hand wraps around my throat. "I can't wait to fuckin ruin you." His other hand slides inside my shorts.

'No matter how scared you are, you must fight!' I hear my mom's voice yelling louder and louder in my head. That's the moment I decide to push my fears away and fight back.

"Fuck you." I spit in his face and it lands on the side of his lip.

"Wow, not so angel-like, love." He licks it clean. Okay, that was gross.

"This won't feel angel-like either," I hiss as I look him right in the eye and smile sweetly before I feel the heat of my power coming alive, rushing through me. His eyes widen in shock as my eyes turn bright red. Everyone finds them creepy, but I don't. I smile widely at the delicious feeling buzzing inside of me.

My hands are swallowed by my flames. I grip the sides of his head and watch as my flames rush into his gaping mouth and begin to burn him from the inside out.

He screams in agony and falls onto his knees, grabbing hold of his head.

"I hope you burn in hell," I whisper. He starts shaking violently, and then blood starts oozing out of his nose and ears, and finally, he stops shaking and takes his last breath as his skin turns to ash.

I drop to my knees as I let go of my flames. Exhaustion hits me from the dark magic I used.

The house grows too quiet.

"Mom." I gasp.

I gasp, sitting up, my shirt clinging to me, damp with sweat. My throat is drier than a desert, shit, I need water.

I wrap my arms around my legs and rest my forehead against my knees as I softly cry. If I weren't a coward, she would still be alive. I used to hate being around Luna. I always thought that she was a spoiled little brat. I used to be so jealous of her.

She was allowed to be a kid and have fun, but not so much for me. My mom always made me stay home so we could practice my magic. If it wasn't that, she was teaching me how to fight. Meanwhile, Luna was able to go out and be with friends. Mom never pushed her because her magic is weak, she never had special abilities, and she didn't have a sociopathic father chasing her. No one looked at her like she was a freak.

Even though she didn't need to work on her powers, Mom should have taught her how to fight, at least so she could take care of herself. I used to argue with my mom about it. She always said, *"Let her be. Let her have fun. We can protect her."*

What I hated the most was that I was made fun of for being different, but I wasn't different. I never had a demon side, never had demon abilities, almost like I wasn't part demon.

A door slams open, jolting me from my thoughts, I get to my feet. The lights flick on, and I slam my eyes shut from the brightness.

"Isabella." I hear a deep voice call out. I slowly blink my eyes open. My father is standing on the other side of my cell.

"Dad? What do you want?" I walk to the cell door, wrapping my arms around my midsection for some type of comfort.

"I think we both know the answer to that." He looks down, his hand rubbing the back of his neck.

"If it's about your obsession with getting revenge, you're wasting your time, mother already told you."

"Why not? They are monsters; they need to be stopped." He grabs hold of the bars and bares his teeth at me, looking like a madman.

"I don't attack someone unless they attack me, I won't help you." I back away, shaking my head.

"They killed your aunt!" He screams, making me flinch at the sudden change.

"I'm sorry, but I can't." I inhale deeply. "Do you really think Auntie would want you to ruin your life for this obsession of yours?"

"She'd want me to get revenge, and revenge I will get, and you will help me."

"You're insane!"

"They need to be stopped! Do you know how many people they kill just for the fun of it?" He snarls at me, the vein in his forehead is pulsing with anger.

"It's impossible. This is the Vampire Prince you're talking about! He's a strong vampire; it's a suicide mission."

"You're stronger! It's not a suicide mission, not with your help. I have thousands of warlocks who will fight with us! We can do it. You can hurt or kill dozens with a flick of your wrist! That kind of power is rare, my love. If I have you on my side, we will win!"

"I won't help!" I shout. "What the prince did to your sister was justified; she shouldn't have stolen from him!"

"You killed over a dozen yesterday, without a single care."

"That was different. They were attacking me and my..." I clear my throat, almost saying my sister. "I refuse to help you!"

"Then you can rot in here for all I care." He turns and opens the door. "When you change your mind, tell the guard, and he'll send for me."

"You can't just leave me here!"

"I can and I will." He shuts off the lights.

"I'd rather rot here forever than help you!" I scream, but all I hear is the door slamming shut.

"Fuck!" I turn and kick the bucket that's in the corner of the cell.

My knees give out, and I drop to the floor. Would I really rather rot in here than help kill someone? Yes, I don't care how cruel the Prince is; I won't stoop to his level and become a killer.

A few hours pass by, and the door opens again, the lights flick on. I see the same man from my house with some food and water. He smirks at me, grabs keys from his front pocket, and unlocks my cell door. Once unlocked, he comes in.

I flinch when he gets closer, and I see his throat; it didn't heal. It looks awful, making me feel bad.

Remember, he attacked you.

"Thank God, I'm so thirsty." I smile; he must be helping me since I let him live.

"Nope." He tsks at me, shaking his head, and holding the water out of my reach. "Only if you're a good girl."

"What the hell are you talking about?"

"If you want this, you'll get on your knees and suck my cock with those pretty lips."

"Ha, funny." I roll my eyes; no way this dumbass really thinks I'll do it.

"Does it look like I'm joking?" He arches his brow, walking towards me slowly. I step back a few times till my back hits the dirt wall.

"It's not happening, so back off," I snap.

"Fine, we'll do this the hard way. You can't use your magic, and you are too weak from not having food or anything to drink in two days." He grins, and then he grips my throat tightly. I lift my knee to knee his dick, but he's faster, blocking the blow and spinning me around, so my face is pressed against the wall. His hips push against my ass, and he wastes no time gripping my shirt, ripping it in half.

My hand swings to his face, and when my palm hits his nose, his grip loosens. I spin around, and I punch the side of his face, he staggers back a little. I kick him in the stomach, and he falls down, landing on his ass. The food and water go flying; what a waste.

Even without food or water, I can still kick ass, but my victory is short-lived when his head snaps up, and my heart stops.

Oh shit.

His fangs are long and sharp, his ears are now pointy, and his nails are now claws. Yep, you pissed off a shifter, good fucking job! He's gonna rip me to shreds.

"Want it the hard way, baby?" He slowly stands up and when he gets close, I shove him and run towards the open cell door. I nearly make it when he grabs a fist full of my long hair and yanks hard enough to make me fall back. The sting of it makes my eyes water. I fall hard onto the ground, and he's right there with his knees forcing my legs open, he settles in between them.

"Let go of me!" I scream as he grips my wrists and holds them above my head with one hand and the other hand assaulting my breast.

"Fuck, baby." He groans. "You have the perfect tits." I look down and see that my white lace bra is on full display. You can see everything.

"Yeah, they are, and you can't have them, asshole." I growl.

"Oh, and who's gonna stop me?" He arches his brow, and then he's gone. I quickly jump up and look around.

Where the fuck did he go?

I see him lying on the floor, scrambling to get up, and I also see another man slowly stalking towards him. The mystery man bends over, and I watch in fascination as the mystery man wraps his large hand around his throat and picks him up like he weighs nothing. Very impressive.

Fuck me, that's so hot.

Really Bella, not the fucking time.

The Greek God has him midair, the asshole is clawing at the stranger's hands trying to get him to loosen his grip. I look at the open cell door. I need to get out of here.

That's when I notice two things: one, the stranger is shirtless, and two, there's a large open portal. It's dark, and I can't see what's on the other side. *Should I jump? It has to be better than this hellhole, right?* I look back at the stranger and gulp.

I know I shouldn't be checking him out at a time like this, but the muscles on this man are incredible. Oh, and don't let me forget to mention the tattoos. I can't suppress the loud, long groan that escapes me. I mentally slap myself.

Seriously, not the time. I step toward the portal ready to make the jump, when his head snaps toward me, and he gives me a sexy, lopsided grin.

He looks like pure sin; I should stay far *far* away.

"Would you like me to kill him?" He asks, arching a sexy brow. His voice is raspy, with a slight Italian accent. I lick my dry lips, and my hand moves to fix my hair, feeling nothing but knots. God, I must look crazy.

Seriously, you're worried about the way you look? Don't let this Greek God affect your head. You need to leave and find Luna.

"Well?" *Oh, um, what did he ask me? Oh yes, right...*

"No, no," I clear my throat. "J-just let him go." I stumble on my words, completely out of breath.

"You want to let him go?" His brows pinch together in confusion before looking back at the man whose face is now blue from the lack of air.

I love how easy he's making it look, like the man is as light as a feather. It's a complete turn-on.

"Yeah." He throws him across the room, and the man lands limp on the floor unconscious.

"I would've killed him." He shrugs.

Yeah, I kind of figured that out already.

"I don't like killing people unless it's necessary." My back slumps against the wall behind me. I feel so freaking exhausted.

Greek God tilts his head to the side, his gaze slowly roams down my body, erupting goosebumps all over. My body has never reacted this way to anyone before. He's not the only person to check me out, but I like it when his eyes are on me.

"You're such a good girl, aren't you?" He licks his upper lip. My breathing picks up, the fire in the pit of my stomach burns wildly, and my mind wonders what those lips would feel like on mine.

God help me; I'm about to sin.

"Um, yeah," that's all I can manage to say. He grins at me. He knows the effect he's having on me right now.

Snap out of it!

"You do have perfect tits," he growls lowly, and he slowly begins stalking towards me like a predator stalking its prey. I feel more than willing to be eaten by this predator. I look down at myself and realize I completely forgot I'm only wearing a skirt and a see-through white lace bra.

"Yeah, yeah, I'm aware." I roll my eyes and cross my arms over them, trying to cover myself from his predatory gaze. Once I do, his gaze connects to mine. And wow, he's so beautiful it's hard to even look at him. *Can a man be beautiful? I don't know, but he is.*

"What kind of beautiful creature are you?" He steps into my personal space, his hands pressed against the wall on either side of my head, boxing me in. His nose grazes my neck as he inhales my scent.

Vampire...

"Uh, ummm...." I can't find my words. My brain becomes completely useless around him. He smells like warm spice with a hint of cinnamon. It's intoxicating and masculine. I just want to wrap myself around his warmth.

"Enough flirting, cousin. Can you get me the hell out of here?" The Godlike man stares at me for a few moments before pushing himself off the wall, backing away. He goes to the other cell where my asshole cellmate is and breaks the door open with one arm.

Can he please stop being all strong and sexy around me?

It's annoying.

My cellmate comes to my cell. He's very handsome, too. They actually look a lot alike, but my cellmate is shorter and bulkier.

Where did these men come from? Wherever it was, they need to go back, they're bad for my health.

"Sooo," I drag it out. "Are we, uh, gonna leave before someone comes and sees the door open and locks us back in?"

"That would be a good idea, little one," my cellmate nods.

"The name is Isabella!" I shout annoyed with all the nicknames.

"Hmm." Godlike one rubs his chin, in deep thought. "Maybe if you say 'please.'" He grins at me.

"Are you freaking serious?" I snap, throwing my hands up.

"Yes, I'm very serious, vixen."

"Urgh! Come on!"

"Okay, I'll shut the door behind us, and we'll leave." He starts turning away.

"You wouldn't dare." I say through clench teeth.

"Oh yes, I would." He looks over his shoulder and smiles widely at me.

"Okay! Jeez!" I clear my throat. "Please help me out of here." He turns back to me, and when he reaches me, he snakes his arm around my waist and picks me up. My breasts smash against his chest. He looks between us and winks.

The area he touches sends an electrical shock through my body, and judging by his confused expression, he feels it too. *He feels so good wrapped around me. God, I'm ready to fuck him here and now.* He buries his face into my neck, giving the sensitive skin below my ear a soft kiss, making me shiver. This intense feeling is all too much.

"Hold on tight, love," He whispers in my ear.

"Don't call me love," I snap. I'm so frustrated with myself and my body's reaction to him. My body is totally betraying me.

My body is acting like a horny bitch in heat, and it's not a good time for that.

"Whatever you say, *love*." He reaches over me and grabs my cellmate's upper arm.

"You mother-" My words cut off. It feels like I'm flying, the world around me blurs, and my hair moves with the wind.

And I feel violently sick.

Chapter 4

We land in a large room. The walls are dark grey, but the back wall is all windows, and all I see are large trees. I'm still wrapped around the stranger like a damn koala bear, so I slowly untangle myself from his body and take a few steps back.

I nearly fall, but my cellmate grips my upper arm, steadying me. I blink a few times to try to get rid of the dizziness. After a couple of minutes, I regain my bearings.

"Whoa." I start walking towards the wall of windows; it's as if we're standing amongst the trees outside.

To the right of me is a large black stone fireplace with a brown leather sectional in front of it. It's all very masculine.

"Welcome to my home," Greek God says. *Of course, it's his house.*

"Who are you?" I ask, looking at them, the only thing they're wearing are jeans—no shoes or shirts.

"You don't know who I am?" the Greek God asked, arching a perfect brow.

"Uhh, nooo?"

"No wonder you've been so snappy. When you find out who I am, you'll be all over me." He gives me a panty dropping lopsided grin. I roll my eyes.

What a cocky bastard.

He's too cocky. *We don't like him*; I try to tell my body.

"You should, since your father is planning on rebelling against him," my cellmate growls angrily. I look at him in shock.

"Wait, her father is Margus?" Greek God spits out angrily as his eyes flash in anger. I take a couple of steps back, ready to run. "Why the fuck did you allow me to bring her here if you knew this whole time, Darren?" He turns to my cellmate, or I guess Darren.

Wait, what did he say? My father is trying to rebel against him?

Oh no... is he the Vampire Prince? Surely, he'd kill me.

Why does this shit happen to me?

I have such crappy luck.

I need to get the fuck out of here.

I scan the room looking for an escape. I see a doorway and start walking back toward it.

"Don't be angry, Azrael." I watch as Darren also backs away from him.

Good, he's the perfect distraction I need to escape.

God, I finally felt attracted to a man, and it's him! No wonder he looks like sin. He's the ultimate sinner. He's made to look the way he does to lure innocent humans.

"How could you allow her to come here?" Greek God, or I mean Azrael, hisses.

Shit, even his name is hot.

"Because her father threw her into that cell because she refused to join him. She's powerful, so I gather we could use her on our side. She's part demon too."

"She is a halfling? Worse, she's a fucking *witch*," he spits out in disgust, making me flinch.

For some reason, my chest squeezes in pain knowing he finds me disgusting. Like everyone else, he hates me, and finds me a disgrace. I bite my trembling lip hard, trying not to cry.

I quickly turn and run down a long hallway. I run into a large entryway, the double doors are right there. I smile widely, wanting to do a little dance, but I don't, obviously. I grab the handle and swing the door open. We're in the middle of nowhere, it looks like, but I have to leave before he kills me.

As soon as I step out, a strong arm wraps around my waist and pulls me back inside, slamming the door shut. I scream in complete frustration.

The front of my body slams against the wall. It knocks the wind out of me, a large body is pressed against my back. I turn my head to look over my shoulder, but he slams my head against the wall, keeping me in place.

"You're not going anywhere, wicked little witch," he hisses in my ear, making me whimper. He pushes his hips against my ass, and he moves my hair to the side. I gasp in shock when he licks the side of my neck, making me shiver. I hate the way my body reacts to him.

He's about to bleed me dry, and I'm getting turned on. What the fuck is wrong with me?

I squeeze my eyes shut, and my body tenses as I prepare myself for the painful bite.

"Let her go, Azrael. We can use her as bait to capture her father."

"No!" I snap angrily. My head is pounding from the pressure of his hold. I need to get out of here, like now, before he drains me. I can't use my magic with these stupid cuffs around my wrist.

"You will help us," Azrael snarls against my neck, and then he spins me around, pushing my back against the wall. The back of my head hits the wall hard, and I clench my teeth to keep myself from crying out in pain.

"I will not!" I straighten my shoulders, lifting my chin to look into his ocean blue eyes.

"I got you out of there; now you owe me." He grips my jaw, and his fingers dig painfully into my cheeks.

I can feel his hot breath against my lips, and a small whimper escapes. "You like this, don't you?"

He smirks; then he thrusts his hips against mine. "Of course, the filthy witch is a little whore."

"No, being manhandled by an asshole isn't a turn on for me, and I could've gotten out on my own." I narrow my eyes. "I didn't ask for your help."

"Fine, I'll take you back." His nose touches my right cheek, and my eyes connect with Darren. I'm about to plead for his help, but I feel a sharp pinch underneath my ear, causing my core to tighten with pleasure.

"Did you just bite me?" I snap, I place my hands against his shoulders trying to push him off me, but he grabs my wrists. He lifts them over my head and holds them there.

"I didn't even break skin. Plus, don't act like you didn't like that. I see the look in your eyes. You almost threw yourself at me like a dirty little whore."

"I wouldn't fuck you if you were the last man alive!" I growl, and my knee rams right into his cock. He hisses in pain and his eyes flash red for a moment, but he doesn't loosen his grip. Well, my mom's boyfriend was wrong. Not every man will drop.

"Just admit it, little witch, admit how turned on you are," he sucks my earlobe into his mouth. *Oh god.* My eyes threaten to flutter shut; *no.* I struggle to get away from him.

"Azrael, that's enough!" Darren snaps. "Isabella, please help us." He pulls Azrael away from me, and I wrap my arms around my midsection.

"To kill my father? Yeah, no thanks."

"We don't want to kill him."

"Speak for yourself." Azrael cuts him off, obviously, he doesn't agree. Darren holds up two fingers, silencing him.

"Like I was saying, he does need to be imprisoned for what he has done. He has gotten out of hand." I nod, agreeing with him. *He has gotten out of hand.*

"No, I'm sorry, but I can't stay, I need to find my sister before he finds her and uses her against me." I look away from them as I start to tear up. I hate not knowing if she is safe or not. "She needs me."

"Look, we can help you find her; it'll be easier with our help. I do apologize for my cousin. He can be an asshole at times." He smiles at me and hands me a grey throw blanket. I look up at him and smile as I grab the blanket and wrap it around my shoulders, covering myself.

"Fine, I'll help you, but first we need to find my sister, and you have to keep us safe."

"Of course." Darren nods in agreement.

"Just stay out of my way," Azrael snaps.

"Fine, not like I want to be near you, asshole." I shrug, acting like it doesn't bother me.

"Just because you're a dirty little witch doesn't mean anything. I'm still a royal, so learn your place and show me some respect," he snarls behind Darren.

"Fine, then stay out of my way." I hold the blanket tighter to my chest, wanting to disappear inside of it.

"With pleasure." He narrows his eyes at me.

I ignore him and turn to Darren, holding out my wrist. "What about these?"

"We're not taking those off," Azrael says to Darren before storming away.

"For now." He clears his throat. "We'll start looking for your sister tomorrow. Let me show you your room." Darren turns and starts walking up the stairs.

"I think I know where she is. Can you at least tell me where we are? And I thank you for your kindness towards me."

"Good, that gives us a place to start. I don't think less of you for being a halfling. You're strong. I can feel your power, don't let anyone shame you for who you are, not even my cousin." That makes me smile, and my heart swells. "We're in Italy."

"No wonder it looks so beautiful outside. Luna, my sister, will be so excited to be here because she always dreamt of coming here." I smile to myself, thinking of her reaction. She'll want to go shopping and eat yummy croissants with a cup of coffee all day.

"What about you?" He looks at me, and I blush, shaking my head in embarrassment.

I've never really thought of what I wanted.

"Me? I'm not sure what I want," I shrug. "It's always been about my sister as long as she's happy and safe."

"That's very kind of you, but you need to be happy as well." He walks me down a long hall, it's dark gray with black doors and no personal touches, just like the rest of the house. "My room is here," he says as we pass the first door. "Your room is here. And Azrael's is there." My room is between the men's rooms, a way to keep an eye on me.

"Thank you." I tuck my hair behind my ear.

"You're welcome, I'll ask my cousin to bring some clothes for you. She's about your size, I think. She doesn't live too far. Now go and rest."

"Thank you," I repeat and open the door.

I walk in, and the walls are a light feather gray. There is a large antique canopy bed in the center of the room and on the other side of it is double glass doors leading out to a balcony, two cozy chairs in front of a stone fireplace. I walk to a door next the bed and see an elegant bathroom, the same color as the room, with marble floors, and a pretty claw-foot tub.

This room is made for a queen.

I go back to the room making a beeline to the glass doors. God, the sight is beautiful, trees and rolling hills. It looks like the balcony wraps around the whole second floor of the house, meaning I share it with the guys. I lean against the railing, enjoying the fresh air for a moment.

I head back inside, straight to the bathroom, turning on the water. I begin removing my dirty clothes. My ID and the tips I made at work drop to the floor when I remove my skirt.

Shit, I'm going to lose my job. I have no way of contacting them; I don't remember anyone's phone number. It doesn't matter. They found us; we'll have to move again.

The bathroom steams up, and I step into the hot water. *God, I needed this.* I close my eyes and force myself to relax. The water back home never got this hot before, and shit, it feels good. I start scrubbing myself off. The bathroom is stocked with everything I needed, thank goodness.

I definitely should take a bath here. I bet it would be amazing!

I can't trust them, but I do pray they actually help me find my sister as soon as possible. It's the only reason I'm staying and not trying to find a way out. It'd be hard on my own getting back to the States, especially without magic and with only a couple hundred dollars.

Do I even want to put my father behind bars? Could I? I'm not sure. Even though he's a bad person, I have always hoped he'd change to be who he was before his sister died.

I loved him so much; he used to be such an amazing dad.

It's crazy how one small thing can change someone so much.

I just wish he loved me enough to be a better man.

After I shower, I wrap the super fluffy white towel around me and go into the bedroom. I let out a loud squeal that sounds like a mouse when I see him sitting on one of the chairs, watching me silently.

"What are you doing here?" I grip the towel tighter, making sure it stays put.

Chapter 5

AZRAEL

"What are you doing here?" she snaps at me; no one has ever spoken to me the way she does. Why do I allow her, too? I'm not too sure, but I love her sassiness. God this girl is gifted, made straight from the devil himself, made to be a temptation you cannot fight and she'll cause you to sin for a simple little taste of her sweet nectar.

I don't answer; instead, my gaze swipes over her body, admiring her long, shapely legs. The towel is way too small for her, and the curve of her neck makes me want to sink my teeth into the soft flesh. My gaze moves up, and I memorize every detail of her face.

She's sucking on her lower lip, making me wish it was me sinking my teeth into those plush lips. I want to rip the towel off and devour every inch of her and punish her sassy ass. No, I remind myself that she's nothing but a witch and, worse of all, my enemy's daughter. I wouldn't touch her if she were the last woman on earth.

"It's my house," I finally reply, and she narrows her stunning forest green eyes.

"You could have knocked, you know."

"Yeah, true, but I wasn't feeling it." I shrug as my thumb rubs my lower lip; she follows the movement. When my sister dropped the clothes off, I volunteered to deliver them, using it as an excuse to see her again. "My sister brought some clothes for you." I held up my hand, showing her the bag of clothes dangling on my index finger.

I don't know what it is about her that makes me feel something different, something I never felt before.

I want her close, and that angers me, more than I'll ever admit.

She shakes her head, throws herself onto the mattress, and lifts one of her legs, inching the towel up, showing me more thigh.

Fuck. Me.

Knowing that she's completely bare underneath makes me want to spread her legs apart and taste her. I wonder if she'd taste as good as she smells. I bet she'd be sweet. I growl in annoyance when my cock hardens uncomfortably in my jeans.

"I'm too tired for this. Can I have the clothes, so I can sleep?" She turns her head to look at me. Every time she looks at me, she takes my breath away, and it pisses me the hell off.

I snarl at myself, and stand. I need to get away from her before I do something stupid. I throw the bag of clothes onto the floor and leave without another word.

I follow my cousin's scent and it leads me to the basement bar, he's already drinking.

"How were you caught?" I ask him as I pour myself a drink.

"I was caught off guard, I guess. I was trapped by the woman I was having sex with. She worked for him." He sighs, staring at the small glass of whiskey.

"You need to be more careful. I told you to stop going home with strange women."

"I won't need to; I have little Bella for now. She's definitely a sweet temptation. I can't wait to fuck her." I grind my teeth together and my hand tightens around my glass, a foreign feeling burns in the pit of my stomach.

"You will do no such thing," I growl. I have the desire to kill anyone who dares to touch her.

"The fuck?" He frowns, brows pinching together. "Why not? You're not interested in her, last I heard, you are disgusted by what she is. Plus, we always share women."

"Because this is business, we cannot mix it up with pleasure. It can get messy," I lie.

"True. I'll think about it because she's too tempting and it might be worth the trouble. Plus, I actually like her. She might be more than sex for me."

"You don't do relationships."

"I don't, but with her, I can see myself in one. She's feisty, strong, and hot."

I don't understand why I'm feeling this way; I hate what she is. I hate her father. I want to strangle her, and at the same time fuck the hell out of her till she's screaming my name, begging me for more.

Making her mine.

Don't be stupid, I'd never make her mine. She's a fucking witch...

He can have her.

"Do what you want." I take a swig of whiskey and walk out.

I'm sitting in my dark room with my legs stretched out in front of me, thinking of her green eyes, full lips, and luscious little body.

Fuck.

I get up, walk to the balcony, leaning my back against the railing, and stare at the glass doors. I check the silver watch on my wrist, and it's a little past midnight, she'll be asleep.

Don't.

I ignore myself and slowly step toward her door, looking through the glass. She's sound asleep in her bed. My hand grips the door handle, but I pause, closing my eyes and placing my forehead against the glass.

I hate everything about this woman, but she's my mate. I knew it as soon as I touched her. The way I feel when I'm close to her, when I touch her, it's... amazing. But we can't. She'll never become my queen. I hate witches, and I'll never allow one to rule beside me. The mate bond is hard to ignore, but not impossible.

Fate is a fucking bitch.

I quickly twist the door handle, and sure enough, it's unlocked. I slowly walk in. I stand at the side of her bed, watching her; she looks peaceful. When she is awake, she looks so stressed; as if the whole world rests on her shoulders.

She moves, kicking the blanket off her and starts thrusting around just a little. I look down, and see that she's only wearing a T-shirt with a red lace thong, red looks good on her brown skin. I swallow, my gaze lowers, looking at her shapely legs, I release a low groan.

My gaze slowly runs up her body, landing on her breasts. I can see the outline of her hard nipples. She has the best pair of tits I have ever laid eyes on, and that bubbly ass is even better. I can imagine my red handprints on each cheek as I smack them.

Fuck. I'm being a complete freak, but I can't bring myself to care.

My phone starts vibrating, I rush out of the room before answering without looking at the caller ID.

"Boss?"

"What?" I snap, pissed at the interruption. I close my eyes and rub my temple.

"We found the snitch."

"Good. Find out who he leaked the information to and kill him. If you can't get him to talk, let me know, and I'll come down. I'll force him to talk." I secretly hope they can't. "You know what? I'll be down in a few." I hang up and text Darren to let him know that I'm leaving.

I get to the warehouse, it's where we do our dirty work. Everyone bows when I enter the metal building. My steps falter when my eyes land on the traitor, who's chained to a metal chair in the middle of the large room. He begins wiggling against the chains, trying to get away from me, and the tape over his mouth muffles his words.

I bend down and rip the tape off his mouth.

"Please, they threatened..."

"I don't care," I interrupt him. "You betrayed me regardless of who they threatened. Now tell me, who did you leak the information to?"

"I can't. They'll kill him," he cries out, eyes begging me to understand, we've been good friends for a long time, I know exactly who he's talking about.

"I would've protected him for you." My nostrils flare, the anger pulses through my veins, making it hard to stay calm. "You were my second in command! You know I would've had your back, Luke."

"I know, I acted out in fear! I'm sorry." He shakes his head, mumbling I'm sorry, over and over.

"Who did you leak the information to, Luke?"

"Prince Gabriel. He wants to take you down. He's pissed that you'll be taking over the crown soon and becoming king. He doesn't want you to wear the crown."

I ball my hands into tight fists. That asshole keeps coming for me, and it's starting to piss me off. We were good friends back in school, but when his mom died, he pushed everyone away. I've been giving him some slack, but enough is enough.

I stare at Luke. What should I do? I get it. He's worried about his father, but he betrayed me. I can't allow this to happen.

I slowly stalk towards him, staring into his eyes.

"You betrayed me. I can never trust you again," I say, as my hand shoots forward, digging into his chest, my fingers wrapping around his beating heart.

"Please..." He chokes out, I don't look away as I rip his heart out. His body slumps forward. This is why I trust no one.

"I don't give a fuck who you are! Friend or not, if you betray me, this is your fate!" I look around the room, staring at the men who work for me. "No one will get mercy!" I look down at the beating heart still in my hand, and I smash it; the blood drips down my arm before I drop it onto the floor.

Chapter 6

BELLA

I'm digging through the bags of clothes, and there's nothing I like; everything is so girly, colorful, and it's mostly dresses.

I release a long, slow frustrated breath, and finally, at the bottom, there's a pair of black jeans and a few tops. I wiggle into the jeans and throw on a white halter top, then turn to look at my reflection. The jeans are skintight, but I look good. I run my finger down the material of the shirt; it feels expensive, soft, buttery, must've cost more than my paycheck.

I finger-comb my long hair as I stare at the dark bags underneath my eyes, I look so freaking tired. I woke up in the middle of the night, and I couldn't fall back asleep. I pull my hair into a messy bun and shrug; it's the best I can do. My stomach growls in hunger.

Alrighty, you can't hide in here forever, Bella.

I put my shoes on and step out of the room. I slowly move down the hall and down the stairs, taking everything in. Honestly, there's really nothing to see. It's a beautiful house, but it's empty, and looks staged. I finally hear voices down a long hallway, I peek around the corner and there they are.

My eyes find Azrael first. He's wearing a shirt this morning, at least. It looks like he just rolled out of bed. His hair is tussled in a sexy way. He sits in a chair on the other side of the room, looking bored, not paying attention to the other two in the room. One hand is tapping the arm of the chair, and the other is holding his cell phone, typing away. His legs are spread widely in front of him.

I want to go to him, slip in between his legs, and sit on his lap. I shake myself mentally and step into the room. He looks up at me, and I swallow when his eyes darken with anger. It looks like he'd kill me if given the chance, but I guess they need me, so I know he won't, at least for now. I need to run as soon as I help him or I'm dead.

He hates me.

I don't care.

Liar.

I truly don't understand why that bothers me so much. Yes, I'm attracted to him, but I don't know him. No matter what it is, I won't allow him to see how much it affects me. I need to show him that I hate him, too; I narrow my eyes at him and lift my chin.

"Oh my gosh! You're beautiful!" I hear a loud screech, turning away from Azrael, I lock eyes with a petite girl with pixie dark hair. "Why didn't you tell me how pretty she is?" She smacks Darren's shoulder, making me smile.

She's one to talk, she's gorgeous. She has the same ocean blue eyes, I'm sure she is Azrael's sister.

"Hi." I smile, waving my fingers awkwardly at her.

"I'm Stella, Azrael's sister! Come have a seat!" She waves me over.

"I'm Isabella. Nice to meet you, and thank you for the clothes." I pick a seat beside Darren, as I feel most comfortable with him.

"You're welcome. They look small on you, we'll need to go shopping so you have your own clothes." She giggles and claps, my eyes widen as I exhale. It's way too early for her perkiness. Plus, I haven't even had coffee. How is she so cheery this early? I wrinkle my nose.

"Good morning," Darren whispers close to my ear. Somehow, I can literally feel Azrael's eyes on me. I look over, and sure enough, he's staring at me, and when our eyes connect, he's not even ashamed that he was caught staring.

I've heard stories of him so many times, and nothing good except for his looks, that he's dangerous and murderous. I've heard that he's going to be taking over his father's crown soon, but they want to wait till he finds a queen first, and after that, women lined up, throwing themselves at him, but he didn't want any of them. They weren't good enough; he's looking for someone with beauty and power.

I see the hatred in his eyes every time he looks at me. He'd never want to be with me. He hates my kind, and to make it worse, my father is his enemy.

Plus, I have too many emotional scars and baggage that no man will ever want to deal with. I finally tear my gaze away from his, and I look down at the food. I'll probably always be alone. Being on the run will never change if I don't help them capture my father.

"Good morning," I finally reply to Darren, looking over at him, his arm is on the back of my chair. It makes me want to move away for a little space, but I don't want to be rude.

"I hope my brother hasn't been too rude. He can be an asshole; he doesn't understand the meaning of manners."

"Oh, uh, yeah, but it doesn't matter, honestly." I shrug it off. "When can we start looking for my sister?" I ask, looking between all three of them.

"Give us the address you think she's at, and Azrael will fetch her," Darren answers. I don't feel comfortable with him being alone with her.

"Can I come?" I ask, looking back at Azrael. He just stares at me with cold, unemotional eyes. I arch my brow after a few minutes.

"No," he snarls at me, lifting his upper lip, which has my heart beating rapidly, feeling fear but also a little bit of excitement.

"Azrael," Stella snaps at him. "Behave." He doesn't look away from me, making me suppress a tremble of fear. I hold his stare, not wanting him to see the fear he causes within me. I have never felt so much power radiating off one person.

"I just really want to be there. She'll be scared, she doesn't know you, it'll make it easier, and I also really want to make sure that she's okay." I pout, and quickly look away, hoping it'll make him feel bad enough to take me along.

I know he probably won't take me; he can't stand being near me. I purse my lips together, looking down at my plate of food. I pick up the fork and play with the food. It looks good. There's eggs, bacon, and toast with a cup of fruit.

"Fine, you can come," he finally says after a few minutes of silence, and shocking the hell out of me, honestly. I look up at him through my lashes.

"Thank you," I whisper. He looks away from me for the first time since I entered the room. The muscle in his jaw ticks quickly, his hands are in a tight fist, and his body looks stiff. He's pissed.

Hell, when isn't he angry?

"When you're done eating, we'll leave," he says to me without looking back at me. He just stares stiffly out the window.

I take the chance to fully look him over, looking at his smooth bronze skin, tattoos running down both arms stopping at the tops of his hands, he is wearing a very expensive-looking silver watch and a ring on his middle finger. I fight the desire to go and curl up on his lap and trace his tattoos with my fingertips, or hell, run my tongue over them. I'm pretty sure he'd cut it out of my mouth before I got too close.

I'm fantasizing about a man who hates me. I lick my lips and pick up the cup of coffee. I pour milk and sugar into it—lots of sugar—my coffee has to be overly sweet.

"Do you mind telling us why you and your sister are running from your father? We have only heard that your mother ran from Margus," Darren breaks the tension in the room.

"You've heard of my family before?" I arch my brows in surprise.

"Of course, we've heard of the powerful witch in hiding with a bounty on her head," Stella says.

"My father, he's not a good man, as you know." I shake my head, it's none of their business, but it might be nice to talk to someone about it. "My mom ran away when she found out she was pregnant with a different man, she cheated and knew if my father found out, there'd be hell to pay. We went into hiding. Honestly, it's all I've ever known. He sent a man after us when I was sixteen. The man murdered my mom, and he tried to rape me." I close my eyes, remembering that horrible day. "I was young, and I froze. I could've saved her. I killed him, but it was already too late. I've been taking care of my sister since." My sister and I never talk about it, but the guilt eats me alive. I blink rapidly, trying to stop my tears from spilling.

"Wow, that's horrible. It's amazing that you're taking care of your sister." Stella reaches across the table and pats the top of my hand.

"I agree that's a lot for someone to deal with at such a young age," Darren agrees.

"I've been so afraid since my mom passed." I sigh. "I hate my father for it. He's dead set on revenge and I swear I was never going to help him. I believe in never judging someone. You never know what they have been through." I stare at Azrael as I say this to them, but he completely ignores me.

"We're grateful for your help," Darren bumps my shoulder.

"And we'll go shopping when we get your sister back; I'm sure she'll need stuff too!" Stella releases my hand and sits back.

"Of course," I mumble as I pick up a piece of bacon and start munching on it. I feel awkward and out of place.

"Okay, I'm ready." I jump up after eating a few bites and slowly walk towards Azrael.

He watches my every move, and my heart starts beating out of rhythm. I chew on my lower lip. He stands up, towering over me, and I've never felt so small. Out of nowhere, he snakes his arm around my waist, pulling me tight against him. My lips parted as I gasp.

God, I love the way he manhandles me; he's strong enough to throw me around.

It's official, I'm going insane...

"Where to?" I pull the address out of my pocket; I wrote it on a piece of paper last night. He looks down at it and nods. Without warning, we take off, and everything around us blurs. I squeeze my eyes closed, feeling sick to my stomach. Thank goodness I didn't eat much.

We finally stop, after what seems like forever. He quickly removes his arms, like holding me caused him pain, which causes me to fall on my knees from the dizziness.

Asshole...

I close my eyes, trying to catch my bearings. I lean forward placing my forehead on something soft and warm. I take a few deep breaths before reopening them. I look up; he's standing there watching me. I watch his pupils dilate, and that's when I realize that I'm on my knees in front of him, my hands are gripping the front pockets of his jeans, and the something warm I am leaning on is his upper thighs. I quickly let go of him, feeling embarrassed.

"Does that ever get easier?" I ask him as I look away, my cheeks are redder than ever.

"Yes." That's all he says as he turns and walks away.

He doesn't even ask me if I need help! He's such a gentleman!

I slowly take in my surroundings; we're in the middle of a large office. The large floor-to-ceiling windows show me that we're currently in a large city. There is no way in hell this is the address I gave him.

What the freaking fuck!

"What are we doing here?" I whisper harshly as I grip his elbow, trying to stop him.

"That's none of your business." He looks at me over his shoulder and yanks his elbow out of my grip.

"No, I guess it's not, but we're supposed to be getting my sister in case you *fucking* forgot!"

"Oh, I didn't forget, but I need to take care of a few things first."

"NO!" I stomp my foot hard, acting overly childish, but I don't freaking care at the moment.

"I don't recall asking your permission," he hisses angrily, getting in my face. I force myself not to take a step back. I refuse to show him that he scares the crap out of me.

"Azrael!" I hear a lady's voice behind him. He straightens his shoulders and turns to face the woman.

Holy moly...

She's gorgeous, looks like a damn model from a magazine cover. She's wearing a black pencil skirt and a white shirt that's very low cut, with red heels, and long wavy blonde hair.

They start talking. I walk towards the large windows. Wherever we are, it's dark out. "Who is she?"

"Her? She's no one, just a filthy *witch*." I flinch at how harshly he said *witch*. I blink back tears. I'm normally not an emotional girl, but he forces emotions out of me. I've heard him say those words before, but hearing him say them to her affects me more than I care to admit.

Why have I been acting like a pushover?! That's not who I am!

Why am I letting him treat me this way?

I don't deserve this.

I don't need him.

Fuck it! And fuck him!

I stomp over and I grab his arm, turning him around to face me. He opens his mouth to say something, but before he gets the chance to, I punch him hard in the throat. He stumbles back a couple of steps, eyes widening in surprise, his hands clutching his throat. Before he gets the chance to recover I turn and rush toward the elevators.

I don't need them. No, I don't need HIM. I'm not useless, I can get Luna on my fucking own. I hit the first-floor button, the doors open automatically, I step inside, and spin around with a smile on my face.

The elevator doors begin to close as I watch him recover from shock. He starts rushing toward me, but he's too late. I tilt my head to the side and flip him the bird.

The doors shut; I grin when I hear a loud roar. I let out a deep breath and lean my back against the wall behind me. *Damn, this building has twenty floors.*

I'm not overly worried about him catching me. We're surrounded by humans. He can't use his speed; it's against the law, and he can't teleport when he doesn't know where I'm going, because I don't even know where I'm going or where I am. He could stake out the address, but it could be days before I get there, and surely, he has more important things to do.

The doors finally open, and I enter a large lobby area with people walking around in fancy suits. They all have cell phones in their hands, not paying any attention.

I head towards the large wall of windows that is at least three stories high.

Whoa.

This place is freaking awesome!

There's a large desk in the middle of the room with two pretty women, both typing away on the computers sitting in front of them.

"Hi, I'm hoping you can tell me where the nearest bus station is and tell me where we are exactly," I ask with a smile.

"Oh yes, we're in Manhattan! Bus stations are everywhere; there's one only a few blocks away, just make a right when you exit the doors. You can't miss it," the redhead says, with a bright white smile.

"Manhattan? As in New York?"

"Um, yes." Her smile disappears, and her brows pinch together.

"Thank you!" I rush out of the building, turning right.

Well, the good thing is, I'm back in America. I'm glad I put my money and ID in one of my pockets this morning when I got ready.

The bad thing is, I can't use my magic. I feel completely bare without it.

Shit.

I'm in downtown New York! I can't freaking believe it. I look around in complete awe, taking my sweet time. Before my mom passed, my dreams were to go to college here and get a job at a publishing house.

I can picture her pretty hazel eyes that always twinkled when she used to tell me, *"You can be anything you want; all you have to do is work hard for it."*

A few weeks before she was murdered, we were making plans for me to graduate high school next year, and picking colleges for us to visit, of course, New York was my top choice.

I mentally shake those memories away and start looking around at all the large buildings filled with lights and large screens that have short videos playing. It's so amazing, and there are so many people walking and enjoying the beautiful night.

I bump into someone, and the man turns around and shouts at me. *Well, the people are rude...*

I make it to the bus station a few blocks later. Surprisingly, it's packed with people. I look around and spot the front desk. I rush over, going straight to the ticket man.

"Hi!"

"Hello, darling. Where will you be heading this evening?"

"One ticket for Massachusetts as close to Salem as we can get."

"We have a bus leaving for Salem in five minutes. You need to hurry if that's the one you want, otherwise, there's one leaving tomorrow."

"No, I really need the one leaving tonight."

"Alright, your total is two hundred twenty dollars, and I also need an ID."

"Oh, yes, of course." I smile at him. Then, I pull out my cash and frown, it's all I have. I push the money towards him. At least I have enough for the ticket. He scans my ID and then hands it back to me with a ticket.

"Thank you." I grab the ticket and start running towards the buses.

I panic when I watch the bus door begins to close. "Wait!" I shout, and thankfully, the older man reopens it for me looking super annoyed. I thank him as I give him my ticket.

The bus is nearly empty, so I go to the very back and pick a seat beside a window.

I relax in my seat and close my eyes happily when the bus starts moving. *I got away from that jerk face; it was too easy. I thought he was the big bad Vampire Prince.*

Pssh, not so badass now. A girl with no magic got away from him.

The bus slams on its brakes, jerking me forward, I almost hit the seat in front of me.

What the flying fuck?

I look out the front window, and I can see him standing in the middle of the road in front of the bus, looking super angry. His arms are at his sides, hands in fists, looking angrier than normal.

Well shit...

I stand up, looking for another way off the bus. No, there's only one way off. I walk to the driver.

"Just go… just drive around." He looks at me like I'm the crazy one. I bend closer to him. "Go around him," I hiss, praying that it'll work, and he nods and starts driving. I'm completely shocked that it actually works, even with these cuffs on. We drive past Azrael, and I flip him the bird, for the second time tonight.

I slump in my seat, resting my head against the window. I don't know who that lady was, but they might be dating. I mean, why else would he visit her?

He's looking for a queen, and she seems perfect for that.

Jealousy burns in the pit of my stomach.

Chapter 7

I'm walking around downtown Salem, looking in the windows of the cute shops as I pass. Of course, the stores are closed since it's six in the morning. That bus ride was the longest four and a half hours of my life.

The shops slowly disappear as I walk further away from town. I pause when I start to feel dark magic in the air. I look around but only see houses around me.

My gaze settles on a two-story black Victorian-style house. The second-story window has a silhouette of a person standing there. At first, I think it's just a mannequin, but then the shadow turns its head in my direction. An uneasy feeling bubbles in my gut, causing goosebumps to rise on my arms.

The house is surrounded with dark magic.

I rush off, wanting to get far away from that place. When I turned the corner, a violet shiver runs down my spine, making me look over my shoulder. My heart stops when I see someone is following me, and that's not even the creepy part. They're wearing a black cloak over their head. I take off running, praying I can get away.

I so don't need this shit.

The map I looked at back at the bus station showed the location is right across this street, in the woods. I look forward, eyes on the tree line.

What do they want from me?

I make it across the street, almost to the tree line, when they shout, "Stop." But I don't stop, I barely pass the first tree when something wraps around my throat and yanks me backwards, I land on my ass with a loud thud.

"You are not welcome here without my permission. This area belongs to my coven," the man hisses, voice low but stern.

"I apologize; I'm just trying to get my sister. I mean no harm." I turn to face him, getting to my knees.

"I don't care."

I look up at the man, his face is hidden beneath the cloak, but I feel a bad aura surrounding him.

"I know who you are. You betrayed my leader, and you are not welcome no matter the reason."

"Your leader?" I try sitting up, but he yanks against the rope, I yelp in shock.

"Yeah, your father."

He's one of my father's followers. He yanks the rope harder and I fall face-first landing on the dirt. I groan, placing my hands flat on the earth to push myself up, but I don't get far. He slams a foot on my upper back, tightening the rope around my throat, hard enough to cut my air supply off. I try loosening it, but I can't get my fingers beneath the rope.

"Please, stop," I choke out. I try to use my magic, but I can't feel it. My vision starts turning dark around the edges, and I can feel my heart rate slowing down.

The pressure from the rope loosens and I start coughing violently, trying to catch my breath quickly while removing the rope with trembling hands. My cheeks are drenched in tears. I never even realized that I started crying. I slowly pull myself up on my knees.

When I look up, I see Azrael, standing there holding the warlock in the air by the throat. I groan in pain. My body hurts. I run my fingers gently across my tender throat. Azrael's gaze snaps toward me.

How the fuck did he find me?

I flinch when I hear a loud crack of bones breaking. It echoes around us. Azrael drops him to the ground, the warlock's neck is at an odd angle.

Azrael steps close to me, and I see a flicker of concern in his eyes, but then it's gone. I must've imagined it. He stops a foot in front of me, eyes on my throat.

"What the fuck?" he snaps at me, crossing his arms, making his muscles bulge. *Nope, that doesn't have any effect on me at all. Did I ever say how hot he is when he's angry?* "You almost got yourself killed by acting childish and leaving."

"I don't need you," I try snapping back, but my throat aches, and it comes out weak and cracked.

"Yeah, it looks like you don't need me." His hand waves to the dead warlock.

"Whatever. How'd you even find me?" I clear my throat as I try getting up, but I fall back due to the dizziness. Azrael grabs my hands, pulling me up. I fall against him, closing my eyes.

"You must've forgotten you gave me the address. I've been waiting in the woods right outside of the cabin until I heard screaming. So, I came to check it out, and I found you on the verge of passing out."

"Thanks, but I'm done. I don't need your help. I'll get there on my own! So why don't you leave me alone and act like we've never met?" I take a step back, crossing my arms over my chest.

"That'll never happen." He steps forward.

"Why not? You fucking hate me. Just let me leave." I poke his chest with my index finger. "Let me go!"

"I more than hate you," he spits out in disgust, making me flinch. It fucking hurts more than I care to admit. *Why am I hated for something I didn't do or something I can't control? It's not my fault who my father is, I shouldn't be punished for his actions.*

"Good, 'cause I hate you, too. Bye." I turn and throw up the peace sign over my shoulder as I storm away, but he grips the back of my shirt, pulling me back until I'm against his front. I pinch my lips together, trying not to moan at the sensation of feeling his hard body against mine.

"You aren't ever leaving me." I feel his lips move against my skin as he talks. He breathes in my scent as his nose grazes my ear. My lips part as my breathing quickens and I shiver from the simple touch.

I'm so totally screwed...

"Why not?" I ask, sounding breathless.

"Because I say so." His fingers grip my hips, and he rubs my exposed skin underneath my shirt. "I won't allow you to ever leave me."

"Well, I refuse to stand around while you talk to your girlfriends. I have better things to do." I ignore the burning desire his fingers are causing me. I step out of his grasp. I hate how jealous I sound. I mean, I am jealous, but that doesn't mean he needs to know that.

"You sound jealous, little witch." He grabs my wrist, pulling me against him. Up close, I can see a scar about an inch long right below his jawline. "You shouldn't be because I'll never want you. I'll never allow you to touch me in such a way." His upper lip raises, and he snarls.

I gasp, and place my hands flat on his chest, shoving him, but he tightens his grip, not allowing me to move. I try to ignore the gut-wrenching feeling that's currently passing through my chest.

"I'll never touch you either. I prefer Darren anyway." *Lie.* His nostrils flare, jaw clenches, and his eyes turn red. I've never seen him this pissed before. So, I decide to push his buttons. "I can't wait to fuck him. I know he wants me too. I see the way he looks at me. I'll make sure I scream his name so you can hear who I desire."

He bares his teeth, grabs my throat and tightens slightly but not enough to cause pain. Burning desire runs through my veins, making me rub my thighs together, and when he sucks in a deep breath, I know he can smell my need.

"Smell that?" I look up at him through my lashes. "That's me fantasizing about me and Darr-"

"Don't fucking say his name." His voice is deeper, raspier. *God, it sounds possessive and sexy.* "You won't ever fuck him."

"Like you can stop us. He wants me. I can see it." I shove him harder, but again, he doesn't budge.

"I'll fucking kill him if he touches you," he snaps, and I watch as his fangs extend. I gasp, and my eyes widen.

Oh shit.

I didn't expect that.

The next thing I know, everything turns blurry as we're teleporting again. It's easier this time around. I still feel dizzy, but I don't fall over when we stop, or maybe it's because I'm holding onto his shoulders for dear life.

His arms are wrapped tightly around me, and my head is resting against his chest. I know we stopped, but we don't let each other go. Why did he sound so jealous? *It wasn't jealousy. He probably hated the thought of me touching his cousin with my dirty witch hands.*

But why would he kill him?

Betrayal maybe?

He slowly pulls away from me, and I already miss his warmth. I clear my throat and look around, trying to distract myself. We're surrounded by trees and a few cabins. They have white rocking chairs on the front porch, and they're rocking back and forth due to the heavy winds. There's a large white picket fence in front of the cabins, and Azrael is already unlocking the gate. I jog to catch up to him, and by the time I do, he's already climbing the wooden stairs.

He lifts his fisted hand and starts banging hard on the door.

Jeez!

"You don't need to bang on the door like that!" I shout as I walk up the wooden stairs. He doesn't answer me. *Whatever.* I roll my eyes and huff. An older woman with gray hair tied in a low bun with red-rimmed glasses open the door. She wearing a long, flowy white dress.

"Hi!" I smile widely, shoving Azrael out of the way, he growls in response. "I'm Isabella! I'm looking for my sister, Luna. Have you seen her? Is she here?" I rush out, looking over her shoulders, trying to look inside.

"Bella!" Luna squeals and pushes her way through to hug me tightly. "I was so worried about you!" I hug her back, holding back tears.

God, I didn't realize how much I needed this.

"I was worried, too, Luna." When Luna hugs me, she pushes my back right into Azrael. I don't move because I honestly love the feeling of him against me. His hands are resting on my hips, I'm sure it's only to make sure I don't fall.

"Tell me what happened!" She pulls back, her hand is wiping the tears that have fallen down her cheeks.

"I'll tell you soon, okay?" She just nods. Her eyes widen when she looks over my shoulder.

"Who is this?" Her brows bunch together as she stares up at Azrael.

"Azrael." I took a step away from him. "He helped me find you."

Her eyes brighten up and her grin widens. "Thank you!" I snort; she wouldn't be thanking him if she knew how big of a jerk he is.

"Thank you for watching her and keeping her safe." I look back over to the older lady, who I assumed is Trisha.

"Of course." She nods once. "Anything for Aurora's daughters. Come inside." She steps back, widening the door for us and waves us in.

"No," Azrael snarls. I narrow my eyes at him over my shoulder, they say, *behave!*

Looking back at Trisha, "We'd love to." I hear a loud sigh behind me, but he doesn't protest. We walk in, and it's tiny but cute, the living room has a white sofa in the center of the room, two white chairs, and no TV in sight.

I can't see the kitchen, but the dining room is past the living room with a large sliding glass door, and the view is to die for. Right outside is a large colorful garden.

"Please have a seat. The tea is about done, let me go check on it." She disappears around the corner, I'm guessing, into the kitchen. I sit beside Luna, gripping her hands tightly in mine.

"Are you okay?" I ask her, looking her over. She's wearing the same long white dress as Trisha.

"Yeah, like I promised, I came straight here. God, I've been so scared, Bella." She sobs, shaking her head. "How'd you get out? I can't believe he did that to you. I thought he'd hurt you."

"I'll tell you everything later, but he helped me escape." I look over towards Azrael who's standing in a wide stance, arms folded over his chest. Every time I move, he moves too, almost like my shadow, except he looks super intimidating.

"Thank you for helping my sister, she's all I have. I owe you!" Luna says.

I press my lips together to hold back a comment. Something along the lines of, "You don't want to owe him anything."

The sliding glass door opens, and we all turn to look over. The man who walks in is tall with short curly brown hair.

Man, he's good-looking with hazel eyes and a strong jawline. He looks to be a couple of years older than me. I bite my lower lip and tuck my hair behind my ear.

Two sexy ass guys in the same room, damn.

Who is he?

"Oh, good, you're here! Meet my son!" Trisha comes out carrying four mugs. "Dante."

"Hiya! I, um, I'm Isabella!" I stand up and straighten my clothes. I never met a warlock that I felt attracted to.

"Hello, Isabella," he replies in a deep Southern boy accent. His gaze slowly takes me in, causing me to blush. He grabs hold of my hand and gently kisses the top of it. I giggle like a schoolgirl.

"Nice to meet you, Dante."

"We're leaving," Azrael snaps. I look over at him, to find him storming over and grabbing my elbow, pulling me away from Dante.

"Oh, don't leave, I made all of this tea!" Trisha holds out a mug for me to grab.

"I'd love to stay and have some." I yank my elbow out of his grip, and grab the mug, taking a sip of it. Luna raises her brows at me in question when I sit beside her, and I shrug my shoulders. Dante sits so close beside me that our thighs touch. I look up to find Azrael's eyes narrowed at the spot where our thighs are touching.

"Wow, this tea is amazing!" I exclaimed, looking over at Trisha.

"You and your mom always did love tea." She sits in the chair nearest to the couch, holding the mug with both hands and blowing the steam to cool it down.

"I know we met before, but I don't remember a thing."

"Yes, you were young the last time you came to visit. You used to come over while your father was away, and you and Dante used to play. You used to have a crush on him." She laughs as she recalls the memory.

"Don't worry, the feeling was very mutual," Dante says.

"Oh yeah?" I look over to Dante, and he nods, staring down at me.

"Your mom and I always thought you two would get married."

"Seriously?" I look over at her.

"Yeah, I think I even asked you to marry me once." Dante grins widely, and then he grips my thigh and squeezes it gently. A low growl rumbles through the small room. I look over, and if looks could kill, Dante would be very much dead right now.

I can feel his anger radiating off him in waves. Even though Dante is good looking, I still prefer the deadly, sinister look Azrael has. I'd choose him hands down, but there's no reason to choose when the feeling isn't mutual. I know he finds me attractive, but the man hates me.

I can picture myself dating someone like Dante to see if we're a good match. Best of all, he knows who and what I am, and still finds me attractive. I don't feel that intense attraction as I do with Azrael, but he's out of the picture. I can't compare other men to him.

"You know you both can stay here." Trisha's voice turns serious. "The other cabin belonged to your mom, and it's yours if you want it."

"She's not staying." Azrael butts in before I can reply.

"I'd love to take you up on your offer, but I made a deal with Azrael. I have to help him with something first, but when I'm done with that, I think we'd love to come back."

"Of course." She eyes Azrael, worry advent in her gaze. "Just be careful."

Azrael's phone rings, and he steps outside, but not before shooting me a warning gaze.

Trisha quickly jumps up and bends down in front of me taking the mug out of my hand. She sits it on the coffee table before gripping both of my hands in between hers.

"Are you in trouble? I can help you. We have a safe house. We can go and put protective wards up to keep his kind out." I stare at our joined hands and ponder on that thought.

I bite the inside of my cheek nervously. It could work. I could get away from him. My brain is telling me to go with her, but my heart squeezes painfully at that thought. I tell myself it's only because I'd break my word I made not only to him, but to Darren, too, and that doesn't feel like the right thing to do.

"I'm okay," I say, finally inhaling deeply. "He saved me, and I owe him. I gave him my word, and I'm tired of running. I need to help him capture my father."

"So much like your momma."

"But if you want to stay until this ends, you can," I say as I turn towards my sister. I think about how much I'd hate leaving her behind, but I need to give her a choice, something I never had, but above all she'd be safe here.

"And miss all the fun? No, thanks. Plus, everywhere you go, I go." She grins wickedly.

"Okay." I nod, fighting the urge to smile, feeling happy that she wants to come with me.

"I have somewhere I need to be. Let's go." Azrael walks back in and stares at our joined hands before his attention turns toward me with a dark predator's stare, his eyes telling me what I need to know: no one can keep me away from him. I wiggle in my seat, feeling anxious under his unwavering attention. I stand up, clearing my throat.

"It was a pleasure seeing both of you again." I smile at them. "Thank you for everything."

"Of course, anything you need." Trisha stands, and straightens her dress, pulling me into a hug. "Here's my number, call me for anything, especially when you want to claim your cabin. I would've taken you in, but you disappeared when your momma passed. I always hoped you'd come here, but you never did, and I had no way of contacting you." She places a paper in my hand.

"I wish I had. I didn't want to be a bother."

"You'll never be a bother." I feel like crying. I should've come here. I had a home; my mom's old cabin sat empty, waiting for us. We wouldn't have been struggling like we were. We probably would've had a better life.

"I'll be seeing you soon, I hope, and maybe I can take you out." Dante rubs the back of his neck and grins at me.

"Let's go," Azrael demands harshly, from close behind me.

He's oh so sweet and polite.

"Jeez, calm down! Thank you again." I lean into Dante and wrap my arms around his waist, hugging him. He smells like cinnamon, yum! He kisses my cheek, and Azrael yanks me away from Dante and grabs hold of Luna's hand.

"Hey, you big goof, don't be such an ass-" He cuts me off by teleporting us again. I don't think I'll ever get used to this.

When we stop, he doesn't release me, surprisingly; my arms are wrapped tightly around his shoulders, and my face is nestled in his neck. I breathe him in, and I groan. My lips part, and they softly rub against his skin, making him tremble. I watch with utter fascination as goosebumps abruptly rise on his skin.

He nuzzles his face against my neck. A deep rumble escapes his throat when he picks me up, I wrap my legs tightly around his waist. His hands grip my ass, pulling me closer as he licks the side of my neck. My lips part with a breathless moan.

"That was in-fucking-sane!" Luna shouts, causing my mind to snap out of this weird daze. I slowly untangle myself from his grasp.

What the hell am I doing? Making a complete fool of myself, that's what I'm doing!

This man hates me!

I take a step back and look at Luna, who's currently trying to get up off the floor. I laugh and stretch my hand out. When I pull her up, she's grinning ear to ear.

"Hey, do you think we can do that again?" Her eyes are bright as she beams. *She enjoyed that? Yeah, she's insane.* We follow Azrael to the room with the wall of windows.

"No," he says and then stalks away without looking in my direction.

"He's such a joy!" she comments sarcastically, rolling her eyes. I snort. *That's the understatement of the damn century.*

"Yeah, tell me about it. He's the Prince of Vampires, so maybe that's why he's always cranky." I walk to the couch, and I snuggle into the cushions. Luna sits beside me.

"How the heck did you get involved with the Prince?" she squeals. "He's as hot as they say, that's for sure, but I feel bad for him; he's probably lonely."

"Pssh, I think he prefers it that way. He's the biggest asshole I have ever met, and that's saying something."

"Well, he probably was raised to be that way." She shrugs. "I see the way he looks at you. Even if he is an ass, he wants to protect you."

"Now, I very much doubt that. He'd kill me if given the chance." I shake my head and turn my body to look out the large windows. It's pouring down rain.

I stand up and walk over to stare outside. Gosh, I wish the fire were on and I had a steamy hot chocolate, or better yet, a vanilla latte and a book to read. I lean against the glass, and close my eyes, listening to the rain hitting the windows. This is peaceful; I could live in this room forever.

"I highly doubt that. You're being overly dramatic, but tell me what happened!"

"After you left, Dad knocked me out," I say, looking away from the window, looking towards her. "I woke up in a dirty cell, and my cellmate was his cousin. He came to rescue him, and he helped me, but when he found out who I was, he regretted it. He hates me for it, just like everyone else does when they find out."

"Well, screw him and everyone else. If they can't see how amazing you are, they don't deserve you. I'm happy he helped you, though."

"Yeah, I guess." I shrug my shoulders, sitting down in the corner piece of the sectional. I kick my shoes off and wrap myself in the fuzzy white throw, looking out the window.

"A book would be pretty amazing right now." Luna curls herself into a ball on the arm of the sectional, looking outside.

"Just what I was thinking, and don't forget a yummy latte."

"Mmm, yess, with whip cream and cinnamon!" She wiggles her brows.

"Yes, and a nice fire going. Goodness, I'm hungry now."

"If that's what you two want, I can make it happen." I look up to see Darren leaning against the doorframe.

"Really?" I grin. "Luna, this is my cellmate, Darren, and Darren, this is Luna, my sister."

"Nice to meet you! Can you really make that happen? Cause I'd love you forever if so!" Luna jumps to her knees and leans against the back of the couch to look at him.

"Not the book part, but the rest, yes. What do you two want for lunch?" He strolls over to the chair by the fireplace and sits down.

Luna turns around, and we both look at each other. At the same time we say, "Ham and cheese croissant!"

"We don't have that, but I'll make Azrael go to the bakery in town, and I'll tell him to get your lattes, too. He'll be fast." He disappears, and I shake my head. I doubt he'd do that for me.

"This place is so cool, and Darren seems very, very nice and super-hot." She licks her lips, grinning.

"You are way too young for him, Luna. Don't even think about it." I wiggle my index finger at her.

"I'm not that young!"

I laugh at her getting up. I wrap the throw around my shoulders and go to the fireplace to see if I can turn it on.

"Here, I'll do that. We don't want you to burn the damn house down. Azrael just left to get the food." I go back to my corner and sit down, watching Darren turn on the fireplace. "I also told him that you're in the mood to read. We'll see what he can do."

Once the fire is lit, he sits down in between us and looks at us both. "You two don't look like sisters."

"Well, like I said, our fathers are different." He nods, and I look back out the window, enjoying the rain and the fire crackling.

"She's here! Yay!" Stella runs into the room. "Time to go SHOPPING!" I cringe at the thought of shopping.

"Luna, this is Stella. She's Azrael's sister." I introduce them.

"Hi!" Stella grabs Luna's hands and pulls her up to give her a tight hug.

"Oh, yay! I love shopping!" Luna hugs her back, they look like old friends, seeing each other after spending years apart.

"Not this second. We sent Azrael for lunch," Darren says, leaning back.

"Wait, we're talking about my brother, Azrael?" She arches a perfect brow.

"Yep, the one and only."

"Well, hopefully, he'll bring me something too." Luna and she sit back down, and at the same time, Azrael pops in, out of nowhere. He has two large bags and two lattes. He places the bags on the coffee table and hands me a cup first. I shyly say thank you as I take the cup, and then he hands one to Luna.

I can't believe he did this...

He sits beside me, and grabs one of the bags, pulling out two things that are wrapped in aluminum. He hands me one, and then leans back to start unwrapping his. We all stare at him in shock.

He's being nice to me...

"What?" he snaps, and everyone looks away, grabbing their own food out of the bag. I slowly unwrap mine and smile when I see the large croissant. I love these, but I bet the ones here are ten times better. I take a bite and release a loud moan when the butteriness hits my tongue.

"God, this is amazing!" My eyes roll back. "Thank you." I look at Azrael, to find him already watching me with dilated pupils. I clear my throat and look away from him.

"Darren told me you wanted some books, so I went to the bookstore in town. The lady showed me books that American girls your age normally like, and I purchased all of them for you," Azrael says, and I look back at him in disbelief, he looks away.

"Thank you, but you didn't have to do that for me," I say in a soft voice.

"I did it more for me, so I didn't have to hear you bitch." His jaw ticks. *Wow, as soon as I thought he had a little kindness, he proves me wrong.*

"Whatever." I roll my eyes. "Whatever the reason, I still thank you for doing it."

"Are we going to be able to explore some while we're here?" Luna asks to change the subject.

"I'm not sure. I need to help them so we can leave as soon as possible. Maybe we'll stay at Mom's cabin and get a fresh start." I hear a low growl beside me, but I ignore him.

"That'll be nice, it's beautiful there. Maybe you and Dante can go out. You need a man in your life, sis. He's a great choice, plus, he's pretty hot."

"Okay, I don't need a man, but I do agree that he's kind of hot and he seems nice." The growl gets louder.

"Oh, please tell me more about this Dante." Stella grins mischievously at me. I'm sure she's using me to mess with her brother because, for whatever reason, he's pissed about this conversation.

"I don't really know him, but he's very good-looking." I wink, taking a sip of the latte. "And he seems super nice, and he likes me too. He asked me out, and I think I'll take him up on his offer."

"Sounds like you need to date him and find out more," Stella agrees.

"Enough," Azrael snarls. "She's not dating anyone."

"Excuse me?!" I snap, standing up and placing my hand on my hip. "Who the hell do you think you are?"

He gets up and bends a little, so that he's eye level with me. "You heard me."

"You can't tell me what to do!" I shove his chest with both hands.

"As long as you're in my house, you will not date him!" He bares his teeth and his eyes flash red for a moment.

"So anywayyyy." Stella jumps up, grabbing me and pulling me away from Azrael. "Would you two like to go shopping now?"

"God, yes!" Luna beams and jumps up. *Yep, these two will get along just great.*

"You two can just go without me." I start walking away, hoping they'll leave without me.

"Not happening. You're coming," Luna says.

I turn around. "Can't you just buy me stuff, Luna? You know my size." I look at Luna with pleading eyes.

"No!" They both say at the exact same time. I roll my eyes, groaning.

Chapter 8

I'm sitting here watching the girls go in and out of the dressing rooms, trying things on and acting like models. I haven't tried anything on. I just told the salesperson my size and showed her everything I liked. I guess Azrael gave Stella his card and told her to get us everything we needed.

I feel bad about spending his money, but those two didn't give a single crap. I cross my legs and lay my head back against the couch.

"This sucks," I groan to myself, even though I did enjoy walking around. This place is beautiful. I'd love to actually be living here. The town is small and historical. There's a small section of designer clothing boutiques, the designer stores are inside beautiful brick buildings. The insides are all updated, giving them a modern look. We're about an hour away from the city.

I wish I could see a place like this decorated for Christmas. I never cared for Christmas. We never really had the means to buy anything. I personally didn't care about the gifts, but it upset Luna a lot, so I worked extra hours just to get her one small thing. But I always enjoyed the lights and decorations.

"I'm hungry!" I shout for the fourth time; they're still in the dressing room. The sales lady refills my glass of champagne, which is the best thing about being here.

"One more outfit!" I throw my head back, with a groan. They said that a few times already.

"Last one! If not, I'm leaving without either of you, I swear on it!" I huff, folding my arms over my chest. They come out wearing the same dress while laughing. They have the same exact taste.

"We picked a few things out for you," Luna says, sitting beside me.

"Me? I already got the things I need."

"Yeah, you did, but nothing fun or sexy!" Stella shakes her breasts at me.

"I don't need anything fun, especially anything sexy. We aren't here to have fun."

"Yes, you do! And we can have fun. There's no reason not to."

"Whatever. Get changed so we can go eat." I'm not going to argue with her. She'd push until I agree, and I'm too hungry to care.

"Okay!" She claps, and they both disappear again.

We're checking out when Stella's phone rings. She hands Luna the card and leaves. When they tell us the amount, I almost crap myself. That's more than I make in a year! I bet that's only chump change to them. I hate spending this much on clothes. I can think of plenty of actual, important things to spend this kind of money on.

"The boys are meeting us for dinner!" Stella skips to us with a big smile. "We need to get you two some bikinis so we can go to the pool!"

"You have a pool?" I ask, I didn't even see it.

"Oh yeah, it's on the east side of the house." We grab the bags and get into the car. We're in a large black SUV. I'm on the passenger side, and Luna is in the back. Stella blasts the music, and they both start singing loudly. I groan as I pinch the tip of my nose.

When we pull into the winery, it takes my breath away. It's three stories and made of large stones with arched doors and windows with dark wood trim. We walk up a couple of steps and then enter.

"Ms. Anderson, the other half of your group is already here. Let me show you." The tall man in a black tux bows to her.

This place is the fanciest restaurant I've ever been in. It has tan large archways and white tile floors with designs. There's a large staircase and the biggest chandelier I have ever seen. We walk up the stairs, and when we get to the landing, the back wall is filled with large windows with black arch designs. It's absolutely breathtaking. The man takes a left and disappears into one of the arched doorways.

Darren and Azrael are inside talking about business. He makes my heart stop. He's in a black tux with the top few buttons undone to show a little skin. His suit jacket is off, and his hair is slicked back.

His eyes connect with mine, and I quickly look away, my face turning hot.

"Little Bella, come sit with me," Darren says patting the chair next to him. I go and sit down, smiling at him. "So how did shopping with my sister go?"

"Honestly, it was pretty boring. What did you do, cellmate?"

"Cellmate, huh? I like the sound of that, it's pretty badass." He grins at me, moving my hair out of my face, his fingers lingering on my jaw. A low growl vibrates through the room, and we all turn to Azrael, who's glaring at us. "Oh, hush," Darren says to Azrael before turning his gaze back to me. "We had a meeting to attend."

"Are you ever going to tell me what got you locked up?" I arch a brow, leaning close so I can whisper in his ear. "What did my naughty cellmate do?" I know that I'm flirting, but I'm curious about how Azrael will react. I've learned that I love to push his buttons. Am I playing with fire? Maybe, but hey, I have every right to. I am single, and Darren is cute.

The next thing I know, Darren is being ripped away from me, and Azrael sits down next to me, leaning back and acting like nothing happened.

"What the fuck, Azrael?" Darren shouts, standing beside Azrael, glaring down at him with his hands in a fists.

"Fuck off," Azrael mutters and picks up a menu. I say nothing as I pick up my own menu and look down at it, trying to find the cheapest thing to eat, which isn't saying much. I chew on my lower lip nervously as I stare at the ridiculous prices.

The waiter comes in and pours each of us a glass of wine and then the food arrives. I guess the guys already ordered food. I get grilled chicken with broccoli and soup. I take a small sip and moan when the flavor hits my tongue. Holy crap, this is the best soup I have ever had.

"So, did you both find what you needed?" Darren asks, looking at me and then Luna.

"Yeah, I want to thank you for doing that, Azrael." He doesn't reply. He just stares at me, I quickly look away, slightly feeling unnerved by his unwavering attention. His stare is so damn intense and intimidating, I love and hate it.

I eat in silence while everyone else talks. I can still feel Azrael's stare burning holes into the side of my face the entire time. It's becoming too much. I can't sit still, and I can't stop fidgeting. Is that what he wants, to make me uncomfortable? I stand quickly, causing everyone to look at me. I need to get away and take a minute to myself.

"I need to use the lady's room." I rush out before anyone can respond.

I get to the restroom and head straight to the sink. I turn on the water and plant my hands flat against the countertop by the sink bowl, staring at my reflection. I look flushed. I splash the cold water on my face, taking slow, even breaths before I gather my nerves and walk back out. I decide to look around, instead of rushing back.

I peek inside a room, and luckily, it's empty. So I step inside and walk towards the arched window, and the view is of the vineyard. I step back a couple of steps, hitting something hard. I quickly spin around, almost tripping on my own two feet, arms wrap around my waist. Startled, I look up to find a man in a black suit and tie.

"Oh my gosh! I'm so sorry. I thought the room was empty and I came in because I needed a moment to myself." *Shut up already, he doesn't care.*

"Hey, calm down, it's okay." He has a heavy accent so it's hard to understand him. "I needed some time to myself as well. I'm the owner of the winery, Stephen. I've never seen you before. It's a small town and I pretty much know everyone. Are you visiting? Let me guess, American?"

"Oh, hi, I'm Isabella. I am visiting, and yes, American." I smile. "It's amazing here, and the wine is delicious."

"Nice to meet you, Isabella." He returns the smile and grabs ahold of my hand, and then I realize that his other hand is still resting on my hip. I want to step back but I don't want to be rude.

"Let me take you out and show you around?" he asks as he leans down and kisses the top of my hand. I fight back a giggle and blush, considering his question. It's weird, lately I have been attracted to more men than I have ever been in my life; it must be something in the water.

"I don't know, I mean, it does sound nice..." A loud growl interrupts me. I look up and see Azrael, staring daggers at Stephan. He walks over and roughly grabs my elbow, yanking me away from Stephen. He pulls me tightly against him, wrapping his arm possessively around my waist.

"Prince Azrael." Stephan bows. "I apologize. I didn't know she was yours." He keeps his head down.

"No, I'm n...." I shake my head, but I'm cut off.

"Now you know," Azrael spits out, and manhandles me out of the room by my elbow, and down the stairs.

"Azrael! Stop!" I try to yank my arm out of his iron grip.

"No," he growls out.

"I didn't even finish my food and what about the others?" Everyone watches as he forces me down the stairs.

"I'll text them and tell them that we're leaving and to pack your food."

"What's the matter with you?" I ask, finally gathering the nerve to ask.

"Do you always let random men put their lips on you?" he snaps, looking down at me, eyes blazing with anger.

"Excuse you?" I gasp. "That is none of your business." He finally releases my elbow and pushes me against the wall, and his arms cage me in.

"It is my fucking business! Two strangers put their lips on you. Do you like strange men touching you? Is that it?"

"Fuck off!" I growl and shove him away from me, storming to the exit, not knowing where I'm going. But it doesn't matter, I keep walking.

"My car is here," he says behind me, and a beeping sound comes from a two-door red sports car. It looks like a very expensive car.

I get in, crossing my arms across my chest, looking out the window, seething. He slams the door and turns on the car, it revs to life.

He pulls out of the parking lot, almost hitting someone. I grab the bar in front of me, death gripping it.

"Holy shit, slow down!" I shout, scared to death as he speeds past every car, nearly hitting them.

"Answer the damn question! Do you always let strange men touch you?" he asks me through clenched teeth.

He has fucking anger issues.

"Are you serious right now?"

"Answer the goddamn question, Bella!" he shouts at me and punches the steering wheel, hard. I flinch back, for the first time, feeling scared of him.

"No, okay? No, I don't always let men put their hands on me. Happy now?" I snap, looking at him with narrowed eyes.

"Yesss, I am happy now!" he hisses, looking at me. I turn around, giving him my back. We finally pull into the house.

God, he makes me so angry. I just want to punch him in the throat.

I jump out of the car, and slam the door shut, stomping into the house, huffing.

Jerk face.

I go to my room and throw myself face-first on the mattress. *I mean, how dare he? He makes it sound like I'm a slut or something! I can do whatever I damn please.*

"Hey, everything okay?" I hear Luna ask, and I look up, and find her and Stella walking into my room.

"No, your brother is a jerk face." I roll onto my back, looking up at the ceiling.

"A jerk face? I've heard people call him so many different types of names, but never jerk face. I can't wait to tell him." She laughs.

"What happened?" Luna asks, jumping onto the bed beside me.

"I don't know. He got angry because I was talking to the owner of the winery, Stephen, and he kissed my hand. Azrael turned into a caveman. I don't understand why he hates me so much."

"Oh, sweetheart, I don't think it's hate he's feeling," Stella comments, sitting in a chair across the room.

I snort. "Sure, whatever you think."

"He may be an asshole, and he hates that you're a witch, but I see the way he looks at you. I know my brother, and he finds you attractive, and it's getting under his skin."

"It's not her fault that she's a witch," Luna says, angrily.

"No, it's not. I don't hold the same hatred for witches, just one in particular. Azrael, on the other hand, decided to hate all of them."

"Why? What happened?" I ask out loud, sitting up, and Luna lays her head on my lap.

"Don't tell him I told you. I won't tell you everything, but my mother's best friend was a witch, and we all trusted her. But she betrayed us and then murdered my mom brutally. She was using my mom the entire time trying to gain her trust." She frowns, looking down at her hands.

"That's awful. I understand, but I agree with you, he can't hate every witch."

"He was close to her; he even called her auntie, and she tried killing him, too, but he was able to fight her off till our father came home." She sighs, looking upset for a minute before cheering up. "Okay, no more sob stories. We have to get ready!" Stella jumps up, grabs the bag she brought in with her, and hands it to me.

"Get ready for what?" I ask as I look in the bag.

"We're going to a club!" Luna beams as she bounces on the bed.

"No, we can't. Luna is too young." I look at her like she's gone crazy.

"Not here. She's allowed to go in, but she can't drink."

"I don't know if that's a good idea..."

"You don't know if what's a good idea?" Darren steps inside my room, and following him is Azrael.

"We're going to the club," Stella shrugs, as if it's none of their concern.

"Fuck yeah!" Darren agrees.

"No, you're not," Azrael says, looking pointily at me, shaking his head.

"That's not your choice to make. We're going." I smirk, agreeing just because he doesn't want us to go.

Chapter 9

AZRAEL

"Come on, relax!" My cousin grips my shoulder, walking out of the room. I follow him as he heads to his room. I still feel pissed about Stephan touching Bella, and she fucking let him. I growl in frustration.

"We shouldn't be going to the damn club."

"Why? Because you don't want anyone touching her?" he smirks before disappearing into his closet.

"I don't know what you mean." I look out of his window, leaning against it.

"Right, you think I'm stupid. I see the way you watch her. I don't blame you, cousin, she's drop-dead gorgeous with the perfect body." Of course, she is. I see how she turns heads everywhere she goes, both men and women. I see both lust and jealousy in their gazes.

"I don't know what you're talking about."

"Sure, you don't. Get ready because even though you hate clubs, we both know she's not walking out of this house without you." I storm out, completely frustrated because it's true. She's not leaving this house without me. I need to be careful, I can't allow myself to catch feelings, especially with a witch. We don't belong together.

I just want to keep her safe till I'm done with her.

I'll be king soon. No one would approve, even if I did want it. I only need her help, then she's gone. I change my shirt to a black button-up, and roll the sleeves to my elbow.

I go downstairs, walking to the bar and pour myself a drink. I sit in my armchair, stretching my legs out in front of me. I crack my neck, trying to relax before we go. I don't care if she dances with someone else as long as she stays out of my way.

I look up when I hear the girls, but my eyes are solely on her as

she walks into the room, pulling her dress down, and my breathing stalls; she's literally taking my breath away. I can tell she's uncomfortable in that tight little red dress that shows off her long, smooth, tan legs. I trail my eyes down her sinful little body, looking at every delicious curve.

Fuck me. I groan.

Why is the universe fucking with me?

The dress is low cut, hardly covering her perky tits. Her lips are painted red and I slowly lick my own, wanting to taste her.

She's not walking out of this house wearing that.

"No," I barely make the word out.

"No, what?" my sister asks, placing a hand on her hip.

"I won't be seen with a fucking whore," I say without taking my eyes off Bella. Her eyes widen as she gasps, and I see the hurt in her gaze.

"Fuck you," she spits out. I can't allow her to know the real reason I don't want her to go out dressed like that.

"You fucking wish. I wouldn't touch you with a ten-foot pole." I stand up and walk towards her, but Stella steps in between us, blocking her from my view.

I'm going to tie her up in my room if I have to.

"Stop being a fucking dick!" Stella's eyes blazed angrily. "You calling me a whore, too? Cause I'm showing the same amount of skin. You can stay home if you don't like it." She shoves me, and grabs Bella and Luna's arms, pulling them out of the room.

"That was fucked up even for you, cousin." Darren follows the girls. I growl out, following them. I'm not letting her out of my sight. My blood is boiling with anger and jealousy.

Darren drives, Stella is in front, Luna sits between Bella, and I in the backseat. I cross my ankle over my knee, and tilted my head back against the headrest, and look over, staring at her exposed thigh. She crosses her leg over the opposite knee, making her dress roll up even more.

Fuck me.

My cock grows painfully hard in my jeans.

She looks at me from beneath her dark lashes, making her look innocent. Her lower lip is pushed out a little, making an adorable pouty face. I want to wrap her long hair around my fist and make her gag on my hard cock.

We pull into the club, and Darren gives the keys to the valet, who stares at Bella for a moment too long. I clear my throat, making him look at me, and he turns away like his ass is on fire.

We go into the club and head straight upstairs through a private entrance. A friend of ours owns the place and there's always a room reserved for us.

"Look who we've got here! How are you guys doing tonight? Ready to party, I see!" Antonio greets us, arms wide open; he's dressed in a black suit. "When Darren called me saying you were coming, I was surprised."

"Needed a night out," I shrug, looking away from him to watch Bella. She's with the girls, looking around. Anytime she is in the room with me, I have a hard time looking away.

"And who is that beauty?" Antonio asks Darren, staring openly at her.

"Stella, I believe you have already met before," Darren answers him, playing dumb.

"No. The one in the red."

"She's mine," I say, stepping in front of him to block his view of her.

"I apologize." He bows his head. "I didn't realize. I mean no disrespect."

"It's alright, Antonio." Darren grabs my arm and pulls me away from him.

"Let me show you your room." He walks away, and we all follow him. I keep my eyes on him. I'm fighting the urge to rip his eyes out. We enter a large black room with its own bar and black leather couches overlooking the dance floor.

"Let me know if there's anything else I can get for you." Antonio bows again and leaves the room.

I sit across from Bella, allowing my gaze to slowly take her in once more. She's fucking perfect, breathtaking, it's hard not to.

Fucking hell, what is she doing to me?

Her sister whispers something in her ear, and she tilts her head back, laughing. Goddamn, I have never heard her laugh before, and fuck, she needs to do it more.

"Earth to Azrael!" my sister snaps her fingers in my face. I turn my head to look at her with narrow eyes. "We're going to the dance floor."

"No, you're not," I reply harshly. Bella doesn't need to be dancing in a room full of people watching her, but I can't allow them to know it's out of jealousy. "Don't you remember your father is looking for you? What if someone sees you and reports back to him?" Bella nibbles her juicy lower lip, which makes my dick twitch. Nothing out of the ordinary, it's always semi-hard around her.

"No one will know. Plus, it's dark down there. It'll be fine!" Stella waves me off, standing up dismissing me. "Come on, girls, let's go!" They leave, and I grind my teeth together.

"Loosen up." Darren smacks my shoulder and disappears with the girls.

Her dress is too fucking short.

It pisses me the fuck off.

I want to take her away, hide her in my bedroom, chain her up if I have to. But then she'd know how much she's affecting me, and I can't allow that.

I might have to settle on killing any mothafucker who dares to touch her. I get up, angry at myself for feeling this way. Why the fuck do I even care?

I walk to the railings, gripping them tightly, looking down at the dance floor, searching for her. I catch sight of my sister first and then find her next. She has her hands in her hair and is moving her sexy little body, swaying her hips to the music. I swallow hard as I force myself to look away from her.

Darren stays close to them since the club is full of all different types of monsters. Humans aren't allowed here. That's the best thing about this club. Monsters can let loose and have no worries about hiding. It's warded with magic, so when a human drives by, they only see a large abandoned building.

I can't help myself as my eyes slowly move back to her.

Goddamn, she knows how to move her hips. My hands grip the railing tighter as I try to stay put.

I smirk each time she shakes her head at the men who ask her to dance.

Good girl.

My eyes move around the club. There's cages hanging down from the ceiling that have half-naked women dancing inside of them. The lights are colorful, and there's a wall of mirrors to my right. The large bar is a circle in the middle of the room with bright blue lights, and the dance floor surrounds the entire bar.

Normally I'd be turned on by the women in the cages, but right now, I can only think of one woman's body. Maybe I should take one home with me to help me get her out of my damn head.

I hate that I'm having this kind of reaction towards her. All I wanted to do is hate her, but it's so damn hard, especially since she's staying with us.

I can't want a witch.

I can't let myself.

I look back at her, to find her dancing with a man, rubbing her body against him like a damn whore. My vision turns red as I let out a loud growl. I watch his hands move down to her hips. He leans down, whispering something in her ear.

I grip the railing harder, and it snaps underneath my hands.

Who fucking cares if she's dancing with him?

Not me.

Chapter 10

BELLA

I'm hella tipsy and I'm actually letting loose and having a blast. I've never gone out and let loose like this before. No wonder people party like this all the time.

On top of that, I'm currently dancing with a hot stranger; his hands are on my hips, my back is against his front, and I'm grinding my ass into him. Goodness, it feels good.

I can feel the man grow hard against me, and that's when I want to stop, but why stop? He's hot, and I want to continue to have fun. He leans in, and I feel his hot breath against my neck.

"Let's go somewhere private, gorgeous." I gasp, and my eyes widen. *Do I want to go somewhere with him? I am having fun with him. A little innocent hot make out session will be fun too, right? There's no harm in it.*

"Yeah, let's go." Making out with a hot stranger sounded thrilling when girls talked about it in the bars where I used to work. He wraps an arm around my waist, everything turns blurry as he uses his vampire speed, and the next thing I know, we're in a dark corner of the club.

He smashes his lips against mine, and I groan as I kiss him back my hands gripping his shoulders tightly. It's for sure better than my first and only kiss in high school, and the feeling is definitely thrilling.

"Wanna go to my place, sweetheart?" he asks against my lips, my eyes open.

I open my mouth to decline, but then he's gone. Azrael grabs me, pushing me behind him and gets in the man's face.

"I was with her first, man. She's mine for the night," the stranger says.

"What the fuck did you say?" Azrael says through clenched teeth.

"You heard me, bro. She's mine for the night."

"In your goddamn dreams, motherfucker." Azrael grips the front of the stranger's shirt, lifting him off the floor and then throws him. He goes flying across the room, slamming into the middle of the dance floor, making the floor vibrate beneath my feet.

Everyone stops dancing and watches the scene unfold in front of them. I'm breathless, and I don't know what to do. Azrael grabs the man's throat. His hand tightens, cutting off his airflow. The stranger claws at his arm, thrusting around, trying to fight him off, but his strength is no match to Azrael's.

"MINE!" Azrael roars, lifting him again, slamming him back down hard, making the floor vibrate again. The man's face is turning grey. Shit, he's going to kill him. I need to stop him.

I rush towards them. "Azrael, please stop." I grab his upper arm, and he turns his head to look at me. His eyes are red, black veins are moving underneath his eyes, and fangs are fully extended; his monster is out. I flinch; I have never seen anything like it before.

He's dangerously beautiful.

"Let him go, Azrael,"

He growls and snaps his teeth at me before looking back at the man. He twists his head in one fluid motion, breaking his neck. I gasp. Did he just kill him?

Shit.

Am I crazy for being so turned on by that?

Yes.

I take a few steps back as Azrael slowly stands and stalks towards me. I look at him through my lashes and lick my upper lip. His red eyes zoom into the movement, and my heart flutters. I'm way too turned on; I blame it on the alcohol.

He grabs me by the waist and picks me up, throwing me over his shoulder. Wind wraps around our bodies. I know that we're teleporting. I slam my eyes shut, trying hard not to get dizzy, and a moment later, my back slams into something soft. I open my eyes and see that we're inside a dark room. I blink, looking to Azrael, who's currently standing there staring at me. His gaze is hungrily roaming down my body, making a delicious shiver run down my spine.

I blush when I look down, my panties are showing since my dress is bunched around my hips. I slam my legs shut, pulling my dress down.

He narrows his gaze and starts pacing in front of me, looking like a caged wild animal; his fingers running through his hair, messing it up.

"Were you trying to make me jealous, little witch?" he asks, looking at me, still pacing.

"What?" I squeal loudly, shaking my head. "No! I was just having fun."

"Why is it that every time I turn around, another man is touching you?" He licks his upper teeth; his vangs are still long and sharp. "Hmm, maybe I should chain you up."

"You're fucking insane." I push myself up and try to walk around him, but he grabs me by the throat and slams my back against the wall. I realize that I'm insane, too. He's manhandling me, and I like it. A lot.

"Did you kill him?"

"Just momentarily. He'll wake up in a couple of hours."

"Okay, good." I look away from him, relieved.

"This is your warning, little vixen." His eyes drop to my lips and leans into me. "I better not see another man touch you; you are staying here, alone."

He hisses in my ear, and then he lets me go, disappearing. I stay still for a second, trying to catch my breath.

I can't believe that just happened.

Chapter 11

Stupid fucking fucker! I can do whatever I want! I'm super livid! Argh! I stomp to the garage. Yes, I'm about to do something stupid, but I don't give a flying fuck. I jump in the car, and just as I assumed, the keys are inside.

I'll show him. He can't just boss me around; he's not my father! I hit the button, and the garage door starts opening. I race down the street, but I slow down because I start swerving a little bit. Yikes, I suck at driving.

I turn on the music and start singing along to it. Ten minutes later, I park in the back.

The bouncer from earlier smiles at me and opens the door for me, letting me in. I go down the same hall we did earlier. It opens up to the large dance floor. I glance up to Azrael's VIP room, and my blood turns cold.

That mother fucking bastard!

How dare he! My hands curl into fists at my side.

He has a woman sitting on his lap and a drink in his other hand. I feel nothing but angry, livid, and jealous.

I storm up to the bar, and the same bartender is there. He grins at me. "Same thing?"

"No, I want something stronger. Surprise me."

"I got just the thing." He winks at me before turning around. He comes back later with two shots. I drink both of them, the liquid burns its way down my throat. I squeeze my eyes shut for a second and then wink at him before walking towards the dance floor.

At first, I am going to find Stella and Luna, but I decide against it because I want to get wild and don't want Luna to witness it.

I look around at all the different creatures here. Warlocks, werewolves, and vampires are all here enjoying themselves.

I want myself a vampire.

I start dancing, swinging my hips side to side. After a couple of songs, I feel hands wrap around me from behind making me grin.

I turn around to face my stranger, and perfect, he's just what I ordered: a six-foot-tall sexy vampire, with hazel eyes, high cheekbones, and lips that can do beautiful things.

We dance together. I grind against him, and he leans down and whispers, "What's your name, beautiful?"

"Bella," I whisper back, my eyes slowly wander, looking up, searching for Azrael. I see him, but this time, he's alone. "Kiss me," I say to my mystery man and he does. It's too sloppy for my liking, though. I don't look away from Azrael, and I watch as one of the bouncers walks behind him, whispering in Azrael's ear as he points right at me!

My eyes widen, I feel so betrayed by the damn bouncer!

"Let's go, dude. Like now. Use your vampire speed too," I whisper in his ears, panicked.

"You're an eager little one, aren't you?"

"Mmhmm." He wraps an arm around me, and we speed off. Once outside, he stops, pushing me against the outside wall, and starts kissing my neck and touching my breasts.

No! Why are you stopping!

I wrinkle my nose, I feel no pleasure at all, absolutely nothing...

I whimper angrily.

"You like that?" he asks, mistaking that for a sound of pleasure and not anger. I can't do this.

"Actually..." I begin, trying to find the right words to let him down easily.

But the next thing I know, he's torn off of me. Darren grabs me, trying to pull me away. I turn my head to find Azrael holding the stranger against the brick wall, hand around his throat.

"Azrael, what the fuck stop!" I scream, but he doesn't look my way. He punches his jaw hard. "Darren, stop him!"

"No can do," he says as he tries pulling me away. I struggle, but I'm no match for him. I look back at Azrael. He looks at me with a sinister smile and without looking away, he rips the man's head off in one quick motion. The man's body slumps onto the ground.

Oh my god, no...

Blood is gushing out of the headless body, and it splatters me. I start screaming.

"His death is on your hands. If you weren't such a slut, he would still be alive," Azrael snarls at me. "This is why I hate your kind so much. You are all so selfish, not caring who you hurt." He stalks towards me, but I shake my head, backing away. His face is covered in so much blood.

"Don't touch me!" I cry out, and he stops. I think I see a little flash of regret or hurt, but then it's gone like I imagined it.

He snarls and storms away.

"Let's go," Darren says, I follow him silently.

That man died because of me...

It feels as if Azrael has stabbed me right in the chest with a knife and twisted it.

Darren opens the back door of the SUV, and I see Luna and Stella are already sitting inside.

"I'll drive the other car home," Darren says and shuts the door. Azrael is in the driver's seat.

I just sit here staring blankly out of the window, biting down on my lower lip hard, trying so hard not to let my tears fall.

He doesn't deserve my tears.

I can feel his gaze on me, occasionally and for once, I don't return it. My heart is roaring loudly in my ear, and it feels like I am on the verge of a panic attack.

I'm not weak, I'm one of the strongest witches known, and that's why my father is after me. I wish I were a normal witch.

Luna is rubbing soothing circles on my left hand. She knows that I'm upset, and she's trying to comfort me.

When we finally get to the house, I rush inside, and as soon as I get to my room, the waterworks start. I'm so freaking angry. How can I let a man affect me so much?

How fucking dare he! He just murdered a man in cold blood!

I jump off the bed and throw my door open. I stomp to his door, throwing it open. He stands by his window, looking out, shirtless, already clean of blood   .

He turns and watches me rush towards him, unaffected. I shove his chest hard, pushing his back against the window.

"Fuck you! You don't get to judge me! If I want a man's lips on me, then I can! If I want to fuck a man, then guess what? I fucking can. It's my body and I can do whatever the fuck I want. If I want to be a whore and sleep with multiple men, then guess what? I CAN!" I hit him again. "It's up to me, and I don't care if you don't like it! You had no right to kill him!"

He laughs! He fucking laughs, hard.

"Ahhh, I *hate* you!" I spin around and start walking away.

"I hate your ass too." He grabs my arm and spins me around, shoving my back against the wall. His hand grips my throat.

"Why? Why do you hate me? I have done nothing to you! I can't help that I'm a witch. I'm not a bad person!"

"I hate the way you make me feel." He leans forward and licks my tears. "Fuck, you are so pretty when you cry," he mutters against my cheek, and then his mouth slams against mine, kissing me roughly. Shock and confusion fire through my veins.

His mouth moves, demanding access, but I'm so stunned that I don't kiss him back.

"Kiss me," he growls against my lips, his grip tightens. I feel his rumble against my chest, and I shake my head the best I can. His fingers move until they dig into my jaw painfully.

"Kiss. Me!" He slams his free hand against the wall beside my head. My lips part as I gasp. He takes the opportunity and slips his tongue in my mouth. I can't stop the moan of approval that slips out. My eyes flutter shut and I completely surrender as I kiss him back, meeting his tongue with my own.

My hands fall to his chest for support. Now this is the type of kiss I needed, I thought to myself as I feel pleasurable tingles snake down, heading straight to my core, causing my pussy to flutter wildly. My body comes alive at the blissful sensation. *Shit, this kiss is the best I've ever had.*

He releases my jaw, and his hands grip the back of my thighs, lifting me. I wrap my legs around his hips.

He grabs my ass with one hand and pulls me tighter against him, rubbing his hard length right where I need it.

"Oh, God," I moan, my eyes rolling back.

"There's no God, just me, baby." Fuck, the way he calls me baby is so fucking sexy. My hands slowly move up his arms to his shoulders, grabbing the back of his hair. The strands feel soft between my fingers.

This is bad, very bad...

I know that he hates me, but I can't bring myself to stop.

His full lips are soft and rough at the same time.

One minute I'm pressed tightly against the wall, and the next, I'm being thrown and slammed against the mattress. He climbs on the bed, grabbing my ankles and spreading my legs apart.

He has a clear view of my black lace thong.

His thumb rubs against my clit over my thong in slow torturous circles as he bites his lower lip. *Damn, he looks so goddamn sexy.*

"Azrael," I cry out, needing more.

"Fuck baby, you're so fucking sexy." He crawls on top of me, then lowers his body and presses his weight onto me. He stares into my eyes for a moment before he claims my lips. His fingers move my panties to the side, and he begins to rub my sensitive clit. I arch my back, clawing his shoulders as I moan his name.

His fingers enter me roughly, making me cry out at the new sensation of being stretched. I tilt my head back. He slowly trails his lips down to my neck, sucking my skin between his teeth.

"You're so fucking wet for me," he groans. His fingers curl inside me and my hips start moving to match his pace. I need more.

"So goddamn tight, I'm going to shove my cock so deep in this wet cunt." He grunts huskily. "You want that baby? You want me to fuck this tight pussy?"

"Yes, oh fuck yes, please." I moan, my eyes fluttering closed. "Don... Don't stop!" My entire body begins trembling with need, and I release an earth-shattering scream as I feel myself explode with pleasure, my body feels high on ecstasy.

"You cum so beautiful, little witch." He rips my panties off. "Fuck, your pussy is the sexiest little thing I've ever seen." I whimper as I watch him lower himself until his face is nestled between my thighs. My lips part when he takes a deep inhale, smelling me, nostrils flaring as he does. It's honestly the sexiest thing I have ever seen before. He looks like a starved animal, and he needs me to survive.

"You're such a needy slut for me." He pulls his fingers out of me. I whimper, missing his touch. "It's okay, baby. I'll make you feel good." He looks into my eyes as he sucks his fingers clean.

"Fuck, that's the best-tasting pussy I've ever had, so damn sweet and all mine," he says, lowly, almost as if he's talking to himself. He starts getting busy undoing his belt, his movements frantic. I should feel nervous since this is my first, but I don't. I'm excited. My body is buzzing with so much damn desire.

His door slams open. He throws himself over me, shielding me from view of whoever interrupted us.

"What?" Azrael's growl is murderous.

"Sorry, boss, but it's important," a man's voice replies.

"It fucking better be, get out." he snarls, standing up, zipping up his pants. I watch as he disappears into his closet.

I slowly sit up, not knowing what to do. He comes back out with a clean black T-shirt. He sits on the bench in front of his bed, and I watch silently as he puts his boots back on without once looking at me. He gets up and stares blankly at the wall behind me but doesn't actually look at me as he clenches his jaw.

"This was a mistake." He sighs, his fingers run through his hair as my heart starts beating wildly. A ringing starts in my head as my chest squeezes uncomfortably making it hard for me to breath. Why does it hurt so bad? I've always known he hated me. And he calls me a mistake. I blink the tears back, so he doesn't see them fall. I refuse to show him the pain he's causing me. He opens his door and pauses. "Be out of here by the time I come back."

Then he walks out. I was about to let him have his way with me, knowing how he feels about me... Am I so depraved of love and affection that I almost let a man that hates me have me?

I'm so stupid...

I swallow hard, slowly getting up on my wobbly legs. I go to my room and head straight to the bathroom, desperately needing to wash him off of me. I turn on the hot water, feeling completely numb.

I sit down on the toilet seat as I wait for the bathtub to fill, feeling utterly stupid. I mean, what did I think was gonna happen?

I'm extremely mad at myself.

I can't even be mad at him. I know how he feels about me; he's made it crystal clear. I also know he's an asshole, and I still let him touch me in a way no man has ever touched me.

How am I ever going to get over the feelings I have for him?

I remember my first crush. He kissed me one day, and then he pushed me, screaming about how shitty my kiss was. I left school early that day, and ran all the way home. My mom found me crying and we talked about it. I remember her telling me that when boys are mean, it usually means they like me but are too scared to admit it, which I believed, but now I think it's total bullshit.

I get up and undress, it's been a horrible night. I let out a sigh, dipping my feet in the hot water and releasing a loud groan when I sink my body in.

I'm just going to pretend nothing happened between us.

Yup!

Love that idea!

I shrug, grinning as I think of the bright side. That was an amazing orgasm.

The next morning, I get dressed, wearing a pair of black jeans and an oversized white shirt that hangs over my shoulder.

I stop on the last step, closing my eyes, and taking a slow, deep breath.

You got this!

Just don't acknowledge him. Don't even look at him!

Easy peasy...

I walk into the dining room and everyone is already at the table talking, and there's only one empty seat, and it's next to *him*.

Dammit, of course, I'm never that lucky.

Don't look at him. I straighten my shoulders, and walk over to the empty chair with a big ass grin plastered on my face.

"Good morning!" I say in a cheery voice.

"Good morning." Everyone replies back, except him, no surprise there. He's a moody bastard.

"How are you, Luna?" I ask as I grab a strawberry, taking a bite out of it. I close my eyes, enjoying its sweet taste.

"Good, it's really amazing here!" she replies with a mouthful of food.

"Where's your room anyway?" I question, I can't believe I don't know where it's located.

"It's down here, I can walk out, and bam, the pool is right there!"

"We should go swimming today." Stella perks up. She looks like roadkill, honestly.

"Yes, that's a great idea!" I nod, then grab my coffee and pour in creamer and lots of sugar.

I reach for the stack of pancakes that are in the center of the table and stack three on my plate, then reach for the syrup, but it's too far, and I accidentally elbow Azrael right in the face.

"Sorry!" I grab the syrup bottle quickly and sit back in my chair. After grabbing more strawberries, I smile at Azrael, who, of course, looks unamused.

"So, Theodore told me you had a woman in your bed last night when he fetched you. Who was it?" Darren asks, and I froze.

"No one important." Azrael shrugs, acting completely nonchalant about it.

"Was she hot, at least?"

"Yeah." He clears his throat. "I guess she was, and she also tasted delicious, but it was a mistake and won't happen again." I blush, knowing he's talking about me. How can he just sit there saying that right in front of me? Is he trying to get a reaction out of me?

"Well, if she tasted good, I'd like a taste." Darren wiggles his brows.

I scrunch my nose, not happening, dude.

"Not going to happen, Darren." I stab the pancakes, imagining that I'm stabbing his eyes.

"Why not?"

"She's not really your type, man, and she's leaving soon." Damn, he's a great liar.

"Maybe next time."

"Alright, can we not talk about this? It's kinda weird," Stella interrupts, thankfully. "We don't want to hear about this."

"Agreed!" Luna giggles, and I nod.

"Not likely," Azrael mutters lowly. I hardly heard him.

"What was that?" Darren questions.

"I said, yeah, whatever." I roll my eyes. If I want to hook up with Darren, I can.

"So, Darren, is there a gym or a walking trail you can take me to? I'd like to go for a run," I ask as I take a sip of coffee, groaning lowly when the warmth hits my throat.

"Hell yeah. I can take you to our gym out back, we also have a nice running trail if you prefer. I'd like to join you if you-"

"No," Azrael interrupts as he types something into his cellphone.

"Why not?" I snap. He doesn't even bother looking up. "You have made it clear you want nothing to do with me, so leave me the fuck alone!" I stand up, grabbing Darren's arm, yanking him up. "Let's go!"

"Jeez, woman!" Darren laughs, shaking his head. "But I have another idea."

"I'm listening." He throws a large arm over my shoulder as we walk away.

"Let's go and shoot some shit."

"Heck yeah, lead the way!" He pulls me outside, and I start looking at my surroundings. I finally see the pool in the distance, and it's massive! It looks like we're in a beautiful villa out here, it's perfect. Honestly, it belongs in a magazine. The exterior of the house is an older home that's been updated, mixed with a modern look with its white wood trim windows that are large and arched.

After a few minutes of walking, we pass a large garden with a fountain in the center. Up ahead, there's a large grey metal building.

"That's where we have our gun range and also a boxing ring and a workout room."

"That's freaking awesome!" I grin. I love to shoot things. I never owned a gun, but when I had extra money, I'd go to the shooting range near our house. It was another thing my mom taught me to do.

She used to say, 'even if we have powers, we should never just rely on them'. She learned the hard way, I guess. Even though it wasn't easy, and she was hard on me, I'm glad she taught me everything she knew instead of babying me.

"Damn, that just made you ten times hotter! Never seen a hot girl like you excited about this type of shit!"

We walk inside, and it's massive. It has everything I need.

He grabs my hand and pulls me over to a side door. We go in. I can't see a single thing, the lights are off, but he flips the lights on. The room has five different sections to shoot, there are targets at each end, and the other wall has a shit load of guns of different types.

"Holy shit! You have an Agency Arms Glock 19!" The gun is beautiful. She has specks of gold details. This baby is worth a couple thousand. My mom had a friend who came over a lot, I think they were more like fuck buddies, but he had one. He let me shoot it if I left them alone and watched Luna.

"Fuck! You just made me harder than a fuckin rock." He comes up behind me and looks down at the gun.

"Oh, shut up!" I smack his chest. "Can I shoot it, please?" I flutter my eyelashes, I'm not opposed to begging.

"Yeah, sure."

I smile and pick up the gun, touching the golden handle, checking to see if it's loaded. After that, I pick one of the stalls, grabbing the earmuffs. "Let's see what you got!"

I pull the safety off and aim it at the target ahead. I shoot a couple of times, laughing like a crazy person. God, shooting is such a stress reliever. It's a fucking blast and the perfect way to get my mind off a certain asshole.

"Damn..." Darren laughs, nodding his head. "That was badass!"

"That was awesome!" I laugh more, placing the gun down, looking at the target; all shots hit the same area, right in the center of its forehead.

"You're good." He comes up behind me and wraps his arm around my shoulder again, and we both admire my work.

"What's going on here?" I jump, spinning around, recognizing that voice, looking like I just got caught with my hand in the cookie jar.

"I was watching her shoot. Look at this shit, man." He points at the target.

Azrael looks, and I'm hoping he'll be impressed like Darren.

"And she knows her guns, man. She knew exactly what your favorite was."

"You're easily impressed, Darren." And just like that, my hopes vanish, and my heart sinks. Of course, he's not impressed. Why the hell does he always show up when I'm having a good time and ruins it like a jerk face?

"Whatever, man." Darren shakes his head.

"Can I have my gun back?" Azrael snaps, holding out his hand. I nod and hand it back to him. "Don't touch it again."

"Fine, jeez, you don't have to be such a dick."

"Then you shouldn't touch other people's shit," he says through clenched teeth, making me roll my eyes. He's so over dramatic.

"I didn't fucking know it was yours! Why don't you just leave, hmm? Darren and I were perfectly happy without you." Darren smiles and wraps an arm around my shoulders and I lean into him.

"You heard my girl. Don't ruin our moment." Darren winks at me, and I see the mischief dancing in his eyes.

"She's not your girl."

"I'm not now, but who knows?" I shrug, playing along.

"It's not going to happen." Azrael grabs my arm and yanks me away from Darren. "Darren, someone is at the door for you," he says to Darren without looking away from me.

I hear Darren leave, and the only sound is our heavy breathing. It's just us now, and I can feel the tension dancing in the air. I try pulling my arm out of his grip, but he won't let me go.

"Let me go!" I hiss.

"We need to talk." He finally releases me, but he steps closer to me, so close that I feel the warmth of his breath. I back away, and he mimics the movement until my back hits the wall.

"There's nothing to talk about." I narrow my eyes at him.

"Whatever happened last night, it won't ever happen again. It was a mistake." He shakes his head in disappointment and then backs away, he has trouble keeping his distance, is it all because I'm a witch? Or is it something else too?

He turns to walk away, but I push. "Agreed. It was a huge mistake, and it'll never happen again, I swear on it." He pauses for a moment, his back tenses up, but then he continues on. I stare at his back till he fully disappears.

"Asshole," I whisper. I let my body slide down the wall until my ass hits the concrete floor and then I pull up my knees, placing my head in between them. I try to act like the way he treats me doesn't affect me, but it does. I have always been belittled, but when he does it, God, it hurts like hell.

I get up and head into the other room. I think of going back to the house, but decide against it. I need to burn off some pent-up energy. I haven't worked out since everything went down. After some stretching, I start running at full speed.

I love the way my heart starts pounding in my chest, the sweat beading down my skin, and the way my muscles are burning as I push them.

After running a few miles, I stop and walk over to the fridge that I see in the corner of the room and open it. Thank goodness, there's water.

I slowly make my way back to the house, taking the long way, wanting a closer look at the pool. I think about removing my shoes and dipping my feet in. It'd be hella nice to take a swim. I hear giggling and look to see a set of French doors open, Luna's room. I walk over to see Stella and her talking. They already have swimsuits on.

"There you are! We were looking for you!" Stella smiles waving me in.

"I went for a run. Mind if I join you?"

"Of course, not, sis!" Luna jumps up and grabs a bag. "We got you a swimsuit!"

"Thanks." I grab the small black bag. "Is that the bathroom?" I point at a closed door by the bed.

"Yep, come out when you're done!" They both walk out. The room is a lot smaller than mine, but it looks the same, and it even has the same furniture. It's just cozier in here. I go to the bathroom. It's a small regular bathroom, nothing fancy like mine, but it's still way nicer than our bathroom back home.

I strip out of my clothes and open the bag, my mouth opens when I pull it out. It's a tiny ass yellow bikini. Seriously? I put it on, and just like I thought, it doesn't cover much. I turn to look at my backside, and it almost looks like a thong on me.

I chew the inside of my mouth, thinking about not swimming. It makes me uncomfortable, but at the same time, it's just us girls, so it'll be fine, right? God, I hope so. I grab a towel and wrap it around my body.

I walk out, and they're already in the pool. I walk to the edge and dip my toes. It shocks me how nice and warm it is.

I feel eyes on me, heavy and intense, Azrael... I look around, and that's when I see him. He's standing in a room, leaning against the window, watching me.

Without looking away, I slowly unwrap and drop the towel, letting it fall to my feet. His eyes stay on me, fighting an internal battle that he loses when his gaze drops, trailing down my body. His stare feels like a gentle caress. My lips part as I start panting, my nipples harden, begging for his touch.

He licks his upper lip. Fuck, those lips felt amazing on me.

His gaze pauses on my chest, and I watch his eyes darken in a sexy, but dangerous way. Yeah, go ahead and look, asshole, you're not touching this again.

I lift my hand and flip him off before jumping in the pool and swimming around as Luna and Stella lounge on floaties, talking about clothes and a new purse that just came out. I ignore them as I float on my back, closing my eyes. His intense stare is on me the entire time.

After a while, I climb out slowly, as I smooth my hair back. I peek at him from beneath my eyelashes, and sure enough, he's still in the same spot watching.

I narrow my eyes at him, and he arches his brows, feeling no shame about watching me. His eye contact game is wild. If he actually liked me, I'd love it. I turn around, showing him my back and swinging my hips. I smile, knowing damn well my ass jiggles when I walk. Not to toot my own horn, but my ass is perfection. It's probably my favorite part of my body.

Doing all those squats paid off.

I lay flat on my stomach on the lounger, even though it's the end of September. The sun is beaming and feels amazing. I close my eyes, enjoying the heat.

"Bella…" I slowly blink my eyes open, and see Luna standing above me, trying to wake me up. I must've fallen asleep.

"How long did I sleep?" I mumble.

"About an hour, but it's time for lunch. You hungry? Darren is making burgers."

"God, yes, please." I roll to lie on my back. Darren is standing by the grill on the other side of the pool. Azrael is sitting on a chair close to him talking on the phone. He's wearing dark sunglasses, but I know his attention is on me. Stella is lying on the lounge chair beside me, and Luna walks to the other one and lays down, too.

Damn, we all look pretty hot. Stella is wearing a sexy red one-piece and Luna has on a black two-piece.

"Darren! My man, long time no see!" I glance up and see two men walk outside from the room Azrael was standing in earlier. The tall one is

American, and then the shorter one has beautiful brown skin, darker than me but he looks like a Latino.

"Stella." The shorter of the two smiles and his eyes brighten up as they land on her. I look at Stella, and she blushes, standing up, walking toward him, giving him a big hug; something is definitely going on between them…

"Ross, these are my friends, Luna and Bella." She points at us, and we wave, smiling. "What are you two doing here?"

"We were in the area, and we finished our mission early, so I wanted to come see you. I should have called."

"Don't be silly." Stella waves him off, giggling.

"Stella is as beautiful as ever! Who are your friends?" The other guy walks over after talking to Darren for a minute.

"Landon, that's Luna." Stella points at her, Luna says a small hello, blushing, and then Stella points at me. "That's Bella."

"Bella," Landon repeats my name, and I smile at him. "Why have you been keeping her from me?" He looks at Stella, looking truly offended. He's freaking gorgeous with green eyes, shaggy blond hair, and kissable lips. The second hottest man I have ever seen, hands down!

"I haven't." She rolls her eyes. "We just met a few days ago."

"New to the area?" He looks back at me and smirks. His smile is swoon-worthy, that's for sure.

"Yeah." I nod, sitting up.

"I'll be more than willing to show you around." Stella walks to him and whispers something in his ear, and he nods, looking surprised.

"She'll be fine, my friend," Azrael says, walking over, gripping Landon's shoulder. He finally hung up the phone and all it took was a man giving me a little attention.

"I think that would be nice, though." Azrael turns his attention to me, and I can almost bet his eyes narrowed. "I think Luna and I would enjoy that."

"Maybe another time," Landon suggests he doesn't sound like he's flirting with me anymore. I wonder what Stella said to him.

Chapter 12

AZRAEL

"So, she's yours, huh?" Landon asks me as we walk to the grill. Darren is cooking burgers for the girls.

"Naw." I shake my head.

"So, you wouldn't mind if I take her out?" I give him a fuck off look, and he laughs. "I knew it. Don't worry, Stella warned me already, but if you don't lay claim to a pretty thing like that, someone else will swoop in and snatch her up. Not everyone is afraid of you, just a warning. 'Cause if you weren't my friend, I would have fought for her. Who knows, I still might."

"No, you wouldn't. She's a *witch,*" I snarl the word witch.

"Only because that matters to you doesn't mean it'll matter to everyone else; I would still want her, witch or not. I don't give a fuck what people say; just remember, she's not the witch that murdered your mom. Don't be stupid and let her slip away, but I'll be more than happy to take her off your hands." He pats me on my back and heads toward Darren.

I look back at Bella, and she's lying on her back, laughing at something Luna said. It's hard not to stare at her. I'm drawn to her, and she's fucking hot in that little bikini. It's as if someone put all of my fantasies inside of her and made her just for me.

Last night was a huge mistake, but I can't stop thinking about her soft skin and the way she responded to my touch. The way she moaned my name. I've never tasted anything as amazing as her. Fuck, the way she came was so sexy. My dick has been hard and it refuses to go down. I want more. No, fuck that. I need more.

I'm becoming obsessed with her, addicted to her.

I hate it when I'm not in the same room as her and don't know what she's doing.

I know what Landon said is true. I know someone will try to take her from me, and I can't stop them all. Plus, she's not mine...

But it makes me see red thinking of another man touching her the way I did. Every single fucking time I even see a man so much as look at her, it makes me want to rip them apart.

No matter how many times I say I don't care, I know deep down it's not true.

"Just stop fighting it already." I tear my gaze away from Bella to find Stella standing beside me. I didn't even see her move from the lounger. "Landon's right. She's not the witch that hurt Mom."

Of course, she was eavesdropping.

I'm not stupid; my father killed that bitch.

"Stay out of it," I snap. She huffs and walks away.

People say I'm an asshole, and I know I am, even to the people I care about, which honestly is only three people: my father, sister, and Darren.

It doesn't matter how much I crave her, we can never be. Fate is a bitch pairing me with a witch. My phone rings, and I head back to my office.

Landon says he doesn't care about what people think, but he isn't the next in line to take the crown. It'd be a lot harder for me.

"Father, what can I do for you?" I sit on my office chair and turn it, so I have my eyes on Bella. They all are now sitting at the table eating.

I close my eyes and groan as I picture her walking away from me. Fuck, her ass literally clapped together as she walked away. Hell, I've never seen an ass so perfect before. I used to think I was a breast man, but with an ass like that....

"Azrael?" My father snaps.

"What?" I clear my throat and straighten my shoulders, like it'll help wipe that memory away. It's not like I'd have to pick when it comes to her, because those tits are perfect too...

"Are you even listening?"

"No, what were you saying?" I turn away from Bella so I can think straight.

"Stella called and told me that you have Marcus's daughter there. Why haven't you called? And why are you keeping the girl's power from her?"

Fucking Stella… "I have it under control."

"You should bring her here. She has been hiding out of fear of her father. She'll be more protected here."

"I'm not trying to protect her. I'm going to use her as bait."

"Azrael, you can't be serious." He makes a sound of disbelief. "Of course you are, you can't use that innocent girl that way."

"I can and I will," I snap as I pinch the bridge of my nose.

"You're putting her in danger. I did not raise you that way."

"Enough!" I yell, punching the desk.

"So what? You're going to do the same thing that evil bitch did to your mother."

"That's not the same." I stand up and begin pacing.

He lets out an unamused laugh. "She was using your mother to get to me and killed her once she did."

"It's not the same!" I growl. "I'm not planning to kill her."

"No, but you're putting her in danger, and that could get her killed, especially without her magic."

"Fuck!" I throw my phone, and it breaks into little pieces. I look back at her again and catch her staring at me. Her cheeks turn a bright red, and she quickly looks away, chewing her lower lip.

What he said, I never thought about it like that. She could possibly be killed... The thought of her being hurt makes the monster inside me roar, wanting to claw his way out to protect her.

"Fuck!" My hands go to my hair, and I yank the strands.

What am I going to do now? I refuse to put her in that kind of danger. We need to let her have her powers back. After a couple hours of pacing. I finally talk to Darren about what was discussed. He agrees with me; I knew he would, though.

I leave my office to talk to Bella, and when I can't find her, I go upstairs to her room, and what I do find has me seeing red. My blood heats up to the point of boiling. My breathing grows rigid, and I want to kill. My monster starts clawing his way out, and I don't think I want to stop him, friend or not.

Chapter 13

BELLA

I don't know what the hell I'm doing; hell, I don't know what I'm even thinking! But here we are, sitting in my bed. This is a bad idea, no scratch that, it's a stupid idea. We began drinking during lunch, and I got pretty tipsy. That's probably why I agreed, but I'm slowly sobering up.

"It's not going to work. I don't even know why we're doing this. It's stupid. Like very, very stupid." I rush out as I shake my head, and look up at Landon. His only response is curling the corner of his lips into an arrogant smirk. "You're insane. Honestly, why are we even doing this?"

"Because I want him to open his damn eyes." He leans his back against the headboard and straightens his legs, crossing them at the ankles, getting extremely too comfortable.

"Open his eyes about what?" I ask for the tenth time. He's driving me in-fucking-sane.

"How he feels about you." I stare at him like he's gone crazy, and then I throw my head back, laughing hysterically.

"Why are you laughing so hard? I'm being serious." He narrows his eyes at me, like *I'm* the crazy one.

"Yeah, sorry, you're right," I say, clenching my side, trying to sober up as I wipe the tears off my sore cheeks. "But you don't understand! You haven't been around. That man hates me, Landon. You are so, so wrong."

"Come on, you're a smart girl. You can't tell me you don't see it."

"See what exactly?" I cross my arms over my chest, lean my back against the headboard, turning my head to face him.

"So, you don't see it either, just like he doesn't."

"See what?" I throw my hands up in frustration.

"Okay, so one," he holds up one index finger, "I have known him my whole life, and he's never been like this towards a woman."

"Maybe because you've never seen him with a woman he hates so much." I shrug.

"And for two," he holds up a second finger, "he wouldn't care if another man touched you. He wouldn't get so murderous when someone touches you. Fuck, when I even looked at you, I felt his anger."

"It's because he wants to protect me so I don't ruin his plan. I'm sure when he's done with me, I'll be tossed aside like the garbage he thinks I am."

"Yeah, because having sex with another man is so dangerous. He told me to stay away from you. He usually shares his women. I see the way he stares at you. It's like he wants to eat you all up, but I don't really blame him." He looks down at my chest, and my face heats up.

"So, what are you saying? Yeah, I already know that he finds me attractive, so what? He still hates me. He's made that very clear."

"He's being stupid. That's what he's doing. He has no reason to hate you." He pulls out a business card and places it on my nightstand. "That has my personal cell phone number, call me if you ever need a place to hide."

"Okay, thank you." I blow out a deep breath. "Look, we don't need to do this. I've changed my mind, I won't help you." I hate that he's right about everything...

"Too late. I hear him. He's close." Then he grabs me, pulling me toward him, and I yelp. My legs are on either side of his hips, I'm straddling him. He grabs the back of my head, and his lips are now against mine. I completely freeze, but I then start kissing him back. I want to kiss him because I need to show myself that I don't need Azrael to make me feel the way he does. Any man can make me feel alive, especially one as hot as Landon.

My hands slowly move up his shoulders, and my fingers tangle in his hair. I start grinding against him slowly. His arms wrap around my hips to cup my ass. He lets out a sexy groan. I completely forgot what we're doing. Fuck, he feels good. His lips are soft and hot, but there are no sparks, no tingles, nothing... That doesn't matter that much because he still feels good. His lips trail down to my neck, and he licks and sucks.

"Fuck, you feel so fucking good," he groans. "I won't lie, it's almost worth fighting Azrael for you. Why do you have to be his?"

"I'm not his," I whisper as I tilt my head back. One of his hands moves off my ass and slowly trails its way up my ribs to the underside of my breast, and his finger moves into my bikini top, grazing my nipple.

"You are. You just don't know it yet. Tell me you don't feel the same about him. Tell me you don't want him, and you'll come with me, bring your sister even, and we'll leave together. I'll fight for you." I gasp, leaning back to look into his eyes. Is he serious? Do I want him to take me away and hide me from Azrael? Do I want to leave Azrael?

No...

Urgh, I don't know!

I lean in to kiss him, delaying my answer because I don't know what I wanted yet. *If I ever need to leave, I'll call him. He says he'll fight for me. God, that alone makes me want to pick him. He actually likes me...*

So why don't I?

I hear my door open, and I freeze. It's dead quiet for a few minutes. Landon is staring over my shoulder. I hear a loud, monstrous growl, and at the same time, I'm being yanked away from Landon. He gets up and looks at me, with a question in those green eyes.

"Bella—" Landon starts but is cut off.

"Get the fuck out of here before I kill you, Landon, I'm serious," Azrael snarls. He sounds different, feral, sinister. It's so damn sexy. It should scare me, but it doesn't. I'm extremely turned on.

Really, bitch? That turns you on and not making out with a hot guy. Goodness, I'm sick of my body betraying me.

Landon rushes out, and I'm alone with a monster. I feel his hot, rigid breath against my ear. His body is tense. I look down to see his hands are trembling.

I swallow hard.

I'm so screwed.

I start walking away and make it a few steps. "Where the hell do you think you're going?" I stop, and my body stiffens, but I don't turn around.

"I'm leaving. I don't want to be near you, and I need to find Landon to make sure he's okay." I say casually and start walking to my closet. I need to change first.

"He's fine. You are not seeing him again unless you want his death on your hands." I gulp. I can't believe he just said that...

"Why the hell not? What if I want to be with him? Huh, what if I like him?" I march over to him and shove his chest with both of my hands. "You can't threaten everyone who wants to be with me. You can't tell me who I can hang out with!"

"Yes, I can, and I will." His lips curl in a sinister smirk.

"No, you will not. It's none of your business!" I am so sick of his shit…

"As long as I'm protecting you, it is my business."

"Yeah, keep telling yourself that. You know what? Landon agreed to take me and Luna and protect us. I'll just take him up on his offer and leave with him. He can keep us safe; I can be your stupid bait without living here."

"No one will or can keep you away from me," he snarls through clenched teeth.

"That's not your choice to make! It's MINE!" I point at myself as I yell.

"You don't get a choice in the matter, and no one is strong enough to stop me."

"Fuck you. I'm horny, so I can fuck whoever I want. Landon is not out to hurt me, so I'm going to go find him so we can finish what you rudely interrupted!" I hate it because he's right, no one can take me away from him. He's too powerful, but deep down, my toxic part won't leave anyway.

He walks past me and disappears inside my bathroom.

"Where the hell do you think you're going?" I follow him into the bathroom, and he's standing by the shower, turning it on. "What are you—"

He picks me up, and he tosses me in the shower.

"Ahhh!" I scream as the cold ass water hits my skin.

"There, that should help with your problem." He lets out a short chuckle and walks out.

J.S. RODRIGUEZ

That motherfucker...

Chapter 14

AZRAEL

I'm fucking furious... How dare he touch her after I told him not to.

She's mine, even if she doesn't know it yet. I know I told her it was a mistake, but once I saw her with Landon, I didn't fucking care. I never want to see her in the arms of another man again. I'll go on a warpath and destroy the world before I let that happen again.

No one else can touch her the way I did. I won't allow it.

The possessiveness and jealousy is eating me alive. Every time I close my eyes, I see them together, causing my anger to worsen. His hands all over her body, ass, tits. I release a low guttural growl.

I can't believe my mate is a witch. The universe is seriously sick and twisted. I sit on her bed waiting for her to come out. She needs to be sober when I tell her that she's my mate.

I'm done fighting it.

She's mine, and she'll know by the end of the night.

She steps out of the bathroom, completely soaked. She's wearing a lace bra and silk shorts. She looks so fucking sexy when she's angry, which makes me smile.

"Why the fuck are you still here?" she snaps as she dries her wet hair with a towel. Body tight with tension.

"We need to talk." I lean against her headboard, showing her that I'm not going anywhere.

"You said enough this morning." She crosses her arms over her chest, making her breasts lift more. I lick my lips slowly.

The way she looks in that lace red bra is spectacular.

I want to devour her, again and again.

"Not nearly enough." I look back up and notice that her cheeks are growing redder by the minute.

"What do you want, Azrael?" She wraps the towel around her body, trying to hide herself from me.

I just need to rip off the Band-Aid and tell her.

"You're my mate, Bella." I keep my eyes locked on hers.

"Yeah, right." She starts laughing, and I'm not going to lie, it hurts. My chest tightens and I grind my teeth trying to calm my rage that's currently pulsing.

"I'm not fucking joking," I snap, getting up, and she looks up at me with wide eyes. "Don't you feel it?" I touch her hand with the back of mine, feeling the electric shock of our touch.

"B... but you hate me."

"I do, I hate what you are," I say truthfully.

"Is there a way for us to reject each other?" She backs away from me and sits down, looking anywhere but at me. My nostrils flare: she wants to fucking reject me.

"There's no way." I lie there are ways to reject the mate bond, but there's no fucking way I'd tell her. I won't take a chance on her rejecting me because of how I've treated her. I honestly wouldn't be surprised if she did.

"So, we're stuck with each other." She looks down at the floor, shoulders slump, looking deflated.

"Seems so." I sit on the chair opposite her and stretch my legs out in front of me.

"So, what do we do?"

"Nothing, you're mine, and I'm yours." I shrug like it's not a big deal. She's stuck with me whether she likes it or not.

"Okay." She nods. "Why wait till now to tell me? You must've known when we first touched." She looks at me through her lashes.

"I did. I wanted to fight the bond. But then I saw you with Landon, and I couldn't... I don't know. I felt jealous, possessive, and angry... I don't want to see you with anyone else. We'll just have to take this one day at a time." I kneel in front of her, grabbing her hand, showing her she's not alone. She nods, biting her lower lip.

"I can leave, and we can forget about each other." She starts playing with her hair, and I feel my fangs extend, the anger rises, flowing through my veins. She still wants to leave me. I'll chain her up before I let that happen. I start to think, I don't have any chains that are long enough for her to reach the bed and the bathroom. I can get them if needed.

"You're not leaving me," I growl, gripping her jaw, and force her to look at me. "Got that? I'll chain you up if I have to," Her eyes widen with fear, and she swallows. Good, let her be afraid. She'll be too scared to run.

I let her go, and she scrambles back, getting as far away from me as she can. I bare my teeth at her, she'll never escape my clutches. "I'll be back."

Part of me is angry with myself. I did that horribly, just because I saw her with Landon. I should've been gentler about it; now she's afraid.

Fuck...

Chapter 15

BELLA

I need to get out of here before this asshole actually chains me up. I wouldn't put it past him; he's fucking crazy. He doesn't want me, if he did, he wouldn't have fought the bond in the first place. It's the jealousy forcing him, and I can't be with someone who hates what I am.

I feel the connection, and God, yes, I want him, but that isn't enough. I want him to want me. I never thought I'd find my mate. It should make me happy, but mine despises me.

I sit here, fidgeting with my fingers, not knowing what to do. I can't be mated to someone who only wants to be with me because he can't stand the idea of another man touching me.

I refuse to be in a loveless relationship.

And I refuse to be chained up, at least without it being in a sexual way.

I grab a small duffel bag and fill it up with the essentials, then I rush to Luna's room. She isn't there, but I grab another duffel bag and start to pack for her. Ten minutes later, she comes in with a large smile.

"Bella?" She looks at me with her brows pinched together in confusion. "What are you doing?"

"We need to leave, now."

"But why?" She follows me to the bathroom.

"I'll explain while we're on the road, but not right now. Just trust me, please." I throw in some essentials from her bathroom.

"Yeah, of course." She nods, chewing her lower lip, and grabs the duffel bag. I squeeze her hand, and we leave the room. Luckily, we don't run into anyone. We go to the garage, and we both search the cars, but none have keys.

Shit.

I run to the last car, silently praying. Thank God, the keys are in the ignition.

"Luna, got one," I whisper, and she rushing over. We get in, and I quickly drive off. I keep looking in the rearview mirror, biting my nails nervously.

After about an hour down the road, I calm down and take a deep breath.

"Okay, tell me what's going on," Luna turns to look at me.

"I don't know how to explain this, but Azrael is my mate, I guess." My grip tightens on the steering wheel.

"Okayyy? That doesn't make any sense. Why would you run?"

"Because Luna... Ugh, what? You don't see how much he hates me? I can't be with someone who hates what I am! He literally told me he tried to fight the bond because of me being a witch. I want someone to love me." A tear slips down my cheeks.

"God, that's true, you do deserve to be loved. I understand. I'm so sorry!" She reaches over and wipes the tear off my cheek.

"And the asshole threatened to chain me up!"

"Are you serious?"

"I used to dream about meeting my mate and falling in love and blah, blah, you know. But that changed after Mom died, and I found him, and he hates everything about me! He doesn't really want me; the bond is forcing him." My hands tremble as I wipe the tears off my face.

"I'll be with you no matter what you decide, sis."

"Am I a coward for running? Am I making the biggest mistake of my life?" It honestly hurts every minute as I get further away. I close my eyes for a moment, thinking about what I just did. Did I overreact? *No, I deserve someone who loves me.*

"You're not a coward, Bella. I think you may have run without thinking about it, but you deserve to be loved, and if you think he won't ever love you, then you made the right choice."

We drive for a few hours. I have no idea where we're going. We stop in a small town, and Luna goes inside a janky motel. She has to use her magic to get us a room since I still don't have access to mine.

Luna comes back out, and we grab our bags and go in to search for our room.

"I called Trisha," Luna says when we find our room.

"Luna! That'll be the first place he'll look!"

"Yeah, but she has other places. She told me she has a house about five hours away from us." She jumps on the bed, and I sit down on the other bed. It's super uncomfortable compared to what I have been sleeping in. God, it's amazing how fast we get used to the luxury things.

I kick off my shoes and glance around. It's small and has two queen beds with red covers and cream walls. A large desk is in front of the beds with a tiny TV on it.

The question which keeps running through my mind is, will he always hate me? Or will he get over the hate and love me one day? Do I risk it and fall in love with him just to have my heart broken?

I squeeze my eyes shut as my chest tightens. I should have stayed and talked to him first, told him my concerns, but I felt like I couldn't chance it if he really was going to chain me up.

My emotions are going all over the place. Half of me agrees with what I did, but I'm so torn. Maybe I just need a couple of days, and then I'll go back. What if he won't forgive me and turns me away?

I know he won't come looking for me. He doesn't care enough. Maybe if I weren't a witch, it could've been different. We could've been happy. The worst part of it all was that he didn't want me to know about us, and that broke my heart.

"So, what then? She wants us to meet her there?" I ask, lying down on the stiff mattress halfway dozing off.

"Yes, tomorrow. She texted me the address."

"Okay…" I roll to my side and pass out.

We've been on the road for a couple of hours. We left around four this morning. We got there at midnight last night, so we didn't get much sleep. Luna is snoring beside me while I listen to music.

Since we got in the car, I've been thinking about turning around and going back to him.

I miss him, honestly, even though he's an asshole most of the time. I enjoy being in the same room as him, and the feeling of his intense gaze on me, watching me.

No! Bella, just give it a couple of days and clear your head. We're ten minutes out from the address Trisha sent. I exit the highway, and we immediately hit a very old-looking town. I can feel the magic in the air, and I can tell most of the residents here are witches. I really pray a psycho doesn't try to chase me out again, but it doesn't feel like dark magic.

The town is a straight line of shops, the buildings dark in color. We drive by a few spell shops, and there are even some tables on the sidewalks with women dressed like witches sitting there. The signs by the tables say they're doing readings.

Destination on the right.

"Luna, wake up." I shake her arm as I turn right.

"I'm up." she groans as she sits up, stretching. I look up, and see a large three-story black Victorian house completely decked out in Halloween decorations. It's completely gorgeous.

"Wow…" Luna whispers.

"Wow is an understatement," I agree as I park the car. We get out, grab our duffel bags, and start walking up the pathway with cute pumpkins lined up.

"Girls, you made it!" Trisha is standing at the open door with a large smile. She has the same style dress on as before.

"Hi again, Trisha." I smile, waving at her.

"Hi, Trisha!" Luna waves, too. The porch has black rocking chairs on the left and a black porch swing on the right. She hugs us both at the same time. I cringe slightly; I'm not really a touchy-feely type of person.

"I'm happy you got away from that horrid vampire. They're nasty bloodsuckers." She shakes her head as she removes her arms off of us. I frown at what she says but keep my mouth shut.

"Thanks so much for inviting us! This place is beautiful!" Luna says, looking around. We follow her inside. There's a large wooden staircase with wood molding surrounding it. It all looks original.

The doors are shut to the left of us, and on the right, there's a large hallway and an opening to a sitting room with a large bay window, two Victorian-style chairs, a wooden coffee table, a sofa in front of it, and a beautiful wooden fireplace mantel with a mirror on top of it.

I see a dining room with a round table with eight chairs. It also has a bay window. This place is beautiful and charming.

"Let me take you to your rooms upstairs. Dante will be joining us for dinner," Trisha says, walking up the stairs. I process what she just said: Dante is coming. I really wanted to be free from boy drama. I guess that's not happening.

My hand is running along the beautiful handcrafted wooden railing as I walk up the stairs.

These walls hold a lot of secrets.

"Each room has its own bathroom. Mine is downstairs. But the door at the end of the hall and the one beside that one, are Dante's bedroom and office. Please, don't enter unless he invites you in. Luna, dear, yours is here." She points to the left. "And Isabella, yours is there." She points at the one next to Dante's. "I'll let you girls get settled, and I'll be downstairs if you need anything. Dinner will be at six."

She then turns and walks down the stairs.

"This place is creepy..." Luna says with a slight tremor in her voice. I smile at her; she hates old places.

"It's just an old house. Let's sleep before dinner," I suggest. I sure could use a couple of hours of sleep. "If you get too scared, you know where my room is," I tease.

"Be nice! It could be haunted..." She grabs my hands and looks around like a ghost is about to jump out at any moment. I laugh.

"Maybe it is, but if there are any ghosts, they aren't evil. I don't feel any negative energy in the house, so go rest." I turn and open the door to my room.

I gasp. It's beautiful. This is more my style than Azrael's modern-looking house. A queen-sized bed is snug in between two windows. On the right side of the bed is a large antique dresser that matches the bedframe, another door, which I assume is the bathroom, and there's a fireplace to the left of me.

I drop the duffel bag on the bench in front of the bed and throw myself on the mattress, which is way better than the one at the motel.

I fall asleep before I even take off my shoes.

"Bella." I wake up, and I see Luna standing by the bed.

"Luna, what's wrong?" I sit up worried.

"Nothing. Dinner is in an hour. I just wanted to wake you."

"Shit, thanks. I'll take a shower." I head to the bathroom. There's an old vanity with two sinks and a clawfoot tub with a shower.

I see a door on the other side, but I just assume it's a closet. I remove my clothes, then turn on the hot water.

Luckily, there's a new bar of soap, so I use it to scrub myself clean. My muscles are super tense, so I stand under the hot water until it turns cold.

I step out and wrap the towel around my body. The door I assumed was a closet opens, and I scream, dropping the towel. I look up, and see Dante standing there, staring at me in shock.

"Oh uh..." He rubs the back of his neck. "I'm sorry, I assume Trisha didn't tell you we have a shared bathroom?"

"Oh n... no she didn't." His gaze drops, looking down my body, and he clears his throat, looking away with a slight red tint on his cheeks.

I look down at myself. "Oh, my goshhh!" I squeal. I forgot I dropped the towel. I bend down and rewrap it around myself. "I, uh, well, I..." I stumble on my words, not really knowing what to say, so I just turn and run out of the bathroom, slamming the door shut, leaning against it without another word.

Stupid, stupid, stupid!

Chapter 16

AZRAEL

She left me! She fucking left! She ran away from me. My body is pulsing with extreme anger. I trash her room when I found her gone. I break almost everything until my sister comes in and stops me, not understanding what is happening.

I have never felt emotionally hurt until now, nor have I felt this strange emptiness I feel. I never expected her to leave me. Yes, I know I was an ass to her, but I thought...

Well, I don't know what I thought.

Darren and my sister keep promising me that we'll find her, but I can't think straight. All I want to do is break shit. I'm high on adrenaline.

I did go to Landon's house, thinking she had left me for him, and went crazy on him. To me, it's his fault she ran and not mine, even though deep down I know it wasn't him, it was me. I destroyed his home looking for her, but she wasn't here. I knew she wasn't, I would've scented her, but I still looked like a madman.

Her leaving made me realize that I don't hate her like I thought I did.

Am I not enough for her?

I thought meeting your mate was a great, joyful moment. Instead, it has been nothing but hell for me. Maybe this is a good thing.

But the thought of never seeing her again makes me crazy.

I didn't know how much I needed her till now.

How happy I was when she was around.

Did she run to the warlock?

Daniel was his name, I believe… or was it Dane?

I'll kill him, but not before I fuck her right in front of him to show him who she belongs to, ME, not him!

Then I'll rip him to shreds right in front of her to teach her a lesson. No one can ever take her from me.

I want to punish her.

I dial the best tracker I know. He's expensive, but I don't give a shit. I'll pay whatever it takes to have her back in my arms.

"Azrael." His rough voice answers on the first ring.

"I need your services, and I need them now." I pace in my office like a wild animal, pushing my hair back with my hand.

"I don't know, man, I'm in the middle of a job."

"I'll pay you double," I growl into the phone, my fist hits the desk, breaking it in half.

"I'll come now. Be there in a couple hours."

I head to the rooftop, where I spent hours putting everything together to surprise her with a date. The candles are all burnt out. The food on the table is cold. I wanted it to be perfect for her. I lined up candles to make a walkway straight to the table and hung up lights.

I made her chicken penne pasta and chocolate cake for dessert.

I pick up the plates of food and throw them, smashing them against the floor, and then kicking the burnt-out candles. I roar before slumping forward, gripping the table.

I sit on the chair and look up, staring at the starry night, clenching my bloody fist that is mixed with my blood and Landon's blood.

What's the best punishment for my little mate when I find her? Because I *will* find her, make sure she never leaves me again, and make sure she'll never want another man. I picture myself stripping her of her clothes, laying her across my lap, ass in the air, and smacking her till her ass is painted red.

I can picture her ass jiggling as I do it. I haven't fucked someone with a big ass before, but I can imagine pounding her in doggy and with each thrust of my hips, her ass shakes.

I have to adjust my jeans as I grow rock hard.

"Azrael." I look up to Darren's voice. He's looking around at the mess I made. "You did all of this?"

"Yesss," I hiss. Landon steps out from behind Darren.

"I'm sorry. I didn't know she was your mate, or I wouldn't have…" Landon starts, but I hold my hand up, shaking my head, cutting him off. I don't want to hear it.

"Andre is here." Stella pushes herself between the guys. She looks sad. She really grew attached to Luna; she isn't used to having women around, especially not one that's oddly similar to her. It's kinda annoying being around two overly preppy girls.

"Good." I nod as I stand and follow her downstairs.

"Prince Azrael," Andre bows.

"Andre."

"How may I assist you?" He straightens. He's a scary man with no mercy. He works for Prince Dimitri and is the best tracker there is. He's a little taller than me and leaner with dark eyes and hair that's pulled back in a man bun.

"I'm looking for my mate, she left yesterday. I want her back." I stare at him while crossing my arms over my chest, wondering if he's the best for the job. He's known to be violent, and I don't want him to be violent with my little witch.

Not long ago, they took down Vampire Prince Julius, who ruled in America. He was a weak ruler, and I disliked him. We usually start wars for killing one of our own rulers, but he deserved it by taking Dimitri's mate, which was a very stupid thing to do and against our laws.

"Why would I look for her if she ran from you? It sounds like she doesn't want to be found," he asks with a smirk. "I like her already."

I growl loudly. He's lucky he's a friend of mine. "Can you find her or not?"

"Of course, I can." He snorts like it's outrageous that I even thought for a second he couldn't find her.

"I'll transfer half to you now and half once you find her." I pull my phone out of my pocket to wire the money to his bank account.

"I will also need something that smells of her."

"I'll go get what she wore earlier," Darren murmurs, already disappearing.

"How long ago did she leave?"

"Late last night, maybe early morning." I look up after transferring the money. "Make sure you don't harm her. I know you handle your business with a lot of violence."

"Not my fault. People can be very whiny and annoying, pushing my patience, but I won't harm an innocent woman who only wishes to be free from a crazy psychopath." He shrugs, pressing his lips together, trying to keep from smiling. I narrow my eyes and grind my teeth. "She couldn't have gone far."

"She's a witch and a strong one at that, but she has no access to her powers. So it should be easy, and her sister Luna is with her." I ignore his comment, not needing to piss him off, making him back away from the deal. "Call me when you get close and make it fast. I'd like to be there when you find her."

"Of course, my Prince." He nods at Darren and Landon. They nod back. I hand one of Bella's shirts to Andre.

"She smells delicious." He groans as he sniffs the shirt. I growl, feeling possessive. She's mine. He disappears before I can threaten him.

I walk to the dry bar and pour myself some whiskey.

This is going to be a long day.

I won't rest till I find her.

I swallow down the whiskey and refill the glass before sitting in my chair, leaning my head back, kicking my feet up, and resting them on the table in front of me.

I was afraid of my father not accepting her, and I just pushed her away. But the more I was around her, the more she melted the ice around my heart and crawled her way into it.

Is she safe? Where did she go?

I checked Trisha's house as soon as I found out she was gone, but there was no trace of her there.

I think about the way her lips felt against mine. They're warm and plump. The way her soft skin felt beneath my fingertips was electrifying. She is made to be worshipped.

And worship is what I will do.

She's exquisite.

She's mine.

She belongs with me.

"Are you okay?" I look over my shoulder to see Darren leaning his shoulder against the wall, his arms folded across his chest. I shake my head, unable to answer as I'm too angry with myself. I pushed her away even though she's the best thing that ever happened to me.

"You can talk to me. I'll never judge you."

"Do you have any idea how much I want her? It's like she's crawled her way into my soul and rooted herself deeply in it. I crave her and ache for her, and I hate myself for it. She's a fucking witch, like what the fuck? But I can't keep pushing her away; it hurts too much, it's physically impossible. I don't care anymore; nothing or anyone else matters. I'll give up my crown for her. I, fuck... I *need* her. But she doesn't want me, but why would she? I have done nothing but be an asshole to her and kept telling her how much I hated her. I'm the reason she ran," I spit out angrily. I despise myself. How can I do something like this to my own mate?

"Just tell her how you fe—"

A knock at the door cuts him off. I get up and open it. My butler stands there, one hand behind his back, and the other holding a note out to me. "This was delivered, and it's addressed to you."

"Thank you, Knox." I grab the note from him.

He bows and leaves. I open it, and see a photo inside. I hiss when I look at it. I can feel my blood boiling with anger.

"What is it?" Darren looks over my shoulder. It's Bella asleep in the middle of a mattress, wearing nothing but a large black T-shirt and white underwear.

> *Prince Azrael,*
> *I have your beautiful mate, but sh won't be yours for long; you see, she's mine, and I will not allow you to take her from me. I met her first. She was made to be my mate, not yours, but it's okay now. She came back to me, and she's here with me, asleep in my bed and not yours. I'm planning on marking her as mine tonight, and you can never have her.*
> *She deserves better. Her mom wanted us to be together, and plans changed when her mom passed away. But now that I have her, I'll never let her go.*
> *She's mine!*
> *Dante*

I growl loudly, my body trembling with anger.

That mother*fucker*.

I throw my glass of whiskey against the wall. I'll fucking kill the bastard. I grab my phone and call Andre. We need to find her tonight before it's too late.

Chapter 17

BELLA

We're sitting at the dining table eating roast beef. I keep looking at Dante, and each time, he's already staring at me. The more I'm around him, the more it feels wrong. My gut is screaming at me something is wrong, but I'm not sure what. I just know I want to leave this house and never come back. Luna and Trisha are talking, but I'm not paying any attention to them.

"So, Bella." I blink, looking up, hearing my name.

"Yeah?" I clear my throat.

"Do you still draw?" Trisha asks, smiling at me.

"Oh... Uh, no, I don't." I take a bite of the food, and it's amazing.

"Your mom used to tell me you drew a lot, and you were getting good at it."

"You talked about me?" I stopped drawing when a teacher told me I wasn't talented enough to enter a contest at school. I remember being heartbroken.

"Yeah, we did, about the both of you. What about shooting? I never understood why your momma taught you when your magic is more effective."

"Yes, I still shoot because there are spells and items that can stop you from using your magic. It's a good thing to make sure you don't just rely on magic."

"Not many people have access to those types of tools, so they are useless."

"Agree to disagree," I say, I refuse to sit here and argue about it. "Plus, I have these." I roll up my sleeves to show them the cuffs.

"That attitude of yours is just like your momma's. It will get you in trouble just like it got her in trouble."

"Excuse me?" I stop chewing, my eyes narrow at her across the table.

"I meant no harm in it. I loved her sassy attitude. Just be careful who you give it to." Both Dante and Luna watch us, eyes moving back and forth.

"She always has an attitude. It won't ever go away, but she's strong, so I doubt anyone will ever put her in her place. I don't think she needs to worry about it." Luna smiles at me with a wink, not reading the tension in the room.

I don't feel like I belong here.

"I can try to remove those. I need to find the spell first." She taps her fingers on the table like she's lost in thought. "I believe it's in one of my spell books. Goddess, I hope so! Don't worry, I'll find it."

I start thinking about Azrael. What is he doing? Is he happy I left? I know now that I made a big mistake. I'm used to running before a problem becomes an issue, but I should have listened to what he had to say before I ran… I get up, excusing myself, walking out before anyone can reply.

I start pacing in my room; I should go back… Yes, tomorrow Luna and I will go back, and I'll apologize to him and admit I ran scared shitless, and hope he forgives me.

"Isabella?" There's a knock at the door. I open it, seeing Dante standing there, his hands above his head, gripping the doorframe. "Can I come in?"

"Oh, uh, yes, of course." I move back, opening the door wider to let him in. I lean my back against the open door as I watch him rub the back of his head nervously.

"I was wondering if tomorrow I can take you out and show you around town?" He gives me a large smile that shows off his perfect white teeth.

"I, uh, will." I push myself off the door. "I think I made a mistake by leaving. We'll be going back tomorrow." I shift side to side nervously. I feel bad, honestly. I asked them for help, and they left the cabin to come here so they could help us hide.

"Are you serious?" he snaps angrily. I look at him in shock. He's always so calm. "You can't be serious. You want to go back to those nasty vampires?!"

he shouts. I shouldn't be too shocked, though. Witches and vampires are enemies. The least I can do is explain myself.

"Look, he's my mate."

"Mate?" he hisses. "He's probably lying to you. That's what they do best." He grabs my upper arms tightly, slightly shaking me like he's trying to knock some sense into me. "No, I won't let you go back."

"Excuse me?" I push at his chest, and he hardly budges. "It's not your choice. Plus, I know he's not lying. I appreciate what you and your mom have done for us, but we're leaving." I rip my arms out of his grip and back away, putting distance between us.

His body grows tense as he straightens. "I understand." He nods, then turns and leaves.

Weird…

I grab the clothes I left on the floor and place them back in the duffel bag. I poke my head out, making sure the hall is empty before heading to Luna's room.

It's empty. She's probably talking to Trisha, so I head back to my room. I'm still so damn tired. I crawl into bed, throwing the blanket over me. A nap sounds pretty damn good.

I groan when I hear another knock at the door. Sleep was so close. I get up and answer it, hoping that it's Luna, but I'm highly disappointed.

"I came with an apology, hot cocoa; it used to be your favorite when we were kids." I smile, looking at the two mugs Dante is holding. I can't be angry when he brings me hot cocoa. I can't believe he still remembers that.

"Come in." I sit on the bed, crossing my legs; he hands me the warm mug, and then he sits in the side chair, which is way too small for his large frame.

"Thank you." I grin when I see small marshmallows in the hot cocoa. I haven't had this since Mom died. She used to make it for us when we were upset or on a rainy day.

"Of course." He grins back, and takes a sip, he watches me over the rim of his mug.

"Wow." I lick my lips. "How did you make this? It's just like Mom's," I say in surprise as I look up at him.

"Your mom stole the receipt from my mom." He shrugs.

"Oh, I see." I laugh. "That makes sense. Your mom makes the best things, and my mom sucks at making food." Heck, she could burn water.

"Trust me, I remember, but my mom taught her step by step when she found out how much you both loved it." I look down at the mug, taking a deep breath. I'd completely forgotten about it.

Goodness, I miss her. I miss talking about her.

"Thank you for this, seriously."

"No, listen, I'm sorry for my reaction. I just care for you. I wish things could be different." He stands up, sits down next to me, and places a hand on top of my knee. "I really like you, and I want you to stay."

"I understand, and maybe if it were different, I could see us being more than friends, but not right now. There's too much going on, and I need to sort things out. You know?" I place a hand over his hand, hoping he'll understand.

"Just take care of yourself, even if he is your mate. Vampires shouldn't be trusted, as you know, our blood makes them more powerful, and that's all they want." I nod, understanding what he means. "Well, drink up and get some good sleep. I know I will." He stands, kissing my forehead, and leaves the room.

I finish my hot cocoa and lie down feeling even more tired. I start closing my eyes, drifting into a deep sleep.

I groan as I slowly open my eyes; it's still dark out. I feel arms around me as they carry me. The problem is, I can't see who's carrying me. I know it's a man by his strong build. I try looking around, but whoever it is tightens their grip on me. My head is pounding like I'm hungover.

"What's going on?" My voice is weak, groggy. Whoever it is doesn't answer me. "Who are you?" I plant my hands flat on his chest and push, trying to get out of his hold, but he only tightens his arms around me, making me flinch. His grip is strong; he'll probably leave a mark. He opens a door, and my heart starts pounding in my ears. I start kicking and struggling, but my body feels weak, and my limbs are heavy.

He lowers me down gently, placing me on something soft. A minute later, the lights flicker on. I blink at the brightness before slowly opening them again. I look up and see him standing there, staring at me. He's wearing a mask, both sides are white, but the center of it is black, it looks like smoke, the black bleeding into the white.

"What... What's going on? Who are you?" I look around, and the only thing in the room is the bed. "What do you want?" I slowly sit up, ignoring my weak muscles screaming at me as I crawl to the other side of the mattress to get away from the stranger.

"I'm sorry my sweet Bella, but I want you to myself." I gasp when I hear his voice.

What the *freaking* hell...

"Dante?" What is he doing?

"Yes, my love. It's me." He starts moving closer, but stops when I hold both of my hands up.

Love? Is he serious?

"What's going on? What do you want?" I jump up, ignoring the protest of my shaking legs, and back away from him. I have a horrible feeling about this.

He stalks towards me once more, and I shake my head, holding my hands up, but he doesn't stop this time. "Don't, stay back. Don't make me hurt you." He stops again, tilting his head to the side like he's confused of my actions. Did he think I'd be happy?

"I don't want to hurt you. I'm sorry, but you were going to leave me again, Bella. I couldn't allow that to happen. Like my mom said, we're meant to be together. You are meant to be *mine,* not his!" he hisses angrily as he slowly pulls the mask off, I see the lower half of his face. He licks his lips and pulls it off the rest of the way. If he wasn't acting crazy, I'd say he looks so damn hot. "You were supposed to be my mate! MINE!" he shouts, and his fist slams against the center of his chest when he says *mine,* and his eyes darken.

"You hardly know me." My back hits the wall, and he laughs softly.

"You may have forgotten me, but I haven't. I do know you. I was older than you, and I always knew you'd be mine one day. I told her we should find you after your mom died, but she refused! Saying we should let you come to us."

"Who?" I pinch my brows together, confused.

"My mom, Bella. She said you'd come to us, and you did, but with him, a damn bloodsucker." He stalks towards me slowly. "It's okay, though. I forgive you."

"Where is Luna?" I whisper, praying he didn't touch her.

"She's sleeping, and she'll be safe as long as you behave. If you don't, well, I guess you don't want to know what will happen to your little sister." He's threatening her. I have to play along, or who knows what he'll do.

"Okay, I'll stay." I nod.

"You actually think I believe you? I know you'll leave me as soon as I let you go." He grabs my face in between his hands and presses his forehead against mine.

"I like you, Dante, but I have a mate." I shake my head.

"I'll be better for you. I promise I'll treat you like the queen you are." Then he kisses me. When I don't kiss him back, he wraps his hand around my throat and tightens his grip, cutting my air supply off. "Kiss me," he growls out. So, I kiss him back, and I hate every moment of it. I squeeze my eyes shut to keep my tears from falling out.

"That's my good girl." He pulls back, just an inch. "I sent him a letter to tell him that you belong to me, and I'm never going to let you go."

"He won't just give up. He'll come for me and make you regret it." I say even though I don't even believe my own words.

"I hope he does. Now I have a few things to deal with. I'll be back." He winks at me, then turns away and leaves. I'm in complete shock. My legs give out, and I slide down the wall. I can't believe this is happening. What should I do?

I get up and try the door, and of course, it's locked. There are no windows in the room. I pace back and forth, my hands gripping my hair.

Will he come for me?

Will he look for me?

No, of course not, you idiot. You ran from him. He can have whoever he wants! He's the Vampire Prince, one of the most powerful vampires out there.

What will Luna do if she wakes up and finds me gone?

Whatever he drugged me with will wear off. I need to gather my strength so I can fight him.

This is why I can't trust anyone.

I'm sitting in the corner of the room when the door finally opens, and Dante steps in, looking at me. He's shirtless. God, why is someone this hot so crazy?

"Like what you see, love?" He arches his brow.

"When can I leave?" I ignore him.

"When that vampire stops looking for you." He shuts the door behind him.

"He's looking for me?" I mutter in shock as I stand up.

"Of course, he is. But don't get your hopes up. He won't find you." He walks up to me. "God, have I ever told you how beautiful you are?" I shake my head, and he kisses me, but I press my lips together. He starts pushing me toward the bed and pushes me onto it. He climbs on the bed, leaning over me. I try pushing him off, but my muscles are still too weak.

"I'm done waiting. I need to claim you as mine so he can't take you away from me."

Oh no...

No, no, no...

Chapter 18

"Wait, please, no I... I'm not ready." My ears begin ringing as tears blur my vision. Don't fucking cry!

"It's okay, love, I'll make you feel good, so good." He gets to his knees and slowly unbuttons his jeans, watching me.

"Dante, please, no. I'm not ready..." I keep shaking my head.

Come on, fight! You are not weak!

Once he's close enough, my arm swings back, and with all my effort, I punch him right in the jaw. His head swings to the side, and he lets out a long hiss, but the punch hardly affected him. He grips both of my wrists with one hand and holds them above my head.

"Shhh baby, it's okay." He grabs my jeans and begins to unbutton them. I start kicking and wiggling hard, hoping his grip will loosen, but it doesn't. He starts pulling them down. His grip loosens when he lowers himself to pull them off.

Once he pulls them off, I pick up my leg and kick his face. He stumbles back, fully letting go of my wrists. I jump off the bed, trying to fight the dizziness off as I swipe his legs out from under him, making him fall with a loud thud.

"Don't make me hurt you," he snarls, standing straight, his jeans hitting the floor. I busted his lip hard enough that there's blood dripping down his chin. His thumb comes up, and he wipes it clean before stalking towards me; I push my back against the wall. I may be weak, but I won't go down without a fight.

"Hurt me? I'm stronger than I look." I lift my chin, refusing to back down.

"Oh, trust me, I know you are." He smirks at me. He's standing, bending a little, so that we're eye to eye. "God, you're fucking stunning." He licks his lips. "Stop making this hard. I know you're attracted to me. I see the way you look at me."

"I have a mate."

"Fuck him!" he growls loudly, hands harshly running through his hair. "I'm done playing your games. If you want this the hard way, then so be it." He grabs my arm tightly, inching me forward, and then slams my back hard against the wall. I cry out in pain, the back of my head throbs from the impact.

"I waited long enough. I can't wait any longer, baby. Don't worry, I'll make sure you enjoy it too, and you'll be begging for more." He grabs my shirt, rips it off me harshly, and then pulls back to look down at me. "I was going to take my time with you, be romantic and shit. Take you out on dates, but you ruined everything when you told me you were going back to him, making me snap."

I yank my knee up and it slams into his balls hard. He groans, knees hitting the floor, holding himself. I pick my knee up again, slamming it into his nose. I hear the satisfying crunch of it breaking. I quickly run to the door, hoping he left it unlocked when he came in earlier, but when I turn the handle, it's still locked.

I growl before walking back toward him, he's still on his knees, cupping himself like his dick is going to fall off. He smirks up at me, his teeth bleeding. "You thought I'd be stupid enough to leave it unlocked?"

I scream in anger as I kick the side of his face. His head snaps back and he falls onto his back. I jump on top of him, gripping the sides of his head, planning on twisting his neck, breaking it.

"If you kill me, you'll die in here alongside me," he rushes out.

"Better than what you have planned for me," I say through clenched teeth, I'd rather die than let him finish what he started.

"Thought you'd say that." He chuckles. "I have someone watching Luna. If I don't leave here in a few hours, they are going to kill her."

"How dare you." My heart stops, but I let go of him and crawl away.

He smirks as he sits up. I don't do anything when he grabs me and tosses me on the bed. I swallow the lump forming in my throat. What do I do?

I squeeze my eyes shut, shaking my head. Don't let him see my tears. I hear a rip, and look down. Tears finally fall when I see that he has ripped my underwear off. He grabs the top of my knees, forcing my legs open. He grins when he sees me bare.

"Fucking beautiful. I bet you taste amazing."

"Don't do this, Dante." I shake my head as my chest tightens. I can't fight him, but I might be able to talk him out of it. "Please, Dante, not like this." I try closing my legs, but his grip is too tight.

He ignores me and leans forward so that his face is between my thighs. He inhales deeply, smelling me. He groans loudly.

He turns his head, and I hiss in pain when he bites my thigh. I clench my teeth hard to keep myself from crying out. He bites me a few more times on both of my thighs before he starts pulling his boxers down. I squeeze my eyes shut, turning my head away.

No, God, please, no!

"Fuckkk…." He groans as he settles between my legs. I start crying when I feel his hardness against me. "I'll be gentle," he mumbles, licking the tears off my cheeks. I keep begging him to stop. My body is trembling with fear; my heart is pounding hard in my chest. It's getting hard to breathe.

Please…

He tries to kiss me, but I press my lips together. I can't fight him, but I refuse to kiss him. He growls and grips my wrists, holding my arms above my head and pulling my bra down to expose my breasts. He grips my breasts tightly, making me cry out in pain. He bites my nipple, causing me to whimper.

Why does he keep biting me?

"I have wanted to mark your flesh ever since I saw you with him." He answers my thoughts as if he can read them.

"Nooo! Please stop!" I scream as I feel him reaching between us. I know what's next and I begin thrusting around. I refuse to let this happen, I need to fight back.

I hear the door burst open, and the next thing I know, Dante is ripped off me. I sit up quickly, scrambling to wrap the sheet around me with trembling hands.

"Mine!" A loud roar vibrates through the room, making me cover my ears. I finally look up and whimper when I see Azrael.

He came for me...

He stalks toward Dante, who's trying to crawl out from a hole in the wall. He finally gets out, standing, shaking the drywall dust off his naked body, baring his teeth at Azrael.

"She's mine!" Dante snarls as he uses his magic to throw Azrael across the room, but Azrael lands on his feet and runs forward to Dante, using his vampire speed. He grabs Dante by the throat, and Dante grabs Azrael by the throat.

They're both holding each other's throats, snarling in each other's faces.

"She is my mate," Azrael growls in his face. His eyes are red, and his fangs are sharp. It's absolutely terrifying.

He looks feral.

Sinister.

Sinful.

And so, fucking sexy.

I can feel his anger pulsing through the room, suffocating me. He'd be scaring the hell out of me if I were sane, but instead, I feel safe. It feels amazing having someone protect me in such a way.

He claimed me as his...

"No! She was supposed to be my mate! She's too good for you!" I watch as Dante tries to use his magic to hurt Azrael, but then someone else blurs into the room, and he stops in front of me, blocking my view.

"You must be Isabella." He smirks at me. I've never met this man before. How can he act so calm at a time like this?

"What are you doing?! Help him!" I yell, pointing at the men fighting behind him.

"You think Azrael needs help? Naw, little one, he doesn't." I look over the man's shoulder, and Azrael has Dante in the air by the throat. His veins are bulging in his arms and hands. He look so strong, so sexy.

"She may be too good for me, and I may not deserve her, but she belongs to me!" he growls.

My eyes widen when he sinks his teeth into Dante's throat, and grips the top of his head, pulling it hard, ripping his head off his shoulders. Blood splatters across the room and paints the white walls red.

It's overly gruesome. The sound of his head ripping off is too much. I scream when the blood splashes me, and I cover my eyes with my hands which are shaking uncontrollably. I'm sobbing like a maniac. I can't bring myself to stop.

Stop fucking crying!

I hate feeling so useless. Why am I crying? I've seen people die. I've killed before, but I think deep down I know it was because of Dante. He wasn't a bad man, he just went crazy.

I feel hands wrap around my wrist to pull my hands away from my eyes.

"Azrael," I throw my arms around his waist and started crying against his neck; he wraps his arms around me. I hear him inhale my scent as he pulls me tighter against him as if he was scared I'd disappeared.

We're both desperate for each other.

"Shhh baby, it's okay. I'm here and I'm sorry. I'm so fucking sorry." He kisses my forehead.

"He... he..." I try to say it, but I can't form the words.

"I know, baby, I know. I'm here now," he growls angrily, and I know it isn't at me. "Are you hurt?" I shake my head. I feel so violated right now, and I hate it. "Let's go home, baby."

"Where's Luna? Is she okay?" He pulls back a little to look down at me, and cups my face with his hands, wiping the tears off my cheeks.

"Trisha has Luna, and no, she didn't know about her son's obsession with you."

He bends down, to wrap the sheet over my shoulders, I didn't even realize that I dropped it. I blush, knowing that I'm naked underneath. I look up, thank God the man that came with Azrael is gone, I don't need someone else to see me nude.

Azrael pulls me into him again, and I feel the uneasiness of his teleportation. It's better this time since my head is still buried in his neck. He places me on something soft and starts to pull away, but I grip his upper arms tightly, not wanting him to leave.

"Plea..." I start to beg him not to leave, but I bite my lower lip to stop myself.

"I'm not going anywhere, baby. I'm just going to start a bath for you. Is that okay?" I nod and look away, feeling embarrassed about acting weak. He turns and disappears into the bathroom. I look around to see that we're in his bedroom.

I never paid attention to his room, but it's just like I had pictured: masculine, dark, and moody, just like him. I still feel tense, as if Dante is going to jump out at any moment, even though I know he's dead. I take a deep breath. I'm safe.

"I started the bath." I gasp, gripping my chest tightly, feeling my heart leap, scared. I didn't hear him come back. He slowly walks toward me, gets down on his knees in front of me, and gently grabs my face in both of his hands.

"I won't let anyone ever touch you again. Anyone who even dares to try will die."

I nod my head, releasing a sob. "I was so scared, Azrael. So, so scared." I wrap my arms around my midsection.

"I'm sorry I didn't get there sooner. It wasn't easy to find you; he hid your scent well." He wraps one of his arms around my waist, and the other hand pushes my hair out of my face. "I do need to go and get Andre and Luna."

"Oh, okay." I look down at my hands, not wanting him to leave. I'm afraid of being alone, but I'll never admit it.

"I won't go, I'll tell them to drive back instead." Without releasing his hold on me, he grabs his phone out of his back pocket.

"It's okay. Go get them." I nod, giving him a sad excuse of a smile.

"Are you sure? I can stay. It's whatever you want." He frowns, which is very adorable. I can tell he's worried about me.

"Yeah," I clear my throat. "I need a bath anyway."

"I'll only be gone for a few minutes. But if you need me to stay, I will. What you want or need is what matters the most to me."

"I'll be fine." I slowly stand, and he watches me. I try to stop my legs from trembling, but he notices.

"Let me help you first." He picks me up bridal style and carries me to the bathroom. Once inside, he gently sits me on the toilet. I watch as he grabs a towel out of the cabinet and lays it on the floor by the tub and hooks one on the hook by the tub for me.

He turns around and adds bubbles to the water. I slowly stand, dropping the sheet, not caring if he sees me. He turns, and his gaze lowers, eyes narrowing before slamming them shut, and his nostrils flare.

Then he's gone. Why is he angry again? I grab a hold of the vanity, using it as support to step in front of the mirror, and look at my reflection. I gasp at what I see. I look at each bruise and mark. All over my ribs and arms where Dante had held me down, bite marks on my thighs, and bruises on my neck. My left nipple has a bite mark. I look horrible; no wonder he got angry.

I stare at myself, looking so weak, and angrily wipe away my tears. My eyes are red and puffy. I squeeze my eyes closed, not wanting to look at myself anymore.

I turn away from my reflection and walk over to the bathtub, turning off the water before climbing in, groaning as I slowly sink into the warmth, and rest my head against the pillow.

I was sexually assaulted by someone I thought I could trust, and I hate myself for it. I'm emotionally drained.

Azrael came for me.

That thought makes me smile.

Chapter 19

AZRAEL

It was extremely hard leaving her like that. The desire to kill is nearly impossible to ignore; my monster is craving more blood. I want to resurrect that fucker, just to kill him over and over. I want to take my time and torture him for touching my mate.

But she needs me. I have to put her before my murderous needs. She's usually strong. I never expected to see her like this, so broken. That pisses me the hell off.

"Is she okay?" a small voice asks when I teleport back into Trisha's living area. I look up to see Luna. Her large doe eyes are red and puffy.

"Physically, she's bruised; emotionally, she's not doing well." I roll my shoulders, not feeling right being here, instead of there. "She's going to need time."

"What happened? What did he do?" My anger roars to life. It's flowing through my veins violently, and I can't shut it off.

What happened replays in my mind again, like a fast movie, not helping with my internal battle, or my need to go on a murderous rampage. When I forced my way through the locked door, I saw my mate crying naked underneath another man, begging him to stop. I don't know if he did.... I can't even say it; did I stop him in time? I swallow down my anger, shaking my head. I need to get back.

"We need to go. Now," I snap at Luna. Not meaning to, but she's not even moving, like we have nowhere to be. I grab Luna and Andre by the arms, and I teleport without warning. We stop outside my bedroom door. "I'll transfer you the rest of the money."

"No need; it was an honor." He nods and turns to leave.

"Go to your room. You can see her tomorrow," I tell Luna, turning my back to her dismissively.

"But—"

"She needs time," I cut her off, looking over my shoulder. Her shoulders slump, and she walks away. I open my door cautiously looking in, but she's not in the room. I head to the bathroom, tapping my knuckles on the wooden door, knocking.

She doesn't answer, but I can hear soft sobbing. I open the door, and there she is, still in the bath, crying and scrubbing her body hard. Her skin is raw and red from scrubbing too hard.

"Baby..." I step into the room; she doesn't look up. She's too focused on scrubbing herself to even notice me. I kneel beside the bathtub, and I gently pry the loofah away from her, and she finally blinks, looking up at me.

"I need to scrub him off. I... I feel so freaking dirty, no matter how hard I scrub," she pouts.

"I know, baby, but you're making yourself bleed. That's enough." I straighten, grabbing the towel off the hook. "Come here." She stands up with zero hesitation. She trusts me. Her body is on full display for me to see. I instantly grow hard and bite my tongue. It's not the time.

Her body is perfection, so fucking beautiful. It's hard not to look. Her breasts are a perfect handful. She has the perfect hourglass shape. You can tell she takes care of her body. I wrap the towel around her, hiding her body from me. I grab another towel, drop to my knees, and start drying her long legs.

This is hard for me because all I want to do is make love to her, make her mine, and rub my scent all over hers since she still smells like him.

I pick her up bridal style and carry her to my closet, grabbing a shirt. I gently pull it over her head, helping her put her arms in the sleeves. It looks like a dress on her, flowing to her mid-thighs.

I reach for a pair of boxers, and hunching down, I help her into them. I look up, her arms are tightly hugging her stomach, her lower lip is sticking out in a small pout, and her eyes are red, from crying. I hate seeing her like this.

I've never been so gentle. Am I doing okay?

I lay her in the bed, pulling the blanket over her. I quickly remove my shoes, pants, and shirt and crawl into bed next to her, wrapping my arms around her, pulling her against me.

I release a long breath. I never knew how much I needed this… My monster and I finally feel at peace. Her head is resting on my chest, and my fingers are running through her long hair, carefully untangling the knots.

She's my little witch and I'm never allowing her to leave me. It's unthinkable to go back to being alone without her. I'd rather die because death would be easier to deal with than living a life without her in it.

She has become my unhealthy addiction. She's the sweetest drug, and I will never get enough of her. My hunger will never be satiated.

Her breathing evens out and slows; she's asleep. I move her off me and roll to my side to watch her sleep. She tosses and turns most of the night.

My phone starts ringing in my jeans pocket, which is on the floor. I keep ignoring it until the tenth time.

I close my eyes and growl in annoyance. I get up to see who's calling me. As soon as I'm out of bed, Bella wakes up.

She looks up at me through her lashes. The moon shining through the dark room against her skin makes her look so fucking erotic, and it makes my heart rate spike.

"Where are you going?" Her voice, low and raspy.

"My phone keeps ringing, but I can ignore it." I crawl back in bed, and she lies her head on my arm and begins tracing the tattoos on my chest, making goose bumps raise. I shudder as pleasure snakes down my spine and runs straight to my cock, making it twitch for attention.

Her fingers slowly crawl down my chest to my abdomen. I reach out, stopping them when they reach the top of my boxers.

"Bella," I warn. "You need to stop. You're driving me fucking insane." She turns so her chin is resting on my chest as she looks up at me with a big pout. I trace her lower lip with my thumb.

"I'm sorry for leaving. I tried coming back, but that's when he locked me away."

"I won't ever allow you to leave me again. That was the worst couple of days of my life. I'd rather die than experience life without you. Tell me what you need from me. I'll do anything you want to make you mine, but know this: you will be mine, willing or not."

"I... I thought you hated me." Her eyes widen with shock.

"I hated what you are, but deep down, I knew I didn't hate you, especially the more I was around you. So, I acted like I did to keep you away, not wanting to give up my crown because my father will never allow a witch to rule. But now I'll give it up. I'll give anything up to have you in my life. All you have to do is ask and it's yours. I'll go on a warpath for you, killing anyone you ask me to, just point at who and I'll do it. No questions asked."

"I need you," she says, her eyes dilating with desire as she licks her lips. My heart starts beating out of rhythm.

"I don't know if that's a good idea right now..." I look away, staring at her is making it too hard. Fuck, denying her is the hardest thing I've probably ever had to do but I can't. She's too vulnerable right now.

"Azrael..."

I close my eyes, grinding my teeth together. God, I'm completely obsessed with the way she says my name. My hand grips the back of her neck, and I lean forward to press a kiss on her soft lips. I shudder as I moan into her mouth. She pulls her body up without removing her lips from mine and throws her leg over my hips, straddling me.

Fuck me. She's trying to drive me into insanity.

"We can't, baby, not like this," I groan. This is too fucking hard. "Don't make this harder than it is."

"Okay..." I see the hurt in her eyes as she pulls away and lays down, placing distance between us so we're not touching. Her back is to me. My chest tightens, knowing I hurt her.

"It's not that I don't want you because I do. Fuck, I do so fucking much, but not right now." I feel horrible for saying no, but I know what she's doing. I need to be strong. I can't allow our first time to be right after a tragic event just because she wants to forget.

She just nods, I wrap my arms around her and pull her against me. She doesn't fight me off. I lie here listening to her breathing until it evens out.

I wake up, rolling over to find the bed beside me empty. I jump up, panicking as I start looking around. The bathroom and closet are empty. It's four in the morning. Where the fuck did she go? I growl as I storm out of my room. My breathing growing frantic.

"Bella!" I shout as I start running down the hall, pushing doors open with a bang while looking in every room I pass. I stalk to Luna's room, but just when I reach her door, it opens, and there she is, still in my shirt. I feel something rush through my body.

Relief...

I grab her, pulling her against my body, circling my arms tightly around her, breathing her in a few times, calming myself.

"I just had to make sure Luna was okay," she whispers. Her hands gripping my chest, looking up at me, her cheeks turn red. "I'm sorry about last night..." She trails off looking away.

"Don't be sorry, I understand." I grab her face, rubbing her cheeks. "Let's go back to bed."

"Okay."

I loop my arm around her shoulders and walk her back to our bed.

Our bed... I like the sound of that. I kiss the top of her head as tuck her in, before pulling her against me until her head is resting on my chest. She slowly falls back to sleep.

I play with her hair for hours, wrapping it around my fingers. It's amazing how things can change so quickly. I wanted nothing to do with her in the beginning, and now I can't imagine my life without her.

I'm not a good man; I have done horrible things and will keep doing so, but for her, I want to be better. One thing Dante said was true...

I don't deserve her, but I'm too selfish to let her go.

She's mine, and I'm hers. It won't be easy, but I'll fight for her.

Chapter 20

BELLA

I wake up, and this time, the sun is up and shining brightly through the large windows in his room. I look around, and see that I'm alone. I sit up, leaning against his headboard, wrapping my arms around my legs.

I think about what Azrael said to me, and I smile. He wants me, and he'll do anything for me. He'll kill for me. I should be scared. He's a dangerous and powerful man, and he's admitted that he'll never let me go, whether I like it or not. The thing is, I'm not. It's what I want. I've always wanted a strong man at my side, and I have one, even if he's a little psycho.

My own vicious Prince, who is brutal and cruel and all mine.

I'm still a little embarrassed for throwing myself at him the way I did, and he said no! But I'm not mad. He knew it wasn't the right time after what I'd been through.

"Bella?" Luna opens the door just enough to peek inside. She doesn't know that I snuck into her room last night to check on her while she was asleep.

"Hi." I smile, putting up a mask, pretending to be okay like I always do around her.

"Are you okay?" She comes in and sits at the edge of the bed. "Trisha feels awful; she didn't know he would do something so evil. She knew he liked you, but didn't think he'd do something like that."

"I'm okay now, and it's not her fault." The door opens again, and this time it's Azrael. He has a tray full of food. He looks at Luna and then me, and he... smiles?

"How are you feeling?" he asks as he walks to my side of the bed. I lower my legs, and he places the tray on my lap, and then he kisses my cheek.

"I'm okay. What is all of this?" I look at the plate. There's a stack of pancakes, a cup full of strawberries, and a mug of coffee with creamer already in it, just the way I like it. I genuinely smile as my heart swells.

"I made you breakfast," Azrael drags his chair to the side of the bed, sitting beside me. He points at the food, eyes serious as he mutters, "Eat."

Still so bossy.

I pick up the fork and take a bite of the pancakes.

"Oh God," I groan. "These are amazing, and you made them?"

"Yes, don't act so surprised." He winks at me.

I clear my throat and grab the coffee, taking a small sip. It has my favorite vanilla creamer, and it's the perfect amount.

"Luna told me how you liked your coffee," he explains as he watches me.

They sit in silence, letting me eat. It feels kind of awkward, honestly, having both of them staring at me, but I get it. I'd be making sure Luna ate if she went through something like that.

"Bella, can you tell me what happened? No one really told me much. What did he do?" Luna asks me when I finish eating, and I glance over to her. I see Azrael tense next to me.

"He was crazy... he wanted me all to himself and said I was supposed to be his mate, and then..." I can't say it; a tear slips, and I shake my head. "I can't."

"Did he force himself on you?" she asks angrily. I bite my lower lip, not wanting to talk about that part in front of Azrael.

"I'll let you two talk." Azrael gets up and leaves, taking the tray with him.

"He did. I mean, he touched me and—" An angry roar cuts me off, and I hear something smash right outside the door. Oh God, Azrael was still listening.

"Oh, Bella..." Luna looks over her shoulder at the door, but there's nothing but silence. "I'm sorry you went through that. I wish... I don't know, but I wish I could have stopped it." She jumps on the bed, sobbing, and wraps her arms around me.

"I couldn't fight back, he said someone would hurt you if I did." I shiver at the memory. "But Azrael stopped him before he was able to go all the way. He almost... he almost got what he wanted. I don't know if I'll ever get over it. I feel so violated, Luna. I feel weak." I cry, burying my face in my hands.

"You're not weak, Bella, you're the strongest person I know. Anyone would breakdown going through what you went through." She starts rubbing my back, and I lean against her shoulder as I cry.

"I wish Mom was still here."

"Me too …" We hold each other for a while, and I start to get worried when Azrael doesn't come back.

"I need to check on Azrael." I start getting up, but she grabs my hand, stopping me.

"No, relax. I'll go get him." She stands, wiping her tears away.

"I'm fine, Luna. I can't stay in bed all day." I get up, too. "We'll go together."

"Fine. Let me go get you some pants and a pair of shoes." I nod, and pace while I wait. I feel cooped up and need some fresh air. She finally comes back with a pair of leggings and my running shoes.

We step into the hallway and see two older women cleaning shattered plates and food that's all over the floor and walls. I frown at the mess he made. Maybe I should be cleaning it up, but Luna shakes her head, knowing what I'm thinking, and pulls me along with her. We excuse ourselves as we pass. We look around, but he's nowhere in sight.

"I think I know where he is," I mumble, staring outside. We walk out and down the trail to the gym that Darren took me to. I open the door and my mouth drops open.

Holy shit balls...

His back is to us. He's punching the punching bag, shirtless and covered in sweat, tattoos nearly covering his upper back, his muscles working hard. Goodness, he's perfect...

A spark of pleasure shoots down my spine at the sight in front of me. My heart leaps, dropping straight to my pussy, making her spasm to life.

"Azrael," I say, it comes out sounding like a plea and a moan. He freezes, his back tenses, and he looks over his shoulder, eyes connecting with mine.

I gasp when I see his eyes, pure red.

He looks deadly like the vicious Prince he is.

"Are you okay?" he asks, looking me over slowly, almost like he's looking for anything wrong.

"Yeah..." I look down at my shoes, feeling anxious. I'm not sure how to act around him. Maybe I should've given him space. Maybe I'm being too clingy. "I came to check on you." I start backing away, heading outside to leave. "I'm sorry for interrupting you; I'll let you continue."

"Why the fuck are you sorry?" I flinch at the harshness in his voice. "Fuck, I'm sorry." He grabs me, pulling me against him.

"I'm going to give you guys some alone time," Luna says behind us; I hear the door shut.

"It's okay," I say softly. "Why are you so angry?"

"Because he touched what's *mine.*" He cups my face in his hands. "I'm pissed I wasn't there to protect you. It's my *job* as your mate to keep you safe, but I kept pushing you away. I was a fucking coward." He smacks his chest with his fist hard a couple of times. "That's on me. If I had grown a pair, you wouldn't have fuckin left me, and *that* never would have happened."

"It's my fault too. I ran because I was scared; we were both scared. I don't blame you. You did protect me, you showed up when I needed you the most, and you stopped him right in time. He didn't go all the way because you came for me." I grab his face, staring into his red eyes.

My glaze lowers to his lips. I want to feel them against mine, taste him...

"Kiss me," I whisper. His hand grabs my chin, tilting my head back. Then, his lips gently press against mine, and everything melts away.

I feel something I haven't felt in a long time, safe.

He groans, and picks me up. I'm smashed between his body and the wall. My fingers run through his hair, gripping the ends. I feel him harden against me.

"Bella," he groans against my lips as I start moving my hips against the hard bulge in his pants, silently demanding more. He pulls back, resting his head against my shoulder. "I won't be able to stop if we keep going."

"Then don't." Please don't...

"Are you sure?" He tilts his head back, gazing into my eyes, the heat in their depths scorches me.

"Yes..." I lick my lips, nodding.

I feel the air shift around us, and then my body bounces on something soft. He grabs my shoes, throwing them off, and then he roughly pulls my leggings off.

"Hell, Bella, you're so beautiful." He presses a kiss on the inside of my knee and then trails his way up my thigh, kissing each bruise. God, those lips feel so good.

His nose runs up the center of my underwear-covered pussy. He deeply inhales, I feel the vibration of his growl against my clit, causing me to shiver. "*Fuck*, your smell is so fucking addicting." I blush, feeling embarrassed.

He grabs the side of my underwear, and the sound of fabric ripping rings through the room. He throws them somewhere over his shoulder, and he grips the tops of my knees, spreading my legs apart. I bite my lip and watch his eyes dilate as he admires me.

"So perfect. Last chance, are you sure? Because I won't be able to stop." He gazes up at me, my lips part in surprise to see how *hungry* his eyes are.

"Yes," I plead, the suspense is killing me. I need him to touch me. He leans in and his tongue slowly runs to my entrance up to my clit. My eyes flutter closed, and I throw my head back, moaning as I lift my hips, needing more. "Please."

"Please, what baby?" He pulls away from me, but I still feel his hot breath against my clit, and I cry out in annoyance.

"More... I need more," I groan; my voice low and breathless. His finger rubs lazy circles around my entrance, before pushing inside, my back arches at the sensation of his finger stretching me.

"Fuck, baby, you're so damn tight." He adds a second one, curling his fingers, hitting the perfect spot. His lips wrap around my clit, devouring me. I try closing my legs, the sensation becoming too much, but he grabs my knees, forcing them to stay open.

I start moving my hips, grinding against his face as my hands reach down to grip his hair, making sure he stays right where I need him. My stomach tightens and my body shivers with need. The feeling is so intense I can hardly take it.

Oh fuck...

"I... I.." I can't even make out the words. I close my eyes, allowing myself to bathe in the pleasure I'm feeling, letting it take control.

"Yes, that's it, love. Cum for me." As soon as those words leave his mouth, I let myself ride the wave of pleasure and explode, wringing the life out of me. My vision goes white, my body is floating in a different universe, one filled with intense pleasure. My legs begin shaking, and my grip in his hair tightens.

When I come down from my high, I moan, blinking my eyes open, and watch as he kisses his way up my stomach. He pulls my shirt up and removes it. He cups my breasts with his hands and lightly squeezes.

"Pure perfection," I watch as he wraps his lips around my nipple, sucking it, his eyes flicker up to meet my gaze, and my breath stalls at the erotic sight. He flicks his tongue; making me delirious. His free hand is playing with my other nipple, rolling it between his fingers. My pussy spasms with need, so much fucking need.

"Azrael…. Please," I moan, closing my eyes as my fingers dig into his strong shoulders.

"What do you need, baby? I need you to say it." His voice, rough and full of need.

"I need *you*, Azrael, please."

"Tell me what you want." His hand wraps around my throat, tightening his grip, making me hiss with pleasure. God, I love this mixture of pleasure and pain.

"Goddammit, just fuck me already, Azrael," I growl, wrapping my legs around his hips, tired of waiting. He smirks as he gets up and pulls down his sweatpants. I gulp when his hard cock smacks his abdomen. It's huge, the large veins are angry with need. How is *that* going to fit? His smirk widens, enjoying my reaction.

He wraps his hand around himself and starts stroking, base to tip, it grows even more. His Adam's apple bobs as he swallows, eyes trailing down my naked body. He crawls on the bed and widens my legs, pushing himself in between them.

"Ready for me, baby?" he asks, watching himself rub the tip of his cock against my clit.

"Yes, Azrael, please." I nod, licking my upper lip. Without warning, he slams himself inside of me with one hard thrust. I scream at the pain. It's intense and painful. I feel full, too full. I shove his shoulders, trying to push him off, but he doesn't budge. I feel tears running down my face. God, that hurts like a bitch.

"Fuck, Bella, I'm so fucking sorry. Why didn't you tell me you were a virgin?" He puts his forehead against my shoulder as he pants. "Are you okay?" He leans back to look down at me. I shake my head no.   "I'll make it feel better." He mumbles as he leans down, licking the tears off my face. "You're so fucking tight. I'll try to be gentle." His lips meet mine as he pulls out almost completely before pushing back in over and over again.

"Jesus fucking Christ, Bella, you feel so fucking good." His eyebrows pinch together, and his jaw clenches tight. I know that he's holding back, and it isn't easy for him, but the pain slowly subsides, turning into unbelievable pleasure. I wrap my legs around him, meeting his slow thrusts, but I need more.

"Harder, Azrael, harder." I dig my nails into his shoulders hard enough to draw blood. He starts moving his hips faster. He places one hand flat on the headboard and the other hand cups my breasts, caressing them. My pussy starts spasming with need, and I know I'm getting close to orgasming again. I chase that feeling, inching closer to the edge.

"That's it, baby, don't fight it." He grunts, he hooks his arm underneath my knee, lifting my leg, pounding harder, faster. The headboard starts banging against the wall, I moan as he fucks the orgasm out of me.

"Azrael!" I scream, closing my eyes, enjoying this blissful feeling.

"Eyes on me when I'm fucking your tight little pussy." He grips my jaw with his hand. "Open your fucking eyes," he growls, and I do as he says, meeting his gaze.

"Fuck…" he throws his head back with a roar, I feel his cock pulse inside me as his hot release fills me. I follow him off the edge, falling into a deep feeling of euphoria, making my toes curl and my lips part in a silent plea.

"Oh God." My body slumps against the bed, breathing hard, staring into his eyes as my body slowly calms down. It was amazing. I think I'm growing addicted to him, the best type of addiction.

"I'm not done with you yet, little witch." He pulls out of me and flips me around. "Put that sexy ass in the air," he growls, and I do as I'm told, arching my back, lifting my ass in the air. His hand rubs my right ass cheek as he groans and spanks me hard, making me hiss at the sting. "Fuck, this ass is amazing. Do you have any idea how many times I dreamt of this? Your ass in the air, this is way better than any dream," he mumbles, amazed and cupping my ass cheek in the palm of his hand. "I can't even fit one ass cheek in my hand; it's too big, baby."

I moan at the praise, arching my back even more. He buries his fingers in my hair as he slams his cock inside me. I groan, feeling myself stretch for him. He mumbles a string of curses as he stills for a moment. He pulls out just to slam back in. He yanks my hair hard, pulling me up until my back is flush against his front. The hand gripping my hip slowly moves its way up, stopping to cup my breast and giving it a little squeeze. I turn to look at him.

"I'll never get enough of this feeling." He groans before slamming his lips against mine, kissing me with so much passion as he keeps pounding into me brutally.

"I'm never letting you go," he says against my lips, and my heart rate spikes as I feel myself tightening around him, feeling pleased with his possessiveness.

He pushes me back down. I turn my head to the side, looking up at him, his hand grips the side of my face, forcing me still, his gaze lowers, and he watches himself fuck me.

"I wish you could see this. The way your pretty pussy wraps around my cock so fucking perfectly," his lips part, and his head tilts back, his gaze still in between us. He's never looked sexier than he does right now. Pure ecstasy is written all over his face.

There's a knock on the door, but he doesn't stop, doesn't look away, like he didn't hear the knock, or he just doesn't care. Another knock at the door, this time more forcefully. His head snaps toward the door with murder in his gaze.

"Go the fuck away," he snarls, never pausing his brutal thrusts. I'm certain the person on the other side of the door can hear the headboard pounding hard against the wall.

"I'm sorry, sir, but it's an emergency." I don't recognize the voice on the other side of the door.

"I don't give a flying *fuck*. It can wait. Now LEAVE!" He looks down at me, and my lips part as he smirks devilishly at me and then spanks me. "Damn, baby, I'll never get enough of the way this ass jiggles when I'm pounding this tight pussy."

"Azrael," I moan, enjoying his dirty mouth and loving his roughness. My stomach tightening is the only warning I get before falling into the deep blissfulness of ecstasy once again. I start mumbling. I don't even know what I'm trying to say. My brain isn't working. He stills as his cock starts throbbing inside me, he whispers my name over and over again like a prayer.

"Oh fuck," he rasps deeply before falling on the bed, pulling me to him until my head is resting on his chest.

"Was I okay?" I ask shyly, needing to know.

"Fuck yeah, baby, that was absolutely amazing. I wish I could be buried deep inside your warmth the rest of my life. You've become my sweetest obsession." He pushes my hair to the side and kisses my shoulder.

He gets up, disappearing into the bathroom. I hear the water turn on, but I'm too sore to get up to clean myself.

"Come here, baby." I scoot closer to him. He spreads my legs open, causing me to whimper. "I'm sorry, baby. I wish I had known. I wouldn't have been so rough on you in the beginning."

He places a warm, wet towel against me and gently cleans me.

"I never thought about telling you. I'm sorry, is that a bad thing?"

He starts laughing. "Fuck no, I'm happy that I'm your first and your last. I'm so possessive of you, Bella, it's driving me crazy. I hate when anyone even looks at you. It makes me want to tear their eyes out." He stands, picking me up, and carries me to the bathroom. He sets me in the half-full bathtub. The water feels good against my sore pussy.

"This should help relieve some of the pain. Lean forward." I oblige, and he slips in behind me. I lay back, resting my head on his shoulder.

He grabs the loofah, and squirts body soap on it, and starts rubbing it against my back. He rubs my shoulders, giving me a massage, and then he wraps his arms around my front and cleans the rest of me. When his hands reach my breasts, he starts massaging them, I bite my lip at the sweet sensation rocking through my body.

"Fuck... I need you so bad again," he pinches my nipple. I tilt my head to the side so I can kiss his sharp jaw as he continues to play with my nipples. I can feel myself growing needy again, my body is begging for more of him. He bites down on my shoulder, and I shiver with need.

"Azrael," I moan, closing my eyes, getting lost in his heat.

"Are you too sore?" He licks my neck before biting my earlobe.

"Yes, but I need you..." I whimper, push my ass against him, he groans. He picks me up by the hips, pushing me forward as he positions his cock at the entrance of my pussy and eases himself inside of me.

I grip the edge of the bathtub and start bouncing up and down on his large cock. The water splashes out of the tub, but neither of us seems to give a shit.

We're both lost in a daze of pleasure.

I throw my head back, screaming his name as I orgasm for the third time.

Chapter 21

AZRAEL

She's standing on shaky legs as I dry her body. I look up at her and still can't believe she's mine. Why did I wait so long? She's fucking amazing, inside and out. I carry her to bed, and she falls asleep before we even make it there. I wore her out.

I lay here watching her sleep. I'm falling for her hard... And fuck... the sex is mind-blowing. I never knew it could feel that good. It's mind-numbing, and I've had a lot of partners. I never take care of any of them, but the need to take care of the body that I worship. The body that brought me otherworldly pleasure that I never knew existed. It's the closest thing to heaven I'll ever be.

I can't get enough of her. Even now, I want more. I know my hunger for her will never be satiated. My hands crave to touch her, to hold her and never let go, but I need to get up no matter how much my body protests. There's an emergency I need to take care of. I kiss the top of her head, moving slowly so I don't wake her. She needs the rest.

After I get dressed, I look at her once more before slipping out. All I wanted to do is go back and cuddle her.

Cuddle? Who the fuck am I turning into? Cuddle has never even been in my vocabulary before.

I slip into the dining room to find Darren, Alexandre, and my father standing there in a heated discussion. They all look up when I step into the room.

"I do not appreciate you ignoring my calls for the past few hours for one of your whores, my son," my father growls, flashing his fangs at me.

"Don't fucking call her that!" I snarl, hitting the table with my fist.

"How dare you speak to me that way!" He gets in my face, grabbing my jaw and pushing it against the wall, but I grip his throat, slamming his body against the table, splitting it in half.

"You may be king, Father, but remember who is stronger. I never want to hear you speak about my MATE in that way again! Do you understand?" His eyes widen, and his mouth opens, but nothing comes out. I wait for him to say something, but then I remember I'm cutting his air supply off, and he can't speak.

"Enough!" My sister runs in, and I let him go, straightening my shirt.

"She's your mate?" My father asks in shock. "I sincerely apologize, my son, I didn't know she was your mate. Why didn't you tell me?"

We're all in shock. My father is the king, and he never apologizes, even to us.

"I was going to, but I've been busy looking for her. Someone took her," I finally say and begin to explain everything that happened since I found her in that cell.

"Kidnapped already? You need to bring her to the castle so we can keep the princess safe." I nod, agreeing. I've already thought about it, but I need to talk to her first. I hate staying at the castle, but it'll be the safest place for her.

"I can't wait to announce it!" Stella grins ear to ear, and I groan, knowing everyone will want to meet her, so we'll have to throw a ball.

"We'll save this discussion for later because there's important business to attend to," my father says seriously, acting as the king and not my father.

It must be important if he's here.

Alexandre, my father's right-hand man, clears his throat. "Someone in the castle is betraying us. We've been attacked every time we leave the castle, so it's someone important who sits in our meetings because they know our every move."

"Who are they leaking the information to? Who's attacking?" I ask, my gaze bouncing between the two.

"Margus. I also believe he's working with Prince Gabriel. I saw someone who works for him there when they attacked us, but he got away," my father answers.

Oh shit, I forgot to mention Luke's betrayal. He wasn't the only one leaking information. Who else, though? We can't trust anyone outside of this room.

"My father already started to attack?" I spin around to see my mate standing there in my oversized shirt, wearing a pair of fuzzy slippers with her hair pulled up in a messy bun.

Beautiful...

"You are?" my father growls, angry at the interruption.

"Isabella. And you?" she snaps with an attitude, arching a brow, looking at him with her hands on her hips.

"Isabella? You're Margus's daughter? Yes, I do recall Azrael mentioning to me that you're going to help him with your father."

"Correct, but what I forgot to mention is that she's also my mate, father." I walk over to her, needing her closer to me. I wrap my arm around her waist, pulling her against me.

"Your mate is Margus's daughter?" I can't tell if he's angry or not, but I don't care. I already made my decision with or without his approval. I'll give up the crown for her. "Interesting," he hums, looking at Isabella closely. His eyes seem to be searching for something.

"Yes, is that a problem?" I tense, but still lift my chin, showing him that I don't give a single fuck if there is a problem. He stares at me for far too long without saying anything. The silence starts getting to me. Everyone in the room stares at him, waiting for some type of reaction.

"No," he finally smiles. "I will not judge you for who your father is, especially if my son finds you noble. I trust his judgment." I release a breath, one that I didn't realize I was holding.

"You're the king?" I feel Bella tense beside me and when I look down, I see a red tint in her cheeks.

"Indeed, I am." My father curtly nods.

"She agreed to help us, but I didn't get the chance to tell her we won't be going through with it." I clear my throat, and her eyes flash, looking up at me in surprise.

"But I thought that was the only reason I was here." She shakes her head; her eyes were turning watery. Why is she on the verge of crying? "He used to be a good person, but I know he needs to be stopped, and I want to help stop him. You can't just make that decision without talking to me!"

"We understand that. We'll still be capturing him, but you're no longer involved. You'd be in too much danger. I promise no harm will come to him." I rub her back, comforting her. "We'll be relocating to the castle till the danger blows over."

"I'm okay with staying at the castle, but I will not sit back and not help!" I stare at her, not knowing what to say, but one thing I do know is that she won't be helping.

"No, it's too dangerous." I shake my head.

"You didn't care about that before. I'm strong. I can handle it. We just need to remove these cuffs." She lifts both of her wrists, showing me the cuffs holding her back. She's not strong enough to go head-to-head with her father and his small army.

"No, I didn't, but my father opened my eyes to what I was doing to you and told me I was wrong for doing it. Regardless of how powerful you are, I'm not letting you help." My voice is stern, but she narrows her eyes, stepping away from me.

"I get that I do, but I'm still helping you." She pushes, I inhale deeply through my nose, closing my eyes. She's going to be the death of me with her stubbornness.

"We'll discuss this later, alone. We need to get ready to leave."

"Fine. Later then." She nods, licking her lips, which makes me want to grab her and kiss her into submission. "I'm going to go change." She gives me a pointed look. I can see the anger burning in her eyes. She turns to leave, and I follow close behind.

"I don't like you making decisions for me! I'm not some weak little girl!" she snaps as soon as I shut the door to our room. She huffs, turning away from me. "Are you sure leaving is the best move for us to take?"

She's made to become a queen, *my* queen. She's strong and special. She puts other people's needs before hers, and she makes sure her next moves are for the best. I don't know the extent of her powers, but I know she has a strong will, and that's what matters to me. I'm strong enough for both of us.

"Yes, I have been thinking about it, and I believe it'll be for the best. The castle is heavily guarded, and you'll be protected." I step in front of her, grabbing her face. "I know you're not weak. Plus, we need to make arrangements for a party so everyone can meet the future queen."

She gasps and her eyes widen with horror. "Queen?" I chuckle at her shock; I assume she didn't think of this.

"Yes, I'm the Prince, soon to be king, and you're my mate. So, you're the princess and soon-to-be queen." I lean in to kiss her parted lips. "I know someone who can remove these cuffs. I'll call him as soon as we get to the castle. I need you to be able to protect yourself if I'm not there. I'll go tell Luna to pack. You go ahead and start."

My cock throbs in my pants. She doesn't understand the effect she has on me. I adjust myself and then head toward Luna's room. She's probably still asleep since it's only five in the morning.

I knock as I call out her name. After a few minutes, she finally answers, rubbing her tired eyes. I tell her to pack, and she doesn't even question it.

Honestly, there are going to be a lot of angry people because she isn't a vampire. That's never happened before a ruler that wasn't their own kind, but there are no laws against it. They just have to deal with it because I refuse to let her go, even for my people.

I walk to the living room to find Stella and Darren sitting on the sofa talking.

"Hey, how is she handling everything?" Stella asks.

"Pretty well, but she never thought about the whole queen thing. She's pretty shocked." I sit on the other section of the sofa, stretching my legs out in front of me.

"Really? I'm surprised she never thought of it."

"I agree." I nod, rubbing my pointer finger across my lower lip, thinking about how sweet she tasted. I want to go up and fuck the shit out of her again, but I ignore the temptation. She needs to recover from our earlier activities.

A loud pitch scream splits through the silence. I jump up.

"Azrael!" I hear Bella scream, and I take off, using my vampire speed. Fear crawls up my throat and tightens its grip, making it hard for me to breathe.

I kick our bedroom door down, to find Luna lying on the floor, not moving, blood gushing badly from a wound on her stomach, and Bella is nowhere in sight.

I roar angrily, Darren and Stella rush in behind me. Darren picks Luna up. He's talking, but with the anger roaring through my veins, I don't hear him. I'm staring at the broken window. They took her...

They took her from me, and they will pay.

I leap out of the window and following their scent.

Chapter 22

BELLA

My eyes flutter open, but my head pounds horribly. I groan, closing my eyes again. I move my hands, searching for Azrael, but the bed is cold. He must have left already. I don't even remember falling asleep.

Packing, I'm supposed to be packing! I must've been exhausted. Maybe going back to sleep for a little longer won't hurt. I'm sure he won't mind.

Why does my head hurt so bad? I roll to my side snuggling into the pillow. Mmm, it's cold and silky. I groan, rubbing the side of my face deeper into it. I blink, wait... Azrael's bed doesn't have silky pillows.

I automatically sit up when last night's events come rushing forward. The window smashed open, and a dozen men ran into the room. I managed to kill a couple of them, but without my magic, there were too many. When Luna was stabbed, I lost concentration, and they knocked me out.

Luna...

I jump up, ignoring the pounding in my head, and rush toward the large wooden door. I try opening it, and of course, it's locked. So, I start banging my fist against the door, screaming at the top of my lungs for someone to open the damn door.

The door flies open, and I'm met with a broad chest. My eyes slowly travel up, and I gasp. He's beautiful, in an icy sort of way. His eyes are icy blue, and his hair is blond, more white than blond, and shaggy.

"Mate," he says in a low, soft, almost soothing voice. He's the opposite of Azrael. Azrael has a dark, sinister, deadly look to him all the time. This man's features are soft. I can picture him in California as a surfer dude.

Wait, did he say mate? Did I hear that right?

"Wait, w-what?" I stumble, completely horrified. There's no way in hell he was my mate.

"You're my mate, little one." He grins at me, showing me a hint of dimples, and then winks. My heart skips a couple of beats at that smile.

No! I have Azrael!

"No, that's impossible." I back up, needing some space. "I have a mate already!" Is this some type of sick joke?!

"You don't have a mate mark," he frowns, looking me over. "Don't you feel the pull?"

"Who are you? Why am I here? Someone stabbed my sister and knocked me out. You have to let me go! I need to check on her!" I decide to change the subject. Obviously, this man has a few screws loose.

"Well, your father has been searching for you, and I owed him a favor, little one. Not that I'm disappointed now that I found you. I'm Prince Gabriel, and now I know that you're my mate, I will not be handing you off to your father. You will stay here with me."

"No! What about my sister?" I shake my head, my mind spinning with panic. What is it with these crazy guys? I have never really received a male's attention, and now they won't leave me alone.

"I can go fetch her for you." He nods, stepping into the room. I step back, maintaining a safe distance. His eyes narrow, and he keeps coming toward me, backing me up until my back hits the wall. Why does this keep happening, me, being cornered?

No, she's safer with Azrael, but I need to know if she is okay.

It all happens so quickly; his lips are on mine, and I feel the same electric zap I feel with Azrael. He really is my mate, but how do I have two mates?

It's impossible...

No, I place my hands against his chest, pushing him back. He looks at me with shock, or is it hurt?

"I'm sorry, but I have a mate. He hasn't marked me yet, but only because I'm not ready. I don't know how it's possible, but you need to let me go. I can't stay here with you!"

"That is impossible!" His voice has an icy edge to it. "Who is this mate of yours? I will kill him. You are mine, and I refuse to share you with another! Mate or not!"

"No, you won't! You won't have to share me because I am his! I choose him!" I snarl for the first time since wearing these cuffs. I can feel a small prickle of my magic when he says he'll kill Azrael.

"I will kill anyone who stands in my way of having you!" He disappears.

Shit! Shit, what the fuck am I going to do?

I pace in the room, feeling completely useless, not knowing what to do, yet again! I need these fucking cuffs off. I run to the large window to open it. I look out and my shoulders slump; disappointment fills me. I can't jump without dying, I'm six stories up. I scream, frustrated.

I have two mates, but I already know who I want. Do I feel bad? Hell no! Maybe if he hadn't kidnapped me, I would've.

No matter what, Azrael is who I pick. If you had asked me a couple of days ago, I would've been confused. But after the last couple of days with Azrael, I know who I want.

I was made for him. Of course, he's going to act possessive. I'm technically his. But Gabriel has no chance in hell of winning over my heart when it already belongs to someone else.

How did my father manage to find me? Darren. He was in the cell with me, and we escaped at the same time. He's smart enough to realize Darren took me with him.

Why haven't I thought of that?

A few hours later, there's a knock at the door, and a lady comes in without waiting for a reply. She looks me up and down with a large ass fake smile plastered on her face. She's beautiful but has a bitchy look.

She wriggles her nose slightly. She doesn't think I look worthy enough to be a princess. I honestly don't blame her because there's no way in hell I look like a normal princess.

"Princess." She bows down. "I'm Prince Gabriel's assistant! He asked me to help you get ready for dinner. Your father will be joining us." She holds up a large black bag with a long zipper down the middle. She carefully lays it on the bed.

"My name is Isabella. And there's no need to bow."

"Oh, but I must! It will be disrespectful not to, Princess!" She looks horrified like I offended her.

"Okay, at least call me Isabella."

"No!" She gasps, and I roll my eyes.

"At least here in private between us girls." I walk over to her as she unzips the black bag.

"Okay, as you wish, but please do not tell Prince Gabriel."

"Of course I won't, it stays between us!" I watch her take out the dress carefully. It's a long ice blue dress with a corset bodice and flowy bottom. Wow, it's beautiful.

It's made for a princess.

"The bath is right over there. I'll go start it for you, Isabella." She heads to the door on the far corner of the room. I sit in the chair by a large mirror. The room is freaking large; it has a bed bigger than Azrael's king-size bed. The bedding is a silky gray, and the walls are white with a massive bay window and two chairs beside a large golden mirror that has gold flowers carved throughout it.

Definitely fit for a princess.

And it's definitely not me. I'm not fit to be one. There's no way in hell! How can I help rule when I can't even keep my sister and I safe?

"The bath is ready!" she shouts from the bathroom. I get up, heading toward the door she disappeared through. Holy shit balls, it's big! It's bigger than my room at Azrael's house—a little overboard if you ask me. "Let me help bathe you."

"Oh no, no, no, that's definitely not necessary!"

"Are you sure?" She looks relieved as she smiles.

"Oh yeah, positive." I nod, and she bows before leaving the room. I walk over and shut the door, locking it. I remove my clothing and step into the bath, loving the hot water.

I close my eyes and lean back. I smile when I remember the last time I was in the bath. Azrael was behind me, massaging my shoulders, cleaning me after we had sex. Sex with him is completely mind-blowing, and the way he took care of me afterward was amazing.

God, I miss him.

Luna will be okay. I know Azrael will take care of her for me.

I'll pretend that I'm giving him a chance and escape.

I feel wrong doing something like that, but he's the one holding me against my will.

I turn around to look at my reflection and gasp. I look like an actual princess. The dress hugs my body perfectly, and all I want is to show Azrael.

"You look beautiful!" She claps, looking at me with a genuine smile.

"You never told me your name." I turn to look at her.

"Many people don't care to know my name. I'm Marisol." She starts putting all the makeup away.

"Marisol, aren't you going to get dressed?"

"Oh no, I don't need to." She lets out a small laugh.

"Why not?" I arch my brow, confused.

"I'm just a servant. We do not get dressed for events. You are so sweet. You will be an amazing queen one day. Now let's go before we're late!" I hear the truth in her words, but also the sadness as well.

I wonder why. Did she have a prior relationship with Gabriel? She hurries me out of the room. I wait for the jealousy to hit, thinking of them together, but I don't feel anything.

We step into a massive hall that's completely bare. There are a couple of doors. "This is Prince Gabriel's office, never walk in without knocking first." She points at the one directly across from mine.

We walk down a flight of curved stairs, and once we hit the landing, we turn right down to another hall, but the walls aren't bare down here. They have large portraits of different people hanging on the walls with large gold frames. We pass them and enter a large formal dining room. It's all black except for the gold accents; the table has a marble top with gold legs, and it probably could fit twentyish people.

It's simple but so beautiful.

"Isabella." I look up to find my father and Gabriel walking towards me. "I heard the wonderful news! You two are mates!" He has the largest smile, and I frown. "We can take down the Vampire King and Prince together!"

"Agreed!" Gabriel nods, stepping closer to me, and wrapping an arm around my waist. They are both in black tuxes.

My father is a handsome and powerful warlock. I'm not surprised that he knows the royal family. I am, however, surprised that they are working together.

"I... Uh, I don't know." I shake my head. "I don't really do the whole violence thing." I look up at Gabriel. My father already knows this.

"That's a funny one! You killed a couple of my best men." He chuckles darkly. He thinks that I'm joking! Who'd joke about something like that?

"Yes, because they were attacking my si... Luna and I. I did what was necessary! I wouldn't kill anyone for less than that." I look at my father. "Look, I loved her too! I understand why you are so angry, but she was a bad person; she broke the law. The Prince had every right to punish her!" I look back at Gabriel. "Don't freaking tell me you wouldn't kill someone that broke into your room and stole something of yours!"

"Of course, I would have, but that's not the reason I want him dead. That's your father's reasoning. Don't even ask." He turns his back, dismissing me. He pulls out a chair, looking back at me. "Please sit."

I take my seat, and he sits to my left, at the head of the table. My father settles across from me.

"You look absolutely beautiful." Gabriel grabs my hand and kisses the top of it. I mutter a thanks, pursing my lips, pulling my hand away. The maids rush out, placing the plates of food in front of us. "I hope you like steak."

"I do," I reply as I stare at the steak and mashed potatoes with broccoli. It does look good. Another maid pours red wine into our glasses. "Thank you." I smile; she looks at me in shock before she hurries away. *I guess no one says thank you here.*

"I sent a man to check on Luna, but the house is now empty."

I bite my inner cheek, tightening my grip on the fabric of the skirt on my dress.

"I need to find her, Prince Gabriel. I need to leave." I look at him with pleading eyes, but it doesn't seem to work.

"Please, call me Gabriel or Gabe, and we're looking for her. No need to worry." He grabs my hand and rubs the top of it. "Now, let's eat."

"Who is this Luna girl to you?" my father asks, and takes a drink of the wine, watching me over the rim. It's as if he's staring deep into my soul. I swallow.

"A very close friend of mine. I've been with her since Mom died." I also take a sip of my wine, and have to suppress a groan. It's not the cheap shit I'm used to.

"I see." He nods, cutting into his steak. I eat half my plate before I get the strength to ask the question, I've been dying to ask.

"Father, I want to ask you something, and you need to be honest with me," I say, sitting up straighter.

"What is it?" He doesn't even bother to look up from his food.

"Did you know that your little thug was going to murder Mom?" I need him to be honest. *Please, be honest...*

"I didn't tell him to kill her, but I did tell my 'little thug' to get to you by any means necessary, no matter what or no matter who got in their way. But I never thought you'd be strong enough to stop them. I was disappointed but proud at the same time."

"Oh yeah, is that why he tried raping me!?" I snap. How can he be so calm? This was the woman he once loved, the woman who carried me.

He pauses his chewing, slightly tensing. "No, I was not aware of that, nor did I think a grown man would want a young girl sexually. I know you killed him, but he's lucky. I would've killed him if I found out he had done that. You may think of me as a monster because of your mother and the fact that I want revenge for your aunt, but I'm no monster; I do love you. You are my daughter, and I missed you. I missed watching you grow up and that kills me. If you don't want to help me, then fine, but I want you in my damn life. I have already missed too fucking much, but I refuse to let you mate with that bloodsucker!" he hisses, his fists hit the table, making it vibrate. How did he know Azrael was my mate?

"That's not your choice. I'll decide which one of them I choose to mate. I'll give you a chance, Gabriel, but I will not promise that I'll choose you. This won't be easy for me, but in the end, it's my choice." I pause, taking a breather. "Will you remove these freaking cuffs?"

"No, not until I know you won't run." I narrow my eyes as I push my chair back, standing, and walking out with my head held high.

I follow the same pathway as earlier and make it back to my room, or I guess, my prison.

I fall onto the bed without removing my dress and stare blankly at the ceiling. I'm exhausted. Today has been too much. I start thinking about an escape plan. There's nothing I want here, including Gabriel. He seems sweet, but there's something I can't place my finger on, but I know he's hiding the evil lurking underneath.

Chapter 23

I can't believe this is where my father has been hiding, behind a prince, no wonder he's untouchable. I'm lying in bed face down, buried in the pillow, trying to fall asleep. I feel hands wrap around my ankles. Startled I spin around and kick whoever it is. Someone groans. I jump up, ready to fight.

It's Gabriel. He's standing at the end of the bed, holding his nose where I kicked him.

"Oh no, I'm so sorry. You scared the living hell outta me!" Why is he lurking around, sneaking into my room and touching me?

"I'm sorry, little one. I didn't mean to scare you." He removes his suit jacket and cranes his neck, grinning at me.

"It's alright. I fell asleep early, didn't I?" I clear my throat. "What can I do for you?"

"Ready for some good sleep. This is my room, after all. I'm assuming my assistant didn't tell you?"

What? No, I don't think so...

"I, um, I don't feel comfortable sleeping in the same bed as you." I cross my arms over my chest. "I don't want to kick you out of your own room, though, so I can sleep elsewhere."

"No, you stay, I'll go. Good night." He smiles at me, it doesn't reach his eyes. "I'll see you in the morning." He leaves the room. I sit back down, rubbing my forehead.

I feel bad for kicking him out of his own room, and maybe I judged him too harshly. He was very understanding. What should I do? I still won't sleep in the same bed as him, but should I go talk to him? I probably should apologize.

I head out of the room, tiptoeing across the hall to his office, and I start knocking on the door. I wait for a reply for a couple of minutes, but I hear nothing.

Maybe he's not in there.

I knock on the door again, placing my ear against the wood. Still nothing but silence. Hmm, maybe he went downstairs again.

I slowly walk down the stairs, hands on the wood railing. I'm surprised to know that I can freely roam around. I pause when I get to the first floor, looking towards where the front door might be. I slowly and quietly head that way and see a large door. I peek down the hall and don't see anyone, so I quickly hurry to the door. My hand stills on the door handle.

I should look outside first. I step to the left, peeking out the window next to the door. Shit, my heart sinks, there are guards. Of course there are, that's why I can roam around.

I turn and head back down the hall. I need to see if there's another way out of here. I shiver; this place is kind of creepy at night.

I make it to the very end of the hall, and I'm about to pass a large archway, but a noise makes me stop. It sounded like something breaking. I stay still and listen; a minute later, I hear a small cry.

What the hell?

I push my back against the wall and slowly step into the room. I see nothing, but there's another door that's partially open. I move towards it. My palms start sweating, and my heart is beating wildly against my ribs. Instead of finding an escape, I need to help whoever is crying out.

Thank goodness I'm not with Vampires. They would've heard me creeping around by now.

"She pissed me off!" A loud growl echoes through the room, sending a chill down my spine. "How can my own mate refuse me?" Gabriel's voice growls. So, he is pissed and just pretended not to be in front of me. I inch towards the opening of the door, covering my mouth to keep quiet.

I find Gabriel standing there with his pants around his ankles, and a woman who I can't see on her knees in front of him. His hands are holding the back of her head, and he forces her head down. She cries out again.

"But don't worry, even though I met my mate, you'll still be my good little side bitch, won't you?"

"Mhm." She nods her head the best she can. Is she really okay with being the side piece? Well, I for one, would not be okay with that. She shouldn't be okay with that, either. I shake my head, feeling sick.

"Get the fuck up, sit on the desk, and spread your legs wide open for me." I watch as she listens and sits on the desk, spreading her legs wide. I avoid looking down at her naked body, but I'm shocked when I look up to see Marisol.

Seriously? That's why she was acting like she was before.

She leans back, resting on her elbows and licks her lips before shaking her head. "I want you, Gabe, but you have a mate now. I can't do this to her," she murmurs.

"I don't fucking care. You'll be my little slut, and you won't say shit. If you tell her, then I'll kill you." He steps in between her legs and wraps her legs around his waist.

It kind of feels like I'm in the middle of a porn film.

"But it's not fair to your mate. I really don't want to be your side bitch for the rest of my life. Even if I love you, I don't think I can," she starts crying. My heart swells. I feel so bad for her. She doesn't deserve this.

"You fucking will because you are no one without me, and you'll fucking like it, you hear me." He grabs her face and squeezes hard, she starts nodding. "Now shut the fuck up." I watch as he enters her and starts pounding into her. I bite my lower lip. What do I even do?

Leave.

No. I'll leave, but I'm going to invite her to come with me. I can't do anything tonight. I'll wait till morning, talk to Marisol, and get the hell out of here.

I stand in the bathroom staring at myself; I look so damn tired. I start splashing cold water onto my face when I finally hear a knock at the door. I hope it's her.

I run to the door, open it, and see Marisol. Her red hair is in a tight, low bun. I can definitely see the appeal there. She has a cute button noise, full lips, and pretty hazel eyes.

"I have your dress for today." She gives me a large smile that doesn't reach her eyes. Everything looks great, except for her eyes, which look dull and sad.

"Come in!" I smile in return and widen the door for her to come in, and when she does, I shut it. "Can we talk?"

"Of course!" I sit in the chair by the large mirror. I watch her as she lays the dress on the bed, and then she sits, crossing her legs.

"I saw you and Gabriel last night, and I heard everything." I get straight to the point.

"What?" She shouts, looking mortified. "It was a total misunders—"

I hold up my hand, cutting her off. "Just stop. There's no misunderstanding. I heard loud and clear. Look, I'm not mad. I know he's my mate, but I have another mate, and my heart belongs to him. I don't want Gabriel. I felt horrible, but after last night, I don't anymore."

"Two mates? That's unheard of." She's nervous, her fingers tapping the arm of the chair, and her legs are bouncing.

"Oh yeah, trust me, I'm shocked too." I laugh a little. "But I love my other mate, and I can't see myself with anyone else." I was becoming so stupid, though. I have been kidnapped twice now. I need to keep my guard up.

"Look, I don't know what you want from me, but he'll kill me if he finds out we're discussing this."

"I want to leave, and I want you to come with me. He doesn't treat you well. You deserve better." I stare into her eyes. "I can help you."

"I can't, Isabella. I know he's rough, but I love him and refuse to leave him." She stands, backing away from me. "You may think it's stupid, but I can change him."

"I won't force you to leave, you can have him and be his one and only, but I need your help. What is the best way out of here?" *Please help...*

"I don't think I can betray him like that." She looks toward the door.

"Don't you want him to yourself?" I arch a brow.

"Well, of course I do."

"Then help me. You know what he's trying to do is wrong." I get up, grabbing her hands, she stares at our joined hands as she chews her bottom lip.

"Okay." She nods, finally. Her gaze keeps moving to the door, like she's scared he'll come in at any moment. "We must do so now; he's not here at the moment as he has an important meeting. Get dressed, and I will show you the best way out. I'll be back." She runs out, and I'm left standing alone. What if she left so she could go find Gabriel and rat me out?

It doesn't matter now.

I pick up the dress off the bed and throw it on. I hate that he dresses me like a damn doll.

It's another beautiful strapless dress, red with a corset top. It hugs my curves, giving it an hourglass look. I put my hair in a high ponytail to keep it out of the way, bending down, I grab the hem of the dress with both hands, ripping it to make a slit so it's easier to kick, just in case.

Marisol comes back in holding a white envelope in her hand. "Isabella, I have about nine hundred dollars in here. Enough for you to get a plane and a couple of nights at a hotel. Where are you going?"

I think for a moment, should I even tell her?

"To Azrael, The Prince of Vampires."

She laughs, and I look at her with narrow eyes. What the hell is so funny? She shakes her head, pursing her lips. "Of course, your other mate is Gabriel's worst enemy. The castle is in London. You'll definitely need a plane. It's too far for a car ride. I cannot take you, but I will show you the way. Let's go."

I follow her down the hall, and down a different set of stairs. We enter a long, creepy hall with candles lining the red brick walls. Shit, what if she's taking me somewhere to lock me up? I have no choice but to follow her; our footsteps echo loudly in the silent hall.

We finally reach the end, and there's a large, old wooden door.

"Okay, hit me hard, so it looks like you knocked me out and stole my keys. Hit this button, so you can hear which one is my car. Do not stop till you make it to the airport. It's about an hour-long drive. There's a GPS in my car; you can use it to take you there."

"Are you sure? I don't really want to hit you that hard."

"You must, or I will be punished for leaving you long enough for you to escape."

"Can I ask another favor?" She stares at me, waiting for me to continue. "Can you cast a removal spell to remove these?"

I lift my wrists, showing her the small silver cuffs on my wrist. She shrugs, nodding her head. She grabs both of my wrists in her hands and closes her eyes, mumbling the spell.

I don't understand a word she's saying, but a second later, her face scrunches, and she begins mumbling faster and louder, panting. I feel the air change around us, filling with magic. The air makes our hair whip from the harsh winds, and I close my eyes, missing the feeling of magic caressing my skin.

I hear something clinging to the ground and I open my eyes to see the cuffs laying besides my feet. I cry out in relief, feeling the heat of my magic rush through my veins. I shiver at the sensation, I grin, staring at my wrists.

"Thank you, Marisol!" I give her a large hug. "If you ever need help, you know where to find me; I owe you one." Then, without warning, I pull back and punch the side of her face hard. She flies back, landing on her ass. I think I actually knocked her out. She lays there as a large bruise starts forming, and her lip splits open.

"Shit! I'm so sorry." I turn and run as soon as I see cars. I hit the alarm button, and her headlights blink. It's a red two-door BMW convertible.

Nice...

I jump in, starting it. This is a very nice car. I punch in the airport. It looks like we're in Ireland, holy Hell.

I'm further away than I thought.

I race down the road following the directions.

It's beautiful here with all the rolling hills. It's October, and it's pretty chilly in this dress. It's a good thing this baby has heated seats and there's a nice leather jacket in the passenger seat. I slow down as I pass a beautiful pond in the middle of the hills. Wow, I wish I had time to stop and enjoy this view longer. I release a long breath and speed up again.

I honestly couldn't wait to see Azrael, but would he even be there? What if he's out looking for me. God, I wish I had his number so I could call him.

It feels like a part of me is missing. I want to feel his lips against mine. I know it's only been two days, but it feels a lot longer than that.

I know Luna is in pain from the stab wound, but I trust Azrael to take good care of her for me.

Chapter 24

AZRAEL

It's been two days without her, and I'm going absolutely insane. I need her more than I ever needed anything. I haven't fed since she was taken; I've been too busy to eat or even sleep. I'm currently pacing in my father's office, waiting for him to come in.

I know where she was taken, and I'm ready to go with or without my father's army of men. I pray he'll help as it'd be easier. If I need to go alone, I will. I'm not scared.

When I received the call a couple of hours ago, I almost left right then and there, but Darren talked me down from the ledge. He's right; I need to be smart about this.

"Jesus, son, you need to feed."

"I will when she's back in my arms, safe," I hiss, running my fingers through my hair.

"You'll need the strength from feeding to retrieve her. Here." He pulls his jacket open and removes a couple of bags from inside it. I inhale, smelling the metallic scent of blood, my fangs extend. I grab them and feed quickly.

"There! Happy now?" I toss the bags aside. "How many men can I borrow? I want to leave as soon as possible."

"Think about this—you will start a war." He sits in his large office chair and starts looking through the stack of paperwork that is piled up on his desk.

"I don't give a fuck!" I roar, growing angrier at how freaking calm he is. "I don't care about burning the whole goddamn world down or going to hell itself to get her back!" I hit his desk with my fist. "I will go with or without your soldiers."

"That would be a suicide mission."

"I don't give a fuck!" I punched his desk again, splitting it in half.

"Calm down, son, you can use however many you need. You should know that. I just want you to know what will happen if you do this, is all. She's a part of this family now." He stands, and I feel relieved. I would have done it without him, but I'm pleased he'll help.

I close my eyes, taking a deep breath. I see her large green eyes with those cute freckles scattered underneath her eyes and on her nose.

I'm coming for you, my love.

Stella runs in and announces, "She's awake."

"Go ahead, I'll tell my soldiers to prepare for a fight." My father walks out of the room.

I want to follow him, but I need to go make sure Luna is okay. I know it's what my mate would want me to do.

I race down to where we're keeping Luna in a guest room. She's been in a coma since she was stabbed, the doctor said it's a good thing that she needed time to rest so she could heal.

When I reach the room, she sees me and smiles. I swallow, not knowing how to tell her that they took Bella and that I failed to protect her once again. I grab Luna's hand, and she frowns.

"What's wrong?" Her voice is raspy, so I grab the glass of water and place it against her mouth while she takes a drink. "Where's Bella?"

"They took her after they attacked you."

"No, no." She rips the IV out of her arm, and blood pours out, making my fangs extract when I smell her blood. She tries standing up, but her legs are too weak to hold her up, and she falls to the ground. "Why are you still here? Go find her!" She screams as I bend to help her, and she hits me.

"I have been looking nonstop, Luna. We just found out where she is this afternoon. We're gathering our soldiers as we speak. I just wanted to come tell you myself. I will bring her back. You have my word."

"You better! She's all I have." She starts crying, shoving me away.

"Oh my…" A nurse runs in. "No, you need rest. Your highness, please help me put her back in bed." She bows, and I stand with Luna in my arms and gently place her back on the bed.

"I must go now. Rest and heal. She'll need you when I bring her back."

"Kill them all. I want blood," she mutters angrily, and I arched a brow. She's always been the sweet one, but I nod anyway. I plan to do just that.

I need to take better care of Bella. She's been taken from me twice now. I'm angry at myself for not doing something.

I'm a shitty mate. I will do better.

I hear someone screaming my name, and my head snaps towards the window.

Chapter 25

An hour earlier

After the long plane ride, I decide to skip the hotel even though it's the middle of the night and I'm so freaking tired, because I need to see him more than I need sleep.

I rent a car and am in town searching for vampires, hoping they'll tell me where the castle is because I have no idea where I'm going, and it's not like I can just Google search the Vampire King's address. Humans don't know about other beings at all.

I walk into a diner and sit on a stool, looking around, wondering what my next move is because I have no idea what to do. I'm sure his castle won't be easy to find.

On top of all that, no one here speaks English, so I have to point at pictures of what I want. The door opens, I turn my head to see a group of men who I'm pretty sure are vampires. The air around them feels different from humans. I grin, that wasn't so hard.

They stop lifting their noses, nostrils flaring. Yep, they smell me. They look around, and their eyes land on me. They smirk and start walking towards me.

"What is a little witch doing in our neck of the woods? Are you lost?" the taller one asks as he takes a seat to my left and leans in towards me, grabbing a strand of my hair, and sniffing it. I shiver, hating that he's so close to me.

"I'm looking for the king's castle."

He snorts, "Are you serious?"

"Yes," I snarl with annoyance. I've never been a patient person…

"They will kill you once you step on the property. You are aware our kind hates your kind, right?" the one to my right says.

"Oh, I'm very aware, but I also don't care. I need to get there." Praying that Azrael would've talked to his guards about me, especially the witch part.

"And what do we get?" the tall one asks as his hand lands on my thigh where my slit is. The third one hasn't said a word; he sits there ignoring me altogether.

"Nothing! If you don't want to tell me, then don't." I stand, throwing money on the bar, I'm not playing their games. Before I get to my car, the two vampires stepped in front of me, blocking my way.

"We'll tell ya if ya give us what we want."

"And what's that?" I cross my arms over my chest.

"Your blood. What else would we want? You know what your blood does to us."

I throw my head back laughing.

"Nah, I'm good." I try passing him, but the taller one grabs me and shoves me against a car door, and wraps his hand around my throat.

"Remove your hand, or you'll regret it," I say calmly.

"Oh yeah? The little witch will cast a spell?" He slaps a hand over my mouth and nose. "There, now you can't. Now you're weak like a human without that sweet voice of yours." He grins, tightening his hold hard enough that I can't breathe, but I don't panic.

I don't need spells like a normal witch, and they'll soon realize it, but why not have a little fun first? The other one presses against my side, and his arm wraps around my waist underneath the leather jacket.

I know I can't win against two vampires without magic, but I'm in the mood to fight the old-fashion way for a few.

I lift my knee and hit the one in front of me in the balls. It doesn't matter that they're vampires; it still hurts when you kick their balls.

He groans, falling to his knees, and I smile, grabbing the back of his head before the other one can react, and I knee his face hard enough that it makes my knee hurt. Blood starts pouring out of his nose. The other vampire snaps out of his shock, slams into me, and we fall to the ground. The back of my head smacks the concrete, and I groan at the sharp pain.

Shit... that fucking hurt. I squeeze my eyes closed, feeling dizzy. He jumps on me, straddling my hips. I watch as his fangs extend. He grabs my wrist with one hand and covers my mouth with the other. He starts leaning in with the full intent of biting me.

I call to my magic and moan as it quickly flows through my veins, heating my insides. I feel the heat of my flames on my hands, running up my arms.

He hisses and quickly releases me, I let my flames flow back into me. "What the fuck?" He looks at his hands and back at me. "What was that?"

"What was what?" I ask innocently. He snarls and tries jumping back on me, but I lift my leg and kick him in the chest, adding the force of my magic to the kick. He flies back, landing on a car across the parking lot, and its alarm starts blaring loudly.

I grin but then flinch from sudden pain as the other one grips my ponytail and starts lifting me up.

"Fuck! Let go of my hair!" I scream. When he pulls me on my feet, I try to kick him in the balls again, but he's prepared for it this time and blocks my knee. But as he pays attention to that, I punch him in the throat, and he starts choking. I spin around and pick up my leg halfway through my spin, and kick the side of his face, sending him to the ground.

I see a blur coming for me at the last minute. I don't have time to move out of the way, and he picks me up by the throat off the ground. I start clawing his hands as I struggle to breathe.

My eyes widen and start to water. I call my magic. I'm losing this fight, and they now want to kill me.

My hands grip the sides of his face, and I let my flames release, wrapping themselves around his face. He drops me as he starts screaming in pain. I hit the ground, landing on my knees, and I start gasping for air, grabbing my neck.

I look up to see the flames continue to spread across his body. He falls to the ground, thrusting around. I call the flames away before they kill him as the other one starts running away.

Fucking coward.

I lean my back against the car, trying to slow my breathing and calm my racing heart. Thank goodness I don't need my voice for spells.

I won't lie; I missed my flames. I look up to see the third guy walking toward me with his hands raised, telling me he isn't looking for a fight.

"I came to give you the address to the castle. Sorry about them, they can be assholes." He hands me a napkin that has an address written on it. I look back up to thank him, but he's already gone.

I fix my ponytail before turning on the car and entering the address in the car's GPS, and I'm about an hour away. Almost there.

I don't bother with the music, needing some peace and quiet. Will they even let me in? Like the vampires said, as soon as they see me, they'll probably kill me, right? They won't let just anyone enter to see the prince, especially a witch. How do I go about this?

I never considered this. I honestly thought I'd drive in, and they'd take me to see Azrael. Stupid right?

Urgh...

But I'm sure Azrael told them to keep a lookout for a witch, right?

I ease my feet off the pedal to slow the car when I see a large black iron gate up ahead, but no one is there standing guard. When I get closer to the gates, the soldiers step out of the shadows one by one. There's at least ten or so of them.

One steps in front of my car and holds a hand up; I slam on the brakes, stopping the car. He stares at me for a moment before walking to the driver's side door, and from the corner of my eye, I see another walk to the passenger side door. I swallow the fear and straighten my shoulders, ignoring my frantic heart rate even though I know they can probably hear it. The one at the driver's side door knocks on my window.

I smile as I push the button to roll it down.

"State your business," he says with a slight growl, flashing his large, pointy fangs, trying to intimidate me, and I have to admit it's working. He's enormous and scary; a large scar runs down his forehead to his cheek, his eyes are red, and it looks like he wants to murder me right there and then.

"Hiya!" I flutter my lashes, trying to look sweet. "I'm here to see Prince Azrael."

"Do you have an appointment?"

"Uh, no?" I laugh nervously, looking around at all these huge ass vampires surrounding the car, staring at me with promises of a violent death lingering in their eyes.

"Then you aren't going in. Turn your ass around now."

"No! I demand you to tell him I'm here!" Okay, being nice isn't helping. I narrow my eyes, dropping my smile.

"You demand?" He arches his brows and then laughs. "You hear that, boys? We must let her through now since she demands it."

They start laughing along with him.

He suddenly stops and snarls, "Get the fuck out of here before I lose my patience."

"No, let me in, dammit. Tell him it's Bella!" I smack the steering wheel with my palm. I'm too close to turn around and just leave.

"I won't repeat myself. Go, or I'll throw your ass in the dungeons." I nod, in agreement. "That's what I thought."

I turn the car back on and look over my shoulder to look out the back window, pretending I'm going to reverse and leave. But I put the car in drive, and slam on the gas pedal, hitting it to the floor. The tires squeal loudly, and the car lurches forward.

The soldiers in front of the car jump out of the way before they get hit, and the car slams into the gate, pushing it down. I start to hear the guards yelling as I drive straight through, running over the gate.

My car crashes into a large water fountain that's in front of the castle doors. I don't have time to look around. I jump out of the car and see the guards running straight towards me.

I run toward the front door, making it halfway before they start closing in on me. They're too fast; I'm not going to make it.

"Azrael!" I scream as loud as I can before they grab me, I start thrusting around, trying to fight them off. "Azrael!" I need to use my magic. I don't want to kill any of the guards, but they're not leaving me much of a choice.

I'm too slow, just as I start calling my magic I feel a sharp pain on the right side of my neck. He's sucking me dry!

My lip's part, but nothing comes out as I start blacking out. He's sucking my blood too fast.

"Let go of her!" I hear a loud roar. He's here. I try prying my eyes open, but my head slumps back, feeling completely drained, literally.

"MINE!" he roars again. The guard must've dropped me because my body hit the ground. I should have called my magic earlier instead of worrying about hurting them when they clearly were out for my blood.

"She was attacking us, Your Highness."

"She's my mate and your princess. You all will be punished for this." I hear before everything turns dark.

Chapter 26

AZRAEL

I kneel beside her, snaking my hand behind her head, slightly lifting her. "Bella!" I yell, grabbing her face with my other hand. "Come on!" I shake her, trying to wake her. My heart shatters seeing her like this. I bite my wrist, ripping it open, and pushing it onto her lips. "Drink!" I demand, but she doesn't.

I pull her into my arms as I stand, cradling her against my chest. "I'll deal with you all later." I snarl at the guards who are on their knees before hissing at the one with my mate's blood running down his face. I want to rip his fucking heart out, but I can't. Not now at least.

I need the doctor! I rush inside using my vampire speed, trying hard to listen to her faint heartbeat. What if I don't save her in time? Do I break the law and turn her?

Yes.

When I reach his room, I kick the door down, rushing in. He's sitting in the corner chair reading.

"Prince Azrael." He stands looking startled before bowing, and looks from me to Bella. "What is goi…"

"Doctor Julius, this is my mate. You must save her." He rushes forward and tries taking her from me, but I snarl, pulling her tighter against me.

"I must take her," he says as he reaches for her again, and this time, I release her. He places her on his bed and starts checking on her.

"Her pulse is too weak. You must give her your blood before she dies."

"I tried already!"

"Try harder!" he snaps and I growl at his disrespect, but I step forward, biting down on my wrist again and placing it against her lips, but nothing happens.

"Fucking drink mi amor." I dig my fingers into her cheeks, forcing her lips open. She's doesn't drink for a minute, a minute too long. "Bella!" I snap, and she moans, her lips opening on their own, sucking my wrist.

"Yeah, that's it, mi amor. Take what you need." I caress the side of her face with my free hand, and I let her take as much as she needs. I start feeling dizzy, but I don't stop her; she can have it all if she needs it.

"She must stop," the doctor says. I growl at him when he tries to force my wrist away from her. After a moment, I let him. "Her pulse is strong now."

"Why isn't she waking up?"

"She lost too much blood; she needs rest." I nod, getting up. I step through the broken door without another word and head straight to our room.

I gently lay her in bed and remove the leather jacket she's wearing. I feel nothing but anger when I see bruises on her neck and the bite wound.

I will take care of them later.

I lick my lips when I see what she's wearing underneath the jacket. The dress hugs her body perfectly. I take off her shoes before removing my jacket, throwing it over my chair by the fireplace, and go to the closet.

I quickly remove my clothes to slip into a pair of sweats, then grab an extra shirt for Bella. I undress her, putting my shirt on her before laying her back down and covering her with the blanket. I inhale her scent. *Fuck, I missed her.*

I know I should get up and deal with the shit that just happened, but I'm not leaving her. I drag a chair to the side of the bed, sitting down to watch her sleep. My legs are bouncing. My anxiety is through the roof. It won't settle till she opens her eyes.

She needs to be okay.

"Azrael." My father knocks before opening the door. He looks at her, then me.

"I know, but I can't leave her side."

"I understand. But..." He nods, his eyes hard. I know he's going to force me to leave her. His shoulders slump slightly. "You know what? You stay here with her, and I'll deal with this mess. Do you want me to call off the fight?"

"For now, yes, but we still need to attack. They will not get away with this. We'll wait till she is feeling better."

"Very well." He turns, shutting the door behind him. I slide into the mattress under the blanket, slipping my right arm beneath her, pulling her tightly against me.

"I'll kill anyone who lays a single finger on you. I fucking swear on it." I mumble against her forehead. I lie here listening to her heart rate, making sure nothing sounds off about it.

I never wanted the mate bond. I always thought it would weaken me, but it didn't, it did the opposite. It's amazing to have someone by your side forever and to have someone to fight for.

To have a reason to live.

I'm a ruthless man. I was never afraid of anything, never afraid of death, never cared if anyone died, not even my family. Dying is the cycle of life; shit happens. But the thought of *her* dying scares the fuck out of me.

I need to mark her. I'm stupid for not doing so yet. If I had, I would've found her sooner, and my scent would be mixed with hers, my guards would've known she is mine.

I won't make the same mistake twice.

Chapter 27

BELLA

I blink a few times, my eyes adjusting to the darkness of the room. The only sliver of light is from the moonlight shining through the large window and the flames crackling in the fireplace. Where am I? I feel something heavy draping across my waist. I lift the dark blanket to find a muscular arm covered in tattoos.

What?

I turn my head to the side nervously and smile when I see him sleeping beside me, causing my heart to flutter.

Azrael.

I roll to my side to stare at him; he looks so peaceful. I trace his lower lip with the pad of my thumb, making him groan.

My head is resting on his bicep, and our legs are tangled with each other's. I close my eyes, snuggling closer, basking in his warmth. He moves onto his back, and his arm pulls me along with him.

"Luna…" I start to sit up, but he tightens his grip, forcing me still.

"She's okay, mi amor," Azrael says in a low, raspy voice.

Holy hell…

I tilt my head back, meeting his blue eyes. "You took care of her for me?"

"Of course, I did." I lick my lips, his eyes dilate as he follows the movement, starving for a taste.

I lean away, pinching my lips together, my brows furrowing. Should I tell him about Gabriel being my mate?

"What's wrong?" he asks in alarm, eyes bouncing between mine. "Are you hurt?"

I need to tell him before he finds out on his own. "I need to tell you something," I finally say, looking away from him, not knowing how to say it. I feel extremely anxious about how he's going to react.

"What is it?" He grabs my chin, tilting my head up to look at him. "Did he hurt you?" he growls, eyes narrowing, nose flaring, jaw clenched tightly together.

"Um, no?" Seriously… *Just ease into it slowly,* my brain tells me. "He's my mate." I blurt out quickly.

What the hell? I thought I said easy into it.

"What?" he snarls, eyes turning red. Shit... "That's not possible. You are *mine*!" He roars when he says *mine*. He jumps up, disappearing behind one of the doors. I get up following him.

"What are you doing?" I walk into a large walk-in closet, to find him throwing on a black button-up shirt.

"I'm going to deal with him."

"No, don't! He's my mate. I felt the bond between us." I rub my neck as my anxiety level goes sky high. His muscles tense, and he slowly turns to face me, pinning me with predatory eyes.

I've never seen him look so murderous...

Fucking fuck...

I lift my chin, keeping my gaze locked on his.

"What did you just say?" he asks, slowly stalking towards me.

"I felt the mate bound with him?" It sounded more like a question, I didn't realize I was backing up till my back hit a wall.

"Do you not feel it with me?" He finally reaches me, caging me in with his arms. "Just so you know, regardless of what your answer is, I refuse to let you go. I'll just get rid of the problem."

"Excuse you?" I snap as my anger roars to life, my magic faring up beneath my skin, warming my insides. *I already picked him, but how dare he act like he can control me?*

"I don't care if he is your mate. I fucking don't care if you want him because I'm not letting you go." He smirks in the evil way of his. I know he sees my eyes turning, glowing with flames, but he doesn't bother backing down like most; no, he seems thrilled with the challenge. I try shoving him away from me, but he doesn't budge.

He's so freakin' infuriating!

"And what if I only came back for Luna and wanted to go back to be with him?" I challenge as I lift my chin. He growls, baring his teeth as his breathing turns rigid.

Stand your ground, even if your anger is turning into lust.

"I'll lock you up and throw away the fucking key because you're *mine* whether you like it or not. No one else will ever have you." He punches the wall beside my head.

He leans his forehead against the wall beside me. I can feel his hot breath against my neck as he breathes me in. Maybe I'm crazy—no scratch that I am crazy. My blood boils with desire, I clench my thighs together as I start to throb with so much need—loving his possessiveness over me.

"And after I lock you up, I'll invite him over, and I'll *fuck* you in front of him before killing him as you watch, and I'll enjoy every second of it. I might even fuck you after in his blood." He bites my ear lobe, making me yelp at the pain.

He's in-fucking-sane, but God, I'm getting so wet over his craziness.

"Good…" I moan. He pulls back, looking at me, confused. He expected me to beg for his life. "Yes, he's my mate, but you are too." I can see the wheels turning as he stares down at me. He shakes his head, pushing away from me.

"I refuse to share you with anyone." He paces in front of me, hands pushing his hair back. "I'll never share you."

"I don't want that. I left him because I choose you. I want—"

He cut me off, "I don't care if you want him… Wait, what?"

"I said I choose you. I never wanted or needed him. I never once thought about leaving you. It's you, Azrael. I want you, not him." I grab the front of his shirt, trying to pull him down for a kiss, but he doesn't budge. He just stares looking dazed, like he doesn't believe me.

"You picked me over him?" he asks, like it's bizarre that I would do something like that.

"Yes, now *kiss* me." And finally, he kisses me passionately as he holds my face between his hands.

"Mine," he mumbles against my lips. "All fucking mine." He picks me up, and I wrap my legs around him. He carries me back to the bedroom and throws me on the bed. He stands at the end of the bed, eyes trailing down my body.

My eyes return the favor slowly taking him in. He's only wearing a button-up shirt, but it isn't buttoned. I can see his toned abs with a pair of grey sweats that hangs low on his hips, the V-line disappearing underneath them. The way his cock looks in those sweats is so fucking sinful.

Fuck me...

He's perfect. He watches me openly admire his body before he slowly removes his button-up shirt.

"I fucking need you," he mutters as he crawls on the bed towards me.

Damn...

My body is begging to be touched by him.

"Please," I whimper.

"Please, what mi amor?" I roll my eyes at him, leaning up to kiss him, taking what I want, but he pulls away as he tsks. "I want you begging for it first."

I smirk as I throw him on his back with a little help from my magic. I climb on him. I'm not begging, I'm going to take what I want.

I straddle his hips, my fingernails dig in his chest, and he releases a sexy groan. I love the sounds he makes. I lean forward, planting a kiss on his collarbone before kissing his jaw. I make my way down his neck, where I suck his skin between my teeth, needing to leave my mark on him.

I start grinding my hips against him, his hands grab my hips controlling my movements, making me grind against him harder and faster.

"Fuck," he hisses. I lean up grabbing the hem of my shirt slowly pulling it off, exposing my breasts to him. He licks his upper lip.

"Did you miss me?" I whisper before biting my lower lip as my nipples harden, feeling the heat of his gaze. I'm fully exposed to him, only wearing a white lace thong.

"More than anything. I went insane without you. I want you to know I'll do anything for you. Tell me you understand that. Tell me you'll never leave me." He looks at me with so much vulnerability in his gaze.

"Never. I'm yours. I need you more than I have ever needed anything. I have always felt that something was missing, but I never knew what till you came into my life."

He sits up, pulling a nipple into his mouth, flicking it with his tongue as his hand cups my other breast. A wave of intense pleasure runs through my body, I throw my head back, letting out a long, breathy moan. I grip his shoulders tightly as I start grinding myself against him again. He bites my nipple, and I scream out from the sting of pain mixed with pleasure.

"Azrael... Please," I whimper, needing more of him. "Please, I... I need..." I can't even form the words. My head is clouded with too much pleasure. His hand releases my breast, grabbing my thong, and I hear it rip; he tosses the shredded pieces off the bed.

I'll need to buy a lot more the way he likes ripping them off.

His hand cups my pussy. "Fuck, Bella, you're soaked for me, you naughty little witch."

My eyes roll back, and I groan when his fingers spread my lower lips, slowly rubbing my achy clit as his mouth moves to give my other nipple attention.

"You're my good girl, aren't you?"

"Yes," I cry out, I'll agree to anything at this point.

"Do you want to bounce on this cock, baby?"

"Ple…" I lick my lips. "Yes." I nod quickly, feeling so desperate for him. He removes his lips and hands, making me whimper, missing his touch.

"Patience, or I'll punish you." I pout but keep quiet. He gently pulls me off his lap before standing. He pulls down his sweatpants and he's bare underneath them. His cock jumps out, slamming against his stomach. I moan at the sight of his large cock and the gleam of precum on the tip.

He grabs his cock and rubs his precum around his tip. "Want it, my naughty little witch?" I nod quickly, not looking away from his hand rubbing himself. "Use your words, Bella," He growls.

"Yes, I want you, Azrael, please."

"Good girl." He lies back down and looks over at me. "Come here." His voice harsh and raspy, filled with hunger. I throw my leg around his hips, straddling him again. He reaches down between us and starts rubbing his tip against me, getting it wet before he places it against my entrance.

"Slide down, baby." I rest my hands against his chest and watch him as I slowly sink down on it, I cry out as I stretch to accommodate his size. My nails dig into his skin, drawing blood.

"Fuck, I missed you so much, baby. Shit, yes, you feel so good. So, fucking perfect, so tight." He breaths heavily as his head tilts back, eyes rolling back in pleasure.

"Oh God," I moan when I finally have him all in. I stay still, trying to adjust when I feel myself clench his cock tightly.

His eyes snap open. They're red, his fangs are slowly extracting. He looks so sinister, and it sends a violent shiver down my spine. I slowly lift myself up before slamming myself down, and then I did it again and again, going faster and harder with each thrust of my hips. His grunts and moans keep me going.

I throw my head back at the amazing sensation. I love being in control and the feeling of making a strong, murderous vampire beg for more and more is indescribable. Having someone so strong and powerful, willing to do anything for me at the snap of a finger.

"Please, fuck, yes, baby, don't stop."

Thousands upon thousands of creatures fall to their knees for him out of fear of his strength and brutality, and he never bows to anyone. He doesn't need to, but he's underneath me at my mercy, begging for more.

"That's it, baby, fuck yeah... Your tight pussy feels too fucking good." He grunts as he watches my breasts bounce. His fingers dig into my hips with a bruising grip.

"Don't you dare fucking stop!" he snarls. I look back down and watch his eyes dilate as his grip on my hips tightens painfully. "I'm going to fucking mark you now," he growls, it isn't a question, it's a warning. I should be afraid, but I'm not. I know he'll never hurt me. He flips me over on my back without pulling out and starts pounding me hard. The bedframe starts banging against the wall.

"Oh God, Azrael...." I moan as he slams into me deeper; it feels so damn good. My toes curl, and my fingers grip the sheets tighter.

"That's right, baby, I'm your fucking God."

"I... Nee..." I'm so close I can't even think straight. I look in between us and watch his strong, defined muscles flex with each relentless thrust. *Oh God.* My head falls back, and my eyes close as I let my body ride this wave of intense pleasure.

"Look. At. Me," he snarls. His hand wraps around my jaw with his fingers digging into my cheeks.

"I... I'm gonn...." A moan slips out before I can finish the sentence.

"I said, look. At. Me!" he snaps, saying each word between each merciless thrust. I open my eyes, looking up at him. My heart pounds hard in my ribs as I try to keep up with his relentless thrusts.

"Pleaseee," I beg, staring into his hungry eyes. My head starts spinning, body trembling, feeling ablaze as he drives me closer to the edge.

"That's it, baby. Now be a good girl and cum on my cock." As soon as he says that, my body explodes. I throw my head back, screaming his name as my nails claw into the sides of his neck. I can feel myself pulsating around him as I cum; powerful waves of pleasure crashing through me.

Azrael turns my face, and in the next moment, I feel the sharp sting of his bite digging into my flesh. I cry out in pain, but a moment later, another wave of pleasure strikes through me like lightning, and I feel our bond snap together.

His cock starts throbbing inside me, making me groan, and my lips part in pleasure when I tighten around him again as an orgasm violently takes control of my body, and he fills me with his warm cum. He slowly retracts his fangs, licking my neck.

My body slumps, the back of my head hits the pillow. Our heavy breathing mingles together as we stare into each other's eyes trying to catch our breath.

"Holy shit." He says pulling out of me, resting his forehead against my shoulder. "That was intense."

"Yeah, it was amazing." I laugh a little. "I missed you."

"I missed you too, my love." He kisses my collarbone before rolling on his back, pulling me to his side.

Holy shit, we're fully mated, is the last thought I have before sleep consumes me.

I feel something tingly against my neck, and I groan trying to roll to my side, but arms wrap around me, keeping me still.

"Bella." I hear Azrael's husky voice. He's kissing the side of my neck on the same spot he marked me.

"A few more minutes," I beg.

"No baby, lunch is ready, and you already skipped breakfast." I pout, but I slowly blink my eyes open. He pulls back just enough to look at me.

"I should've asked for your permission. But the monster inside me demanded that I mark you, and I didn't stop him. I didn't ask because I was afraid you'd say no," he says, his gaze filled with regret

"It's okay, I was ready for it. I needed it, too." My hand cups the side of his face, and my thumb runs across his lower lip. "I missed you so much, Azrael."

"I missed you more than you'll ever know. Those were the most miserable two days of my existence. I fucking love you." I gasp, shocked that he said those three little words. My heart swells and I lean up, smashing my lips against his.

"I love you, too," I say against his soft lips. He pulls back grinning ear to ear.

"Say it again."

"I love you, Azrael." He wraps his arms around my waist, lifting me up out of bed, spinning us around with a large smile as I laugh.

Chapter 28

AZRAEL

I'm sitting in the dining room watching my mate eat. She's laughing at something Luna said, and I press my lips together to hide my smile. It's such an angelic sound, but I'm not paying any attention to their conversation. She's wearing her hair in a high ponytail like she wants to show off my mark.

I just sit here staring. Creepy? Yeah, I know, but I don't give a fuck. The way I feel about her is impossible to describe. I just know I'd do anything for her, and I'll do anything to keep her. I hate that I have to share her, even with her sister.

I want to keep her all to myself. Hell, I don't even want her near Luna. I want to fuck her in every room and then lock her away in my room for my fucking eyes only.

I'm too obsessed with her.

She laughs again, and this time, she turns to look at me. My heart speeds up, the blood beneath my skin heats, and my cock hardens. I bite down on my tongue hard enough to taste the metallic taste of blood to suppress a groan.

She's too fucking beautiful.

My fucking angel.

She winks at me, and I snap. I get up to take her to my room. As I step in front of her, her eyes widen, and her cheeks redden; I smirk. That's right, my wicked little witch, be afraid. I'm about to fuck the shit out of you.

"Azrael." I bare my teeth when my father calls out my name from somewhere behind me. I let out a slow, long sigh, and my little witch decides to laugh at me, finding my anger amusing. I narrow my eyes at her.

"What? I'm in the middle of something." I finally turn to face him.

"We need to talk."

"Can it not wait? I need to take care of something. I can meet you in a couple of hours." Yes, that will be enough time to punish my wicked witch.

"Getting your dick wet can wait." I hear Bella gasp behind me.

"Fine, but let's make this quick." I turn back to Bella and lift her up against me. "Be ready, my wicked witch, because I'm going to punish you for teasing me." I caressed her lower lip before walking out of the dining room with my father following close behind.

We enter my office. I sit on my office chair, and he sits across from me, folding his fingers together, resting them on his stomach, bouncing his knees.

"Prince Gabriel sent an invitation for us to join a ball in his plaza, commenting that we should bring Isabella as your guest. He knows she's here." He clears his throat. "I'm leaving this decision up to you. How do you want to proceed"

"It's a setup," I say, placing my elbows on the desk, and rubbing my jaw. He wants to take my mate from me and keep her as his. I curl my upper lip in a snarl.

I see red.

I'm going to fucking kill him....

My fists slam against the desk.

"It is indeed." My father nods, ignoring my outburst. He's used to my anger. "If I were you, I'd go, but I wouldn't take her. That's exactly what he wants."

"I agree, but she won't stay. I know without a doubt she'll come whether I like it or not." That's one of the reasons I love her, but except in these cases. She's too stubborn.

"Then keep it from her! You must not give in to what he wants, which is your mate, and you must go, or it'll show weakness."

I inhale deeply through my nostrils, trying to calm down, tapping my knuckles against my desk. I need to figure out what I want to do. I am thinking of withholding this information, but I quickly shake my head, knowing I can't keep this from her.

"I refuse to lie to her."

"Good, because I'd never forgive you if you kept something like this from me." I hear Bella's voice. I look up to find her standing in the doorway. I stand, holding my hand out, and she walks up to me. "I heard a bang, rushed over to see what was wrong, and I heard you." She looks at my father. "You told him to hide something from me. What is it?"

"I wouldn't hide something like this from you, mi amor." I grab her face with both hands, staring into her eyes. "Prince Gabriel invited us to a ball, but we know it's a trap."

"Of course, it is. He wants me back. We'll go, and we'll be prepared." She smiles.

"No, I will go, but you will not," I say, and her smile completely disappears. She takes a few steps away from me, eyes narrowing.

"Actually, I will go, whether you like it or not!" She sets her hands on her hips, lifting her chin, stubbornly. She's feisty as hell.

I love that she stands up to me and challenges me like this. No one challenges me, except my father occasionally.

"Father, leave us," I say, not looking away from my feisty mate, who's not backing down even under my intense glare, which would have any other grown man on his knees begging for mercy. He leaves the room without saying another word, shaking his head with a grin.

I sit on my chair without saying a word, spreading my legs out in front of me, patting my lap for her to come sit, but she shakes her head.

"You're a naughty little witch, aren't you?" I arch a brow, feeling excitement grow deep in my veins, warming my blood from the challenge.

"I'm being serious, Azrael. You can't really believe that sex will make me drop this conversation, roll over, and do whatever you say!" she shouts in frustration, stomping her foot down hard like a child. I know that she's being serious, but I don't give a shit.

I get up slowly, stalking towards her.

I need her bent over my desk now.

"Azr—" She starts, but I cut her off by grabbing her neck and squeezing lightly, cutting her air supply off, leaning down to lick her jaw. She releases a sexy little moan. My thumb runs across her pouty lips, and then I shove my ring and middle fingers in her mouth, making her gag and her eyes water. I grip her long ponytail, wrapping it around my fist a few times before yanking on it, forcing her head back so I can suck on the mark on her neck. I smirk when I feel her shiver.

"Be a good girl for me and get on your knees and gag on my cock. It's about time I fuck that feisty mouth of yours." Her eyes widen, filling with desire, but she shakes her head in defiance. I click my tongue. "*Now*, Bella," I growl. She swallows but drops to her knees.

"Good girl," I praise. "Now unbutton my jeans."

"You can unbutton your own damn jeans," she says with attitude, looking up at me through her lashes, innocently licking her lips. Fuck, she's sexy as hell.

My dick twitches in my jeans.

"Bella," I warn through clenched teeth.

"You didn't say please." She flutters her lashes and cups my cock through my jeans, making me groan. I never say please.

"Unbutton my jeans," I rub the side of her face. "Before I bend you over and spank you."

She rolls her eyes at me, making me growl, but she starts unbuttoning my jeans. She pulls them down along with my boxers, and I wrap my fingers around the base of my cock, then up to the tip, slowly stroking it. "Wrap those pretty lips around my cock."

I grab her ponytail, pulling her closely, rubbing my cock against her mouth. She parts her lips, sucking me in. I shove myself in forcing my cock to the back of her throat, making her gag. "Breathe through your nose and relax your throat for me, baby." She does as I say, and I grab her hand wrapping it around my cock, squeezing it for her. "Fuck yes, good fucking girl." I tip my head back; my voice sounds deeper and raspier from pleasure. I repeat the movement, fucking her mouth.

Her mouth feels so fucking good...

"Shit," I groan loudly. "Those sinful lips feel fucking amazing, baby."

She looks up at me, and tears are running down her cheeks. Fuck me, that makes me almost explode. *Almost.*

"So, fucking sexy. Get up and bend over," I growl, I don't want to explode in her mouth; that's for that sweet pussy. She stands doing as she was told, bending over my desk. I reach around her and unbutton her jeans, slowly pulling them off, throwing them over my shoulder.

I grab her ass with my hand, and then... *whack*.

The sound of her gasp fills the empty room. I massage where I spanked her. "That's for talking back," And then I do it again, this time harder. I spank her five more times, growling as I stare at her ass cheeks that *I* painted red. She gasps and moans each time I spank her.

My little witch enjoyed her punishment too much.

Fucking perfect.

"Naughty little witch," I tsk at her.

I lower myself down to my knees, looking up. She's wearing a pink silk thong, and it is soaked already. I lick my bottom lip, dying to taste her.

Later, I'll taste her later. I need to feel her around me again. My body is shaking in anticipation, like an addict waiting for his next hit.

"Damn, your ass is too fucking perfect." I slap it again, watching it jiggle. I grin; it's the best part. I love her curvy body. "This body is made to be worship, and that's exactly what I plan to do, day and night. Even though that'll never be enough, not for me at least. You've made me lose my mind, my fucking sanity, and I'll never be the same. I never want to be, not as long as I have you."

I stand, ripping her thong off before spreading her legs with my foot and rubbing my cock against her wet little pussy.

"You ready for me, baby?" I ask as I lean over, licking the side of her neck, making her shiver.

"Yes," she moans. "Please, Azrael."

Fuck, I love when she moans my name. I grip the back of her neck, pushing her down so her face is buried in all of my paperwork. My other hand grabs my cock, placing it against her opening, pushing the tip in.

I grind my teeth, wanting to go slow to torture her a little, but as soon as I slip into her warmth, she clenches around me, sucking me deeper, my control snaps completely.

I need to fuck her.

I need to show her no one can make her feel the way I do.

I force myself in with an all-in-one hard thrust. She screams; I pull back out a little and thrust in again even harder. She's so goddamn wet and tight. It's the best pussy I've ever had, hands down. I've never experienced something so fucking good. It's an out-of-this-world, mind-blowing pleasure. I release her neck to grip her hips, straightening my back, watching myself fuck her.

I slow my thrusts to watch her ass jiggle, and her pussy stretch open for my cock, hugging it perfectly. This is the closest thing a ruthless man like me will get to heaven. She's fucking flawless.

"Azrael," she moans. I look up to find her looking at me over her shoulder, biting her juicy lip. "Harder, baby."

I groan and pound into her harder and deeper. She screams again, and I growl. Someone is going to hear her pleasure. I grip her ponytail and pull her up till her back is against me, and I cover her mouth with my hand.

"Shhh, baby, someone will hear your moans, and those are only for me to hear and only for me to enjoy," I say, still pounding her. "Tell me you're mine," I hiss, removing my hand from her mouth before biting my mark on her beautiful skin.

She mumbles something that almost sounds like a plea. I release her hair, running my fingertips down her side till I get to her ass, and then I smack it hard, making her cry out. "Tell me."

"I'm yours, all yours. Please don't stop!"

"No one else can ever make you feel this good."

"No one," she agrees, nodding quickly, and starts meeting my every thrust.

I don't know how much longer I'll be able to last. She feels too fucking incredible. She clenches my cock, making me groan loudly.

Someone opens my office door, and a guard pokes his head in.

"Get the fuck out," I roar. His eyes widen in fear, and he slams the door shut.

The *fuck?*

Her pussy starts pulsating around my cock, and a sharp spark of pleasure rams into me intensely. She screams out, arching her back. I slap my palm against her mouth harsher than I meant to.

"That's right, cum all over this cock, baby." And she does as she screams my name into my hand.

"Fuck yes." Stars blast behind my eyes, and all I can even think about is this euphoric feeling spreading through my veins, causing me to tremble violently. The feeling is like taking a bite of a sweet, enchanting fruit and savoring it because you can't get enough.

I roar as I violently spill my release deep into her tight pussy.

I am still inside her, my forehead falls against her shoulder blade, and I close my eyes, feeling completely fucking spent.

Feeling completely numb, I grab her around her waist, spinning her around and lifting her, and I fall onto my chair. She lays her head on my chest, closing her eyes. I rub her jaw before kissing her forehead.

I never say please, I never beg, but for her, I will. She can have me crawling on my hands and knees, begging her for a little taste.

Chapter 29

BELLA

When I wake up, I'm alone in our room. I decide to lie here for a moment, thinking about what happened. I was so relieved when I heard Azrael say he wouldn't hide anything from me. I walk by the door looking for him right as his dad told him to hide it from me. I was so angry I almost burst into his office and yelled at them, but I didn't. I had to hear his reply. I knew he wouldn't, but I had to make sure of it.

Why is Gabriel inviting us to his ball? Azrael believes it's a trap, but he wouldn't hurt us, would he? He should respect my wishes. He can't force me to be with him.

Plus, Azrael marked me.

If it's a trap, we need to prepare for a fight, but once he sees that Azrael has marked me as his mate, he'll surely leave us alone.

I also need to figure out a way to get Azrael to allow me to go because I'll be going either way, even if I have to go without him knowing.

I was relieved he wouldn't hide anything from me, but here I am, sitting, thinking of ways to go behind his back to sneak into the ball... I'm so messed up.

The way he fucked me yesterday, I know that he's trying to prove to me that he's the only one who can pleasure me. That I don't need Gabriel; he must be feeling insecure about it. I know I would be if the tables were turned.

I won't lie; I loved every minute of it. The roughness was mind-blowing; no wonder I like darker romance instead of something sweet.

My stomach growls, and I pout, rolling over to my side to look at the clock. I slept all day yesterday and all night. I stretch, groaning at the same time.

I go to the bathroom to brush my teeth. As I do, I stare at myself. My eyes look bright and happy. I turn my head to the right a little to look at my mark that's on my neck, and I feel so happy. I squeal loudly and giggle.

I never thought I'd feel whole again after my mom died, but I do with him in my life. It makes me feel sad that she'd never meet him.

But I just know she would've loved him. I spit my toothpaste out and rinse my mouth. I throw my hair in a messy bun since I want to show off my mark and head to the closet. I put on a pair of black leggings and grin as I grab one of his white button-up shirts and put it on. I let one side hang off my shoulder and tuck half of it into the waistband of my leggings.

I'm so grateful for Azrael and his family. They helped Luna and took care of her while I was gone. I feel like I don't need to take care of us alone anymore. I have help now. She really likes being around them, and I do too. We talked a lot yesterday and agreed she'll finish her senior year online, and she'll graduate in a few months. She already started to look at colleges around Azrael's house.

Stella says there are two different options: a human college she can get into easily or a supernatural college that'll be harder. Stella says it's pretty exclusive, but Azrael can get her in. The downside is, she'd have to stay there on campus. It's only a couple of hours away, so we can visit. But we never thought we'd be away from each other, and it makes us both nervous, especially her.

But I think the supernatural college will be the best option for her. Stella says I should apply since I never went to college, but Azrael shut that idea down quickly, too quickly.

When I enter the dining room, Azrael is on the phone standing by the window with one hand holding the phone to his ear and the other hand on the window as he stares out of it, snapping at the poor person on the other end of the call.

It's as if he can sense me. He turns his head to look over his shoulder, and his gaze slowly trails down my body. He hangs up without another word and walks towards me with a grin.

"Morning, baby. I was just about to wake you." He grabs my waist, pulling me against him. "That shirt looks amazing on you. It makes me want to eat you all up."

"You like it?" I ask, grinning as I wrap my arms around him.

"Like it? No baby, I fucking love it. Wearing my clothes makes you smell even more like me, and everyone knows you're mine, especially when you show off my mark." He kisses the top of my head. He's so freaking gentle with me and sometimes it surprises me. I never pictured him like this. If you had told me this was the way he was going to treat me a week ago, I would've laughed in your face.

My stomach rumbles, making him chuckle. He grabs my hand, taking me to the dining table. He pulls out a chair for me, and I sit down. He sits beside me, grabbing a plate, and starts piling pancakes on it for me.

"Good morning, sis." Luna winks at me. She eyes my mark with a smile, and I groan. She knows exactly what happened between us; we talked about it yesterday, and she's been teasing me. It's like someone stamped my forehead with "Just freshly fucked."

"Good morning," I reply as Azrael places the plate in front of me, and then gets up, disappearing into the kitchen. Stella walks in, looking like she just rolled out of bed.

"So, how's mated life treating you? Is my brother being too rough?"

"Uh, no?" I clear my throat as I cut into my pancakes. This is not a conversation I want with Azrael's sister.

"Well, how do you feel? Feeling the change?"

"I'm fine." I shrug, hoping she can read my body language or notice that I don't want to have this discussion with her.

"Well, you'll need some blood to fully transition, so you won't need so much sleep." My head snaps up, and I start having a coughing fit. Luna jumps up and starts hitting my back.

"What the *fuck* did you just say?" I squeal. "I need blood to *what*?"

"You don't know? No one ever explained what being fully mated to a vampire will mean? Azrael should've discussed this with you." She smacks her forehead.

"So, I'm transitioning to a vampire. That's why I'm so tired?" I wish someone fucking told me.

"Yes." I turn to see Azrael leaning against the door frame. "I thought you knew. I would've explained it already if I had known." He shrugs like it's no big deal. "That's why most don't mate outside of their kind." He takes the chair beside me and places the coffee in front of me. I grab it, taking a sip. My mind is turning, this is crazy!

"It's okay, Bella, don't freak out. I can tell you're panicking." My sister rubs my back in a circle softly. I nod, taking a deep, shaky breath. This is too much, and there's no going back. How can a witch be part vampire, our enemy? My kind will never forgive it.

"What will people think? I'll never be respected," I rush out.

It's not like witches ever showed me any respect in the first place...

"Look at me, Anima gemella." I do as he says, and he cups my face in his hands and places his forehead against mine, I close my eyes. "It's okay. No one will dare disrespect you."

"What does that mean? Anima ge…?" I can't say it right.

"My soulmate," he whispers, and my heart swells. Everything will be okay. I have him, so who fucking cares what other people think?

"Soulmate," I breathe, opening my eyes to stare into his. How did I get so lucky with him? He's everything I need, even if we started out rough.

Our relationship wasn't supposed to happen. It's not common for a witch and a vampire to be together. Our kind hate each other.

He's a prince. Vampires will never accept me. God, we rushed into this without even putting any thought into it, but I would still choose him.

"So, what happens now?"

"We'll announce that I've found my mate, and you'll be my queen."

"Wait, I'm not ready for the whole queen thing. I was hoping you'll push back getting crowned so I can get used to this whole royal thing and be the princess first. What if your kind doesn't accept me? I'm a witch, they'll hate me the same way you did."

"It's not up to them. That decision is up to me." I look up and see Azrael's father standing there. "I'm the one who passes the crown to the next in line, and if my son finds you worthy, then you are. If anyone has an issue with that, they'll have to get through us, and no one is that stupid. We are family now, witch or not." He smirks, "I guess part witch now."

I try holding the tears back, but one slips. I look away, trying to hide it.

"What's wrong?" Azrael asks, of course, he freaking noticed.

"Nothing, it's just that…" I shake my head, forcing the tears back. "We've been alone for so long, and now we're not. We don't have to keep running in fear."

"No more running. You have me now and my family." He gently rubs my cheek.

"We're okay now," Luna says as she wraps her arms around my shoulders, and I smile, hugging her back.

"We do need to plan for Gabriel's ball," his father says, sitting across from us.

"I refuse to sit back and not help," I stare in his eyes, refusing to back down. He stares back with power, and I feel it rushing through me, but I push back, lifting my chin. He's the king; it's disrespectful to stare into their eyes. You're supposed to submit. But he needs to know I'm not the one to submit, and I won't take any shit from anyone, powerful or not.

Out of nowhere, he starts laughing. "You got yourself a feisty one, Azrael. I've never met anyone who can stare into my eyes that long and not submit to my power. I like her."

"That's one of many reasons I love her. She's strong and stands her ground and doesn't back down. She definitely doesn't take my shit." He grabs my hand, intertwining our fingers. I look down at our joined hands, smiling and tightening my hold.

"If you want to come, you can, but only if Azrael is okay with it. It's a dangerous situation; we'll have to keep a close eye on you. It won't be easy."

"I can take care of myself."

"I haven't decided yet," Azrael says. I rip my hand away, giving him a death glare. "If I agree, you will not leave my side." I cross my arms over my chest. They're both being unfair, treating me like a child. "Do you hear me, Bella? This is not negotiable. If you can't do that, then you're staying here."

"Fine! Jeez." Not leaving his side is better than not going, I guess, but I'm still pissed.

"We have plans to discuss, so ladies, excuse us," his father says, standing up.

Azrael tries kissing me, but I turn away from him. He grabs my chin, forcing me still, and kisses me, but I press my lips together and don't kiss him back. He growls lowly, baring his teeth before turning around, storming out of the room.

I stare down at my pancakes. I've only had a couple of bites, but I lost my appetite. I push the plate away, grinding my teeth together. I'm so angry that he wants to control everything.

Maybe I'm being unfair, but I don't like being told what to do like I'm a damn child. I get everyone jumps when he says jump, but I'm his mate, his equal.

"At least he's allowing you to go," Stella says, shrugging.

"Allowing me?" I laugh harshly.

"Bella hates being told what to do; she always has," Luna mumbles with her mouth full.

"Look, I know you're not used to having people around that care about you, but when someone loses a mate, they go insane. Most go on a rampage, killing thousands from the grief of it. He doesn't want you to go, and he's probably holding himself back from locking you up to keep you here where it's safe but he's not because he wants you happy," she says, sounding annoyed that I'm angry about this, but I don't give a crap. I don't remember asking for her input.

"I understand that, but I'm no child. I don't need to be told what to do; I can handle myself."

"You can handle yourself against normal beings, I'm sure. You've made it this far, but remember, you were out there, now you're here, and you'll be going against the strongest monsters out there. You don't become a royal because you're weak." She scowls at me the way you'll scowl at a toddler doing something bad. "You literally got kidnapped twice. You don't know how to handle yourself against the strong monsters out there." Okay, she got me there.

"She's right, Bella. I know you're strong, but in a roomful of equally strong or even stronger monsters, you can get hurt. We want to protect you and keep you safe."

"If he can meet you in the middle, I feel like you should meet him in the middle as well." I chew my lower lip. She's fucking right.

I still won't be told what to do, but I do need to meet him in the middle, especially if he's willing to. I finally look at Stella and nod.

"Most people can't stand up against the two of them, especially Azrael, but you do. That shows me that you're strong because the energy they put off makes most people drop to their knees and show respect. My brother isn't used to the push back, and I've got to say it's going to be fun to watch." She grins at me.

"He makes me want to pee myself, honestly. It's hard not to bow when he enters the room. He's freaking scary," Luna's entire body shivers.

"Who?" I ask in surprise.

"Both, but especially Azrael."

"Seriously, he's not that scary."

Luna snorts.

"See? That's exactly it. When either of them enters a room, people's first response is to bow, and they do. You'll see it. We sense their power."

"I don't sense that." I've seen people bow, but I didn't think it was because of that. I just thought they knew who he was and did it out of respect.

"Because you are equally as strong. You're meant to be a queen, and queens don't bow down to anyone. You may not know this, but your power does. That's why Azrael's presence doesn't scare you; your soul knows he's your mate, and that he'll never hurt you."

"Does he scare you?" I ask, leaning closer to her.

"Yeah, he does sometimes if he's angry, but I'm used to it. You're not around our kind a lot, are you?"

"No, never." I shake my head, finding this new information interesting.

"She was always near humans," my sister says, like she hated it. I glare at her, and she shrugs. "It's true."

"There's nothing wrong with that," I protested.

"No, but being surrounded by them is why you don't know any of this. You wouldn't be shocked if you hung out with us more."

"They hated me!" I shout.

"No, they didn't. They were afraid of you! They felt the strength of your powers, and they didn't like being around you, but you didn't even give them a chance to get to know you."

Stella nods, "They probably wanted to bow but didn't because they thought you were a nobody and didn't respect you. You do feel like a royal."

"Then why haven't you ever told me?"

"I've tried telling you, but you always roll your eyes and change the subject." Okay, that does sound like something I would do.

"Okay, but if I do feel royal, as you say, why doesn't Luna feel royal? I mean, yeah, we have different dads, but to be a strong royal, the way you're saying, both parents would need to be full royals, right?"

"Well, actually, yes." Stella frowns, looking at Luna, and it seems like she's looking for something, staring deep into her soul. "I don't sense anything in her. Did your mother ever discuss family history? Anything?"

I thought about it for a few minutes. She never mentioned her family. Actually, come to think of it, she never talked about her past before me being born.

"No, never, I have never met her side of the family. I just know my father's family worked for a royal family, but Prince Gabriel's parents attacked the castle, killing everyone to steal the crown. The only two survivors were my father and his sister, and now my father works for Prince Gabriel."

"I find it strange that they killed everyone except your father and his sister." Stella stands, walking to the window, playing with her short hair.

"That's why he took her death as badly as he did. She was all he had left."

"His sister was evil. My father forgave her for stealing, and she paid us back by murdering our mother," she hisses angrily. "She deserved it."

"Wait, a moment, I knew she stole from your father, but I never knew she was the witch that murdered your mom!" Why didn't Azrael tell me? He had to have known.

"Have you seen Azrael?" I ask one of the guards. It's nearly midnight and I haven't seen him all day. I can't fall asleep knowing he might still be angry about this morning.

"Yes, Princess Isabella. Please, follow me." He turns, walking down the hall.

"Please, just call me Isabella," I say as I follow him, but he doesn't reply.

Alrighty then...

"How's your night going?" I try making conversation, as we head down a flight of stairs one I've never even noticed, but to be fair, I haven't explored much.

He doesn't even reply. Duly noted, guards aren't very talkative.

He stops in a long, dark hall, gesturing down it with his hand. "Prince Azrael and his company are down the hall to the left." He bows before turning and leaving. His company? This late at night. My heart leaps in my chest.

Don't think like that. He'd never cheat on me; he's nothing like Gabriel.

Right?

I creep down the hall when I hear laughter. My shoulders relax; it sounds like a bunch of guys laughing. He probably has a few friends over. I get closer, finding the door wide open.

"She's fucking hot, man. I saw her earlier exploring the gardens, and I have to say you're damn fucking lucky."

"Thanks, man. I know I am." Azrael's reply makes me grin widely. I should leave and let him be with his friends. I turn to go, but the next words out of the man's mouth stop me.

"If you ever wanna share, let me know. That ass is delectable."

"What the fuck did you say?" Azrael snaps.

"Hey, it's not my fault. She's fucking hot, don't shoot a man for trying!" Everyone laughs.

"If I ever hear you talking about her like that again, you're dead, friend or not." The laughter dies, and there's a long, very awkward silence. I hear Azrael asking for a refill.

"I think you had enough to drink, sir."

"How dare you disrespect me?" Azrael hisses.

"I apologize, sir—"

"Pour me another one, I won't ask again." Azrael cuts him off, not caring to hear the rest of his poor excuse of an apology.

"It's sad that you need to be this intoxicated to lie in bed with a *witch*. Even a hot one." My heart clenches painfully at the disgust in the man's voice. A loud bang makes me jump, and someone is thrown into the hall. I see a man in a tuxedo slump down the wall, landing on the floor in front of me, and Azrael steps into the hall, lifting the man by the throat.

He hasn't noticed me yet.

The man in front of me is not the man I came to know, not the man who holds me at night, whispering sweet things in my ear. No, this is the ruthless, brutal, heartless prince everyone claims him to be.

"Azrael," I shout. He looks over his shoulder, and there's a murderous look in his eyes. "Let him go."

"What are you doing down here?" his voice low and deadly. "Stay out of this."

The man looks at me with a pleading look, wanting me to help him. "Let him go, Azrael."

"Fine," he smirks, slamming his fist into the man's chest, ripping his heart out before dropping his lifeless body on the floor. I gasp, covering my mouth with a shaky hand. "There, happy now?" I start backing away.

I turn, rushing down the hall. I can't be around him when he's acting like this, like a drunk psychopath. He starts laughing, it's dull, no humor to it. "Can't handle a little blood, baby?"

Why is he being so cruel? I know the man was disrespecting me, but I'm used to it, and he didn't deserve that.

I make it to our room, but before I can shut the door, Azrael slams a hand on it, keeping it open. He walks into the room, slamming the door closed behind him. Our relationship is filled with... madness, and it's overall toxic. He has me questioning my sanity.

"How could you do that to that poor man? Why are you being so cruel?"

He snorts. "He knew just like every-fucking-one else, I don't do well with disrespect, and I'm learning very quickly that I'm even worse when they disrespect you. No one disrespects you and gets away with it." He blocks me in a corner of the room. "And I'm a cruel man. I never acted like I wasn't. I'm just not cruel with you." He smirks.

He's right. He has never pretended not to be, and for some reason, my stomach tightens with desire. He coldheartedly killed that man simply for disrespecting me. He cups my face with his bloody hands.

I place my hands on his chest to push him away, when he pleads, voice filled with longing. "Please, don't push me away."

He says, "please…"

I realize that I want the toxicity of our relationship, I want to question my sanity. I crave his madness. I don't want normal.

"Why did you stay away from me all day?"

"I was angry with you. I know you don't like being bossed around, but you don't understand." He runs a hand down his face, looking away. "I can't handle the thought of you getting hurt; it pains me." Instead of pushing him away, I grab a fist full of his shirt, yanking him toward me, smashing my lips against his.

He groans against my lips, picking me up, pushing my back against the wall. "You know how hard it was to stay away from you all day? This obsession I have with you is going to be the death of me." He rips my shirt in half, and the buttons fly in all directions. "Fuck, I need to bury my cock in you more than I need my next breath."

He reaches behind me, pulling my bra off before carrying me to the bed without removing his lips from mine, and sets me down on the edge of it. He pulls back, ripping my leggings off like he's in a hurry, but he slowly removes his clothes while his intense gaze drinks me in.

"My friends all want a piece of you because I've shared with them before." I shake my head, afraid of what he might say next. "Don't worry, baby. Not you, never you. You're mine. All mine." He mumbles as he wraps his hands around each of my ankles, throwing each one over his shoulders before brutally slamming his cock into me without warning. I cry at the burning sensation as I stretch open for him.

"Fuck," he groans, slamming his eyes shut and throwing his head back, and he bites his lower lip. I watch his throat muscles bob as he swallows. After savoring the sensation for a minute, he begins to pound mercilessly into me.

I stare at his face, twisting with desire as he watches my tits bounce. He licks his upper lip, and fuck, I can't take it anymore. I need those lips on me. I sit up, slipping my legs off his shoulders, gripping the back of his head as I wrap my legs around his hips, and I press my lips to his.

His assault on my pussy never once wavers as his arms wrap around me, gripping the back of my neck and the other gripping my lower back, keeping me tight against him.

"This tight little pussy is mine."

"Azrael," I moan, feeling myself pulsate around his cock. I scream his name against his mouth as my orgasm takes control and waves of intense pleasure smash into me.

"Holy fucking shit," he groans, quickening his pace. "I'm gonna cum so fucking deep in your pussy." Then, he does.

Chapter 30

BELLA

I stand here getting more annoyed by the minute. The seamstress has poked me with the damn pen for the millionth freaking time! She keeps telling me to hold still, so that I don't get poked, but I'm feeling on edge, and I can't help the fidgeting.

It's been ten days since Azrael killed that man for disrespecting me, and every day has been perfect. Except for the last three days, I haven't seen Azrael; hell, I haven't even heard his voice. He's been off preparing for the ball. They even managed to get a map of the place. I only know this because Stella has been relaying this information to me.

Azrael is supposed to be back tomorrow. This is another reason I'm so damn annoyed. This dress fitting is taking forever. All I want to do is go to bed because when I wake up, he should be here. However, the ball is tomorrow night, so she needs to do the final touches.

Stella is getting annoyed with me. I keep asking her if she's heard from him, and she keeps saying no each time.

She also told me this is normal; whenever he's distracted like this, he falls off the planet. No one hears from him, and the only reason she even knows what's going on is because of their dad. I guess we're meeting them at the ball, which is on Halloween.

What I don't understand is why he hasn't come to see me. I mean, he can literally teleport and be here in less than a minute! Like he doesn't have five damn minutes to spare for his mate! I'd be happy with a fucking phone call!

"Alright, no more pouting or whining over my brother!" Stella walks in with her long, silk green dress. It's simple but beautiful. The dress has a slit on the right leg that runs all the way up her thigh and a halter top, which has a very low-cut neckline.

I look at myself in the mirror. I have on the most beautiful gown I've ever seen, it's totally me. It's sleeveless with black lace. It also has a slit, but mine is all the way up to my hip, showing off my entire right leg. The best part is the see-through lace corset. Plus, I have a matching black lace mask.

It covers half my face. You can see my jawline and lips. I'll be wearing red lipstick, so I look sexy and mysterious. Luna isn't coming, which she's pretty pissed about.

"We're going to get our nails done!" Luna jumps into the room behind Stella. I look away from my reflection. Well, at least that'll take my mind off of him.

"Alright, I'm in." They both jump up and down excitedly, and I roll my eyes. "Let's get this dress off," I say to the seamstress. She nods and starts removing the dress.

An hour later, we're in the back seat of an SUV, and there's two guards in front. I guess we can't leave without them, or more like *I* can't leave without them because of Azrael.

"We don't need babysitters!" Stella pouts, slumping in her seat. She and I threw a huge fit when they manhandled us into the backseat. "Just wait till Azrael hears you put your hands on Bella!" My head snaps to look at her. Wow, really? She's using me.

"We apologize, but Prince Azrael is the one who told us to use force if you threw a fit. And told me to tell Princess Isabella to behave or he'll punish you." The driver has a large scar across his face, and he's the one who tried bleeding me dry.

I huff, crossing my arms around my chest. Azrael calls him but is too busy to call me.

"And you can tell him that I said bring it on!"

"Yeah!" Stella nods making Luna laugh.

Oh, and he let it slip that he's been watching me for the last few days. I guess he's been my very own silent bodyguard, making sure I never wander off the property.

"When did you talk to him?" I look at him, and he looks back at me through the rear-view mirror. He's already apologized to me for almost sucking me dry earlier.

"He called me an hour ago, asking me to accompany you into town."

"And how many times *exactly* have you talked to him since he left?" I lean forward, daring him to lie with my death glare. He clears his throat, shoulders tensing. I'm clearly making him super uncomfortable.

"He calls me every couple of hours to ask what you are doing."

"Are you fucking serious!" He flinches at my outburst.

"Yeah, like, what the fuck, Jeremy?" Stella shouts, I'm not really sure why that upset her, but I think she just wants an excuse to yell at him.

"Really, Jeremy? First, you try to bleed me dry, and now you're keeping *shit* from me!"

"I said I was sorry for that!" His hazel eyes widen.

"Prove it and give us some alone time!" Stella grins, bumping her shoulder to mine. The other guard, who hasn't said a word, looks at Jeremy.

"Yeah!" Luna jumps in.

"He'll kill me!"

"He'll never have to know. We won't say anything. Right, girls?" I ask, looking at the girls, and they both nod, but he shakes his head, clearly stressing. I'm starting to feel bad for ganging up on him.

We park in front of the salon and walk into the salon together. Jeremy follows us in while the other guard stands outside by the door.

It looks like they closed the salon for us. We get our nails done, all getting a French tip plus massages, and there's also champagne. It's pretty damn relaxing. I've never done something like this, but it's something I'd like to do more.

"What's next?" Luna asks, looking between Stella and me.

"Just watch and learn," Stella whispers, standing up.

"We need to pee," Stella says, walking toward Jeremy. "So, give us a moment to pee. I'm sure Azrael won't be pleased if you watched her use the bathroom since you know that involves her taking off her pants."

"Fine. You have a couple of minutes. I'll be right outside the door." We get up and head to the bathroom. The door shuts behind us, and Stella disappears around the corner for a second before popping her head back out.

"Come on, we don't have much time!" she whispers. Luna and I look at each other. I think this is a stupid idea, but I'm mad at Azrael, so I shrug. We step towards Stella, looking in the stall. She already has a window open. One by one, we jump out. We're in a back alleyway. There's a sign that says employees only.

We giggle, taking off. We don't stop running for another mile. Luna bends over with her hands on her knees, breathing hard.

"See why I tell you that you need to run more, Luna?"

"And get all sticky and sweaty? No thanks," Luna says, finally catching her breath.

"Agreed." Stella nods, and I shake my head at them.

"So, what's next?"

"We're going to the bar!" Stella starts walking down the road, and we follow her. Around the corner is a large bar, it doesn't look very busy. It's only nine, but that's okay. We're just here to have fun, not to meet people.

We walk in, going straight to the bar.

"So, Stella, are you seeing anyone?" I ask after ordering drinks. I don't know much about her.

"I wish. My ex and I broke it off because he's a close friend of Azrael's." She takes her shot, and we do, too. Yes, Luna is drinking, too. The bartender didn't ask for IDs, which is a good thing because I don't have mine at the moment.

"So, what? Azrael isn't happy about the relationship?"

"No, he doesn't even know about it. I broke up with him because he wanted to keep us a secret, I was okay with it at first, but I started to fall in love, so I backed off."

"Good. No one should be kept a secret," Luna says.

"Amen!" I agree, doing my second shot. "I would have just told Azrael."

"I couldn't. He begged me not to, he's afraid of losing his friendship with him. So, he let me go. That was a few months ago, so I'm still trying to move on."

"We'll find you some dick tonight!" Luna shouts with a grin.

"Luna!" I smack her shoulder.

"What? I didn't say for me, oh, Stella you should call Landon. He's hotter than sin itself. He'll be a yummy rebound." I look at her like she grew a third head. Is this my little sister?

"I mean, she's not wrong," Stella says between giggles. "But he has a thing for Bella."

"Well, she's taken. We just need him to pay attention to one of us. She can't keep all the hot ones."

"Still sitting right here, you guys! If you want him then call him. He knows I'm with Azrael even if I'm pissed at him."

"My brother is an ass so I can't really blame you." her phone vibrates. "Speak of the devil!" She grins, holding up the phone, and I read the word *asshole* on the screen.

Who's asshole? Azrael or Landon.

"Hello, dear brother of mine!" I jump up, putting my ear against the phone to hear what he's saying. When I hear his voice, my heart skips a beat, how can I miss him so much when he hardly misses me.

"Where the fuck did you take her?"

"Who are you talking about?" Stella says innocently.

"You know damn well who I'm talking about."

"Oh, she's busy right now, dancing, but I can tell her that you finally decided to call her. But you know she's pretty pissed at you for not calling her. So, she probably won't call you back."

"Dancefloor?" he yells. "Are there other men there? Wait is she dancing with someone?" He sounds hysterical, I cover my mouth to keep myself from laughing.

"She was dancing with a sexy beast the last time I saw her, but I haven't seen her in a while. Hmm, where did she go?" She stays quiet for a moment, tapping her chin with her index finger. "Oh, here she is and no longer dancing with the sexy beast."

"Can I get you ladies a drink?" a man asks behind us. Perfect timing!

"Who the fuck is that?" He roars; I didn't need to be close to the phone to hear that. Stella flinches, taking the phone away from her ear. She mutes her phone, saying no to the guy, and he walks off. She unmutes her phone.

"You want to buy Bella a drink? Yeah, she's free. Go buy her a drink and meet her on the dance floor."

"The fuck?" I hear him scream. "I'll kill him!"

"Damn, you want some sisterly advice? You really shouldn't leave a girl hanging for days. We get lonely, you know. Sorry bro, but it's loud, and we're pretty busy! Byeee!" I hear him scream her name, but she hangs up.

"That makes me feel so much better, but I really should get a phone."

"Agreed." Luna nods. Stella waves her hand, asking for more shots.

"Wait, what happens if he finds us?" I ask, swallowing nervously. Her phone keeps vibrating, and she keeps ignoring it.

"Eh, he won't. Don't worry so much! Here, drink some more!" I shrug; downing two more shots. Stella picks up the phone, calling someone.

"Who are you calling?" I ask, leaning against her.

"My ex."

"Ohhhh." Luna giggles, wiggling her brows.

"Hi!" She giggles when he answers. "I'm at a bar and I'm gonna let a man take me home tonight and dick me down," she puts her phone on speaker.

"The hell you are," a man growls into the phone. But she just laughs, hanging up.

"Asshole. We broke up and he still wants to control me! Well, fuck him. Come on, girls, I'm getting laid tonight!"

"Cheers! We're getting laid!" I shout.

"Not you," Stella points at me, and I pout, but she still yanks me toward the small dance floor. I'm drunk off my ass. We're the only ones dancing, but an hour later, more people start dancing with us.

We're having a blast, dancing with cute guys.

"Let's get out of here," a man mutters to Stella, but she shakes her head no and grabs Luna and me by our arms, pulling us off the dance floor, leading us outside.

"Sorry girls, I can't." she frowns, looking down.

"Can't what?" Luna asks leaning her head against my shoulder, looking exhausted.

"Sleep with someone else."

My heart feels sad for her. I know what she means. She's in love.

"It's okay, we understand." I grab her hand.

We call a cab, agreeing to sit outside as we wait for it. The doors to the bar open, and the men we were dancing with step out.

"We've been looking for you girls."

"We're not interested."

"We bought all of your drinks. You owe us."

"We owe you nothing." Stella narrows her eyes.

"Get the fuck out of here!" I turn to see the man who was with Landon that day at the pool standing behind us.

"Ross," Stella whispers. "How did you find us?"

"Let's go." He turns, walking towards a car. Luna and I jump in the back seat, and Stella starts to climb in behind us, but Ross stops her. "You're in front."

She swallows, and nods, going to sit in the passenger seat.

"What the fuck were you thinking, Stella?" Ross shouts as we start driving.

"Hey, don't talk to her that way! She can do whatever she pleases." Luna leans forward and my eyes widen.

"I'm done waiting for you. It's time for me to move on," Stella mumbles in a small voice.

"Fuck that," Ross growls.

"Excuse you?" Luna snaps, taking it personally.

"You can't tell her she can't move on!" I decide to get involved.

"You two need to stay out of this." Ross says, looking at us through the rearview mirror.

"No, she's our friend." I lift my chin without backing down.

"Yeah." Luna agrees, grabbing Stella's shoulder. He stays quit, hands tightening on the steering wheel.

"So, unless you want to tell Azrael about the two of you, she's going to move on, and we'll help her," Luna pushes.

"She's tired of waiting and I can't blame her, honestly. So, you need to decide what you want because you can't have it both ways," I snap.

We pull up to the gate. The guards must've recognize the car because the gates automaticity open. It looks like nothing had happened to the gates or the water fountain.

He parks, and I sigh in relief, I'm exhausted, nearly falling asleep on the way here. I move to open the car door, but it flings open with force. I groan in annoyance when I see who it is, can I not catch a break, Jesus.

He grabs my upper arm, yanking me out.

"Let go of me!" I growl, trying to pull my arm out of his grip.

"What the hell were you thinking?" He snaps, getting in my face, lightly shaking me.

"Leave me alone, Azrael!" I turn away, storming inside. "You can go back to wherever you've been the last few days because I don't want you here!"

I stomp my way upstairs, hoping he leaves me alone, I need sleep. I get to the room, and I try to slam the door shut behind me, but he stops it, forcing his way in.

"Leave!" I shove his chest angrily.

"Why the fuck are you so angry?"

"I said *leave*!"

"Did he touch you?" He ignores me, gripping my face with one hand, squeezing my cheeks, forcing me to look up at him. I bared my teeth at him, my blood boiling.

"You know what? Yeah, he did! While we were dancing his hands were all over me!" I stumble forward as he disappears.

Shit...

Chapter 31

I wake up with a groan, my head is pounding, urgh! I've never been hungover before. I have always known my limit, stopping before I get drunk. I rub my forehead as I look at the clock on the nightstand. It's only five a.m.

I grab a pillow, pushing it against my face, I feel like absolute shit!

Never *ever* again.

I just need more sleep. I roll onto my stomach, closing my eyes, but the pounding in my head hurts too freaking bad; I can't even get comfortable. My brows slam together. How did I even get to bed?

The last thing I remember is shouting at Ross about something and...

Oh no, Azrael. He was mad... very mad.

"Shit... fucking shit!" I groan, sitting up, and the room spins. I need a glass of water and maybe something to relieve the pain, which probably won't happen because vampires don't need Advil or pain relievers.

I blink a few times, trying to clear my blurry vision. I see a glass of water on the nightstand and two pills beside it. I smile, knowing exactly who put these here, immediately feeling guilty about last night. I was in the wrong, but it doesn't mean that I'm still not pissed. He still ignored me for days.

I grab the pills, swallowing them down with water. In the bathroom, I turn on the sink faucet, leaning down to splash my face with cold water.

I straighten my back, looking in the mirror, my heart leaps as I let out a high-pitched scream when I see Azrael standing behind me. I spin around, smacking his chest for scaring the crap out of me.

"God! Give me some type of damn warning next time. I almost had a freaking heart attack." He just stares at me with predator, angry eyes. Reminding me of how he used to stare at me in the beginning. He's angry? He has no right to be.

But, fuck, why does he have to be so damn sexy? Nope. I have to remind myself that I'm still angry.

Don't have sex with him...

He doesn't deserve me.

I huff, spinning around, walking out of the bathroom.

Asshole!

I open the bedroom door, wanting to leave, before I say something I regret. But before I even take my first step, Azrael picks me up, slamming the door shut before throwing me on the bed.

I punch the bed with my fist, before sitting up, I open my mouth about to give him a piece of my mind when he pushes me back down and grabs both of my wrists, pinning them above my head. I narrow my eyes, giving him the meanest look I can muster.

"Let go of me!" I shout as I try wiggling my way out of his grip.

"You have been a very naughty girl, and naughty girls don't get what they want."

"I'm not playing your stupid games, Azrael! I'm so mad at you, I don't even want to see you right now." My body slumps against the mattress, knowing damn well I can't fight him off and look away from him.

"Why the fuck are you mad at me?" He pinches my chin, forcing me to look at him.

"You up and left without even saying bye, not even a note! You were just gone! You didn't even pick up the phone to call me to explain or anything!"

"I was busy."

"Yeah, so busy that you called Jeremy every few hours to find out what I was doing. You never once asked to talk to me, didn't come to see me even for a couple of minutes!"

"You missed me?" He smirks, looking cocky.

"Yeah, I guess so, but you didn't miss me."

"Why would you say that?" He frowns, looking confused.

"Didn't you hear anything I just said!" I'm on the verge of freaking out, growing more and more frustrated with this man.

"I came back every night, and each time you were already asleep. I watched you for a couple of hours, kissing these sinful lips before leaving." His thumb brushes my lower lip, eyes filling with desire.

"Okay. Well, why didn't you call?"

He smirks, eyes sparkling with amusement. "There's no cell phone service where we were."

"So, how'd you call Jeremy?" I arch a brow, catching him in a lie.

"You need to learn, my love." He shakes his head. "My security and I did a blood ritual with a witch; it allows us to communicate with each other through our minds. Same as the werewolves in how they communicate with their pack members. And it wasn't as easy as popping in and out like I do here. It takes a lot of energy to come and go." I press my lips together, looking away, feeling embarrassed. I do need to learn more.

I've been mad for nothing.

"Okay, so where were you? Why did it take so much energy?" I say in a low voice, looking back at him. Fuck, I missed him. I want to touch him, but he still has my hands captured over my head.

"The underworld." I gasp, my lips and eyes widen in shock. It's nearly impossible to come and go, even for demons.

"What, why?"

"I needed to see Dimitri."

"Like *the* Dimitri, the one with the hellhounds?" Dimitri is very well known. He's a freaking badass and a completely crazy demon. And his mate, Rosa, is also pretty badass.

I've always wanted to meet her. I'd seen photos of them once, and let me tell you, he's a hottie! He can have anyone crawling on their hands and knees, doing whatever he wants. Yes, including me.

I've always prayed a man like that would come into my life, willing to do anything for me like he does for Rosa.

And I guess that did happen, didn't it?

I have my very own Dark Prince Charming.

"Why did you say that like he's the most amazing man on earth?" he grumbles.

"Because he is. He's strong, sexy as hell, and a fucking badass! Rosa is so lucky," I mumble breathlessly.

"You're mine!" he rumbles darkly, chest vibrating as he pushes his hips against mine. Then it clicks, he's jealous.

"I know that! I feel the same about you. Except I find you even sexier, no one compares to you. When I first saw you, all I wanted to do was rip off my clothes and let you have your wicked way with me. I have never been so attracted to a man like I am with you."

"Is that right?" He buries his face in my neck, grinding slightly into me.

"Yes, my heart skips a beat every time I see you." I all but moan.

"Every single time I see you, you take my breath away. You are so beautiful, stunning, sinfully so, and sassy as fuck. I have never felt this way before. You scare me, and I have never been afraid of anything before. I'm completely obsessed with you," he says as he runs a single finger down my face, over my lips. "But you're still going to receive your punishment."

"Pun... punishment?" I gasp. "For *what*?"

"For allowing another man to touch what belongs to me," he snarls, gripping my neck. "And sneaking away like a naughty girl."

I whimper, shaking my head.

"Oh yes." He nods, smirking evilly, making me nervous. I swallow hard, even though I know he'd never hurt me.

He jumps up, stepping away from the bed, not once looking away from me. I try getting up, but I still can't move my hands. I tilt my head back, looking at my hands, shrieking. "Azrael!" My hands are tied to the headboard.

Using his vampire speed, he rips off my clothes until I'm completely naked. He straightens, looking at his handiwork with lust-filled eyes, and he mumbles to himself, "Fucking perfection." I think that's what he says, at least.

He slowly removes his clothes, his heated gaze on my naked flesh. "Did I tell you how fucking much I missed the feeling of that pussy squeezing my cock?" His voice is low with desire, making me moan.

My body heats, shivering underneath his intense gaze. "No. Why don't you show me?" I moan, and he growls, exposing his cock to me. I lick my lips, feeling excitement bubble up inside me. He pushes my thighs apart, slipping in between them.

"I need to touch you, please," I whimper. "Take off the cuffs. I'm sorry."

"Fuck, it's hard to deny you, but this is your punishment. I'm going to keep pushing you to the edge of ecstasy, but I won't allow you to fall."

Chapter 32

AZRAEL

I watch my naughty little witch squirm, pleading for me to give in, but she won't be having any release tonight.

She arches her back, moaning my name, and my gaze snaps up to hers. I watch as she licks her lips. I pull away, looking between her parted legs, and I groan as my gaze runs over her sweet pussy. It's swollen, glistering with wetness, making my cock jump in excitement.

I lean down in between her thighs, slowly licking her achy clit. I groan as I taste her; she tastes so fucking good, better than anything I've ever had. I'll never get enough; it's my new addiction. My tongue laps hungrily against her, circling her clit, devouring her hungrily. Her hips lift off the mattress, trying to get more friction, but my hands grip her hips, pushing her back down. I'm in charge.

I lower my mouth, sucking her clit into my mouth, feasting on her as I push two fingers in her tight pussy. Fuck, this is going to be harder than I thought.

I don't know if I can bring myself to stop. Why am I punishing myself?

I start pumping my fingers in and out. She starts wiggling, making sexy little sounds and whimpers. It's music to my ears, the sweetest little melodies I've ever heard.

Her pussy starts pulsating around my fingers, and I can tell she's about to fall into a deep hole of ecstasy. I sadly have to pull out before she orgasms.

"Why are you stopping? I was so, *so* fucking close!" she cries out, completely frustrated.

"It's your punishment for being a naughty little witch."

"*Please.*" She pouts, eyes full of desperation.

"No, you were very naughty last night." I groan as I suck on the two fingers that were fingering her. Why does she have to taste so fucking delicious?

"I promise to be good. To be your good, little witch. Just please..." she pleads as she lifts her hips. My gaze drops to her perky tits when they bounce as she thrusts her hips up.

I groan; she's making this extremely hard on me. I lean down, my tongue circling her hard nipple, while my fingers roll her other nipple.

Her hips start rubbing against my cock, forcing a growl out of me. My control is about to snap. This was supposed to last all night, but I can't do it. She's too fucking tempting. I jump off her, stalking angrily into the bathroom, slamming the door shut. I turn on the cold water, taking a much-needed shower.

I grip my cock and start stroking, closing my eyes as I picture her on her knees sucking me deep in her throat as she stares up at me with those large innocent eyes filling up with tears and, fuck...

I release a grunt as I cum in my hands.

She screams my name angrily in the other room, making me grin. I open the bathroom door, stepping into the room, not bothering to look at her, as I head to the closet, throwing on some clothes.

"I'll be back later," I say over my shoulder as I leave our room with her still naked, tied to my bed.

I head straight to the bar, desperately needing a drink. I sit down after pouring myself some whiskey, trying to relax.

I left a few days ago to ask Dimitri for help. He said no at first, but Rosa forced him to help us because they were in the same type of trouble last year. After batting her lashes at him, he melted and agreed. I know exactly how he felt because I would've done the same for Bella.

He's coming to the ball, and he's going to help me stop Prince Gabriel. Dimitri also hates the man, but I honestly think Dimitri hates a lot of people. His trusted circle is tighter than mine.

The sun starts rising, and I decide to relieve my mate from her punishment. Fuck, I can't wait to relieve her, fucking her until we both fall into ecstasy.

I smirk, getting up and rushing upstairs with excitement running through me.

When I get to the room, my smirk widens as I open the door, walking in, but when I look at the bed, she's gone.

My heart sinks.

Did she get out of the ropes alone? No, she would've come looking for me. I step deeper into the room, taking a deep inhale, and I smell someone else's scent.

None that I recognized...

Chapter 33

BELLA

I start waking up, feeling completely dazed. I fell asleep after screaming for Azrael for what seemed like hours. I'm so freaking mad at him. How dare he leave me tied up and naked! I'm going to kill him! My wrists literally went numb!

At least he let me loose sometime after I fell asleep.

I try rolling to my side, but someone grips my knees, spreading my legs open. I open my eyes, but it's still dark. I can't see anything but outlines. I blink, trying to adjust, looking down to see the shape of Azrael kissing my inner thigh; I moan at the feather-light kisses. His kisses were usually rougher, but maybe he's apologizing, taking his time.

Or he was still teasing me for being a naughty girl. I won't lie, I kind of liked it.

I arch my back, lifting my hips, begging for more. "Please," I whimper. He gives me what I want, lapping my clit like he's a starving man. His tongue feels so good, but not like last night. I pinch my brows together. Why does it feel so different?

I grind my hips against his mouth, trying to get more, to get what I need from him. Why is he being so gentle? I need him to devour me like last night.

He releases a groan as his fingertips brush against my nipples, lightly pinching them, and rolling them. I whimper in annoyance.

I need more; I need his roughness.

He gently and slowly pushes his fingers into me, slowly fingering me, and curling his fingers. It feels good, but not the same, not mind-blowing. He's doing a great job torturing me! I'm ready to get down on my knees and beg for his forgiveness.

"Faster, please," I plead, I can't take it anymore. He thankfully shoves another finger in, moving them faster, while sucking my clit, his other hand still rolling my nipple.

"Yesss!" Now we're getting somewhere.

His lips start traveling up my body, stopping at my breasts, giving each nipple a soft kiss. My hands grip his hair as he kisses my lips. I can taste myself on him.

But something is different, something is off. His hair feels different, and his lips feel smaller. My gut twists in horror.

"Azrael?" I question against his lips, pulling as far back as I can against the mattress, trying to look at his face, but I can't see. He pulls back slightly, opening his eyes.

No...

No.

Blue, his eyes are icy blue not ocean blue like Azrael's. I screech in horror as my hands push against his chest, trying to push him off me as I shake my head. Horror clawing my throat, making it hard to breathe.

What the fuck is happening?

"No *mate,*" he spits in pure disgust. "Never say his name again; you're mine. Goodness, baby, you taste so damn good. I can't wait till you're wrapped around my dick. Baby, this body is definitely made for me. Best damn body I've ever seen," he mumbles, looking down my body.

"Get off me!" I cry, pushing his chest. He just laughs at me. I taste acid in my throat, I swallow, trying hard not to throw up, oh my god! I let him do all of those things to me.

How the fuck did I get here?

"Don't act like that didn't feel good, don't act like you don't like this."

I growl as my horror turns to anger. I'm sick of this! I call to my magic, feeling my flames heat my body, running through my veins. I smile at the sensation.

I watch as his eyes widen in horror as he sees my eye color change to the same color as my flames. The flames cover my hands that are against his chest, and he hisses as they burn his flesh.

I push my flames into him, and he's thrown back, hitting the wall, crumbs of drywall drop on him. I grab the blanket, wrapping it around my body as I stand, one hand clenching the blanket together, the other out in front of me. Flames dancing around my hand, ready to strike.

The lights flicker on, and I see Marisol standing there, watching in horror. Gabriel groans as he slowly stands. His body left a hole in the wall.

He looks at me, and I shiver in disgust. I let him touch me. I still can see my wetness glistering on his mouth, evidence of what just happened. I blast flames at him, but this time he's ready and quickly responds by lifting his hands, creating a shield between him and the flames. I growl; I need both of my hands.

Fuck it.

I let the blanket drop down my body, lifting my other hand, pushing more flames toward him. I roll my hands together as if holding a ball and slowly push them toward each other, creating force against his shield.

"Didn't I tell you to pack your shit?" Gabriel hisses, looking away from me, his eyes harden. My brows furrow, not knowing what he means.

"You don't mean that," Marisol whimpers.

"I don't need you anymore. *Leave,*" he says, looking back at me, and his gaze softens. "Please don't leave again," his voice laced with pain. And just like that, I sort of feel bad for him. I'm his mate, too. Even though I want Azrael, it doesn't mean Gabriel isn't hurting from my choice. "I won't let you leave again."

I drop my flames, frowning, picking up the blanket and wrapping it around me.

"Gab..." Marisol cries. I look over at her to find her crying.

"I need her! Not you, what don't you understand? Now leave," he snaps at her without looking away from me. "Don't hide from me. I've already seen everything. I rescued you from him! He had you tied to that bed naked; I'll treat you better than that, I swear on it."

"I don't want to stay. I want to go back." I say in my sweetest voice, begging him to understand as I blink back the tears that threaten to escape. I look around for an escape route, but they're all blocked. I feel like a caged animal.

"I knew I couldn't get you to stay willingly. I have leverage to keep you here with me." He walks towards the front of the bed and picks up his pants. He reaches into his pocket, pulling his cell phone out, his fingers quickly tapping the phone screen. I step back, but my back hits the wall.

I fist my hands, my fingernails digging into my palm. I start feeling scared. What does he have that'd make me stay?

"Hello," I hear a raspy male voice through the speaker.

"Do it," Gabriel says as his eyes met mine, and I swallow hard. I look at Marisol, but her gaze is stuck on Gabriel.

I hear a loud scream, making my heart leap. I jump forward, eyes bouncing between him and the phone. "Who... Wh- what's going on?"

"I have your little sister here with Damion, who will torture her if you even try to escape or leave me."

"Please stop!" I hear Luna's voice cry out; her voice laced with pain and exhaustion.

"Luna!" I run to Gabriel, ripping the phone out of his hand. "You touch her again and I'll kill you!" I scream into the phone, and Damion starts chuckling darkly. I hear a crack and Luna cries out again, making my eyes fill with tears, unable to stop them. I feel so useless.

"You can stop now, Damion. I think our message is loud and clear." He grabs the phone out of my hand, tossing it on his bed. My legs give out, and my body crumbles onto the floor. Marisol runs to me, wrapping her arms around me.

"How dare you! I never thought you were this evil!" she screams at Gabriel.

"I did what I had to. So, I can keep her here with me; I'll do anything. I'm sorry, Bella, I didn't want it to be this way. I hate that I'm hurting you, but you're mine. Did you honestly think I'll let you be with someone else? I'll do whatever it takes. One day, you'll realize that." He kneels in front of me, trying to grab my face. I flinch back, but he forcefully grabs it with his hands, making me look at him. This man is so beautiful, but there is so much evil lurking underneath.

"Why would you want someone who already loves someone else?" I scream. "I'll never want you! You can't keep Luna locked up forever! I'll leave the first chance I get!"

"It doesn't matter if you love him; you're here with me. If I have to keep her locked up forever, I will! You are mine. You hear me! You'll never leave me again!" he growls, violently shaking my head. "Don't make me call Damion again! I'm sure he'd love to strip her down and take her innocence." His smirk is evil, and boy, do I want to punch the smirk right off his face!

"Don't, please, don't let him touch her," I whimper. I'll do anything. Whatever he wants.

"Good girl." He leans in, kissing me softly, and I let him, but I don't kiss him back. "Marisol, get her cleaned up and ready for the ball tonight. We'll be announcing you as my queen this evening, isn't that wonderful?"

"But..." Marisol begins, but he cuts her off.

"Shut up and do as I say, or you'll be banished."

"Yes, of course." She looks down at her hands. He walks out of the room, and a minute later, she turns to me, grabbing my hands. "I'm so sorry," she whispers.

"It's not your fault. We need to find Luna and find a way out of here," I mumble, wiping my face clean as I look at her.

"We can't. It won't be nearly as easy as before. She's locked away tight." She shakes her head. "I even tried to check on her for you, but I can't even get past. The only people who are allowed down there are Damion and Gabriel. Plus, the castle is heavily guarded."

"Azrael will be attending the ball. He'll get us out." I nod. "And you are coming with us." She just nods, and I get up to take a bath. I need to listen to him for now to keep them away from Luna.

How did he get into Azrael's castle? And leave with two women? It's heavily guarded... Unless someone on the inside helped him.

But who?

I wasn't there long enough to meet anyone to point blame at. I just know Darren, Stella, Landon, and Ross. They all had easy access to the castle, but I can't picture any of them doing this. I mean, Ross is an ass, but you can tell he cares about Stella too much to betray her, right?

It had to be someone else. Jeremy? It has to be him. He has been watching me to keep me safe, but Azrael trusts him enough to be around me, and he seems nice enough; he went out of his way to get me to forgive him. Where was he when we were taken? He was always near one of us. He's a strong vampire. There's no way Gabriel could get past him with two women. Unless he helped him.

I thought I'd grown on him once he found out that I'm Azrael's mate, but maybe it was just a front, and maybe he doesn't think I'm princess material, which I agree with, but that's a good reason for him to want to get rid of me.

I get out of the bath, stand in front of the large mirror. There's bruising on both of my wrists and bruises on my upper thighs.

Did Gabriel do this? No, he's too gentle, a little too gentle. It had to have been Azrael; he's always rough, just the way I like it. I bite my lower lip, touching my mate mark.

Crying won't do any good

I keep telling myself, but it doesn't stop the tears running down my face.

Marisol runs into the bathroom with a large smile on her face.

"A close friend of mine is working as the guard in the dungeon tonight. He'll let me in and help me sneak her out, but we won't get far on foot. You said Prince Azrael will be coming?" I nod. "Will he help us escape?"

"Yes, without a doubt."

"You have to go along with everything he says. Once he comes to escort you to the ball, I will get your sister, but everything else is on you."

Freaking wonderful!

Chapter 34

AZRAEL

A couple of hours earlier

I pace back and forth in my office. It's been two hours and fifteen minutes since I found Bella missing, and not just her, but Luna is missing as well. I have a feeling that Prince Gabriel did this. She's his mate as well. Of course, he wants her. I just thought that was the reason he invited us tonight to get his filthy hands on her.

He wanted our guards down, letting us think he wouldn't attack till we got to the ball. Damn, it's smart, and I feel stupid doing exactly what he wanted by letting my guard down.

And I tied her to my bed, making it easy for him to grab her. I swallow the lump forming in my throat, remembering her screaming my name. Was she screaming for me to help her, and I just ignored her?

Fuck!

I throw my glass against the wall.

Sitting down, I run my fingers through my hair, and that's when I feel it, the pain in my gut… I growl loudly… There's no fucking way.

I can feel her pleasure.

She's fucking him!

I roar loudly, standing up and throwing my desk across the room, it smashes against the window, and the glass shatters into pieces. Landon runs into the room.

"What the fuck, man?" He looks at me, then to the window, walking towards it, the glass crackles beneath his feet as he looks out of the broken window. "You threw your damn desk out of the window?"

I clench my teeth together, feeling the pleasure that she's feeling, and I roar again, not able to contain my emotions. My heart squeezes painfully in my chest at the thought of him touching her.

She said she picked me…

Without a word, I walk out of the room.

"Where the fuck are you going?" he asks, following me.

"I'm going to kill him."

"Kill who?"

"Fucking Prince Gabriel, who fucking else?!" I snap.

"No, you know it's best to wait till the ball. Only a couple more hours." Another wave of pleasure runs through my body, making me stop dead in my tracks. My monster will take over soon.

How dare she fuck him!

How dare she let him touch her!

She's mine!

I roar once more, and this time, the ground shakes beneath our feet.

"What's going on here?" I look up, meeting my father's gaze, snapping my teeth at him in warning as I push past him.

"I don't know, he won't tell me." I hear Landon behind me.

"Tell me what's going on. Now." I stop to stare at him. How dare he demand me? I see Stella run into the hall, looking worried. She heads straight to me, and I snarl at her, making her flinch.

"She's fucking him! I can feel her pleasure!" I spit out, feeling another wave, this one is the most intense, making me fall to my knees. I growl out loudly, punching the floor. The tile cracks underneath the force of my fist.

"Oh no..." I hear Stella gasp. She drops to her knees, slowly crawling towards me. She reaches out like she is approaching a wild animal.

I let her come close to me, and she wraps her arms around me. I grab her and hug her tight to me.

The next wave crashes into me with a mixture of emotions: confusion, hurt, and then pain. She's horrified.

What the fuck is going on?

Did she decide she doesn't want me? Did she finally see that she is too good for me? Did she leave me willingly?

"We'll get her back." Stella rubs my back in small circles, making a light humming sound just like Mom used to when she tried calming us down.

"She left me. She doesn't want me," I seethe angrily. I'm masking my sadness with anger. Maybe she ran after what I did last night. Maybe tying her up was too harsh, and she left me for it.

I need to go and beg for her forgiveness.

"She wouldn't do that," Stella says in such a soft, soothing voice. I've never in my life felt like this, never felt the urge to cry, but I'm so close to breaking down.

"She did. She left me."

"We'll go and ask her ourselves." I just nod, taking a deep breath, standing up, and walking away without another word. I head straight to my room, sitting on the edge of our bed. Her scent is still so strong, wrapping around me. She found out I'm a monster, and now she wants nothing to do with me.

I can feel my monster trying to claw his way out. I keep him at bay, but I know what he's thinking, what he wants.

If we can't have her, neither can he.

I will kill him and then chain her up. Forcing her to stay with me until I can prove myself to her.

She will be mine even if I have to force her to be...

I get up, going down to the dungeons where we used to imprison vampires. We haven't used it in a while. I walk into the guard's old office. It's dark in here, but when my eyes adjust to the darkness, I look around. I find what I'm looking for, the chains are covered in dust and dirt. I pick them up and the screws that go with them.

They're the best of the best. They can even hold down werewolves. Not even magic can break through them. Perfect for *my* witch. I grab the keys that unlock the chains and nod. This will do.

Am I a psychopath? Yeah, maybe. Some people might call me that, but I call it love. If that makes me a psychopath, then so be it.

As I walk back to my room with the large chains dragging behind me, everyone I pass openly stares, eying the large chains.

I look around my room, looking for the perfect place. I find one on her side of our bed, I drop to my knees, to get to work. I hammer the bolts into the hardwood floors. Once that's done, I wrap the cuff around my ankle and I walk around first to the closet and then to the bathroom, into the shower and bathtub. Good, it's long enough to walk around the whole room.

I hate that it came to this. I never thought I'd do something like this. Hell, my close friend, the fey prince, did this when a woman he was obsessed with rejected him. She was human, and yes, she's a very pretty woman. He met her at an event, and he grew obsessed with her at first sight. I thought he was in-fucking-sane, but now I understand.

I look at the Rolex on my left wrist, and it's time to get ready. Time to get my woman. I head to the bathroom, grabbing my hair gel so I can slick back my hair. I shave, clean my face, and then go to the closet, putting on one of my all-black tailored suits.

After putting on my leather shoes, I head down to meet everyone. They're all standing there. Darren is in a black suit as well, but with a white under-shirt matching my father's suit and my sister has on a green silk long gown with a slit.

"Ready?" I ask, feeling impatient.

"Yes, brother, we are, and I must say, you clean up nicely." She smiles, looping her arm around mine.

"Landon, Jeremy, Dimitri, and a man named Caspian are already there," my father says. I nod at them. They all touch me, and I teleport us.

We land at the back of the castle, where they held their parties and events, etc.

We walk inside, and it's already packed, mostly witches and warlocks, it seems like, but there are other creatures here, mostly the royal families.

I spot Lucien, the fey Prince, and Anastasia, yes, the woman he held hostage. I walk over to them, and they greet me by kissing my cheeks. Lucien is dressed similarly to me, and Anastasia is in a bright red sleeveless dress with a corset that lifts her breasts nicely, showing off her curvy body, with a long slit on the right leg. I have always thought she was stunning and understood Lucien's obsession with her. But that was before Bella, and now I find her looks dull.

"Something rather important is going on. He wants every royal family to be a part of this. Honestly, I'm pretty pissed that my father made me come to this shit," Lucien snarls. He's a fucking asshole but definitely powerful. I'd never want to get on his bad side, but most of my close friends are.

"Oh, shut it, Lucien, you're only saying that because you want to spend all night in bed! It's nice to go out sometimes. Let's enjoy it, mi amor. We'll have some alone time later." She kisses his jawline and then winks at him. They're always like this, teasing each other, but no one ever talks to Lucien the way she does.

I never knew why he let her talk to him with attitude and disrespect until Bella. She gets away with that smart mouth and disrespect, and she's the only one who could.

"You're lucky I even let you out of the house wearing that dress. Behave, or we're leaving." He sounds possessive as hell, but that's not shocking. Honestly, I'm also surprised that she's out wearing that dress. He never lets her out wearing clothes that are too revealing. She enjoys winding him up, though.

"I'm only here to kill that bastard," I say casually as I look around, searching for my mate.

"Kill him? What the heck are you talkin' about, man?" I look back at Lucien.

"Exactly what I said. He took my mate, and I'm here to get her back. I'll kill him for touching her," I snarl loudly. A few people nearby look over at us, but I ignore them. I haven't seen her or him yet.

"How do you know he has her, or that he even touched her?" Anastasia asks gently.

"Because she's his mate as well, and she went missing yesterday. I felt her pleasure when she was with him."

"Fuck man, that's fucking horrible. Feeling her pleasure with another man and fighting for your own mate. I wouldn't even give her a damn choice." He shakes his head, running a hand through his hair as if he were stressed just thinking about it.

"Seems to me like she chose him over you. Shouldn't you let her be?" Anastasia asks innocently, but I want to rip her tongue out for saying something so horrible. I growl at the thought, and Lucien wraps his arm around her waist protectively, tightly, pulling her against his body.

"Seriously? After what happened between us, do you think we're the type of men to just give up? You know, Azrael and I are a lot alike in that way. We won't stop till we get what we want unless someone kills us." He looks at me, smirking. "You want me to help you find the chains that I used for her and help you set up?"

"Already done." I smirk back at him. "Just so you know, Dimitri is here as well, and there's going to be a lot of blood spilled, my friend, if you want to leave, now is your chance." I need to warn him. He's the only one here whom I want to warn.

"And miss the fun? Nah, man." He looks down at Anastasia. "You probably should leave, beautiful."

"And miss the fun? Yeah, right, in your dreams, big man." She snorts, rolling her eyes, and her hand taps his chest. "Just so you know, even if at first, I hated him for keeping me trapped, I'm glad he did. I was running in the beginning because I was afraid of love." I nod at her before looking away, hoping this will have the same outcome.

I feel guilty as hell for doing this to Bella. I don't want to hurt her, but I don't see any other way, and I refuse to let her go.

I'll prove to her that I'm doing this for us and our love, and hopefully one day she'll see it my way. I'll show her how good I can treat her.

I'm a monster underneath, and she's the only one that can tame the beast, and I'll kill anyone who stands in my way.

"Ladies and gentlemen, here comes Prince Gabriel!" The speaker shouts with the sounds of trumpets. I huff at the ridiculous entrance, and Lucien snarks; Stella steps beside me, lightly touching my arm. I look down at her, and she nods to me. Good, everything is in place.

The doors at the top of the grand staircase open, and I see the man I will murder tonight. He walks out the door with a large, smug smile. The bastard is full of confidence. Right next to him is Markus. I snarl loudly, wanting to kill them, but I need to wait a little longer.

Shit, I promised Bella I wouldn't kill Marcus. Oh, fucking well, she'll get over it.

Where is she?

"Hello everyone!" Prince Gabriel speaks into a microphone, and everyone claps. "Thank you for coming! We have a celebration tonight! We are all here, so I can introduce you to my mate, Isabella, your new princess and the future queen!" Roars of excitement sound throughout the crowd, making my blood boil.

She is *mine*.

The doors open. The trumpets sounded once more, and I see her.

Everyone else seems to fade; she takes my breath away. She's always been beautiful, but tonight she looks like a true queen, not his queen, *my* queen.

She's wearing a tight gown with a long skirt that has two long slits showing off her sexy legs; the top is a low-cut V showing off her perfect tits going down almost to her naval. The dress is all black with gold beaded details. She has on a large golden crown, and her hair is up in a low bun with a few strands framing her face and neck.

I swallow the hard lump as I stare at her. My feelings are between anger and happiness that she is okay, except I see some bruises on her wrists. I can't remember if I gave those to her or not.

"Wow, Azrael," Anastasia says breathlessly, "I can see why both of you are fighting over her. She is truly stunning."

"Yeah, man. She's fucking stunning." Anastasia smacks his arm. "What? I just repeated what you said. You know I got eyes only for you, baby." He kisses her lips.

I stare into her eyes, and they look…

Scared?

Her chin is high, and her shoulders are back; she looks beautiful and confident. You wouldn't know she was scared unless you knew her. Her eyes quickly scan the floor.

She is almost to me, but then Prince Gabriel grabs her hand, pulling her closer to him, and his arm wraps around her waist. I see her eyes twist in pain. She quickly masks her pain and smiles widely.

My eyes narrow as I snarl. He's hurting her.

My heart swells. She didn't come willingly.

Chapter 35

BELLA

I stand on a large balcony looking down at so many important people from all different kinds of creatures. Gabriel told me his plan; he's going to kill Azrael and mark me soon after, since the only way to remove a mark from a mate is to kill the one who placed the mark. I anxiously start looking through the large crowd for Azrael, trying to send a message through my eyes, hoping he'll understand.

But before I can find him, I'm dragged backward. He wraps his arm around me, grabbing the exposed skin on my back, and he pinches my back, twisting hard, making me flinch. I quickly mask the pain with a smile.

I have to for Luna. I look up, placing my hand on Gabriel's chest to make him happy. I know Azrael is here. I feel his energy nearby. I start where I left off, looking for him, and after a few minutes, my eyes land on him. God, he takes my breath away. He looks stunning wearing a black suit with his hair slicked back. His ocean blue eyes are lethal, his anger radiating off him in waves. It leaves me breathless.

I look past him to see some of Gabriel's guards making their way through the crowd toward him. I nudge my head to the right a few times, trying to tell him, and he arches a brow in confusion.

For fuck's sake!

He's not understanding.

Gabriel grabs my chin, forcing me to look at him.

"He's dead," he whispers so lowly that I can hardly hear him. Fuck him, fuck this. Azrael is in danger, and they're creeping up on him quickly. Time for plan B: Marisol is downstairs with Luna, waiting for the signal.

The signal is going to be people screaming.

Hopefully, she's already there because it's happening before we both thought. I smile up at Gabriel, a man who looks like an angel, but he's the fucking devil.

My hand slowly trails down his arm, and I lick my lips seductively. I hate every second because I can feel Azrael's gaze burning into me.

"If he's that weak and can be killed that easily, then I don't want him," I whisper in Gabriel's ear. My lips graze his earlobe as I talk, sending shivers down his body. I see goose bumps rise on his skin.

My smile widens as my hands slowly trail up his chest. I usually don't like killing, but he has been a threat to everyone I love, and he took me twice without consent. I'm done being messed with. Plus, he's torturing my sister.

But I'm still hesitating.

I look over to Azrael, and his eyes are full of anger. He isn't paying any attention to the guards closing in on him. He's in danger, and so is Luna. I need to do this.

He's an evil person.

Fuck me, I don't know if I can do this.

Do it.

For Luna and Azrael.

I close my eyes before calling to my magic, so he isn't given any warning. My hands flare up with flames, and they dance their way to Gabriel's mouth. His eyes widen in shock when he feels the heat of them against his flesh. He doesn't even have a chance to fight back before they enter his mouth, literally burning him from the inside out. He screams in agony before falling to the ground limp.

I notice the deadly silence in the air, so I turn to look at everyone to find them all staring up at me in wonder. I just killed the most powerful warlock without so much as breaking a sweat.

The guards snap out of their shock and grab Azrael and Stella around their necks, holding a knife to their throats. I growl, jumping off the balcony and landing in front of them, tilting my head to the side, looking at them.

"Let them go." I look between them. If they didn't have Luna, I would've done this long ago. I need to stop feeling bad for killing people who hurt the people I care about because it's holding me back.

Not anymore.

I'm fucking done.

"You killed our Prince."

"He shouldn't have kidnapped me." Why the fuck am I even trying to reason with them? Azrael looks pissed, and Stella is crying.

"Run, Bella," Azrael hisses through clenched teeth, and I smile, with a single flick of my wrist, my flames rush toward the guards, entering them before they even know what is happening and dropping their knives. Azrael spins around, breaking both of their necks at once before my flames even have a chance to finish the job.

And that's when all Hell breaks loose. Everyone is screaming and running toward the exit while guards run in. We're surrounded.

The next thing I know, I'm being flipped around, strong arms wrapping around me, and I scream, but then hands clamp my mouth shut before the world blurs. I'm about to burn the fucker, but his masculine scent floods around me, making me relax.

I'm flipped around once more before he shoves my back against a wall. I don't see anything at first, but then the light flickers on, making me flinch at the brightness. We're in a closet full of coats. I finally look up, locking eyes with Azrael. I cry out as I throw my arms around his shoulders.

"Shh, it's okay, my little witch." He grabs my face in between his hands, pulling my head back to look down at me.

"I had to kill him." I blurt out quickly, panicking. "He wanted to kill you and hurt Luna!" I don't want him to think I'm a monster just like my father.

"You had no choice, my love." He leans in, kissing me with so much longing. I grip his tuxedo, pulling him tighter against me. He pulls back, wiping the tears from my face. "I thought you left me. I thought you chose him." His voice turns rough, like it pained him to say those words.

"I'll never leave you, Azrael. You're stuck with me till I die." I joke, smiling.

"Good." He rests his forehead against mine. "I wasn't letting you go that easily. I came to beg you to come back, and if you didn't, I was going to force your sexy ass back and chain you up in my room."

"You were gonna chain me?" I gasp, leaning back, arching my brows.

"Yes, and I don't feel any shame in admitting it. You're mine. Whether you like it or not."

"You are so possessive." I roll my eyes.

"I am, but that doesn't answer why I felt your *pleasure* when you were with him." He spits out the word 'pleasure' like it was such a dirty word.

"Felt my pleasure?" I ask, not understanding what he was talking about. He just stared at me through narrowed eyes. After a minute, I know exactly what he's talking about. "You felt that?" I gasp.

"Yes," he hisses out through his teeth; his eyes are slowly turning red. I don't know what to say or how to explain it.

What do I say? Oh yeah, I did let him touch me, but I thought it was you, no biggie...

"We have to go back out there," I rush out, trying to change the subject.

"You think I'll let you walk out there in all that danger?" He scowls at me. "I'm taking your ass home and coming back, but not until you tell me why you *fucked* him." He pushes me back, creating space between us, like he can't stand being close to me, and it hurts.

"It's not what you think." I shake my head; my eyes start to water again from fear. He'll hate me if he knows.

"Then fucking tell me!" he roars. He punches the door before placing both of his hands against the door frame, breathing raggedly. His back is facing me, and his body is trembling with anger.

"I... I..." I stumble, not knowing how to start. "I thought it was you. I don't know. One minute I fell asleep chained to our bed, and the next minute I woke up and it was dark. I couldn't see anything, and I thought you came back... Please, don't hate me! His head was between my legs, and he was licking me down there, fingering me, and well, you know, but when he crawled up my body and kissed me. That's when I realized it wasn't you. He tricked me, Azrael."

His body is tense. He is leaning against the door and not saying a word. I swallow the large lump in my throat. My entire body is trembling slightly, and my anxiety is going haywire.

"Azrael, please," I cry out, feeling hurt and scared. I reach my hand out and touch his back, but he immediately flinches away from me.

Someone starts knocking at the door, making me jump. Without looking back at me, he opens the door and walks out to talk to whoever is on the other side. I can't hear what they're saying because of the loud buzzing in my ears. My legs give out, and I fall to the floor, panting hard on the verge of a panic attack.

I haven't cried this hard since my mom died. I wrap my arms around my legs, putting my face on my knees, rocking back and forth.

I close my eyes and think of my mom.

We're sitting at my mom's vanity. She has my hair in her hands and is brushing it while she hums. Luna had fallen asleep on Mom's bed. We're all in here because it started storming badly, and we both got scared. I was fifteen at the time.

"Momma?"

"Hmmm?" I look at her through the mirror. Her hair was long and brown, just like Luna's. It's braided down her back like normal. She has very pretty hazel eyes and high cheekbones. She was so beautiful.

"How do I know if a boy likes me?" I ask her, and she looks into my eyes and smiles.

"Depends on the boy, honey. Some boys bully you, and some just outright tell you or show you by flirting and teasing you. Why is that?"

"Because there's a boy I like." I blush, looking down at my hands. "He kissed me and then told me it was horrible, and teased me in front of his friends." I shrugged like it wasn't a big deal when it was.

"I really don't know, but if he kissed you, he obviously likes you, and I think maybe he was just too scared and tried pushing you away."

"Do you think I'm pretty? That I'm worthy of love one day?" I turn around to look up at her. I don't have any friends. Girls stay away from me, and boys do too, except for James. When I finally told him I liked him and kissed him, they all laughed at me, and I ran away crying.

"You are beautiful and very worthy of love. If a boy or man ever makes you feel like you aren't, they don't deserve you, and you're better off without him." She grabs my face, wiping off my tears. "You may find out things about me or, I guess, secrets when you are older, and you may hate me for them, but just know, I'll always love you, and nothing changes that."

She always said that, and I never figured out what secrets she meant. She'd never tell me what they were. God, I miss her. She always made me feel good about myself, even when the kids were so mean to me.

Enough crying! You are stronger than this.

I get up, cleaning my face. I'm sure my eyes are red and puffy, but oh well. She's right. If anyone makes me feel as if I'm below them, then they don't deserve me, not that Azrael is doing that. He's just hurt, and understandably so. Hell, if I felt his pleasure—I shake my head. Don't think about that. But crying here and doing nothing won't fix anything. Once we get out of here and back to safety, I'll take some time alone to feel sorry for myself.

I step closer to the door, opening it an inch, trying to listen to their conversation. I need to go find Marisol to make sure Luna is safe.

"She murdered him. She needs to be put on trial and take her punishment," a man shouts, making Azrael snarl at him.

I look at the tall man. He's freaking intimidating. His anger is so strong that I feel it from here, but Azrael doesn't even flinch. I never thought about being punished for what I've done. I killed a royal prince! I'll probably be put to death for it. My trembling hands cover my mouth as fear crawls up my throat. I just signed my own death warrant to save Azrael and Luna.

It's worth it...

"Anyone who touches her will receive my wrath, and a lot of people will die at my hands," Azrael growls.

"Someone will answer for my son's death," the man growls back. His evil eyes turn to me. I swallow hard, but I don't look away.

"No one will answer for your son's death." I turn to see Azrael's father. "My son and I are both witnesses, and I will stand trial with her. She is my son's mate, and your son had an obsession with her, kidnapping her from her own room. You know the rules on mates; if you mess with a mate bond, it warrants death. She had every right to defend herself and her mate."

"And my sister, who he was torturing to keep me here," I say, my voice low but strong, which surprises me compared to how weak I feel.

"Impossible! My son would never kidnap a woman, especially a mated one." They ignore me, acting as if I'm not even standing here.

"Just look at her. You can clearly see the mark that I put there! Smell her. She's mine." Azrael grabs my wrist, harshly pushes me between him and Gabriel's father. He eyes me with hatred as he steps toward me and looks at my neck. He leans in close, and I hear him inhale. What the fuck? Is he smelling me?

"Impossible. You could have easily just placed it there. She will be taken until the council can gather, and they will decide." He turns, leaving the room. The guards behind him step closer, reaching out as if they're going to grab me, but Azrael snaps his teeth at them, like a wild animal. They take a step back with fear in their eyes.

"It's okay." I grab his arm with a smile, trying to soothe him before stepping towards the guards. I wince with pain when one grabs my arm tightly.

"Hurt her again, and I'll kill you," Azrael warns in a dark, low voice.

"Get your hands off me. I'm coming willing," I snap, he drops my arm but stays close to me.

Four guards are surrounding me, and I start following them down the hall. I look over my shoulder to look at Azrael once more. His father and sister are both talking to him, but his eyes are on me. His jaw clenches tightly, his body trembling, and his fangs are sharp, ready to kill. I can tell he's trying his best to keep his vampire in check.

We turn the corner, and I lose sight of him. We suddenly stop in front of a large mirror. I raise my brows, wondering why we stopped. The man in front waves his hand in front of the mirror, mumbling something that sounds like, "*Ensenarme que es occulta.*"

I'm pretty sure that's Spanish. With a click, the ground trembles slightly, and the mirror opens a crack. The guard reaches the edge of the mirror, and he pulls it open slowly. The door loudly screeches, making me cringe.

He steps back, and the guard behind me pushes me in, making me stumble. It's a large dark hall with torches lit up on the walls. Our steps echo loudly. I swallow but continue forward until I stop when I hit a flight of stairs. I look down at them, and it seems like they continue on forever, leading into pitch darkness. I bite my tongue hard enough to make it bleed.

I don't want to go down there; the unknown is scary. "Move!" One of the guards' voices echoes loudly in the silence, making me jump.

I almost turn to run back to Azrael, knowing he'll do anything in his power to keep me safe. I don't want to put him in that situation.

I swallow the fear clawing at my throat, taking the first step down the stairs. When I finally hit the end of the stairs, I see six cells in total, plus another door at the end of the hall. A guard unlocks one of the cell doors and shoves me inside with enough force to knock me over. I land on my ass, groaning at the impact.

"How long will I be waiting?" I ask them as they slam the door shut, locking it. They ignore me and turn to leave the way we came. "Hey! I asked a question!" I shout, but there's no response except the sound of their footsteps disappearing.

I spin around, looking around the cell. It's made out of old grey brick. The three walls are bare. I can't see into the other cells, but mine has a twin metal bed, a sink, and a small metal toilet; I wrinkle my nose. At least it's clean. I have been in way worse. I slump on the metal bed, which makes a scratchy sound when it moves against the floor. I take several breaths, trying hard not to break down. I look up to find someone watching me silently in the cell across from mine, sitting on their bed, resting against the wall behind them.

"What did you do to land in this hellhole?" she asks in a scratchy, rough voice as if she hasn't talked in a while. She is wearing grey sweatpants, a white T-shirt with a grey cardigan, and grey slippers; her hair is long, dark, and messy like she hasn't combed it in a while.

"Murder," is all I decide to say.

"Hmm, interesting." She tilts her head to the side a little, looking me up and down with pierced lips.

"Why is that?"

"You look like a queen or someone important wearing that crown and that dress. Normally, you people get away with that sort of thing."

"Judgmental, aren't you?" I look away from her, staring down at my hands clenching tightly together. "I guess I am of sorts, but Prince Gabriel kidnapped me, taking me from my mate, and I killed him for trying to force his mark on me."

"Prince Gabriel is dead?" She gasps. "And a little thing like you is the one to do it? Color me impressed." She smirks.

"Thanks, I guess." I chuckle lowly, not knowing whether to take that as a compliment or take offense to it.

"So, who's your mate?"

"Prince Azrael." She gasps again. "Yeah, I know, shocking, huh? I never thought I'd be mated to someone as strong as him."

"Oh, don't forget, so damn sexy. Now, that should be a crime on its own. Don't worry about staying here. They won't do anything; you'll leave scratch-free. It's highly frowned upon around here to mess with another creature's mate. Royal family or not. Since it's a royal family, you'll be out within a couple of hours.

"So, I have heard." I nod, looking back at her. She's now sitting on the edge of her bed, still focused on me. She's probably a little older than me, but not by much, maybe a year or two. "Enough about me. What about you? What evil things have you done to end up here for judgment?"

She snorts, licking her lips. "It was so stupid." She shakes her head as she hunches slightly, looking at the ground. "I'm low class. Don't have shit to my name. I work at the plaza, to you know, pay my bills and shit. Well, you probably don't know what it's like. So, anyway, the king, you know, Prince Gabriel's father, likes to get a little too handsy with me, and he offered me to be his mistress, and when I declined, telling him I was going to tell his wife, the queen, he threw me in here, saying I stole from him. He said if I change my mind, he'll take me back, but I will never. I'll rather rot here."

"Seriously? Fuck, that's bullshit."

"Yeah, tell me about it. Stupid royals think they can control everyone beneath them." She looks up at me. "No offense."

"None taken, and you are wrong. I do understand what it's like. My sister and I have always struggled with money until I found my mate. It's hardly been a month, and my life has completely changed. Did a fucking one-eighty." I lift my hand, rolling it in a small circle.

"You lucky bitch!"

"At first, it was rocky. Man, did he hate me." I laugh, remembering it. It feels like forever ago. "You know, because he hates witches. I don't know how it's going to work. I mean, there has never been a witch to rule the vampire species. They will hate it, and maybe even try to stop it."

"Who gives a damn? People are always bitchin' about something; people suck, you'll never make everyone happy."

"Well, on top of everything, I'm also a halfling." She looks at me in shock. "Yeah, yeah, I know." I roll my eyes.

"No, it's not that. You're not a halfling. You're a full-blooded witch and a very powerful one. I can sense it."

"No, I'm not. My mom is a demon." I stand up, walking to the cell door.

"You're joking, right? Have you never been around our kind before?"

"I was when I was younger, but they usually liked staying away from me."

"They stayed away because they feel how strong you are. It makes them uneasy; you must have been around lowly witches.

Sorry, girl, but I'm not wrong. You're a full-blooded witch. I don't know what to tell you."

Impossible. I know my mom was a demon.

"How—" I start to say, but the side door opens, cutting me off. Two guards step in, coming straight to my cell. The taller one waves his hand in front of the lock, and it clicks open. He opens the door, letting me step out. That was faster than I thought it'd be, but I'm not complaining.

I stop to say something to the girl, but the guard pushes me forward. "Move it." I narrow my eyes at him, but I don't move. So, he grabs my upper arm, dragging me out forcefully. I start struggling, trying to get out of his hold.

Chapter 36

"Let her go!" A loud growl booms out in the silent space. The guard immediately tosses me, and I fall to the ground.

"Azrael!" I cry out, looking toward where I heard his voice, but it's too dark, I can't see anything, and he doesn't respond.

There's a loud pounding sound. I snap my head to that side of the room; the torches light up one by one around the room. That's when I see a large podium with five cloaked figures. I slowly get to my feet, staring at each one, hoping to see a glimpse of their faces, but nothing.

This is some creepy cult shit.

The one in the middle stands, and I can feel their gaze staring back down at me. I shiver but don't look away.

"I am Prince Dimitri, and we are gathered here for the murder of Prince Gabriel." A loud male voice says, full of authority. "Isabella is here on trial for his murder."

Shit, I am so screwed. Prince Dimitri has no mercy.

"Which I am very pissed about!" he hisses. Fuck, he might just kill me on the spot. "This is a complete waste of my time."

I hear a few mutters behind me, but I keep my eyes on Prince Dimitri. I see the cloaked figure beside him gripping his hand and squeezing it, trying to calm him. That must be Rosa.

"Tell me why you insist on wasting my time, King of Warlocks."

"She murdered my son!" I turn my head to see Gabriel's father sitting on a large stone bench. It's filled with others. I try looking for Azrael in the sea of strange faces, but Prince Dimitri speaks again, forcing my attention back to him.

"She had every right to murder him!" he growls out loudly, making me sigh in relief. He's on my side. "Prince Gabriel took her from her fated mate and wanted to force his mark on a woman who is clearly marked!" he gestures his hand toward me.

"There is no proof she was mated prior to him taking her."

"We have plenty of proof. Prince Azrael is her fated mate, and she is marked by him. On top of that, we found her sister, who was beaten by one of Prince Gabriel's assassins. The King of Vampires stepped forward as a witness; he saw her mating mark before she was taken. They drank truth serum before we interrogated them."

"There is no way my son would do such a thing."

"I smell Prince Azrael's scent on this young lady. That wouldn't be possible if they were not mated." The cloaked figure that clenched Dimitri's hand says, Rosa's voice sounds angelic.

"Impossible." I look over to see the king shaking his head.

"Are you calling my mate a liar?" Dimitri's deadly voice sends a shiver down my spine. "Do you not smell her scent mixed with Prince Azrael's?"

"No, of course not. I apologize. And yes, I smell it, but he could have marked her after his death. There was plenty of time for him to do so."

"We are done! I do apologize for this nonsense, Princess Isabella," Dimitri turns towards me, and for some reason, his calling me Princess Isabella makes it real.

I'm a goddamn princess.

"No, someone must pay for my son's death! I request Mirthal to look in her mind."

"Mirthal? Will you do the honors?"

"No!" Azrael's voice shouts out.

"Quiet! Or you'll be escorted out."

I swallow nervously. Why doesn't Azrael want Mirthal to do this? We're not hiding anything.

"Of course." Another cloaked member stands. I know she's a female by the sound of her voice.

She slowly steps around the podium and stands in front of me. She looks up at me since she's a few inches shorter than me. Her hood falls back, and I see her. She's older, around my mother's age, and her blue eyes are glowing.

"May I?" She asks me with a small smile.

"Of course." I give a small nod. She lifts her hand; her pointer and middle fingers are touching my forehead.

A second later, I feel a painful zap. It feels like she's splitting my forehead in half, and the most agonizing pain I have ever felt before shoots down my spine. My body paralyzes in pain. I can't even scream. When she finally let's go of my forehead, I release a high-pitched scream as I fall to my knees.

That's why Azrael didn't want her to do it.

"She is telling the truth. She was marked before he took her."

"Very well. You are free to go." Arms wrap tightly around me, curling me into a masculine chest. "Court is adjourned!" They all stand, turning away, ready to leave.

"Wait!" I shout, and they pause. I try wiggling out of Azrael's arms, but he refuses to let me go. I wait till Prince Dimitri turns around.

"Yes?" he hisses, voice dripping in annoyance.

"There is a young lady that the king is keeping prisoner all because she refused to be his mistress," I rush out, knowing Dimitri is running out of patience.

"Is this true? King of Warlocks?"

"Of course, it is not! That young lady stole from me."

"Why not bring her forth to us? Stealing from a royal is for us to judge, not you!"

"Because he has no proof!" I say, believing every word that girl told me.

"And you do?" Rosa gently asks me.

"I don't, but I believe the girl. Mirthal wouldn't mind looking in her head." My gaze snaps to hers with a pleading look.

"Of course not, but this will have to wait till tomorrow. It takes a lot of energy to look into minds, young one." She bows her head before walking out.

"We shall meet tomorrow at the same time; we'll have my guards keep an eye on the young lady as protection," Prince Dimitri says and then turns, wrapping an arm around Rosa, and they disappear. And so does everyone else.

I groan from the pain I feel. I could really use some rest.

"Bella," Azrael whispers in my ear as he walks us out of the room, his voice laced with worry.

"My head hurts," I whisper, resting my head against him.

"I know, my love." I close my eyes, drifting to sleep, feeling safe in his warm arms.

"Luna?"

"She's okay. Stella is with her."

I wake up groaning, my head is still pounding, but not as bad as it was. That shit was super intense. I hope I never have to go through a judgment again.

Being in a roomful of the most powerful people was in-fucking-sane. Man, what she did to my head was hella cool. I literally felt her roaming through my memories before finding what she needed. She could've watched a movie of my entire life if she really wanted to.

I start sitting up, but an arm that I didn't notice tightens its grip around me, keeping me in place. I turn, looking beside me to find Azrael sleeping peacefully, making me smile. His lips are slightly parted, and it makes him look extremely adorable. His arm is under my head, which I'm using as a pillow, the other is around my waist, and our legs are tangled together.

I notice he removed my dress and dressed me in one of his T-shirts.

Relief spreads through my body. My finger slowly traces the tattoo on his naked chest. I smile when goose bumps erupt on his skin.

"Mmm, good morning, little witch." I look up to find him staring down at me. "I can get used to waking up with us snuggling like this."

"Yeah?" I giggle, tilting my head back to kiss his throat. "I can, too." I give his throat a lick, he releases a low rumble, and I feel his chest vibrate beneath me.

"I need you," he pulls his lower lip between his teeth, and desire awakens in me, spreading through me like wildfire.

"Then take me." I enjoy watching his pupils dilate with the need for me.

I slowly kiss my way down his chest, and when I reach his delicious abs, I slowly trace them with my tongue. His fingers bury themselves in my hair, and he tries pushing me lower, but I look up, shaking my head slightly, tsking at him.

"You are such a damn little tease," he rumbles in a husky voice that makes me shiver. Goodness, he sounds so sexy, it should be a crime.

I get to my knees, looking him in the eyes as I grab the edge of my shirt, slowly removing it, exposing my naked body to him. I toss it behind me as I bite my lower lip, feeling shy now that I'm completely exposed to him aside from my small black panties. My hands itch to reach up to cover myself from him.

His eyes darken while his gaze slowly roams over my breasts, making them harden from his attention. He reaches up to touch me, but I smack his hands away; his eyes snap up to meet mine, and they narrow at me. The way he's watching me is making me feel confident.

I lick my lips, slowly moving back, and my fingers curl around the waistband of his sweats, slowly pulling them down until his cock pops out, smacking his lower stomach. I bend down, looking back up to stare into his eyes as my tongue licks the entire length of him. His groan sounds desperate, and I feel him tense beneath me as his hands fist the sheets.

"Enough teasing, little witch, and fuck my cock with that pretty mouth." So, I do as he commands, opening my mouth wider as I swirl my tongue over his tip, my fingers curl around his cock, and my other hand cups his balls, massaging them. I suck him into my mouth, stopping halfway down before moving back up, teasing him purposely. I do it again, but he grabs the back of my head, snarling, "More, you can fucking take it." He lifts his hips; making me gag. I whimper as my eyes water.

"Good girl," he says through clenched teeth and continues to mercilessly thrust his cock into my mouth. "Look at me as I fuck your mouth." My eyes snap up, meeting his. My pussy begins to throb with desire at how dangerously sexy he looks with his upper lip curled up with a feral, possessive look in his dark eyes, turning me on to no end.

"Fuck, you look so pretty choking on my cock." He finally lets me up, and I try taking a breather before he slams himself back in.

"Relax, baby, open that throat for me and let me fuck it deeper; just breathe through your nose." Deeper? How?

He starts throbbing and pushes me faster and harder. My throat is starting to hurt from his savage thrusts. "That's it, baby, you're such a good girl for me." His praise makes me shiver with complete need. I moan around him.

"Fuck!" he growls as he stills, cumming deep in my throat. I swallow half of it, and the other half spills out as he pulls out. I look at him when I grab his spilled cum with my fingers, sucking my fingers back in my mouth, licking them clean.

"Damn, that's sexy." I smile at him. "Now, it's your turn." Before I can even ask him what he means, he grabs me by the hips, flipping me on my back.

I look down to find him between my thighs, with the waistband of my panties in between his teeth. He stares up at me with a smirk, and then I watch him tear my panties apart.

Okay, fuck me, that's too damn sexy.

I groan when I feel his tongue on my clit, devouring me like he was starving for me. My head rolls back and I moan, "Oh God, please, yes!"

"That's right, baby. I'm your god," he murmurs as he continues to lick me.

My core tightens, and my body starts trembling. I'm so damn close to the edge; I'm about to fall, and I'm so ready for it.

"That's right, baby." He pushes two fingers inside of me, curling them, hitting the perfect spot. I close my eyes, ready to explode. "Look at me! Look at who makes you feel this way. Scream my name so everyone can hear who makes you writher in pleasure," he growls. I snap my eyes open, finding his red eyes staring up at me as he lightly bites my clit.

"Oh God!" My toes curl. "Don't you dare fucking stop, Azrael!" I scream out, gripping the back of his head, pushing him closer to me, needing more. "Yes, yes!"

I see stars as I finally let go, falling off the edge, cumming so hard. It feels as if my body is falling into a deep hole of pleasure.

"Fuck, you taste so good." My limbs loosen, and I slump against the mattress, closing my eyes, coming down from that intense pleasure.

He slumps next to me, wrapping me tightly in his arms like he's afraid I'll disappear.

"Tell me that it felt better than when he did it." My eyes snap open when I hear the vulnerability in his voice.

"Azrael, you feel so much better. There is no comparison to the way you make me feel."

"I'm sorry I haven't been taking care of you like I should be."

"What are you talking about?" I look up, meeting his gaze. He brushes the hair out of my face and stares at me like I'm the most precious thing in the world.

"You've been kidnapped three times. Two of which you were in my house. I'm doing a horrible fucking job keeping you safe."

"It's not your fault. I don't blame you at all."

"If I were keeping you close and safe, it would never have happened." He looks away, jaw ticking angrily. He gets up, sitting on the edge of the bed, hunching over with his hands covering his face. "I wouldn't blame you if you blamed me; as your mate, I'm supposed to protect you."

"I understand what you're saying, but they would have kept trying. I have to be alone once in a while. You can't be with me every second of the day."

"I can try to be."

I sigh, rolling my eyes. "Azrael, you have so many responsibilities. You can't."

"I can make you follow me around." He turns to look at me over his shoulder.

"I love you, Azrael." I decide to change the subject. There is no way in hell I will follow him around like a lost puppy.

"Fuck, say it again."

"I love you, Azrael."

"Damn, baby. I'm hard again." He lies back down, pulling me on top of him, but I shake my head, saying no, and he pouts at me, making me laugh.

"I need to see Luna."

"Fine, we can go, I'll share you with her for an hour only. Afterwards, I'm bringing you back here, to have you all to myself."

"Deal."

Chapter 37

Azrael and I are walking down the hall when he suddenly grabs hold of my hand, intertwining our fingers. I look up in shock, but he's staring straight ahead, looking casual. Everyone we pass either nods or bows their head to us. Honestly, it's something I need to get used to.

I'm worried about the judgment tonight. Hopefully, they'll let her go. She doesn't deserve to be locked up or alone down there for nothing.

I find it disgusting that they use their powers to get what they want, punishing people for saying no and getting away with it. I mean, who do they think they are?

"Azrael?"

"Yes, baby?" He looks down at me, his thumb starts to rub the top of my hand.

"Tonight, when it's judgment time for that girl…" I trailed off, not knowing how to ask him or if he'll even agree. He stops walking and grabs my chin, forcing me to look back up at him. His other hand cups the side of my neck.

"Never be afraid to ask me something. Tell me what you're thinking."

"I don't think she'll have anywhere to stay; she's been struggling just like I did, and I don't know, is there any way she can stay here? There's plenty of work around here." I stop when I realize that I'm rambling.

"Of course, she can. Whatever you want. You'll be a perfect queen, my perfect queen." He smiles, making my heart skip a beat.

"You should do that more." I reach up, laying my hand on his chest.

"Do what more?" he asks, scrunching his brows together.

"Smile."

"Anything for you." He smiles again.

"Anything?" I bat my lashes at him, making his smile widen, and he nods.

"Then kiss me." And he does slowly and passionately. It's full of love and need, making my heart swell with happiness.

We start walking again, but this time, he tucks me under his arm, and I wrap my arm around his waist. Azrael stops a little down the hall, opening a door for me. He steps aside so I can walk past, and he winks at me when I do. I try not to blush. Will I ever get used to his beauty?

I look around the room, and my eyes land on a sleeping Luna. I rush over to her, grab her hand, and sit on the chair by the bed. The room is light grey, with white tile floors and machines. It looks a lot like a hospital room.

"She's been passed out since we got her. We did give her some blood to heal her wounds. She'll be fine. She's just resting from the trauma her body went through."

"Your blood?" I blink, feeling disgusted by the jealousy that's rising in the pit of my stomach. I feel bad for feeling that way. I'm happy if he did because it'll help her with the pain, but for some reason, I still feel jealous.

"Of course, not." He rushes to my side and stares into my eyes, looking dead serious. "I'd never do that. Once you find your mate, you never give your blood to anyone else. It's way too intimate. To a vampire, that is betraying your mate. It's almost as bad as cheating, don't you know that?"

"No. I don't know much about mates or anything like that."

"I'll teach you what you need to know along the way." He gently runs his fingers through my hair, curling a piece around one. "I'd rather die than live without you. I'll sacrifice my life for you, I'll rip my own heart out and give it to you if that's what you want. I'll do anything for you. All you have to do is ask. You're the most precious thing to me, Bella." My breathing stalls, and I melt into a puddle. I can't believe this brutal, savage, ruthless prince will do anything for *me*.

"Azrael, I'll do anything for you, too." God, now I'm wishing we were alone.

"Enough with the lovey-dovey crap," Luna groans. "It's disgusting."

"Luna!" I push Azrael away, running to the bed where I start soothing her hair. "Are you okay?"

"Yeah, I feel tired and sore, but other than that, I'm fine." She hasn't opened her eyes yet. "What about you? Did that dude hurt you?"

"No, not in that way; I was mostly worried about you."

"I'm fine now, sis, but can I have some water?"

"I'll go get you some," Azrael says, already heading out of the room.

"I'm sorry," I say, my voice low with pain.

"For what?" She finally blinks her eyes open, pretty hazel eyes that remind me so much of our mom's eyes.

"I don't know. Shit, it's my fault you were there." I shrug, looking away from her.

"Naw, sis. It's his fault. He was fucking crazy. I don't blame you one bit. What time is it?"

"Good, that makes me so happy to hear." I smile, looking back at her. "It's six. It's too damn early, but I needed to make sure you were okay."

"One water coming up!" Azrael steps beside me, opening the water bottle and hands it to her. When she has a hard time leaning up, he reaches over and helps her up. Once she's done, he closes it, setting it on the table beside the bed. "I'll find the remote that moves the bed. I know it goes up and down. Plus, a straw."

I chew on my lower lip. God, this man just got ten times hotter; I'll be rewarding him later.

He smirks at me, winking, like he knows what I am thinking. Damn cocky bastard.

He clears his throat, looking between us. "Did you happen to see who took you?"

"Nope, I was tied up and asleep; they took advantage of it. I don't know how they got me out of here without waking me up. Until well, you know." Azrael releases a possessive growl, wrapping an arm around me, pulling me off the bed and tightly against his body.

"I never got to apologize for that."

"No need to. I know that it was never your intention to leave me vulnerable for a man to have his way with me."

"Never. I wish I could've tortured him for laying his disgusting hands and lips on you." His eyes flash red from anger.

"Is that why you were passed out and naked?" Luna gasps. "And yes, it was Jeremy and the man who tortured me. They enjoyed the fact that you were naked."

"Fuck!" Azrael roars. "I'm so sorry for leaving you like that. Your naked body is for my eyes only! I'll make them pay, and I'll rip their eyes out before I kill them. You have my word," he snarls, and in a blur, he's gone.

"Holy shit. That was hot. I hope my mate will rip someone's eyes out for looking at me naked."

I wanted to tell her that it isn't easy being with someone as possessive as Azrael, but I wouldn't change it for the world.

I step into our room, wrapping a towel around my body. I frown. It's almost eight, and I haven't seen Azrael since he ran off earlier. The judgment starts at nine. Where the hell is he?

The door slams open, I jump, my heart leaping in fear until I see a savage-looking Azrael standing there covered in blood, my mouth parts in shock.

"It's not my blood." He answers the question in my eyes as he kicks the door shut with his foot. He throws something on the floor between us, and four small round objects roll over to me. I pinch my brows together, bending down to look at them, and I scream in horror, jumping back.

"I promised you I'd rip their fucking eyes out, and I enjoyed every moment of it."

"You took their eyes out? Were they…" I lick my dry lips. "Were they alive?"

"Yes." His lips curl in a cruel smirk. "I made them suffer, baby, just for you." I take a step back, and then another, looking into his dark feral eyes, and his cruel smirk drops intensely. "Are you afraid of me? You know I'll never hurt you."

Am I afraid of him?

No.

I just can't believe he did something so brutal like ripping their eyes out for seeing me naked, but at the same time, I feel something wild running through my veins, heating me up with so much desire, knowing he'd do something so vicious like that just for me and bringing me the proof of his brutal actions.

"Don't be af—"

"I'm not afraid of you. Did you make them suffer for looking at my naked body?" My voice is low and rough.

"Yes, for hours," he hisses. I move closer to him, stopping just out of reach. I bite my lower lip, and he watches me as he starts panting with need. I drop the towel, exposing my wet, naked flesh to him.

His eyes trail down my body, leaving a trail of goose bumps as he does, he rushes toward me in a blur, picking me up and slamming my body against the wall. I wrap my legs around his hips when I hear his pants hit the floor, he thrusts into me with such brutal force I scream.

His bloody hands grip my hips painfully. They'll for sure leave a mark. I arch my back, making his gaze drop to my bouncing tits.

He pulls a nipple into his mouth, swirling his tongue as his hands release my hips to grip my ass.

"Bite me Azrael," I moan. His thrust is slow as he looks up at me with a wild glint in his eyes. "Please." I can feel his fangs extract against my nipple, making me moan.

A deep primal groan escapes his mouth as his eyes dilate and then he bites me right above my nipple. I scream the pain overwhelming, but it only lasts a moment before the pleasure slams into me like a hurricane. My hands grip his hair, pulling it slightly. He pulls out his fangs, licking his bite mark, and pulls me off the wall. He sits in his chair by the window and leans back.

"Ride me, baby." I rest my hands on his chest for support and adjust my knees. I start bouncing on his cock. He leans forward and his hand grips my hair tightly, forcing my head back, and my back arches as I hiss from the slight pain.

I feel him cupping my breast. I try to look at him, but he tightens his grip on my hair, keeping my head back, and my gaze locked on the ceiling.

"Fuck, the way this tight pussy squeezes my cock is my goddamn addiction. I literally want my dick inside you all day, every day. Best pussy I've ever fucking had," his voice guttural and wild as if he's about to lose control as he pinches my nipple. "And the way these titties bounce as you're riding me should be against the law. Thank fuck, I'm a sinner." His words are making me crazed and so fucking hot. I'm about to burst. I grip the arms of the chair with my hands. I can't handle it.

"Azrael, your cock feels so fucking amazing!" I cry out before screaming his name as I literally burst. Large, wicked flames dance around my hands as I scream in ecstasy.

Azrael follows, mumbling my name over and over again like a fucking prayer, not giving a shit about the flames circling around us.

We stare at each other as we pant. He starts laughing as he eyes the flames dancing around us in a perfect circle.

"Well, fuck, that was literally the hottest orgasm we've ever fucking shared." I blush, flicking my wrist, making the flames disappear as I bury my face in his chest.

"Don't make fun of me," I mumble against his chest.

"I'm not, baby. Don't be shy, I loved every damn second of it."

"I could've hurt you."

"Good thing I've never been afraid of fire. It takes a lot more than that to hurt me. You have no idea what that did to my ego, making you lose control like that." He stands with me, and we both look at the damaged chair.

"I'm sorry." I melted the hell out of the leather.

"It's just a fucking chair; it can be replaced." He walks me into the bathroom, gently sitting me on the bathroom vanity. He grabs a hand towel, wetting it before settling in between my legs, and starts scrubbing the blood off my skin. He tries to get me to open my legs to clean me down there, but I shake my head.

"I need a shower."

"We need to leave. The judgment starts in ten minutes. You don't have time for one, and they won't wait for us." He rewets the towel and continues cleaning me off. He lifts me back up, walking me to the closet, and tries to put panties on me.

"I'm not fully clean!" I try to push him back, but he doesn't budge, forcing the panties up my legs.

"I offered to clean that sexy little pussy, but you declined. It's too late for a shower, and we need to get dressed." He begins to put my legs through a pair of leggings and pulls them up. He grabs a bra to put on me, then a large, oversized, fluffy sweater.

"But I'll smell," I blush as he finishes and starts to get himself dressed. I won't lie; I love his need to take care of me.

"Yes, of sex, and my cum will be dripping out of your delicious pussy, and everyone will smell exactly how much I pleasure you." He smirks as he dresses himself in blue jeans, a white V-neck, and a leather jacket.

I groan before walking to our room, throwing on my ankle boots. I can feel his cum on my thighs as it slowly leaks out. He's leaning against the doorframe, still smirking.

"You're an ass for not letting me clean up."

"Yeah, I am, but I'm your ass." So true, all mine. He grabs me, pulling my body against his, and we teleport. I don't even get sick this time, fuck yeah! I look around, we're in the judgment room. This time, I'm in the stands.

"How do I know they'll be fair?" I whisper once we're both sitting on a stone bench. I see the other benches are full of people.

"I trust Prince Dimitri's judgment. If I didn't, I would never have allowed you to be here yesterday."

"Okay." I nod, feeling better since I trust him with all my being. "There's no way you could've stopped what happened yesterday, even if you didn't trust him." I point out.

"Yes, the fuck I could have. I would've killed every motherfucker." My eyes widen, and I truly believe he would've.

I feel a slight breeze in the air, and when I look to my left, I see Stella sitting next to me. I need to get used to their speed.

"Father couldn't make it." She leans into me slightly, wrinkling her nose. "Really, Azrael." He looks over at me, looking so damn smug as he wraps his arm around my back. I blush, suddenly realizing what she was talking about.

Everything turns dark and silent. I straighten as I look forward, footsteps echo loudly in the quiet space, and I see shadows coming from the side door. I imagine it's her coming in.

Chapter 38

The candles light up one by one, and I see the council sitting behind the large podium. They are all in the same hooded cloaks; they look scary and mysterious.

"We call upon the King of Warlocks." Prince Dimitri's voice booms.

"I am here, my Prince." I glance over to see him sitting alone in the back corner of the room.

"Very well, we shall begin." One of the cloaked figures gets up, and I assume it is Mirthal walking towards the woman whose name I never got.

Mirthal lifts her hand and places the tips of her fingers against the woman's forehead, just like she did to me. Azrael's arm tightens around me, but I don't look away from the scene. The woman's back arches, and her eyes are wide open looking up at the ceiling, after a few minutes, she screams, falling to her knees. Well, shit, I could've sworn it was way longer than just a few minutes when it happened to me.

"I need the king now," Mirthal demands, and the king stands slowly, taking slow calculated steps towards her, taking his sweet time. He looks nervous; I'm sure everyone else can tell, too. Once he stops in front of Mirthal, she places her fingers against his forehead.

I thought it completely drained her if she did more than one.

"He has his mind blocked," Mirthal hisses angrily, which surprises me since she looks like a sweet grandma. "I will pass your attempts to hide from me." She clenches her jaw, and I can see her body tense as she struggles to break the barrier. The king falls to his knees and his mouth opens in a silent scream; his face twisted in agony. Mirthal drops to her knees, hunching over, but never removes her fingers; they both start shaking. Holy fuck, my hand jumps out and squeezes Azrael's knee.

"Enough, Mirthal!" I hear Lord Dimitri shout.

"I almost got it!" She doesn't sound like herself, but a minute later, she removes her fingers, and her hands hit the floor as she pants heavily

Someone who is sitting at the end of the podium stands, walks to Mirthal, and picks her up. I saw Mirthal whisper something in his ear, and she points at me, making Azrael tense slightly beside me. I look up at him, but he's listening to their conversation. I grow nervous and my hands tremble with anxiety as I wish I could hear what she is saying and why she pointed at me.

"I'm highly disappointed in you. How dare you attempt to withhold the truth from us!" Dimitri's voice booms out of nowhere, making me jump. I swallow; he sounds so terrifying. "Mirthal was able to see the truth, and I am disgusted. You used your royal status to try to force this young lady to be your mistress, and when she refused, you threw her in the dungeons. I now see where your son learned his abuse of power."

"My Prince, I can explain."

"No, you cannot. There is nothing you can say that will help your case. You will be on a thin line from here on out. One little mistake and your crown will be removed from your head."

"You can't remove my crown!"

"Yes, we can, and we will if you step out of line again." He looks away from the king and looks toward the woman. "Aurora, we apologize for any misunderstanding. You are free to go." He turns and leaves. I jump up wanting to protest.

That's all he gets? A slap on the wrist like a toddler who took a cookie from the cookie jar! But Azrael slams a hand over my mouth. I look up, and he shakes his head. Once Dimitri disappears, the lights turn back on. Azrael removes his hand, and I narrow my eyes at him. We will talk about this later. I walk away, rushing to Aurora's side. She sees me coming and smiles widely.

"Thank you for what you did! You set me free. I can never repay you." She giggles and hugs me tightly, and I hug her back, smiling. I'm so happy that I was able to help her.

"Don't worry about it." I pull back. "Anyone would've helped you."

"Nope, I highly doubt that." She looks over my shoulder. Her eyes widen with fear. I look behind me to find Azrael standing a few feet away, watching us with his arms crossed. I can see why everyone finds him intimidating. "That's Prince Azrael, isn't it? He's your mate, right?" she whispers like he wouldn't hear her.

I laugh. "Yes, and yes. Do you have anywhere to go? Any family?"

"No, no family and I highly doubt that my landlord saved my room this long. It's been months down there, and I haven't paid, so no, not really, but don't worry, I'll figure it out. I refuse to work in that castle again. I'll rather sleep in the park until I find a new job."

"Well, why not come with us? We have plenty of room, and Azrael says we can find you a job. There's plenty of different jobs you can choose from."

"Seriously?" Her eyes grow big with shock. "You'll do that? For me?"

"Yes, of course we will." I smile.

"I never had anyone help me like this. Not even my own family." She starts to tear up. "Of course, I'll come, and I'll work hard, I swear it! You guys won't regret it." She looks between Azrael and me.

"I know you will," I say. Azrael wraps his arm around my shoulder, and I look up at him to find him already watching me. I can tell he's ready to leave.

"I owe you both."

"No, you don't. Let's get going. I should warn you, though, we're going to teleport, and if you've never done it, you'll feel a little sick."

"Never done it. I really believed teleporting was some type of myth. It's so cool you can!" She smiles at Azrael, and he grunts but doesn't say anything. He's still so rude.

I frown, ready to teleport, but he has to touch her. I lay my hand possessively on his abdomen. Shit, am I jealous of the thought of them touching each other? Yes, yes, I am.

"Grab Bella's arm," Azrael says to her. I sigh in relief, looking up at him to find him smirking as he leans down, whispering in my ear. "Don't worry, little witch, I get jealous when anyone touches you, too, but fuck, it's hot as hell seeing you possessive of me. Don't worry though, I have eyes only for you." Of course, he knew exactly what I was thinking. I should be embarrassed, but I'm not, I'm just happy that the feeling is mutual.

I sigh, as I lay my head back, loving this overly warm bath full of bubbles. A long day is an understatement; I feel like a weight is lifted off my shoulders, and Azrael and I can start our lives together.

After showing Aurora her room, Azrael ran me a bath, which I took full advantage of, pairing it with a really good dark romance book. The man in the book is insane and stalks the poor girl, but I freaking love it. I guess I have a thing for bad boys. After all, my man is crazier than this man.

I smile, remembering when we came home, and I saw the chain he was going to use on me because he didn't want to let me go. Honestly, it turns me on, and yeah, maybe I'm a little crazy for being turned on by the thought of being chained up by the man I love, but I really don't care.

I love the fact that *I'm* his obsession because he's mine as well.

"How did I get so damn lucky?" Azrael's voice makes me jump slightly, and bubbles spray over the edge of the bathtub onto the floor. I look up to see a shirtless Azrael leaning against the door frame. He's holding two wine glasses in one hand and a bottle of wine in his other hand. My eyes start to roam over his muscular body. Jesus, this man is sinfully sexy.

"You keep staring at me with those fuck me eyes, I'll fuck you," he warns as he pushes off the door frame, and I giggle.

"That doesn't sound like much of a threat to me," I whisper, my voice sounding low and husky.

"May I join you?" He sets the glasses down on the little side table by the tub, and I nod. He opens the wine bottle and pours us both a glass, handing me one. I take a sip as I watch him over the rim as he slowly unbuttons his jeans. When he goes to unzip himself, someone starts banging on our bedroom door, making me groan at the interruption. He releases an aggravated sigh, buttoning his jeans up, and I pout, looking up at him through my lashes. He bends over, pressing a soft kiss to my pouted lips.

"Patient, my little witch. I'll send them away," He mumbles against my lips, and then disappears.

"Hurry up!" I shout after him, and his only reply is a dark chuckle. I swear he totally gets off on my misery.

I take another sip of wine, trying to relax. I pick up the book to start reading again, but I keep eying the clock on the wall by the vanity. I've already drunk the whole bottle of wine while waiting for him.

"Ugh!" I shout impatiently after about ten minutes. Yeah, just leave me naked in the tub, why don't you? Asshole. I get up, grab my silk robe, put it on, and tie the belt around my waist, not bothering to dry myself.

I walk out, but our room is empty. I march to the door and yank it open. I see Azrael, his back towards me, talking to Cain. I was introduced to him once before; he's the leader of the guards. His eyes slowly trail down my body, making his fangs extend and he groans with desire. Azrael looks over his shoulder, and he growls when his eyes lower, seeing what I have on, or in this case, what I *don't* have on. I don't see the problem; all the goodies are hidden. Narrowing his eyes, he steps in front of me to cover Cain's view of me.

"If you don't want me to tear your eyes out, then you'd better look away," his voice has a dangerous edge to it as he shoves Cain away before turning to me. "Get inside *now.*" He snaps at me. I grind my teeth to keep myself from snapping back. I spin around, walking back into the room.

"I'm sorry, my prince, I wasn't trying to disrespect you." I hear Cain apologize, before I shut the door. I go to the mirror to glance at myself. *Oh,* the silk robe is clingy to my body, and my nipples are hard; it's practically see-through. I can pretty much see every curve of my body.

Shit...

No wonder he flipped. I settle on the edge of the bed, waiting for him since there's no longer a chair in the room. He comes in a couple of minutes later, and he stares at me with such intensity, his jaw ticking. After a minute, I look down at my hands that are fidgeting with the end of the robe.

"Don't you *ever* fucking walk out of this room like that again!" He snaps, his voice vibrating with rage, making me flinch. "Unless you want me to kill everyone who looks at you."

My skin tingles, knowing damn well he would kill everyone, so I decide to push, just a little. "Why? It looked like he enjoyed it." I purr, looking back at him innocently.

"No one is allowed to see you dressed like that! I don't give a shit if he enjoyed it. It's for my eyes only." I slowly lick my lips, my skin tingles with anticipation, ready for him to punish me. He fucks me so viciously good when he's jealous.

I stand slowly, biting my lower lip. "Is that right?" I untie my robe, letting it open so he can see what's underneath, begging for his touch.

My hands start taking it off when he growls, "Stop." I freeze for a second, then retie it, swallowing down the hurt. "I need to deal with something first. I'll be back."

"What do you need to deal with this late?" I wrap my arms around my midsection. I hate it when he's mad at me; he's so cold.

"Nothing." He disappears into the closet without looking at me and comes back out with a black T-shirt on. "I'll be back." He crosses the room to the door.

"So, what? You're not gonna tell me?" I snap angrily as he opens the door. Why do I feel like he's trying to hide something from me? I walk up behind him, grabbing his elbow to stop him from leaving.

"Enough questions!" he turns to face me with bare teeth, seething. I don't ever remember feeling afraid of him, until now. I take a step away from him, eyes wide.

"Then leave, and don't come back!" I yell, shoving his back, pushing him into the hall.

"Fine, I fucking won't!"

"Good!" I hiss, a lone tear falls down my cheek. His eyes soften, and he steps forward, but Cain blurs between us.

"Give me a fucking moment!" Azrael snaps at him, but I slam the door shut, locking it with magic, knowing nothing can get through, even with his strength. I watch the handle shake as he tries opening it, and then he slams against it, vibrating the walls with an angry roar.

I turn away from the door, using my magic to lock the windows as well, just in case, and close the curtains.

"Open the fucking door, Isabella!" I slide down the wall. I don't ever recall him using my full name. "Please, I'm begging you, baby. I'm sorry," he says in a calmer voice, filled with remorse. I slowly get up, stepping to the door, considering it. He never begs or apologizes. It's not in his nature to do so. He must really feel bad. My fingers wrap around the doorknob, about to yank it open.

"Fuck!" He hits the door hard enough to vibrate the wall again, making me flinch, and back away from the door. A minute later, he leaves, and I don't feel his presence on the other side of the door.

I'm sitting in bed with my back resting against the headboard, staring out the window. I haven't been able to fall asleep after our fight; I mostly cried my eyes out, it hurt when he flipped out on me, and then tried hiding something from me.

My stomach starts rumbling with hunger, so I decide to get up. I dress myself in grey joggers and a blue long-sleeve V-neck shirt and fuzzy slippers. I slowly walk down the stairs and head to the kitchen, feeling jittery, like Azrael will pop out from around the corner. I'm not ready to face him.

I make myself a turkey sandwich and grab a bag of Cheetos before sitting on the countertop, swinging my feet. Guards come around the corner, whispering to each other as they walk past the kitchen. I quietly hop down to follow them. They stop by the front door, and I press my back against the wall, listening.

"Can you believe Prince Dimitri is here? I'm staying away, dude scares me."

"Yeah, but do you think they'll kill the princess's father?" another guard whispers, making my heart rate spike. Does he mean my father?

"Dunno... They said they were going to." I hear the front door open, and it closes a moment later. I wait a minute before peeking out from the corner. I let out a deep breath. Does that mean my father is here? No, Azrael wouldn't keep something like that from me, and he surely wouldn't kill him, he promised me.

But why is Prince Dimitri here?

I remember when Stella pointed down a dark stairwell, warning me to never go down there. It's where they held interrogations, and it's not something I ever want to witness. She told me Azrael can be pretty brutal.

I quickly head that way, continuously looking over my shoulder, anxious about being caught. I open the door, pausing before walking down the steps.

I hit the landing, but there's a large metal door with a pin pad, and it's slightly open. Someone didn't shut it all the way.

Turn around...

No, I push the anxious voice away, pushing the heavy metal door open, and when I peek my head inside, it doesn't seem like I'm in the castle anymore. The floors, walls, and ceiling are all metal and sparkly clean. There's only one way to go, so I carefully shut the door, leaving it open slightly so I can escape if needed. I creep down the long hall, the only sound is my footsteps bouncing off the walls. The further down I make it, the more it smells like blood, making me wrinkle my nose.

This shit is straight out of a horror movie...

I stop at the end, looking right to left, not knowing which way to go, but I hear a scream. It makes a chill snake up my spine and around my neck, tightening its grip, making it hard for me to breathe. I look behind me, thinking of running back the way I came. I swallow before turning down the hall to the left. After a minute, I see the end of the hall, and there's a door to the right.

It's shut all the way, and I can't get it to open, but there's a large window beside it with chairs to sit in facing the window. I walk into the small room, peering inside the window, and what I see makes my blood turn ice cold.

I cover my mouth with the palm of my hand to stop the gasp from spilling out. My father is hanging unconscious in the middle of the room, his wrists bound by chains that are hanging from the ceiling. Dimitri and Azrael are circling him. Neither of them is wearing a shirt, and their skin is covered in blood.

I stare at Azrael, and he looks like a wild, untamed animal circling his prey.

"You cannot tell your mate about the information we found."

"You expect me to keep this from her?" Azrael snarls, stopping in his tracks, looking at Dimitri. They are both the same height, and they both look dangerously psychotic, unhinged. There's a reason both males are known to be dangerous and extremely deadly. "Would you keep something like this from your mate?"

"This is not about my mate." Dimitri lifts his chin, growling at Azrael.

"Exactly, you know you wouldn't." Azrael also lifts his chin as he straightens his shoulders.

"If it'd keep her safe, I would keep it from her. If word gets out that she is the daughter of the previous Queen and King of the Warlocks, the rightful heir of the crown, the current King will try to kill her to keep her from claiming the crown, even if she doesn't want it. He won't take the risk, and as you know, he doesn't follow the rules."

Azrael growls, and I see his body physically shaking from the rage he is feeling. My body turns numb from what I just heard. There is no way that's true. I don't believe it.

"You need to kill him." Dimitri's chin points to my father, and Azrael nods in agreement, making my heart stop.

"Azrael, you made a promise to your mate." Darren steps out from a dark corner.

"Promises need to be broken sometimes."

"She won't forgive you." But Azrael turns his back on him, a clear dismissal. In a flash, his hand is buried in my father's chest, and then he pulls his heart out. He stares at the beating heart for a moment, jaw clenching angrily before squeezing it, making the blood seep down his arm, to his elbow, to the floor.

I let out a cry, my knees buckle, making me fall.

"I know that may have looked cruel, but our mates are cruel; they are ferocious monsters that have a fierce desire to keep us safe no matter the cost." I turn to look over my shoulder to see Rosa standing in a corner of the room, leaning her shoulder against the wall.

"He only did that to keep you safe, not to hurt you. There's a feral need in their beast that they can't control, and they'll do anything to keep us safe."

"He just killed my father!" I shout, pointing toward the murder room.

"To keep you safe, it's not like he was a good man." Rosa shrugs, like it's no biggie. "Although I understand your pain. I also understand why he did it." I look back at the window and watch Azrael pull down my father's lifeless body. I wonder why they can't hear us.

"It's a one-way mirror. You can hear and see them, but they can't hear or see us. We have to click the button to talk to them." She answers me, knowing exactly where my train of thought went.

"Are you asking me to forgive him?" I know my father was a bad man, but I never once gave up on him, praying he'd one day be the man he once was, the man my mom fell in love with. Now that's been taken from me by my own mate.

"No, I'm asking you to keep an open mind. Know that he did it to keep you safe, not to hurt you." She comes over and drops to her knees beside me. "I know it can be wonderful, but hard as hell to be mated to one of the strongest royals out there. They are pigheaded, assholes, and wild creatures, but they love us so ferociously. It's amazing to see how gentle they are with us, even when they aren't with anything or anyone else, and nothing can ever hurt us because they'll keep us safe, no matter what, and that's a blessing. Dimitri will do anything for me. All I need to do is snap my fingers, and I know Azrael will for you, too. Those two are a lot alike."

"I can't think straight right now. I need time away," I whisper, looking down at the ground.

"You can come stay with us if you need to. Dimitri is strong enough to keep him away for a couple of days with the help of our hellhounds, if you need room to think and breathe."

"And my sister? And wouldn't Dimitri be upset?"

"She's more than welcome, and no, if it makes me happy."

The door opens, and the three men walk out. Azrael freezes, staring at me, but all I can see is my father's lifeless body over his shoulder.

"Bella," his voice full of remorse, he drops my father, and I flinch when his lifeless body hits the ground. Azrael steps towards me, but I fall to my ass, scrambling to back away, pushing myself behind Rosa as if she'll keep me safe.

"Don't!" I scream. "Don't touch me." Looking away from him, I can't stand the sight of him covered in my father's blood.

"I think she wants to come with us, Dimitri," Rosa says, hiding me from Azrael. I can't see them anymore; my eyes stay glued on the window, staring at the horrible scene in the other room.

"No!" Azrael shouts. "You can't leave me. I won't allow you to."

"Rosa, we shouldn't be inv—"

"Dimitri!" Rosa snaps at him, cutting him off. "She needs time to process everything, time away from you."

"You're not taking her from me!" Azrael roars at Rosa.

"Don't talk to my mate that way," Dimitri snarls, and Azrael's body goes straight through the window, but it doesn't faze him. He jumps right back up, lifting Dimitri up by the throat.

"You will not take my mate away from me," his teeth snap in Dimitri's face, and Dimitri punches the side of Azrael's face, and they both fall to the ground fighting.

"Enough!" Darren snaps, but they ignore him. Dimitri is on top of Azrael, punching him over and over again until Azrael gets the upper hand and flips them over and starts punching Dimitri in the face with a deadly glint in his eyes.

"Stop!" Rosa and I scream at the same time, and they both freeze mid-punch, listening to us. They shove each other off with a growl.

"I'll stay," I whisper to Rosa. I don't want to cause trouble.

"Okay, I'll give you my number before we leave. Call me if you ever change your mind or even if you just need someone to talk to." I nod, getting up and walking away.

Azrael grabs me, and I try to pull away, but he refuses to release me. "Don't touch me." I look in his eyes as I call to my flames. They burn his hand, making him hiss in pain as he releases me.

I leave without looking back, going straight to Luna's room. There is no way in hell I'm sleeping in the same bed as Azrael. Luna and I shared beds before.

Chapter 39

I'm sitting outside on a stone bench in the garden, enjoying a peaceful day. I tilt my head back, basking in the morning sunlight as I listen to the birds sing their beautiful melody.

It's been two weeks since I saw Azrael murder my father, fourteen days of hell. I haven't talked to him or even looked in his direction.

My body aches for him.

But I can't find it in me to forgive him. I trusted him like a fool. I can't unsee the image of him holding my father's heart in his hand or the blood dripping on the floor.

The first week I stayed locked in Luna's room, but I missed being outside, so now I come here. He always watches me, like right now. I can feel his eyes burning into me, even though he isn't out here. He must be hiding in the trees somewhere.

My sister is pissed at him, too, and so are Stella and Darren.

Stella and Darren got me my own bed in Luna's room, so we no longer have to share. Stella told me that Azrael is doing bad, and he's even refusing blood.

I look up when I hear voices to see Luna, Stella, and Darren walking towards me. Well, they found my hiding spot. I force a smile. They sit down; Luna beside me and the other two across from me.

"I have decided that it is time for you to hear what your father had to say when we interrogated him."

"Oh." I suck in a deep breath, digging my nails into the palm of my hands. I haven't asked, and I don't know if I want to know. "What, did Azrael finally permit you to tell me? Or is he still trying to keep things from me?" I say it loud enough so that wherever he's hiding, he can hear me.

"He knows I'm telling you, but doesn't want me to, but I think it's wrong to keep it from you."

"He's just trying to keep you safe," Stella says in a small voice, making me snort.

"I need to know. Are you ready, Luna?" I ask her, and she nods.

"Your father was a guard for the King and Queen of Witches and Warlocks before they died at the hands of Prince Gabriel's father." I nod, waiting for him to continue; everyone knows that. Luna's hand grips mine, and she leans into me.

"Well, he was there that fatal night, hiding. He's the one who found them dead and noticed their newborn daughter was still alive. So, he took her and fled, taking her home. He showed his wife, and they both decided to keep her because if the king found out she lived, the king would have killed the baby."

"But where is she? Did she end up dying? She'd be Bella's age, wouldn't she?" Luna asks, straightening her back, slightly leaning forward.

Stella nods, but neither of them says anything. They just stare at me for some reason. I replay what he said…

No.

No…

"No," I shake my head. "I know what you're about to say, but don't, because it's not true."

"What?" Luna asks, not catching on.

"It's true, we gave him truth serum."

"What?" Luna shouts, getting frustrated. "What am I missing?"

"Bella is the baby," Stella says, and Luna's mouth pops open, looking at me.

"That's why you're so powerful. No wonder we don't look alike." She stares at me with wild eyes, like she's looking at me for the first time.

That means we're not real sisters…

Why would my mom keep something like this a secret?

"We can't let anyone else know. Only we know, plus my father, Azrael, Dimitri, and his mate," Stella says, looking between us. "It'll put you in danger. The crown will instantly be handed to you, and the King will try to kill you if he finds out you're alive."

"My father never told anyone?" I question, needing to know why.

"No, he was crazy, but he truly wanted to keep you safe. He came that night willingly, demanding to see you but…"

"Let me guess, Azrael refused." I cross my arms, turning away, my blood heating from the anger boiling inside of me.

"Yes…" Stella nods, piercing her lips into a thin line.

"He came to apologize and wanted to tell you the truth."

He was going to apologize to me…

Tears begin flowing down my face uncontrollably.

"I fucking hate you, Azrael!" I scream as loud as I can before turning to run. I open the back door, and I hear Azrael roaring my name. I look over my shoulder to find him running towards me, eyes full of horror.

It almost makes me stop.

I call to my magic, throwing a wall of fire up so he can't get to me, but my heart stops when he runs headfirst into it, not caring about getting burned. I want to yell at him for being so fucking reckless.

Holy shit…

I pause quickly to cast a spell to lock the glass door before running to Luna's room. When I'm halfway up the stairs, I hear glass shatter. I push myself faster, finally making it to Luna's room, and slamming the door shut before locking it magically right as Azrael's body slams against it, making it rattle.

"Bella!" He keeps slamming the door with his body over and over again. I honestly think that it's not going to keep him out. "Open the fucking door!" he roars.

He's not going to stop.

My phone!

I grab it from where it's charging on the nightstand. I rush to the furthest corner of the room, sliding down the wall, drawing my knees tightly against my chest.

My trembling fingers turn it on, and a loud roar shakes the ground beneath me, my magic shatters along with the door, and wood pieces hit the opposite wall.

My eyes widen when I see him. He looks so, so, I don't even know…

Broken…

His skin is pale, and he has lost some weight from not feeding. It looks like he hasn't shaved and now has a light stubble. His eyes flick to the phone in my hands, and they flash red for a moment. He knows what I was trying to do.

"Please, Bella. I can't do this anymore." He cries out, falling to his knees, hunching over, and gripping his hair, face full of sorrow, making my heart shatter. "Don't fucking leave me. I'm so fucking sorry. If I could go back and change what I did, I would, I swear I would."

I look down at my phone as my thumb hovers over Rosa's number before looking at the broken man in front of me.

"Please, don't leave. I *need* you; I love you." A single tear falls, and I watch it slowly run down his cheek.

I drop the phone, and it bounces off the floor.

"Azrael," I whisper, my eyes start blurring, and I cry out his name again as my tears keep falling like the dam broke. He rushes towards me, his arms snake tightly around me, and his scent covers me like a warm blanket in the freezing cold. I cling to him desperately.

I feel him lifting me up, but I don't look, I don't freaking care. I stay clinging to his shirt, burying my face into his neck, crying hysterically. He rushes out of the room, away from prying eyes.

He lays me down on something soft and pulls back, looking into my eyes before softly kissing my lips. I grip the sides of his face, feeling his rough stubble against my skin.

I pull back, looking up at him.

"Drink," I whisper, moving my hair away from my neck as I tilt my head to the side, offering him access. He looks at me with hesitation. "Please."

This time, he listens, leans down, and places a soft kiss on the sensitive skin beneath my ear, making my body shiver. "I love you," he mumbles against me, and I hiss as I feel his teeth puncture my skin. He groans deeply, and he tangles his fingers in my hair, tilting my head back further.

I arch my back, releasing a needy moan as I wrap my arms around him, nails digging into his shoulder blades. He pulls me tighter against him, and I spread my legs farther apart for him.

He releases my neck, and his lips trail their way to my lips, claiming them desperately, like he needs to feel me.

"I need you," I whisper and start rubbing myself against his large bulge for some much-needed friction. He pulls back, his eyes dilate with desire, making them darken. I run my hands down his back, feeling his body shudder and his back muscles tighten as my fingers slide past them.

"Are you sure?" he asks roughly, and I answer by cupping his cock with my hand, making him moan. He closes his eyes, digging his teeth into his full, luscious lip.

"Make love to me, please," I beg. He sits back on his knees and reaches behind him to grip the back of his shirt, pulling it off before he desperately claws my clothes off. He stares at my naked body underneath him for way too long.

"Azrael, please." His eyes snap back to mine as he gets up and hurriedly removes his jeans and boxers at the same time.

His cock is standing tall, begging for attention. My heart pounds in my chest, and I start panting as he crawls back between my legs. He grabs a pillow, placing it under my lower back. He's still on his knees as he curls his arms beneath my knees, spreading me wide and thrusts into me, making me groan as I stretch to accommodate him.

"Bella," he grunts as he pulls slightly back out before thrusting into me again, taking his sweet time as he gazes into my eyes.

My eyes drop to his lips as he licks them.

"Kiss me." I grip the back of his head, and he releases my legs, placing each elbow beside my head as support before he kisses me with so much passion. I swear my heart is about to explode with love.

"Tell me you love me," he begs. "Tell me you forgive me for hurting you." He pulls back to look at me, still slowly thrusting into me. My hands move to cup the sides of his face, and he thrusts deeper, making me cry out. "Tell me."

"I love you," I breathe. "So, so much, Azrael, and I forgive you." His hands lace together at the top of my head. He stops thrusting slowly and begins to thrust deeper and harder, making my hands curl around his hard biceps, needing something to cling to as he shakes the bed with his hard thrusts.

"Holy fucking shit," he growls and starts going faster. I'm pretty sure he's using some of his vampire speed because he has never fucked me this fast before.

My lips part in a silent scream as I let go of his biceps, feeling myself lose control of my magic, and I set the bed around us alight. I hear something snap, and the bed falls on the floor with a loud thud, but he still doesn't stop. He keeps going. His hand grips the headboard, and he pushes off of me a little.

I control the flames so they don't burn him. I open my legs, spreading them wider for him. Somehow his cock hits me even deeper, and I chant his name over and over as I cum, spasming and clenching him tighter. I arch my back as the intense pleasure takes over my body.

"Bella! Fuck!" he roars, slamming his other hand on the headboard, sitting up even higher. He looks at me and roars again. I'm pretty sure the entire castle can hear us.

Chapter 40

AZRAEL

Bella passes out immediately after having the greatest makeup sex I've ever had. Fuck, every time we have sex, it's intoxicating. No one compares, not by miles. I stand, looking at our ruined bed. Bella set the mattress alight, and I broke the bedframe. I shake my head, chuckling. I hurriedly throw on some sweatpants and a shirt, as fast as my vampire speed allows me. I'm missing her already.

I get her dressed, like I always do. Picking her up, I carry her to the guest room next to mine that I had set up for Bella when we first arrived, but I never told her because I wanted her to sleep with me. Selfish, I know, right, but I need to be selfish with her. There's no other way around it.

A maid walks past, and she blushes when she looks at me, then down at my sleeping mate, and I immediately know she heard us. Fuck, every vampire in and out of the castle heard. I have no doubt about that, and it makes me smirk, feeling extremely cocky. *I'm* the one who makes her scream and lose control.

I enter the room, shutting the door with my foot before heading to the bed, pulling the blanket back, and laying my mate down as gently as possible, like she's something fragile. After I tuck her in, I stand here watching her sleep.

These past couple of weeks were the worst fucking days of my life; knowing I hurt her literally broke me. I watched her as much as I could. Hell, every damn minute I had free, I spent fucking stalking her, watching her every fucking move like a psychopath. When she shouted that she hated me, it literally felt like a knife cut me open, stabbing me in my damn cold heart.

Worst fucking pain ever, I would rather be tortured for weeks than go through what I had to these last couple of weeks.

Not fucking joking, dead serious.

I truly did what I thought was best for her.

Taking a deep breath, trying to relax. It's okay, she's here now, and she forgives me. She'll be hungry when she wakes up, so I call my assistant and tell her to get me a new bed, bedframe, and a damn chair, and order everything with flame resistance, no matter the cost. I smirk while giving the order. She laughs but catches on quickly that I'm not joking; Aurora makes a good assistant, not the best, though. I only keep her around because of Bella. She thinks everything is a joke, and I don't joke, and fuck, she talks too damn much; the girl never shuts up. Before hanging up, I order Bella her favorite pasta and dessert. Plus, expensive champagne.

I go outside to the rooftop and start working, making sure everything is fucking perfect for my Queen, hanging lights, setting the table, and making a walkway of candles. Stella and I get into an argument because I don't like the way she arranged the flowers, and now she's cursing at me under her breath as she fixes them.

I rush down to the room to hang the red dress on the door for her before sitting on the chair beside the bed and watching her sleep.

She begins waking up, and she reaches her hand out to my side of the bed, looking for me. I grin, grabbing her hand, pulling her out of bed, making her yelp in surprise. I set her on my lap, and she looks down at me with tired eyes.

Fuck, she's fucking breathtaking.

I'm so damn lucky.

I never thought love was for someone like me, but ever since she walked into my life, she slowly cracked my rough exterior, melting my cold heart by warming it with her love.

She smiles at me, making my heart skip a beat.

"I have a surprise for you." She gasps, and her smile widens. Wider than I've ever seen it before, and her eyes were shimmering brighter than the moon with excitement. Fuck, I need to surprise her more if I get gifted with that look. She starts bouncing on my lap innocently with happiness, but I grip her hips to stop her. She's making me harder than fuck.

I look down at my watch. Fucking dammit, there's no time to slip into her, even for a quickie. I groan with annoyance.

"I'm sorry."

"Fuck, baby, it's alright. Go get ready." I point at the red dress hanging on the bathroom door, and she jumps up and rushes off. I watch her ass as she runs, but she turns around, and she kisses my lips softly before running off again, grabbing the dress, disappearing into the bathroom.

"I'll be back," I shout, and she replies with a giggle. Fuck, she really does love surprises. I just hope she loves it. I know she isn't into jewelry, but I custom-made her a diamond necklace. It's a large yellow square diamond as the pendant with small diamonds surrounding it. She thinks her birthday is in March, but it's not; it's a week away, but I can't wait to give it to her.

It cost a couple million because of the rare yellow diamond, but she's more than worth it.

I shave the beard I let grow out the last couple of weeks; I didn't really take care of myself because I was too busy stalking her. I open the black velvet box and look at the necklace before placing it in my suit jacket. I swallow nervously. I've never done this before; luckily, I have Stella's help.

I need to talk to that girl. One of my closest friends told me they were in a secret relationship a couple of months ago, and he wants permission to start dating her again. I was busy dealing with too much shit to really talk to him about it, and didn't give him an answer. I want to make sure it's what she wants, and if it is, then I'd be more than happy to grant him permission. He's a good man, and he'll protect her.

I want to tell her to wait for her mate, but I don't want to get her hopes up. I know how rare mates are, but they are definitely worth the wait.

My heart starts pounding like a damn war drum as I knock on the door, hoping she's ready to go. She shouts, "Coming!" Then, a minute later, she swings the door open.

My breath leaves my chest when I make eye contact, making the cold blood in my veins warm with desire. Now all I want to do is rip the dress off and fucking worship her. Her hair is in a low bun with small wavy strands framing her face, and her red lipstick is the same color as the dress that hugs her every curve perfectly.

She clears her throat, making me realize I've been drooling, and my attention shoots up, meeting her gaze. "Do I look okay?" she asks shyly as she blushes, making me smile. She's so cute when she grows shy.

"Do you look okay? No, baby, you look breathtaking. All I want to do is rip that sexy little dress off and fuck you till you light up." Her cheeks turn redder as she sucks on her lower lip.

"Shall we?" I offer her my arm, and she curls hers around it. I lead her up a couple flights of stairs, feeling so goddamn nervous, my heart is beating faster than ever, and I keep running my hand through my hair. I've never been so nervous about anything in my life. What if she doesn't like it? What if she'd rather go to a fancy restaurant? Shit, I should've just taken her to a restaurant like a normal person.

I pause at the door that leads out to the rooftop, and Bella stands there with a face full of excitement. I don't want to disappoint her.

"Let's go, I'll take you somewhere nice," I clear my throat, pulling her away from the door, and she frowns, not letting me pull her away.

"But…" She looks at me and then at the door.

"It's just a stupid idea. Let's go. You need food, baby."

"Please, Azrael. I want to see." She tugs me towards her, and I let her. "Please."

"Okay." I nod once, straightening my shoulders. I pull the door open and I place a hand on her lower back, pushing her forward. She steps up the couple of steps. She freezes at the top, taking everything in slowly. I grind my back teeth together at her silence. I can't see her facial expression, and it's driving me insane.

Finally, she steps forward, looking up at the lights, her lips part as she rounds the table, slowly bending over to smell the flowers, then her eyes flicker to mine.

"I told you it was stupid," I say through clenched teeth in a rough voice. "Let's go. I'll take you somewhere fancy." I turn before she can reply, heading down the steps. I don't want her to see how much her silence is affecting me.

"Azrael." I hear her steps rushing toward me, but I don't stop. My hands are trembling, and my feelings are heading in different directions. Extremely angry at myself for coming up with such a ridiculous idea, making a fool out of myself. "Stop!" she shouts, and I do, but I don't turn around. "This is the most amazing thing anyone has ever done for me. It's beautiful, so magical." She breathes, and I turn to face her with my heart pounding hard.

She loves it.

I stalk toward her with purpose, staring into her beautiful green eyes that are lit up with happiness and an expression full of love. An expression that I now crave to see, and I swear I'll make sure that it stays there. I grip the back of her neck, slamming my lips against hers, making her moan, and fuck, it has me hard, putting all my love into the kiss. She slides her hands underneath my suit jacket and slowly moves past my sides to my back, where she digs her fingernails, marking me.

"I love you," I whisper, pulling back, resting my forehead against hers as I stare into her beautiful eyes.

"I love you," she whispers back. Her stomach rumbles, making me chuckle. I place a soft kiss on her forehead before tugging her to the table and pulling out her chair for her.

"I don't think we ever had an actual date," she says as she sits.

"You're right, tell me if I do something wrong because I've never taken a girl out," I mumble as I move to the other side of the table, sitting down across from her.

"Really? You seem like such a ladies' man." She rests her elbows on the table, leaning forward.

"I've never had to try really hard to get them into bed; I never was with the same woman twice."

"Oh," her eyes flash with jealousy, making me realize I'm talking about my history of having sex with other women casually, but if it were the other way around, I'd be murderous. Let's just say, it's a good thing I was her first, or I'd want to hunt down the others.

"Shit, baby, I'm sorry."

"No, don't be. I know you've been with other women." She clears her throat. "But I have to ask, have you done so in our bed?" Her body tenses as if she's preparing for impact.

"Never," I frown, how can she think I'd disrespect her by fucking her in the same bed as I did with a whore? "I never brought a whore into my house, *our* house, and if I did, I would've burnt the bed before laying you in it."

"Have you had sex with someone else since we've met?" She looks away like she can't bear to look at me when I respond. The door opens, and a couple of my butlers walk in with the plates of food.

"Thank you," she mutters as they place the food in front of her. They bow before leaving.

"Don't answer that question. I don't want to know. I'm not sure why I even asked." She licks her lips and smiles down at the pasta. "My favorite! It looks delicious!"

"No," I answer her at last.

"No, what?" she asks as she picks up the fork.

"No, I haven't slept with anyone else since we met. Fuck, Bella, I haven't even looked at another woman. You're all I see."

"You had someone on your lap when I walked back into that nightclub." I scrunch my brows together, trying to remember.

I chuckle when it clicks. "Baby, she sat on my lap offering me the time of my life, and I declined. She kept trying, so I pushed her off."

"You pushed her off." She laughs like it's the funniest thing ever. We start eating, and she moans after every bite. She does that often, moaning whenever she eats something good. I always find it adorable.

"That's literally the best chocolate cake ever." She groans, rolling her eyes back, taking the last bite. She looks at mine, which I haven't touched. "Are you finishing that?" Her eyes are hopeful, making me laugh. My booming laugh catches her off guard, and the corners of her mouth twitch as she watches me.

"You can have it if you come here." Scooting my chair back, I tap my right thigh. She stands, walking over, sits on my lap, and starts eating my cake. As she does, my hand slowly runs down her exposed back, making her body shiver as the other hand slides beneath her dress, caressing the soft skin between her thighs.

She drops the fork with a breathless moan, widening her legs for me, the cake long forgotten. I lift her dress till it's bundled around her hips, groaning when I see her red lace panties. I pick her up, turning her so that she's straddling me. Her breathing quickens, and she glances at the door before asking, "What if someone comes up?"

"No one is coming up," I mumble as I pull the top of her dress down, exposing her tits to me. Her nipples harden when I do due to the cool night air. "Fuck, baby." I sound desperate, and fuck, I'm not even going to lie, I am extremely desperate for her.

I reach up with both of my hands cupping her perky tits, my tongue swirls around her perfect brown nipple before biting down, making her moan louder. The noises she makes are the most erotic sounds I've ever heard. Fuck, how did I ever get so lucky? I'm a fucking asshole who doesn't deserve something so pure, so perfect. She's definitely the better half of me.

"You drive me insane with those sexy little sounds you make." I want to take my time with her, but my balls are aching, needing release. I can't take it anymore. Her knees tighten around me as she arches her back, making the jewelry box dig into my side. I completely forgot about it.

"Ready for your surprise, mi amor?" I pull the box out of my pocket, and she looks down at it, eyes wide in shock. I open the lid without removing my gaze from hers, and she gasps, covering her mouth with the palm of her hand.

"Azrael, it's beautiful." She reaches out and gently touches the yellow diamond.

"It's a one-of-a-kind diamond; the stone matches your birthday."

"My birthday? It's in March, and the birthstone is blue."

"No, that's the birthday they gave you because that's the month they took you, but you were born in November, a week from now, but I couldn't wait." I take the necklace out of the box. "Come here." She leans into me, resting her head on my shoulder, and I clasp it around her neck. It nestles beautifully between her perky tits.

"I need you," she pleads as she starts pulling my suit jacket off and I swirl her nipple with my tongue. "Urgh!" She growls impatiently as she tries to unbutton my shirt before grabbing it and yanking it hard, ripping my shirt in half.

Fuck, that was hella sexy.

I unzip my zipper, pulling my hard cock out, not caring about removing my pants. I'm too desperate. I suck my lower lip between my teeth as I pull her panties aside, lining myself at her entrance.

"Slide down, baby." She slowly slides down, making me growl impatiently. I jerk my hips up, thrusting deep into her. She screams my name, clawing her nails into my chest, and starts bouncing on my cock.

"That's right, baby, scream *my* fucking name," I say between clenched teeth.

"Azrael," she cries, and I feel her tighten around me. Fuck, she's already going to cum. She starts bouncing faster, and I watch her eyes light up, turning colors, and I know she's about to lose control.

And she does, her flames explode out of her as she pants my name over and over again.

Fuck, yes...

I almost fall into the abyss, but I force myself to stop. I'm not ready for this to be over. I stand flipping her over, pushing her front onto the table, and slam myself back into her tight pussy, making me feel completely insane with need. I start pounding hard, and she grips the tablecloth, begging me to pound her harder, so I do.

I watch the flames spread across the table, slowly burning the red roses I got her, turning the petals black before they turn into ashes.

"Tell me who owns this sweet pussy. Tell me who you belong to."

"You, Azrael! She's yours, I'm yours, please!" she whimpers as she squirts, and I see stars in my vision as I groan her name. She tightens around me perfectly, squeezing me with such force, too tight, too fucking perfect.

"Your pussy is choking my fucking cock," I clench my teeth. Just a little longer, I need to make her cum once more before I can allow myself to finish.

"You're such a needy little slut for my cock, aren't you?" I pull back to watch myself fuck her pussy, my nostrils flare as I watch her ass jiggle with each thrust.

Fuck me, that ass is everything.

"Yes..." she mumbles when I spank her ass. "Only for you." Her pussy starts pulsating around me. I need her to finish. The pleasure is too much for me to handle. I'm about to explode and I don't think I can hold back this time; it's too intense.

"Cum. For. Me." I growl between my teeth, saying each word with a hard thrust. "Holy fucking shit!" I hiss, gripping her ass tightly, pounding harder, and she explodes around me, making me see double. The pleasure hits me like a Mack truck. "Fucking hell, Bella!" I roar out my release as we both let the intense ecstasy claim our bodies.

We both slump over as our limbs turn to jelly. "Good girl." I kiss her shoulder before lifting her, and she flicks her wrist, making the flames disappear.

Chapter 41

BELLA

Three months later

"I now name Isabella our new princess!" The vampires below scream our names as Azrael's father places a diamond Tiara on the top of my head, and the vampires accept me with open arms. Something I never thought possible, and people say vampires are horrible. They say if we are mates, then it's meant to be.

Tears fill my eyes as I look at everyone below us. Azrael stands by my side, hands entwined with mine.

"My gods, you are so beautiful." Azrael breathes as he pulls me against him. He grips my jaw with his large hand and tilts my head back, pressing a possessive kiss against my lips.

"Get a room!" Someone screams, and I turn, glaring at Aurora, who has become important to me. My first true best friend. I can't believe I have a girlfriend to gossip about stupid things. We got closer after Luna left for school. She's happy, learning to use her magic, but I missed her.

I finally feel accepted. I have friends, family, and most importantly, Azrael.

I fully transitioned, and now, I'm part vampire. The only difference is that I'm faster, stronger, and can hear and see better.

We kept our other secret; no one knows I'm the rightful heir of the warlocks and witches. I have no intention of taking that crown anyway, especially when they told me that it meant leaving Azrael. It was one of the reasons he didn't want me to find out; he thought I would leave him.

He's still gentle with me and still very, very possessive of me. That'll never change. Rosa told me Dimitri is still overly possessive even after years of being together, but secretly, I never want that to change.

Just last week, he broke a man's hand for touching me when I was walking to the bathroom in a restaurant during one of Azrael's meetings. The man's mistake was assuming Azrael wasn't paying any attention to me.

One thing I know is that if I leave Azrael's side, no matter if he's busy or doing something important, he's always paying attention to me like a fucking hawk. If I am not out of the bathroom or if I'm out of his line of sight for more than a few minutes, he'll come looking for me. No matter what.

Not that I'd dare test it...

Fine, maybe I did test it.

I just love testing his patience, and it's not my fault he's so hot when he's angry.

Well, anyway, I tried to warn the guy and told him that if he didn't take his hands off me, he'd regret it, but he didn't listen.

And as a bonus, Azrael fucked me in the bathroom after breaking the man's hand. It's his way of claiming me. Showing everyone in that restaurant that I'm his. He wanted them to know he's the only one who can bring me such pleasure while reminding me of that, too, like I'd ever forget.

Every freaking time a man touched me, accidentally or not, within minutes, he took me somewhere private and started fucking me, no matter where we were, as long as no one could see me, like he needed to erase the man's touch, replacing it with his own.

He never leaves the house without me, and sometimes when I get bored during one of his many meetings, I'd get a man to accidentally touch me. Nowhere inappropriately, just my hand or arm. Don't judge, sometimes his meetings run on too long, and I need his attention. Evil right?

But if you were ever at a boring ass meeting for hours and craving your man's attention, and that's the only way to do it, you would do it too, don't lie bitch.

Especially when he makes you cum so fucking hard your soul leaves your body.

The end...

About J.S. Rodriguez

J.S. Rodriguez lives in the beautiful countryside of Pennsylvania with her amazing husband and their four wonderful children. A lifelong romance enthusiast, she proudly calls herself a romance junkie who is fueled by strong coffee, good music, and the occasional spontaneous dance break.

Born in California, Rodriguez spent much of her childhood moving from place to place. Those early experiences sparked her deep love of reading and storytelling, eventually planting the dream of becoming an author. As she grew older, that dream only intensified, shaping her passion for writing heartfelt, imaginative romance.

Rodriguez now enjoys life in a spacious farmhouse, where the peaceful view of the creek from her front porch often inspires her stories. When she's not writing, she loves baking with her family, unwinding during cozy, lazy afternoons, and cherishing quality time with the people she loves most.

My adoptive father hates me and blames me for the death of my adoptive mother. I am hurt and feel lonely. I have my best friend, Cassie, and she is the only one who keeps me sane. I can't wait to leave this town full of bad memories to get a fresh start. But then, I met him. Now, I crave his touch. He is everything I didn't even know I needed. I can finally breathe when I'm around him, but he keeps pushing me away. He doesn't believe he's good enough for me.